THE TROUBLE WITH PARADISE

*To learn more about the author and her books,
please visit cynthiahamiltonbooks.com*

THE TROUBLE WITH PARADISE

CYNTHIA HAMILTON

Copyright © 2019 by Cynthia Hamilton
All rights reserved. This book, or parts thereof, may not be reproduced in any form without the author's permission.

First Published 2019
Woodstock Press

ISBN: 978-0-9904046-8-2 (paperback)

Cover design and formatting by Six Penny Graphics

This book is dedicated to all the readers who have allowed me to entertain them with my tales. I thank you with all my heart for your trust and support!

Cynthia

ONE

Mike watched as the dark blue sedan pulled onto the dirt shoulder off HWY 1, just outside Lompoc city limits. He remained watchful behind his Ray-Bans until he got a clear look at the driver. The vehicle came to a stop amid a trail of dust and the engine was cut. Mike pushed away from his 1964 Mercedes convertible and walked slowly toward his assignation with the man he despised most in the world. It was going to take every bit of self-restraint to keep from beating him to a bloody pulp.

As if feeling the hostile vibes emanating from Mike, Steven Ridley faltered before stepping away from his rental car. Mike made note of the hesitation and was satisfied. He kept his expression neutral but let his posture and slow, deliberate gait send the message that one word or action put wrongly would end this confab and may result in a sound thrashing, regardless of the consequences.

"Thank you for meeting with me," Steven said, futilely holding out his hand. A wave of Mike's seething hatred made him drop it to his side.

"You've got exactly sixty seconds to convince me this wasn't a waste of my time," Mike warned him.

"I'll get right to the point, then," Steven replied with as much aplomb as he could muster, nervously shifting the manila folder from his left hand to his right. "The warden at the women's prison in Chowchilla spoke off the record to me about an inmate she feels doesn't belong there. She has serious doubts that the woman—Lindsay Bartholomew—committed the crime for which she is serving a twenty-year sentence. Because of the work I've been doing since my release, she thought I might have access to resources to assist in clearing this woman's name and reuniting her with her child."

"What crime was she convicted of?" Mike asked, arms folded across his chest.

"Murdering her husband."

Mike let out a disdainful huff as he continued to glare at Steven. "What makes you think I'd be interested in this?"

Steven fought back a bemused smile while Mike struggled to retain his saintly composure. "You and Madeline have proven yourselves to be superheroes when it comes to righting wrongs and fighting for the underdog. Given what I put Madeline through, and the price I've had to pay for my crimes, I appreciate where her sentiments lie. I'm no detective, but I did a little poking around into Lindsay's background and I would have to agree it seems like her trial was a bit of a farce." He glanced down at the file, hoping it would give him a modicum of credibility.

Mike wagged his head slightly to convey his skepticism. "I still don't see why we should get involved."

"I think if you look at the file, you might agree that this woman just isn't the type to kill anyone," Steven said, clearly not enjoying having to grovel while trying to do a good deed.

"Almost no one is as they appear," Mike said pointedly, "despite how they might come across. Look at you, Steven. You were God's gift to investors and borrowers until the truth came out. Even Madeline—who once adored you—was completely unaware of what a sociopath you are until you degraded her in the worst possible way before trying to have her killed."

Flashbacks of Madeline covered with ligature marks, red wine, brambles and dirt when she arrived at the District Attorney's office filled him with rage and remorse. With obvious effort, Mike fought the temptation to secure some real justice for the woman he'd loved for more than twenty years. He turned and strode purposefully back to his car. As satisfying as it would be to unleash on Steven, it would not make Madeline happy to know that he'd taken this meeting in the first place.

After absorbing the hateful vibes, Steven gathered his courage and set out after him.

Mike swung around, barely able to control himself. There was only so much a man could take before every fiber of his being screamed for justice.

"I think if you could just set aside the past for a moment and listen to this woman's story, I—"

The power traveling through Mike's arm and out his fist delivered a punch that knocked Steven sideways. The folder flew out of his hand and cartwheeled over the low brush, papers tumbling out among the patchy weeds as the satisfying sound of bone colliding with bone engendered a deep craving for more. Mike caught himself as the desire to let his feet participate in this much-deserved punishment almost overwhelmed his restraint. He glared down at the pathetic man cowering in the dirt, and his anger seeped away, leaving a contemptuous pity in its place.

Steven gingerly rubbed his face as Mike gave him one final look of disgust and turned back to his old Mercedes. Steven staggered to his feet and went to retrieve the contents of the file from the brush.

"Wait," he called through jaws that barely functioned as Mike reached for the door handle. Searing pain and the taste of blood made him suspect a loose molar. "Just hear me out."

Mike turned with deliberate slowness as many conflicting reactions flooded through him. He moved slowly, threateningly toward Steven.

"Forget that I'm the one who brought you this case," Steven said as he rocked unsteadily on weak legs. "You can speak directly to the warden, get her take on it. You can imagine how rare it is for someone in her capacity to speak out on behalf of an inmate."

The intermittent drone of the sparse traffic filled the void in the conversation. Neither man said anything for nearly a minute.

"Look, just imagine for a moment that you're me." Mike's sneer strengthened Steven's resolve. "No, seriously. Imagine that you destroyed every relationship you ever had—and I think you have an inkling of what I'm talking about." Steven paused to let that sink in. He recognized the flicker of shame that passed quickly across Mike's features.

"You remember how hard it was to regain Madeline's love and trust. Just think how much further down I've sunk and all the lives I've ruined and what I had to face while being in the hell of my own making."

Sensing he'd gotten his point across, Steven paused and took two heaving breaths. "I worked my way out of prison knowing I must walk a very fine line in order to keep my freedom. The only way I have of using my...*creativity* and hard-won knowledge is by making a positive difference in other people's lives."

Mike barked out a sharp laugh, shaking his head at Steven's impudence.

A reasonable facsimile of shame showed on Steven's face before he hung his head and concentrated on the ground beneath his feet.

"As hard as it might be for you to trust me, just keep in mind I have nothing to gain or lose here. Though I went through most of my life focused on what I needed to be happy, I can honestly say that I feel...*fulfilled* whenever I find placement for an inmate. But even if you don't believe that, my record speaks for itself. Over three-hundred convicts have been assimilated back into society without recidivism in the eighteen months I've been doing this. But even that's a drop in the bucket compared to what can happen now that I've got a government agency behind me. It's—"

Mike held up his hand in protest. "Spare me the self-aggrandizing bullshit, Ridley."

Steven absorbed the slight and changed his tack. "Please...just take the file. Look it over and do whatever you feel is right. That's all I'm asking."

Mike glared at him through narrowed eyes, as if he could penetrate the scheming mind behind the placid façade. In the end, he realized he had no need to commit anything to this man. He reached out and snatched the file out of Steven's hand, sending a powerful message that going back to prison would be a better choice than doing anything that might jeopardize Madeline's safety or peace of mind.

"If I'm interested in this case, I will make contact with the warden up in Chowchilla, but I'm making no promises."

With that, Mike headed to his Mercedes. Before he reached it, he turned back to Steven. "Don't ever contact me again, for any reason."

He divided his time between tapping out a text and keeping an eye on the ex-jailbird before starting the car. He pulled back onto the pavement with enough speed to generate a cloud of dirt that settled slowly on Steven. He couldn't help finding a small comfort in the sight of a former back-stabbing leech reduced to such humble circumstances. Still, prison is where Ridley belonged, and no amount of good deeds would ever settle the score as far as he and Madeline were concerned.

TWO

The euphoria Madeline felt as she mounted the first four steps had steadily given way to weakness and doubt. It was not in her nature to struggle in front of others, which was precisely why she hadn't told anyone she was coming into the office. Such an announcement would've been met with fanfare and expectation from her employees, and concern from Mike. He knew better than to openly doubt her decision, but she would pick up on his anxiety. Only she knew when she was ready to get back to work. And only she knew how important it was to reclaim her life and her former mobility. Her sense of self required it.

By the fifteenth step, her counterbalance of tote and computer bag felt unreasonably heavy, as though they encased slabs of concrete. The combination of pain and weakness in her legs and back would've alarmed her if she could've afforded such a luxury.

She counted the remaining steps. Drawing in ragged breaths, she mentally girded herself. Only seven more to go. She lowered her head, her jaw quivering from the effort as she stepped with her left foot. She indulged in a few quick pants as she forced the right foot to follow suit. She didn't remember this exercise feeling so difficult in physical therapy.

It must be the shoes, she decided, regretting her choice of footwear. But the designer heels were emblematic of her style and her attitude. To give up anything would be a concession, a sign of compromise. If she were back in action, then she'd be back one hundred percent.

Voices coming from somewhere on the second floor amplified along the hallway walls, growing louder as they approached the stairs. Madeline straightened up, a forced smile and erect posture masking her weakness. She held her pose as the architect and his draftsman from the office down the hall appeared at the top of the stairs. The sight of Madeline halted their conversation mid-sentence.

"Hey…" Rob Lindstrom called out as he realized the significance of what he was seeing. "You're back," he concluded happily as he came to a stop on the same step as Madeline, all smiles. His employee kept a respectful distance two steps up. Madeline beamed as confidently as her achiness would allow.

"Yes, the vacation's over," she joked, not knowing how much of what she'd been through had made its way around the building. Given her former notoriety, anyone who knew her—or knew of her—had probably heard all the salacious details of having been shot by a deranged client. And it had been less than a year since she'd made the gossip circuit for having killed a psychopathic fugitive with her bare feet. By now, half the town must've known of her unsavory escapades. It was a wonder she was able to have any sort of private life at all.

Belatedly recalling the outcome of Madeline's most recent sleuthing adventure, Rob's expression shifted to one of concern. "You doing okay?" he asked, wanting to show his concern without prying or coming across as pitying.

"Good as new," she replied blithely as she stepped up the next riser with a lightness in her step that cost her dearly. Tamping down her reflex to yelp, she gave Rob's draftsman a breezy smile as she passed him.

"Glad to hear it," Rob replied before continuing down the stairs.

"Thanks!" Madeline answered heartily as her eyes stung from her efforts. She kept her head up and planted one Manolo, then another, keeping her progress steady until she heard the creak of the glass door's hinges and the sounds of the street intensify as she reached the landing.

Being on a flat plane again allowed her to catch her breath. She took a gulp of air and pushed on, counting the steps. Having conquered the hardest part, her muscles tingled and slowly recovered. By the time she reached the entrance to her office, excitement welled in the pit of her stomach, replacing earlier trepidation. She had done it. She had overcome so much to get to this point and it all seemed worth the struggle.

After drawing a final deep breath, she opened the door, her eyes eager to see the remodeling efforts she'd barely glimpsed before lapsing into a coma.

"Welcome back!"

The unexpected chorus caused Madeline to flinch and stagger backwards.

With mouth agape, she scanned the six expectant faces beaming back at her. Her obvious bewilderment elicited a few laughs before Mike stepped forward to help with her bags.

"We're so glad you're back, Maddie," Lauren said as she came over to give her boss a gentle hug.

"How did you know I would be coming in?" Madeline asked, focusing her suspicious gaze on Mike. He pursed his lips, keeping his pleasure of having ambushed her to a minimum. His reticence said it all. "What did you do—install cameras outside my house?"

As soon as the words left her tongue, she got her confirmation via Mike's guilty half-smile. He'd been smart to surround himself with innocent bystanders, one of whom was Santa Barbara D.A. Conrad Adams. His attendance at this spur of the moment welcome back party touched her, as had his visits to the hospital when no one knew what her future held.

The enthusiastic welcome—even by the two employees hired in her absence—caused her throat to constrict and her eyes to sting again.

Hanging conspicuously behind Lauren and the two new members of the Current Affairs and MDPI staff was Samir, his unease palpable as he averted his gaze anywhere but at Madeline. Though she had tried to assure him it wasn't his fault she had been shot while wrapping up the Cavanaugh case, he couldn't forgive himself for taking his eyes off her for a few life-altering seconds.

"I knew not even a coma could keep you away from here for long," Conrad said, placing a hand on her shoulder in lieu of a hug, something Madeline was becoming used to. Everyone seemed leery of embracing her for fear of somehow damaging her. The entry and exit wounds had healed, and the scars had shrunk to a fraction of their original size. But to those who knew her, those holes would always exist, symbolically if not physically. In reality, they were more vivid to those who cared about her than they were to her. The tight knots had become more like badges of honor than a reminder of how close she'd come to dying, or worse, living in a vegetative state indefinitely.

"Conrad, I'm touched," Madeline said, keeping her tone light and jocular, as if this show of support was flattering but unnecessary.

"I'm just here to collect on the bet I made with Mike," he joked right back. "He said you'd be out six months, I said four."

"That sounds more plausible," Madeline said, a pleased smile lighting up her face. "I appreciate the show of support, either way. But seriously, how did you get here so quickly?"

The D.A. seemed unsure of himself for a moment, a sight Madeline had never witnessed.

"There's something I wanted to discuss with…Mike…and now that you're back, I can go over it with both of you," Conrad said, sensing the oddness Madeline must be feeling after being out of her domain during her extended absence.

Madeline smiled nonchalantly, as if having the District Attorney drop by their office was a common occurrence. "Sounds good," she said. "Let me just say hello to the new members of our staff and I'll be right there."

"Oh sure," Conrad said.

Judging by their voices on the phone, it was easy to put the names of the new support staff with their faces. She rightly guessed that the husky voice of the receptionist belonged to the tall brunette.

"Sydney?" Madeline asked as she extended her hand.

"Yes, and it's great to finally meet you, Madeline."

After exchanging pleased and welcoming looks, Madeline turned to the petite redhead, a good six inches shorter than the other new hire.

"I'm Jessica. Most of my friends call me Jessie. Welcome back! It's so good to finally meet you." Another warm hand clasp and Madeline was satisfied with the newest members of the MDPI/Current Affairs team.

"Thank you. It's so nice to meet both of you. I'd say my colleagues did well when they brought you on board. Glad to have you on our team."

The phone rang, reminding everyone that it was a regular business day. No sooner had that line been answered, a second call came in. Lauren gave Madeline a warm smile before ducking back into the office she now shared with Jessica. With everyone manning their posts, and Mike and Conrad waiting for her to join them, Samir stood conspicuously alone. His nervousness radiated off him as if he'd been caught by a searchlight, facing the inevitable.

"Welcome back!" he said with what he hoped came off as genuine enthusiasm. But the cheeriness in his voice couldn't mask the haunted look in his eyes, a sight Madeline had never seen in him before she was shot. With all the concern that had flowed her way after the shooting, she wondered if any of it had found its way to Samir.

Without a word, Madeline put her arms around him, giving him a heartfelt embrace. She felt Samir stiffen, then relax as sorrow was replaced by relief. With reluctant arms, he slowly returned Madeline's hug.

"My hero," she whispered in his ear. With her chest next to his, she felt the spasm of anguish mixed with relief as the erroneous guilt he'd been harboring was slowly exorcised.

After several long seconds, Madeline released him and looked into his eyes. Samir shyly met her gaze between swipes at his tears.

"I'm sorry, Mad—"

"Don't say that, Samir," Madeline whispered. "You saved my life. That's not something you should apologize for. If you hadn't come to my rescue, I wouldn't be here. Don't ever forget that. Okay?" she asked as his gaze went to the floor. "Okay?"

Samir nodded until he could find his voice. "Okay," he managed to say, then drew in a ragged breath. "I just wish I could've done a better job," he said softly.

"I'm here, aren't I?" Madeline asked, her tone playful, making it impossible for Samir to do anything but smile. "Thanks for holding down the fort. Guess I better find out what Conrad wanted to see us about."

Samir nodded again and Madeline headed into the original portion of the office in search of Mike and the D.A.

"I put your bags on your chair," Samir called out.

"Thank you, Samir," Madeline answered over her shoulder as she stepped inside what had become Samir's makeshift office now that the reception desk was manned by Sydney. It had become the conference room after the remodel, which was finished a day before she was shot. The staff had grown in her absence, *because* of her absence, and now she wondered if they'd already outgrown the additional space. If the pace of new cases and events continued, they might have to figure out a better use of space.

Anticipating that Mike and Conrad would be waiting for her on the other side of her desk, she was surprised to catch a glimpse of Conrad sitting on the client's side of Mike's desk. A hollowness resonated through her as the reality of her four-month absence hit home. MDPI and Current Affairs, two companies she had started and worked tirelessly to build, had gone on despite the fact she'd been out of commission. Whatever brand she had established had become a thing of its own. She knew she should be happy her businesses could survive without her, but the euphoria she'd felt just minutes earlier evaporated, leaving her with a gnawing emptiness inside.

Conrad caught sight of her and smiled. "Ready when you are," he said, snapping her out of her melancholy funk enough to mask her fears.

"Be right there," she called back before continuing on to her private office. She scanned her desk, file cabinets, credenza as she tried to tamp down feelings of loss.

Stop being pathetic, she warned herself as she quickly glanced at the stacks of mail that had been deemed non-urgent during her absence. *You're here now. Things will shift back to normal.*

Samir appeared at her doorway with a latte in one hand and a glass of mineral water in the other.

"I'll set them in there?" he asked with a nod toward Mike's office.

"Sure, Samir. Thank you." When she realized he was still hovering in her doorway, she glanced back up.

"Sorry I've got my stuff all over the conference table now."

"No problem." Madeline gave him a reassuring smile. "We'll figure things out," she said as she rounded her desk and took the latte off Samir's hands.

"It's so good to have you back, Madeline. The place just isn't the same without you."

Joy stabbed at Madeline's heart, beating her insecurities back.

"Thank you, Samir. It's good to be back."

THREE

Madeline pulled out the chair next to Conrad Adams and sat down across the desk from her partner.

"I was just telling Mike about a woman who came to my office a few months ago. Her husband had been found dead in their bedroom, apparently from a self-inflicted gunshot wound to the head. She'd been the one to find him. His death had been ruled a suicide by the Coroner's Office, mainly because police detectives were unable to find any evidence to the contrary. The ruling didn't sit well with his wife, Natalie Sheckle. She worked her way through my staff with such dogged determination, I finally agreed to meet with her personally.

"Natalie is quite convincing in her belief that her late-husband would never take his own life. According to her, Andrew had never owned a gun, never used one, never even held one. He wasn't raised around guns, and he was a staunch advocate against the use of firearms. He held the strong belief that taking one's own life was an unforgivable sin."

Mike and Madeline eyes sought each other's, trying to gauge their thoughts. It wasn't their typical case, but neither of them was opposed to taking a deeper look at this apparent suicide, especially if it could bring about closure for the widow.

"There were none of the red flags associated with a suicide. He was a man in the prime of his life. He had no financial worries or health issues. No history of depression, except for a short period after their son died, which is completely understandable. All the Sheckle's bank accounts had ample funds. The Sheckles weren't rich by any means, but they were financially secure. There was no note, absolutely zero indication that something was bothering him. He'd left for work that morning in his usual chipper mood.

"Any other children?" Madeline asked.

"No."

"What kind of work did Mr. Sheckle do?" Mike asked.

"He was an art framer. He had his own shop, The Frame Job, for fifteen years. Andrew's assistant is managing it for Natalie now. She told me that Andrew's death haunts her around the clock, but there really isn't anything else the law can do for her at this juncture. The detectives have looked into the case from every angle, but there was no evidence that he was being blackmailed or had anything to run away from. Obviously, they couldn't do a deep dive into his past based on the absence of evidence, but they did do an extensive background check. Nothing. By all accounts, he was a model citizen."

"Does Mrs. Sheckle want to hire us to take a deeper look?" Madeline asked.

"I suggested it to her, just as a means for finding closure, if nothing else. From the law's point of view, if it appears to be a suicide, and there's absolutely nothing that suggests homicide or accidental death by misadventure, then there are no grounds for further investigation. I know Mrs. Sheckle is devastated by her husband's death, but I get the strong impression she'd accept that Andrew took his own life if she could find a reason for it. That's what's got her so tormented."

Glancing down at his watch, Conrad got to his feet. "I've got to get back."

"Give her our contact info and we'll take it from there," Mike said as he and Madeline stood to see him out.

"Thanks. I appreciate that. I have no idea what good might come of it, but I think I've started looking past the surface of almost everything these days, mainly due to your influence," he said as he turned around to face them.

Conrad's words managed to underscore a point that no one had had the time to articulate. Both Mike and Madeline had uncovered wrongs and set the records straight on the two cases they had solved right before Madeline's hospitalization. But they believed there was no such thing as a small case. If their services could help someone resolve a problem or get to the truth, then giving the situation a closer look was the right thing to do.

After seeing the D.A. out, Mike came and leaned against the doorjamb to Madeline's office, watching her as she sifted through the stacks of paperwork. Madeline glanced up at him with the distracted look he knew so well. Reading her mood as approachable, he entered and folded his tall frame into a chair on the other side of the desk.

"Lots of stuff," he surmised.

"Yes, lots of *stuff.*" Madeline looked at what she had in each hand, and deeming it all of low importance, she dropped it back on the piles, which she then located to the credenza behind her.

"So..." Mike said tentatively, as if he wasn't sure what to say under the circumstances.

"I'm fine," Madeline replied in the same offhand manner.

"Are you mad at me because I had surveillance on your house?"

The corners of Madeline's lips twitched, but she did her best not to smile. "That was rather presumptuous of you."

"Why would it be 'presumptuous' of me to want to make sure you were safe?" This question earned Mike a superior, eyebrows-arched stare that forced him to try a different tactic. "Look, I didn't even think of putting up my own cameras until we got the news about Steven's release."

Though this remark took him out of the hot seat, it cast a pall on a day that should've been celebrated. "I'm sorry. I didn't mean to—"

"It's all right," Madeline said, her head moving from side to side as if she were engaged in some internal debate.

Aggravated with himself, Mike got to his feet. "I screwed this all up. I just wanted to give you a big welcome back. I'm going to go disable those cameras right now," he said, turning to leave.

Madeline let out a laugh. She stood up, hands on her hips, looking at him with an expression that held twenty-plus years of knowing Mike Delaney better than anyone on the planet.

"I'm not upset with you for setting up your own surveillance on my property. I can understand why you'd be concerned. It just caught me off-guard, is all."

"I can understand that." He rested his hands on the chair he'd just vacated. "Anyway, welcome back," he said with a sheepish smile.

"Thank you," she smiled back. "It feels good to be here again."

"So, got any initial thoughts about this potential case of Conrad's?"

Drawing in a deep breath and letting it out slowly, Madeline sat back down at her desk. "Well…I hope she calls us. Sounds like she's dealing with a lot of conflicting emotions. I would not want to be in her shoes."

"No, me neither. We'll see what happens. I'll let you get settled back in. Let me know if you need anything."

"Thanks. I will. And thanks for the surprise. I really wasn't expecting to be the one on the receiving end."

Mike gave her a big, slightly goofy smile that warmed her heart. Glancing at each other like the young college students they once were, their smiles turned to soft chuckles, then almost shy awkwardness, bringing back feelings of being bitten by love for the first time. Madeline blushed and Mike dithered in the doorway until Madeline finally shooed him away.

"Don't forget to take those cameras down," she called after him, earning a bark of a laugh in response.

Madeline listened as Lauren detailed some of the ideas she had for a new event proposal, a corporate awards ceremony spread over three days. It was to be lavish while keeping a low profile. Madeline had done these kinds of events before, and one thing she had learned is that the emphasis needed to be on lavish with a nod to discretion. After all, what those Fortune 100 companies wanted more than anything was a high profile, especially where their financial muscle was concerned. More exposure equaled more revenue, which in turn equaled more success.

In Madeline's absence—especially while she'd been comatose—Lauren had risen to the occasion, soldiering on with the event side of the operations while her boss's future was uncertain. With a few solo events under her belt, she now had to show Madeline her competence without appearing to usurp her role. What Lauren didn't realize was Madeline's growing apathy for that line of work.

Must've been all those years of fundraising, she thought before envisioning a few ideas to add real snob appeal to the proceedings. As the company in question was founded in the early '80s, a few big names in the music industry from that era—especially performers who seldom made public appearances anymore—would really generate some excitement.

Mike rapped on the doorjamb. "When you get a minute," he said to Madeline.

"I'll be right there," she said, quickly tapping out a few suggestions on her tablet before sending them to Lauren. "Just some ideas," she said after she heard her message come through on Lauren's screen.

"Thanks," Lauren said as she watched Madeline stand up.

"All your ideas sound great. See if you can incorporate what I sent you, and we'll get the proposal out tomorrow."

"Okay…sure…thanks!" Lauren said, clearly buoyed by Madeline's confidence in her.

Mike was just outside Lauren's office, discussing a surveillance assignment with Samir at the desk that used to be his, now occupied by Sydney. Madeline could tell Samir was feeling a bit like a citizen without a homeland.

"What's up?" Madeline asked after Mike finished his confab.

"I already heard back from Natalie Sheckle. She can meet with us at two o'clock. I told her we'd go out to her place. I thought it would make her feel more comfortable."

"Good idea," Madeline replied as a familiar fluttering in her stomach made her realize how happy she was to be back to work. Though the circumstances surrounding this possible case were tragic, she experienced the same buzz she got whenever she sensed they could make a positive difference in someone's life. The truth, no matter how painful, was always better than living in limbo, not ever really knowing what you should be feeling or doing.

"You want to grab a bite to eat on the way out there?"

Madeline thought this over, then declined.

"There are so many things I'd like to go over before we leave," she said as they came to a halt in the conference room, each of them poised to head to their separate offices. "But maybe we could have an early dinner…?"

Mike had karate class that night, but this one he'd be happy to miss. "Be thinking about where you want to go," he leaned in and whispered to her. They held each other's eyes while sly smiles lit up their faces. "Just make sure it's somewhere intimate and expensive," he added before backing toward his office. "We've got some celebrating to do."

FOUR

Madeline stared out the window while Mike drove her Audi to their appointment. She hadn't been in that section of Santa Barbara in years. It was a nice, quiet, respectable area, one of the last bastions offering housing for average-income families, though the values had gone up many times over since they were built.

Made up mostly of subdivisions and condo projects built in the seventies and eighties, this was where middleclass families made their home. She could make out a repeat model every fifth or sixth house, tweaked slightly to hide the similarities. Each lot had front and back yards of varying sizes, with shady green spaces set aside at strategic intervals to give the development a more bucolic, less congested feel.

Though most of the homes had retained a modest look in keeping with their decidedly dated styles, the Sheckle house was one that had been recently upgraded with custom windows and doors, fresh paint and hardscapes, and a new roof. Only the landscaping, although fairly new, showed any sign of neglect. Weeds crowded the shrubs and infiltrated the grass, which had gone brown in large sections. As if mirroring the bereavement of the sole occupant, the exterior sent a warning that life was not as it should be in the Sheckle household.

Receiving a hint of what was in store for them, they glanced at each other and drew in deep breaths before getting out of the SUV. A cool wind kicked up and swirled fallen leaves, causing Madeline to pull her sweater tighter around herself. After descending the stairs from their office and sitting down for the short drive, her back ached with her first few steps, but she did her best to walk as naturally as possible.

Within seconds of ringing the bell, they could hear footfalls on the other side of the door. After they came to a stop, there was a moment of scrutiny as the detectives were studied through the peephole. The door opened, revealing a trim woman in her mid- to late-thirties with dark brown hair pulled back in a ponytail, standing roughly the same height as Madeline's 5'7" minus the heels. Dressed in black leggings and tank top—not an ounce of fat in sight—Natalie Sheckle came across as a woman of conviction, motivation and focus.

Madeline wasn't sure what she'd been expecting, but the person standing before them was not quite what she imagined. From the look on Natalie's face, Madeline gathered the same could be said about her and Mike. After a brief moment of reconciling the anomalies, Natalie Sheckle greeted them and pulled the door open wide.

"Thank you for coming," she said, brushing back stray hairs as she closed the door. Mike and Madeline followed Mrs. Sheckle down a hallway to the left of the entry and into a large space that comprised the kitchen, family room and dining room.

"You'll have to excuse the way I look—I just got back from teaching my Pilates class. Please have a seat. Can I get you something to drink? Water, coffee?"

"We're fine, thank you," Madeline said. Though she usually preferred to let Mike do all the talking during initial interviews so she could do the observing, they had agreed that in light of what this prospective client had been through, Madeline should be the one to take the lead. They glanced at the sofa behind them, but neither of them made a move to sit down.

"I'm sorry," Natalie said with a self-conscious laugh, "I don't know where my brain's at. I'm Natalie Sheckle," she said, left hand to her chest as she offered her right.

"I'm Madeline Dawkins, and this is my partner, Mike Delaney."

After the ritual handshakes, Natalie said, "I appreciate you agreeing to see me. I hope it won't be a waste of your time."

"We're glad to offer whatever help we can," Madeline tried to reassure her without making promises.

Natalie exhaled deeply and attempted to smile, but it wouldn't stick. "I don't know how much D.A. Adams told you…"

"Please just tell us everything in your own words," Madeline said, taking a seat on the sofa. Mike followed her lead.

Once seated, Natalie swallowed with effort and closed her eyes briefly as she prepared to make her case against the conclusion law enforcement had come to.

"You know that Andrew—my husband…my late-husband." The words caught in Natalie's throat, and her eyes became glassy with tears. "He…" Natalie coughed to cover her emotions and tried again. "He was found dead in this house with a bullet wound to the head…" Madeline and Mike both nodded their understanding of these facts.

"We're very sorry for your loss," Mike said.

Natalie nodded her thanks, then drew in a deep, shaky breath and let it out slowly before forcing herself to continue. "His death was ruled a suicide, but I *know* that can't be the case," Natalie said, her left hand covering her heart, a gesture of both conviction and love.

"An act like that was so *completely* contrary to Andrew's character. Anyone who knew him knew he could never get so low that he'd want to end his own life. He was…too optimistic. I never once saw him get so beaten down by life that he felt there was no hope of ever feeling better again. Plus, he thought suicide is a cowardly act, and Andrew was no coward. He believed every trial we face is an opportunity to learn and grow. Even when we lost our son Jeremy to leukemia in 2015, which is really the hardest thing any parent can go through," Natalie said, both hands clutched to her chest, her face reflecting the painful memories that time brought back, "even then, he…he never stopped thinking about or working toward the future. Our future. He always believed 'tomorrow' would be a better day."

Reflexively, Natalie reached for a tissue, lowering her eyes. After blotting her tears and wiping her nose, she seemed more composed, more focused on getting to the truth as a means of combatting her grief.

"Andrew and I had been married for fourteen years. We shared everything with each other, no matter how difficult or embarrassing it was. We knew how to read each other's moods without even speaking. If something was ever troubling him, I could tell right way."

Natalie paused, forearms resting on her thighs, her gaze to the floor. She suddenly came back to herself and stood. "I need some water. Are you sure I can't get you anything?"

"Water sounds good," Mike said. Madeline nodded in agreement.

"I'll be right back."

"What do you think?" Mike whispered.

Madeline answered with a shrug as she studied their surroundings. She smiled warmly as Natalie came toward them, her long fingers clasping three glasses. She set them on the sofa table, then passed out three coasters to set them on.

Getting the interview back on track, Madeline asked, "Was there anything going on around the time of Andrew's death that upset him in any way?"

Natalie shook her head. "Nothing that I can think of—certainly nothing that would cause him to kill himself." She took a moment to collect herself. "Until you go through something like this, it's hard to understand what it really feels like to live inside a nightmare." Natalie's eyes grew large with the effort of holding back unwanted tears. "I feel…*obsessed* with the need to understand what happened here."

Though she had spent considerable time bracing herself for another interview regarding Andrew's death, Natalie Sheckle's emotions were still right on the surface.

"I'm sorry," she sputtered. "I just need a moment…"

"We've got plenty of time," Madeline assured her.

"I promised myself I wasn't going to do this. It just never gets any easier."

Instead of stemming the flow of Natalie tears, the compassion written on her visitors' faces unleashed a torrent of pain. Madeline glanced at Mike as she rose and went to sit in the chair next to Natalie. She handed her another tissue and let her hand rest on Natalie's. These gestures seemed to help, and soon Natalie's breathing relaxed and the tears abated.

"Could you show us where you found him?"

Natalie hesitated for a moment, mentally girding herself for the painful task. "He was in our bedroom," she said as she stood and led them back the way they had come in, turning left down another hallway to the master suite.

"I had everything replaced after the investigation and had the floors refinished and the walls painted. But I can't sleep in here anymore," Natalie said, standing just inside the room, clearly uncomfortable.

Madeline glanced around, taking in the floorplan. The bedroom itself was roomy—twenty-feet square by her estimation.

"Is everything arranged as it was before?"

"Yes, the same layout."

"Do you mind if I take some photos?" Madeline asked as she withdrew her phone from her handbag.

"No, please do whatever you need to," Natalie replied, her tightly crossed arms betraying her discomfort at sharing the worst day of her life with strangers. Still, underneath it all, it was apparent how important it was for her to travel down this path for the sake of the man she had dearly loved. Madeline knew she would do the same thing if she were in Natalie's shoes.

"Take us through what you did after you came in here and found Andrew," Madeline said, keeping her tone professional in hopes of getting Natalie through the process with as little trauma as possible.

Natalie drew in a deep breath, summoning the strength to get this done and behind her. She stepped back to the threshold and envisioned what she saw that horrific day four months earlier, the scene she'd been trying to expunge from her memory ever since. Madeline and Mike watched her as she reacted to the thoughts flitting across her mind. With slightly jerky motions, her body played its part in reacting to what she'd seen and done.

"I had been calling out to him. His car was out front, so I knew he was here…though it was unusual for him to be home at that time of day," she said as she walked into the room, her eyes fixed on a spot to the right of the French doors that opened out to a patio. "For one freaky second, I couldn't tell what I was looking at. I remember the burning in my throat. I could hear the echo of my screams in my ears." Natalie's body shook with the painful memory. She gained control of her emotions and focused on mentally recreating the tragic scene as she had found it.

"He was sprawled on the recliner that used to belong to his father, about two feet from that door," Natalie said, motioning with her chin to indicate the spot, while her arms wrapped protectively around herself. "I…" Her voice trailed off as she relived the worst moment of her life.

"There was blood…on the wall…a horrible spray of dark red and…" Natalie gulped air and pressed on. "I couldn't make sense of what I was seeing. There was a gun lying right below where his left arm was hanging over the recliner. Um…his…face…" Tears began to stream down her cheeks. "I ran over and threw my arms around him. I remember trying to feel for a pulse in his neck. I don't know why…he was so obviously dead, his eyes staring at nothing, his mouth open, the back of his head… I don't know how long I held him in my arms before it occurred to me to call the police."

"We're sorry to put you through this," Madeline said.

Natalie shook her head as she wiped roughly at her tears. "No, it's okay, really," she said with a sniff. "I totally understand that you need to know all the facts. How else could you find out what really happened?"

"I take it Andrew was lefthanded…?"

"Yes, he was a southpaw, and so was his son," Natalie replied with the beginnings of a smile, her eyes averted as she entertained fond memories.

"Is there anything else you remember about that scene? Anything else that struck you as out of the ordinary?" The question sounded inane to Madeline's own ears, but she had to ask it.

Natalie shook her head slowly, her lips pursed. "No."

Madeline looked to Mike to see if there was anything he wanted to ask.

"Wait," Natalie said, becoming animated. "This may mean nothing, but I thought it was strange that the recliner had been pulled away from the corner." Her eyes roved back and forth as if she were scanning unseen thoughts for clues. "I don't know," she said at length, "it probably means nothing. I just had a flash of the first thing I noticed when I walked in. It was like, why is that chair *there?*" She shook her head as divergent emotions assailed her. "Such a beat-up old thing," her voice broke into a half-laugh, half-sob, "but it had been his father's, so I think he took special comfort in it. I can't believe I miss that ugly thing so much." Her voice gave out as more tears filled her eyes. She wiped at them roughly and stared down at the floor.

"What about the gun?" Mike asked. "Were the police able to trace the ownership?"

"Yes. It had been reported stolen a couple years ago. Andrew would no more know where to buy a black-market gun than I would," Natalie declared with a derisive huff.

"So…the blood splatter was approximately here…" Madeline speculated as she went over to the now barren wall near the French doors. Natalie nodded, her expression devoid of emotion.

"Thank you. I appreciate how hard this must be," she said, giving Natalie a sympathetic smile. She looked out the French doors that opened onto a flagstone patio. She could see an outdoor fireplace and a built-in barbeque fabricated of sandstone. These finishes spoke of current trends and an infusion of money.

"How long have you lived here?" she asked.

"It'll be eight years in January," Natalie replied, drawing a deep breath to calm herself.

"I take it you and Andrew made all the upgrades...?"

"Yes, we just finished them last year. We had to stretch to buy this place, so we just did what we could as the money came in."

"We understand Andrew owned a frame shop...?"

"Yes, he did custom framing. He opened the shop over on Turnpike fifteen years ago. His hobby was photography, but he specialized in framing oil paintings, watercolors, prints and photographs. I don't know anything about framing, so I had to hire someone to take over. I'm not sure how that's going to work out." Natalie's strained sigh seemed to encapsulate all the complexities that come with an unexpected death.

Madeline asked Natalie if they could have a look around the back of the property. They would learn more about the crime scene when they read the police report.

The detectives followed Natalie outside. About fifteen feet from where they exited was a hot tub, sunk into the earth to blend in with the hardscape. Natalie studied the scene attached to countless memories, hands clutching her bare arms tightly, recalling good times that would never be repeated.

"We saw the home security sign in your front yard. Was your security breached the day of your husband's death?" Madeline asked.

"I had the alarm system installed after Andrew's death," she admitted, wiping a fresh tear from her eye. As they moved farther out onto the patio, another door came into view, presumably to the master bathroom.

"Is that door unlocked?" Madeline asked.

"No. I'll go unlock it while you have a look around."

Once Natalie was back in the house, Mike voiced what they'd both been thinking. "Two ways to enter the house without being seen from the street, not counting the windows."

Madeline took more photos as they continued along the flagstone deck past the kitchen and family rooms. Mike and Madeline upped the tally to three sets of doors not visible by the neighbors.

They passed the second bedroom and turned in the direction of the street as they made their way toward the front of the house. They passed a small window positioned high, a second bathroom. Farther on, a third bedroom could be glimpsed through the side window. Judging by a few items of clothing strewn across the bed, this was the room Natalie Sheckle had chosen in lieu of the one she had shared with her husband.

Mike stood on his toes to peer over the fence at the front yard and street beyond, noting the high hedge that separated the Sheckle property from their neighbor's. The hedge, plus the huge jacaranda tree spanning twelve feet of the front yard, would provide enough cover for someone to slip in from the street and hop the fence without being seen.

"I'm going to check out the other side," Mike said.

"I'm coming with you," Madeline replied.

"Why don't you go back inside? I'll be right there."

Madeline knew what he was trying to do, but she wasn't going to play along. "I'd rather see for myself, if you don't mind."

"I do mind, actually," Mike said, coming to a halt before they rounded the corner to the backyard. "I think you've had enough of a workout for one day."

"I'll be the judge of that," Madeline said under her breath.

"Look, I'm not trying to pull a power trip here…I just don't want to see you give up the gains you've made."

Madeline narrowed her eyes at Mike, then walked around him. Each step accused her of vanity, but she wouldn't relent at this point.

I'll have a long soak tonight, she promised herself as her determined stride shrank to careful, mincing steps once she'd rounded the back of the house and was temporarily out of Mike's sight.

After a quick look inside the master bath and adjoining walk-in closet, Madeline led the way to the other side of the house, doing her best to conceal her pain with self-assured strides that cost her plenty before she came to a grateful stop in front of a wooden gate. On the other side of the gate, garbage and recycle cans flanked the two-car garage. The simple latch securing the gate was operated by a string that could easily be pulled up by someone standing on the outside, as long as they were tall enough to reach over the top.

They became aware of Natalie's presence as she came up behind them.

"We'd like to take a look at the other rooms in the house, and the garage too, while we're at it," Madeline said.

Natalie led the tour, starting with the garage. Two vehicles—a Jeep Wrangler and a Subaru—sat side by side, the Subaru's engine still letting off heat in the closed-up garage. Storage cupboards and a work countertop under an orderly display of tools filled the available wall space. There were no other doors besides the overhead garage door that opened to the driveway and the single door that led into the house.

Madeline's earlier guess was confirmed when they inspected the two other bedrooms. It seemed natural for Natalie to choose the room farthest from the spot where her husband's life had ended. She wondered if she could manage to stay in the same house under those circumstances. But Natalie might not have had any other options. She wondered if Andrew had life insurance and if so, was the suicide clause still in effect. There could be more at stake here than just needing peace of mind.

"Did Andrew carry life insurance?" Madeline asked bluntly, figuring the circumstances warranted such forthrightness.

"We both carried enough coverage to pay off our mortgage, thinking that would make life more secure for the surviving spouse. We let it go when the bills for Jeremy's treatments started to pile up. Once we got back on our feet financially, we got new policies."

Madeline studied Natalie's face, willing her to offer what she really wanted to know. When Natalie didn't, she had to ask.

"Were you beyond the mandatory two-year suicide exclusion period before Andrew's death?" Natalie pursed her lips to hold back her emotions as she confirmed Madeline's suspicion with a forlorn shake of her head. Madeline could tell the loss of her son and her husband, plus the added financial burden, was almost more than she could bear.

"I don't know what I'm going to do," Natalie admitted. "I guess I'll have to sell this house." She looked as though she was about to say more, but apparently lost her words or the resolve to deliver them.

All Madeline could offer was a compassionate half-smile. The only thing she could really do for this woman who'd lost so much was to find out why her husband was dead. She motioned for Natalie to continue the tour.

One look at the third bedroom offered another explanation for why Natalie hadn't preferred it to the one closest to the street. The room was a time capsule, a shrine to the Sheckles' only child. A twin bed jutted into the room from the wall shared with the hallway. The comforter and coordinated sheet set depicted every mode of transportation likely to catch a young boy's fancy. Cars, helicopters, trains, tractors, fire engines, cranes and cement trucks repeated down the length of the bed in colors of red, blue, green and yellow on a khaki field.

Next to the closet stood a white shelving unit arranged with royal blue bins, each housing a variety of stuffed and plastic toys, a lot of them mirroring the vehicles pictured on the bed linens. Photographs of a beaming young boy with dark hair like his mother and father were arranged on top of a red dresser with blue drawer fronts.

One photo in particular caught Madeline's eye. Her hand gravitated to it, bringing it closer so she could better examine it. "Is this Andrew?" she asked.

Besides being a terrific shot of Natalie's husband holding their toddler high over his head, it also contained the beat-up recliner that meant so much to him in the corner, as Natalie had mentioned. The exuberance father and son were experiencing had been frozen in one perfect moment while Jeremy was having his first flying lesson.

"Yeah, that's one of my favorite photos of them together," Natalie said, her radiant smile at war with the tears brimming in her eyes. Though examining her past happiness was like a physical wound to her chest, her smile grew as she luxuriated in the love she still had for the two men in her life, both now gone from this world.

Madeline replaced the picture on the dresser and took a photo of it and the four others next to it.

"Jeremy sure looks like you and Andrew," Mike observed.

"No one could accuse us of not being his real parents," Natalie quipped with a weak laugh.

It was hard not to express their sympathy for all Natalie had lost in recent years, but they knew their roles in this situation required that they use their skills instead of their empathy in order to achieve what they were being hired to do.

"What year did Jeremy become sick?" Madeline asked.

"2013. He was three when our pediatrician started to suspect his chronic colds and respiratory infections were not normal. Plus, he just couldn't gain any weight." Natalie kissed her fingertips and placed them first on Jeremy and then on Andrew. After drawing a fortifying breath, she led her visitors back into the family room.

"You can imagine how devastated we were with the diagnosis, but we were reassured by every doctor we saw that the cure rate for childhood leukemia is very high—almost ninety-percent. We really believed that our odds were good, but there was always something that set our little guy back. He was such a trooper, that little dude."

"Did the medical expenses for Jeremy's treatment create a financial hardship for your family?" Madeline asked.

"Well…yes, they did. The cost of his care was staggering."

"Could that financial burden have gotten to be too much for Andrew?"

"We had set up a payment plan to cover what our health insurance didn't. It meant no trips and splurges, but we got it all paid off in less than two years after…after…" Natalie covered her mouth with a fist while she cleared her throat, trying her best to choke down her emotions.

"And you don't think Andrew was harboring any pain due to the loss of Jeremy that he wasn't sharing with you? Guilt, perhaps?" When Natalie's features hardened into a grimace, Madeline added, "Sorry, I just have to ask."

Running her hand roughly over her hair, Natalie considered Madeline's question at face value and how to respond. "If I'm wrong about Andrew not committing suicide, then I can't pretend to know anything about my late husband."

Madeline studied Natalie's face for a moment and was satisfied with her assessment. She nodded her acceptance of Natalie's conviction before asking the next question.

"Are any of Andrew's family here in town?"

"No. His dad died in a car accident when he was in high school. His mom lives in Florida with Andrew's stepfather. Andrew was an only child."

"How about your family?"

"My dad lives in Seattle. My mom passed away last year. I have a brother in Palo Alto, but I hardly ever see him."

"Can you think of anything else that might help us put together the pieces of Andrew's life?" Mike asked.

The question spurred Natalie into action. "Actually…I've got a couple boxes of stuff that might help," she said over her shoulder as she headed to a pair of bi-fold louver doors that concealed a washer and dryer in the hallway just off the kitchen and family room. Sitting on top of the appliances were two cardboard boxes, a laptop computer and a smart phone.

"This is all Andrew's personal stuff—financial records, mostly, but some stuff going back to high school and college, just in case that'd be of any help. That's assuming you're willing to take on this case." Natalie's hands clasped her arms, fingers tapping nervously. "These are Andrew's logons for the phone and the computer," she said, pointing to the piece of paper taped on top of one of the boxes.

"Thank you," Madeline said, lifting a lid to peek inside. "I'm sure this will be very helpful." She could read the trepidation on their new client's face at sending off bits of her husband's past—the tangible links to his life—for them to dissect.

Pushing despair aside in favor of being constructive, Natalie added, "And my contact info is there too, in case you have any other questions for me." Her arms fell to her sides, as if exhausted by the process and having to relive the past.

"It's impossible to know if anything we find will shed light on Andrew's death, but we'll go through everything thoroughly and follow any possible leads. I imagine we'll probably have questions as we familiarize ourselves with Andrew's life, but I want to be clear that we all understand what we're trying to achieve," Madeline said as Mike stacked the boxes in preparation of taking them to the Audi. The way she had framed the statement told him to not get ahead of himself.

Natalie understood Madeline's remark was a prelude to a question she probably wasn't going to be comfortable with.

"Go ahead," she said, her voice heavy with resignation.

Madeline watched Natalie closely, knowing her physical reaction to the question would be as telling as her verbal response.

"In order for us to prove that your husband didn't kill himself, we have to prove that someone else did. That gun didn't go off on its own, and since Andrew's prints were apparently the only ones found on the gun, it will be up to us to find out who had a motive to end Andrew's life." Madeline let that statement hang in the air for a moment.

"Is there anything you're not telling us, any disagreement Andrew had with someone?" When that question didn't provoke any response other than a bewildered shake of Natalie's head, she kept probing. "Could he have borrowed money from a dubious source to pay off the medical bills, or do the improvements around the house or keep the business afloat?"

Natalie fought to keep her composure as tears gathered and fell in large drops. Madeline's eyes stayed trained on Natalie's face, searching for any hints that their new client was trying to hide something. Madeline had no idea what she could possibly achieve by sending them on a fruitless quest, but she wanted to get a reading on this woman before they put too much time and energy into her case.

"I don't know," she said, breaking down. She held a hand over her mouth as sobs shook her whole frame. "I honestly don't know." Mike and Madeline watched with neutral expressions as Natalie fought to pull herself together. "I don't know how I could've known Andrew for so long and not really known him." She shook her head from side to side, eyes closed tightly as if trying to erase the events of the last four months.

"How involved were you in household finances before Andrew's death?"

"Not that involved," Natalie admitted. "Andrew paid the bills. I mean, I knew how much was in our checking account. Andrew would sometimes tell me if we got a high credit card bill. I deposited the checks from my Pilates classes, and Andrew took anywhere between twelve and fifteen-thousand a month from the shop. We were never rolling in it, but we could pay our bills and take short vacations every now and then. To answer your question, I wasn't aware of any financial problems."

"Thank you for your honesty. We'll email you a contract to the address you've given us. Once you get it back to us, we can get started on your case. We'll also need your consent to order a credit report for what it might reveal about your financial obligations," Madeline said, waiting for Natalie to acknowledge what they were asking. Natalie nodded, making eye contact and holding it long enough for Madeline to glimpse the depth of her pain.

"We can only imagine how difficult this must be for you. Mike and I will get started as soon as we get your written authorization." Mike took this as his cue to grab the boxes. Madeline picked up the laptop and the cell phone.

"Thank you," Natalie said, wiping her eyes. "Anything you can find out has to be better than this purgatory of not knowing."

"We'll be in touch," Madeline said as Natalie opened the door to let them out. Once outside, she used her key fob to unlock the Audi and open the lift-gate so Mike could set down the boxes. She followed behind him at a leisurely pace to appease her complaining muscles. She handed him Andrew's laptop and phone, then headed for the passenger's seat.

"Think we should talk to the neighbors now to see what, if anything, they heard or saw the day of Andrew's death?" Mike asked once they were both inside the vehicle.

Madeline considered the idea as she glanced around at the houses on the Natalie's street. In order to be thorough, they would have to speak to the neighbors on both sides, those directly across the street, and the three that intersected with the Sheckle's property in the back.

"I think we're going to have to save that for a later date," she said, giving up the pretense that she was one hundred percent back to normal. Mike nodded, careful not to gloat as he started the Audi and pulled away from the curb.

Madeline turned to appraise Natalie Sheckle one last time. Their new client stayed in the same spot until the SUV disappeared from view. It took all her effort to turn around and go back inside to face a house that was no longer a home.

FIVE

"What do you think?" Mike asked, breaking into Madeline's thoughts as he turned onto Turnpike Road.

"My inclination is to believe Natalie's sixth sense. Sounds like she knew Andrew better than anyone. The big sticking point will be in finding a plausible reason for someone to kill him."

Mike had to agree with her. Even if they could find a reason for someone to want Andrew Sheckle dead, there certainly weren't a lot of clues to work from at this stage. But he knew just by Madeline's distracted state that she was already invested in finding out the truth, one way or another. He signaled and glided into the left lane to get back on the freeway.

"Let's go check out Andrew's frame shop, since we're out this way. I think it's around here somewhere," Madeline said, pulling out her phone to do a search. Mike executed a quick lane change and sped up to cross the intersection on a yellow light. "Looks like it's up here at the next corner, on the right." She looked up to get the lay of the land. "Must be in that shopping center."

Mike turned into the first entrance and crept along as Madeline surveyed the complex. A row of small businesses flanked a supermarket on both sides. Wooden signs hanging out in front announced each establishment.

"Must be on the other side," Madeline said as Mike stopped to let foot traffic cross from the grocery store to the parking lot and vice versa. "There it is."

"Want to go check it out?" Mike asked as he pulled up in front and leaned toward her side to get a better look.

"No," Madeline said, scrutinizing the storefront that was about twenty feet wide. She reached into her tote for her tablet and began to tap out some notes. She spotted a woman behind a long counter talking to a male, presumably a customer.

On top of losing her husband, Natalie Sheckle also had to face a drop in household income. Even if the frame shop could bring in the same amount of revenue as before Andrew's death, the cost of hiring someone to do his job would cut into that.

"Seen enough?"

Madeline nodded, still distracted as she tried to assimilate the pieces.

"Where to now?"

"Home, please," she said, giving Mike a sheepish smile.

~~~

The hot bath Madeline had promised herself did wonders for the soreness in her back and legs. She dried off and wrapped up in a cashmere robe and slipped her aching feet into plush slippers, questioning her decades-long habit of wearing high heels.

"Don't you look comfy," Mike remarked as she entered the living room, though he only glanced up briefly from his laptop. "I ordered some Indian food. I figured you'd prefer that to going out. Should be here in a few minutes," he added as he continued to read the police report.

"Excellent thinking. You're right, I sort of overdid it today," she admitted as she sat down next to him on the sofa and pulled her legs up underneath her. "What have you been able to find out so far?"

"The bullet that killed Andrew Sheckle was a 9mm cartridge fired from a Glock 19." He handed his laptop to her so she could see the grisly aftermath of Andrew's death for herself. She winced as her stomach lurched. She felt sick and dizzy as she tried to imagine being the one to discover a scene like that.

"Oh, God. Poor Natalie." She studied the gory close-up for another few seconds before handing the computer back to Mike. "I think I need a glass of wine," she said as she untucked her legs. Fortification was a must if they were going to get into the gruesome details of Andrew Sheckle's demise.

"Stay there, I'll get it for you." Mike stood up and set the laptop down where he'd been sitting. "Red or white?" he called out as he disappeared into the kitchen.

"There's an open bottle of pinot on the counter," she called back. Despite her reservations, she picked up Mike's laptop again and skimmed the police report, noting the approximate time of death: 2:15 pm. There had been no signs of forced entry. No fingerprints around the house except those of Natalie Sheckle, Tanya Ramirez and the victim himself. No fingerprints on the gun except Andrew's.

Mike returned with a generous glassful of wine.

"Thank you, kind sir," Madeline said, taking a grateful sip.

"What do you think?"

"About the wine, or this…?" she asked as she passed the laptop to him. "This."

Madeline took another long sip before answering. "I think if someone else killed Andrew in the middle of the day and made it look like a suicide, then he or she would be careful not to draw attention to themselves."

"Are you thinking about the noise?"

Madeline nodded.

"Since nothing like pillow stuffing was in evidence, a silencer could've been used, and the killer could've easily pocketed that," Mike surmised.

"If we go on the assumption that Andrew was killed, we have to come up with a motive." Both looked at the two cardboard boxes on the sofa table in front of them.

"Might as well get started," Madeline said as she abandoned her wine and took the box closest to her to the dining table. A manila envelope labeled "Financial Records" was on top. Sensing this was going to be tedious work, she went back for her wine glass and took a generous swallow before sifting through the contents of the box.

Mike traded his laptop for Andrew Sheckle's and went to sit next to Madeline. After logging on, he pressed the start button to see what kinds of programs Andrew had loaded on his computer. He opened his mail and spreadsheets for starters. It gave him an eerie feeling to look at personal emails sent to the deceased, especially the ones in the Inbox that came in after Andrew's death, emails from individuals and companies that weren't aware the person they were trying to communicate with was no longer able to reply.

Clicking on "Sent Items," he started with the most recent and worked his way back. "Is your printer on?" he asked.

"Yes," Madeline replied distractedly as she sifted through the contents of the first box.

She couldn't help but be impressed with the way Natalie had put Andrew's personal records in order. She could empathize with their client's situation, knowing *she* would not let anything stop her from learning the truth if she were in Natalie's situation.

Underneath the bank statements were the credit card bills. Beneath those were separate folders for each service provider: power, water, trash, gardening, gas, insurance. A separate folder held the monthly credit card statements. Nothing unusual on any of these, just everyday charges for goods and services.

A check register underneath the monthly bills gave credence to Madeline's hunch that Tanya Ramirez was probably the cleaning lady. There was an entry every week for seventy-five dollars up until the time of Andrew's death.

Madeline took a moment to imagine Natalie breaking the news to the cleaning lady. Would Natalie have told Tanya her services were no longer needed, or would Tanya be the one to break off the arrangement? A house that had been the scene of a violent death was also a victim of the tragedy. Anyone selling a home where a suicide took place was required by California law to disclose that information to prospective buyers for three years after the fact. Few people relished the idea of paying big money to reside with ghosts or bad juju.

Suddenly feeling the tedium of studying financial records, Madeline took a look inside the second box. This one seemed to hold more memorabilia than records, including Andrew's high school yearbooks. She took out one and flipped through it for a minute before putting it back in the box. She would save that for the morning. Spotting Andrew's cell phone, she gravitated to it, thinking it might hold more relevant clues than keepsakes decades old.

"Find anything interesting?" Mike asked, his eyes scanning the computer screen.

"Not yet," Madeline answered, craning to look at the passcode Natalie had taped to the top of the box. The code was of no use because the phone was dead. She was just going to get her charger when the doorbell rang.

"Can you get that?" she asked as she headed into her bedroom. She was glad for the distraction dinner would provide. It was probably too late to be digging through a dead man's personal affects, anyway. She brought the charger back into the living room just as Mike was carrying a large brown paper bag into the kitchen.

"That smells heavenly," she said, suddenly weak from hunger.

"Can I make you a plate?" Mike called out.

"Please." Madeline pushed Andrew Sheckle's paperwork aside to clear enough space for the feast Mike had been thoughtful enough to procure. After a few more contemplative sips of her wine, Mike appeared with two plates heaped with chicken tikka masala, lamb saag, shrimp curry, raita and naan. They wasted no time digging into their feast.

"Well, your first day back certainly wasn't boring," Mike observed between mouthfuls.

Madeline let out a sigh of contentment mixed with wistfulness. Some cases were definitely more challenging and complex than others. What Natalie Sheckle was asking them to prove would be no easy feat. And what if they couldn't give her the answer she was looking for?

Though she had a soft spot for longshots and was always game to champion an underdog, she was starting to have reservations about taking on this case. She was trying to keep an open mind, simply because the D.A. had personally brought it to them. Fortunately, Conrad had supplied the photos of the crime scene and the police report. But she had serious doubts that Natalie missed something among all this paperwork that would shed light on what led to Andrew's death.

Belatedly remembering to check her emails for Natalie's consent to run their credit report, Madeline got up to retrieve her cell phone. Finding what she was looking for, she went to the hall table to get her laptop. Mike knew better than to remind her that the food was getting cold. Once Madeline got focused on work, it was fruitless to attempt to dissuade her.

"What are you doing?" he asked innocently.

"Running the Sheckles' credit," she replied, her eyes never leaving the screen as she took another bite of her rapidly cooling dinner.

Watching Madeline's eyes as they roved over the screen, Mike had a good guess of what she was seeing. "Find anything interesting?" he asked between forkfuls. He already could tell by her expression that she hadn't found any red flags.

"Not really," she admitted. "Middle credit scores for both are in the mid-seven-hundreds. Two credit cards. No lates. No derogatories of any kind. I can see that a payment plan was filed with the hospital a few years back, but even that's factored into the scores. Looks like that was paid in full, like Natalie said."

She doubted if the cause of Andrew's death could be found in his financial data. And there was no way to know for certain that he didn't succumb to depression over the loss of his little boy. Some people put up a good front for others, to make *them* feel better. He may have hidden his pain from his wife in order to spare her any more suffering than she had already endured.

What a horrible thing for a wife to go through, to find your husband dead from a gunshot wound to the head, she thought as she tried to put herself in Natalie's shoes. *I know I could never get rid of a visual like that.* She let out a heavy sigh, her empathy sparking her resolve.

"Did the police report mention the collection of GSR from the victim?"

"I can check, but Andrew would've had gunshot residue on him regardless if he'd pulled the trigger or not," Mike said as he scrolled through the report. "Especially if the killer placed the gun in his hand afterwards to get his prints on it."

"I know. I'm just curious as to how they approached the investigation," Madeline replied.

Mike toggled to that screen and scanned through the report.

"Yeah, GSR was collected from both hands. Looks like left had more antimony, barium and lead than the other, which I guess could support either suicide or a murder disguised as one."

"Right," Madeline acknowledged distractedly, her mind already moving on to something else. She thought back to the photo of Andrew holding Jeremy aloft. The joy on both their faces was unmistakable. Poor Natalie, left with only snapshots of her once happy life. She picked up her phone and scrolled through the photos she'd taken at the Sheckle residence.

Mike was watching her closely as he ate, idly wondering what she was thinking. Her eyes traveled from side to side as she scanned each frame.

"The chair," she uttered so quietly, Mike almost didn't hear her.

"What about it?" he asked as she got up and came over to his side of the table.

"I want to see that report," she said, her hand on his shoulder as she bent down to look at his screen. After reading the written report, she examined the photos. She picked up his laptop and moved it to the other side of the table so she could sit down and study each frame. A look of recognition registered, which slowly transitioned to something approaching a smile.

"See those splatter marks? They're roughly at standing height, which would be inconsistent with him pulling the trigger while sitting in the chair. He would've had to be standing up when the shot was fired." Mike got up and came around to look over her shoulder.

"You're right."

To give credence to her theory, she went to retrieve her phone. "Natalie remembered that detail about the location of the chair while we were there. Her subconscious picked up on that anomaly, but it was pushed aside during the horror of finding her husband dead." Madeline flicked to the photo she'd taken earlier.

"Here's Andrew giving Jeremy 'flying lessons,'" she said as she held out her phone so Mike could see it. "This is where the old recliner was prior to Andrew's death, in the corner of the room, closer to the dresser." Mike nodded. "And this is where the chair is in the police photo."

"Yeah, I see what you're saying. But maybe Andrew wanted that view to be the last thing he saw when he pulled the trigger," Mike speculated.

"But why wouldn't he just shoot himself while he was sitting down, if that was the reason he brought the chair over in the first place?" Madeline asked. She and Mike stared at each other, the reality of what had taken place that day becoming more apparent.

Neither said anything as their thoughts roved over all the elements of the crime scene and what they might be trying to tell them. Madeline looked at the photos taken from various angles, making note of the absence of blood on the hardwood floor.

Had the crime scene investigators tested the floor beneath the chair for blood residue?

In a case that had all the hallmarks of suicide, it was probably unlikely, especially since Natalie admittedly disturbed the scene as she rushed to her husband's body to see if he was still breathing.

Because Natalie had disturbed Andrew's body, the scene the forensic team found had been tainted. Having become cynical due to her line of work, Madeline couldn't help but wonder if that had been intentional on Natalie's part.

Madeline studied the photos taken at the scene a moment longer.

"It's entirely possible that Andrew was put in the chair after he was shot, which means someone could've wanted this to look like suicide, after the fact," she maintained. She got up to pace as she followed that line of thinking.

"Let's say the scene hadn't played out the way the assailant had planned it. That could explain why the chair was brought away from its usual spot in the corner and positioned to line up with the blood splatter," Madeline speculated.

"I don't think there's any way we can prove that, but yeah, I think you're right. The positioning of the chair is an anomaly, though probably not suspicious enough to warrant law enforcement opening a murder inquiry."

"I agree," Madeline said, arms folded in front of her. "But I still feel like the scene is trying to tell us something, though any conjecture about Andrew's motive for moving the chair is just that. And dead men tell no tales."

"So…that pretty much puts us back to where we started," Mike said.

"At least now I feel more comfortable with the possibility that Andrew's death was a murder disguised as suicide. We don't really have to get into the finer points of the forensic evidence at this juncture. Suffice it to say that we're now open to the idea that Andrew may have been killed by someone other than himself. Now we have the task of figuring out who could've had a motive for wanting him dead."

Madeline gave Mike a wan look as she went over to her computer.

"I'm going to let Natalie know that we think she's right about Andrew's death and that we'll work this case until we find out who killed him. Let her go to sleep with a little peace of mind for a change," she said as she tapped out an email to their new client.

"But now she has to face the fact that someone wanted Andrew dead," Mike countered.

"We're going to find out who that someone is. She deserves at least that."

"Isn't it better to under-promise and over-deliver?"

Madeline scoffed. "We've never under-delivered, and we're not about to start," she said, her fingers scrambling to keep up with her thoughts.

Mike shook his head in resignation and collected the dinner plates.

Madeline looked up from her computer, her thoughts divided. "I'll get that," she said as he headed into the kitchen.

Mike scraped the remnants into the trash and put the plates in the dishwasher. "I'm going to head home," he said as he came back into the dining room.

"You're not staying?"

"I think it's better to let you get a good night's sleep. You've had a long first day back," he said, giving her shoulders an affectionate squeeze as he kissed the top of her head on his way to the living room.

Madeline found it hard to argue. It had been a full day, and she had pushed herself too hard. She should've been grateful that Mike had made the decision rather than her having to send him on his way. Instead, she felt an emptiness settle in the pit of her stomach.

"You're right," she said after sending the email. "I guess I'll see you in the morning."

She stood and tightened her robe as she moved toward him distractedly until she was standing right in front of him. He gave her a real kiss, then gently folded her into his arms. She hugged him back, letting her head rest against his shoulder, basking in his warmth and his protective embrace. Her body was often at odds with her brain, preferring comfort and a sense of protection instead of fiercely maintaining her independence.

"Want me to pick you up in the morning?"

"No, that's okay. I'm fine driving. I'll be in early," Madeline said, pulling away.

Mike nodded and headed for the front door. "Sleep well."

"You too."

They exchanged somewhat somber glances before Mike headed down the front walk. Madeline watched until he got into his car, then closed the door, securing all three locks before arming the alarm. She stood in the entry, listening as the sound of Mike's old Mercedes faded into the night, wondering if she was always going to be her heart's worst enemy.

SIX

True to her word, Madeline made it to the office before anyone else. Despite all that she had on her mind, she'd fallen asleep as soon as she laid her head on the pillow. She slept through the night, a clear indication she'd pushed her body to the limit. She woke just after six and was out of the house before seven, seizing the day with the same level of competence and gusto as she had before a bullet put her life on hold.

Having the office to herself for an hour gave her a chance to get acquainted with all the changes that had taken place in her four-month absence. She'd had little time her first day back to assess things due to the new case Conrad Adams had steered their way.

By the time Mike and the support staff arrived, she had already gotten up to speed with all the events in the Current Affairs pipeline and had begun familiarizing herself with the various cases MDPI had taken on during her convalescence. Getting a handle on what had taken place while she was out of commission put her in a good frame of mind, reaffirming for her that being in control of her dual businesses was vital to her peace of mind and self-worth.

Being in before anyone else also conveyed a message to her support staff. The burble of casual chitchat came to an abrupt halt once Madeline's presence was detected. Focused industry replaced the lackadaisical habits that had taken root and bloomed while Mike was in charge. Suddenly, there was an effort to exhibit proof that four bodies were now needed instead of two.

This change in the atmosphere wasn't lost on Mike when he showed up at eight-thirty. He worked at concealing his amusement as he went in search of his partner. She wasn't in her office, as he expected; instead, she was seated behind his desk, skimming through recently closed cases.

Now that she had reviewed the open cases—mostly background checks and a corporate theft investigation—she was grateful to have the Sheckle case to come back to. She sent Samir down to her vehicle to fetch the two boxes containing Andrew's personal records so he could start making copies of everything for their files.

"Good morning," she said cheerfully as she put one file down in exchange for another. Mike gave her a bemused smile and took a seat in one of the visitor chairs on the other side of his desk.

"I take it you had a good night's sleep."

"I did," Madeline replied smugly.

"I'm glad to see you feeling so chipper."

Madeline laughed. "I wouldn't go that far, but it is good to be back." She quickly skimmed the file she'd opened, checking to make sure it had been properly audited before she put it in a stack of case files that needed to go in the "closed" drawer.

Mike watched her with evident pleasure as her hand went for the last folder. With a jolt of recognition, he reached for it a second too late. Madeline stared at him as he hovered over the desk, locked in a tug of war with her over the mystery file. Her surprised expression quickly turned to one of apprehension.

"I need to talk to you about this case." He held his ground until Madeline let go of the folder. She leaned back in his chair, regarding him with a mix of concern and suspicion.

"What is it?"

Mike chewed the inside of his lip, silently cursing himself for not broaching this subject sooner, though in reality, there would never be a good time to confess his clandestine meeting with her detestable ex. He had yet to find an acceptable way to spin what he had done.

"What?" Madeline prompted again. After another beat of continued silence, she lunged for the file, an awkward move that rewarded her with a sharp pain that she was unable to disguise.

Feeling guilty and childish, Mike sank back into the chair opposite her and cleared his throat.

"This case came to me outside of the normal channels," he said, grasping the file in both hands, as if that could contain the explosion that was sure to follow.

Madeline held her tongue for a few beats before prompting him to continue. "Let's hear it…"

"It has to do with a woman who's serving time for her husband's murder."

Madeline's eyes widened expectantly. With an air of thinning patience, she waited for further details that would hopefully explain how Mike came to be involved in a case like this. It was obvious from the way he was behaving there was something peculiar about this file.

"The referral came from someone who interacts with prisoners in his line of work. His involvement started when he was contacted by the warden of the Chowchilla women's prison. According to our source, the warden believes the woman doesn't belong there."

While Mike struggled to get this preamble out, he watched Madeline's features as she took in what he was saying. He knew how her mind worked, and he knew that she'd already made the connection before he finished his spiel. She let out a breathy snort, her jaw slack, as she stared at him incredulously.

"Don't tell me you've taken on a case referred to us by that worm I used to be married to," she fairly spat.

Mike let out a defeated sigh. "I haven't committed to anything yet," he backpedaled, which Madeline rightly interpreted to mean her suspicion wasn't wrong. Several emotions flickered across her face as she abruptly stood up. Shock, disbelief, disgust and loathing were followed by disappointment and exasperation.

"Look, before you have me drawn and quartered, let me just tell you why I even entertained meeting with Steven."

Mike's boldness left Madeline momentarily speechless. She couldn't decide who she was angrier with, her partner-lover-best friend or her pathological ex. After what she'd been put through by Steven, she was justifiably suspicious of anything he was involved in.

"Maddie, please just hear me out," Mike said as he slowly rose out of the chair. He tossed the folder on the middle of the desk and held up his hands in a placating manner.

After smoldering a moment longer, Madeline managed to tamp down her anger. With an arched brow and a tight-lipped nod, she grudgingly gave her consent for him to continue. She leaned back into his chair, her eyes never leaving his face, though it was hard to read her thoughts through all the static. Only the pensive jiggling of her leg under the desk betrayed how hard she was working to remain civil and give him the benefit of the doubt.

Mike sucked in a deep breath and held it as he pondered the best tack to take. It bothered him that he had allowed Steven to dump this case on him. He was mad at himself for meeting with Steven in the first place. His gaze went inward, searching his heart for the right thing to say.

"I can imagine how betrayed you must feel," he said at length. Staring down at the desk, his right hand clenched in a fist, he put his feelings into words. "I was actually prepared to go to jail for the chance of a one-on-one with Ridley. I didn't even care what his pretense was for the meeting. To me it was just an opportunity to beat the living hell out of him."

Madeline gave nothing away as she stared at Mike, waiting for him to dispel the limbo he had put her in.

"When he got there, I remembered what you told me while you were still in the hospital, about how pathetic and weak he was in your eyes, how he no longer held the power to frighten or hurt you again. It made me look at him the same way, and actually, there was a small part of me that was hoping he would screw up, throw a punch at me or travel into your thirty-mile safe zone, which would trigger a return to prison."

Mike huffed at the irony of Steven Ridley actually walking a fine line, as if his life depended on it.

"At first, I wasn't really even listening to what he had to say. Then, when he started talking about this woman who might have been wrongly imprisoned, I could almost feel you standing next to me." He looked at Madeline, trying to gauge her reaction as he continued.

"This may seem convoluted to you, and maybe even self-serving, but I thought of you a lot before I met with Steven. When he contacted me, he prefaced the conversation by saying that this was the kind of situation you would want to champion."

Madeline's mouth dropped open, indignant that Steven would make such a claim, as if he actually knew anything about her and how she felt.

"I know...let me finish. He said that he could see a parallel between what had happened to Lindsay's life and what he had done to yours."

Madeline sat stock-still as she assimilated this remark. Like anything else that came out of Steven's mouth, she didn't trust it.

"That's when it hit me. I *knew* that had you been there, you would've immediately focused on the woman serving time for a murder she might not have committed. Everything else that was happening seemed immaterial. I knew in my heart that you would've wanted to investigate this case to determine for yourself if this woman—the mother of a nine-year-old girl—was serving someone else's prison sentence."

There was a charge in the air surrounding Mike's desk, an electric current that made the hair on Madeline's arms stand up. Subliminal messages passed back and forth between her and Mike.

"Have you started investigating this claim?" she asked.

"A little. I was able to speak with the warden yesterday morning, and she confirmed that she has her doubts about this prisoner's conviction," he said. "You want some water?"

"Sure," Madeline said, wrapping her arms around herself.

Mike pressed the intercom button on his desk phone and asked Samir to bring a mineral water for both of them. Knowing Samir's agility, they remained silent until he popped in and set the bottles and two glasses on the side of the desk and beamed his irrepressible smile at each of them. He backed out and pulled the door closed with his customary discretion, making both Madeline and Mike chuckle affectionately, effectively dispelling the tension in the room.

"Fortunately, some people are very easy to read," Mike quipped as he twisted off a cap and poured water into a glass for Madeline. She managed a tight smile for the water and the levity. Without further distractions, Mike got back to the topic at hand.

"I could tell by the way she spoke that wardens aren't supposed to have opinions about their charges' guilt or innocence. What little I've learned so far is that the prisoner, Lindsay Bartholomew, had been married to her husband, Nick Bartholomew, for only three years prior to his death, during which he had legally adopted Joni, Lindsay's daughter."

"How did Mr. Bartholomew die?"

"In a tractor accident, on their ranch." Madeline gave Mike a quizzical look.

"Okay, I'll bite. How did a tractor accident garner a murder conviction?"

"I don't have all the details yet. I was going to speak with Conrad about the case to get some background before I told you about it, but I hadn't expected you back in the office so soon." After letting that hang in the air for a moment, he took his phone out of his pocket. "I'll send him a text, see what light he can shed on the matter."

After listening to the whooshing sound of a text taking flight, Madeline shifted in her chair, struggling with her mixed emotions. She bristled with hate at the idea of her ex-husband having the nerve to refer cases to them. To her, this was a red flag as well as an affront. The fact that he could worm his way into her life through her partner made her want to scream. After all he'd put her through, was there no justice?

Madeline fought down her anger. She couldn't tell who she was more furious with, Mike or Steven. But as hard as she tried to wallow in her righteous indignation, her better side was struggling with turning her back on a woman who might be serving time for a murder she hadn't committed. Having direct contact with the warden took Steven out of the loop. Maybe that was something she could work with.

"Although I loathe the way this case came to us, I guess there's no harm in looking into it—as long as we can be assured Steven won't be involved," she said, feeling some of the poison coursing through her dissipate. "In the meantime, I say we canvas Natalie's neighborhood, see if any of her neighbors remember hearing or seeing anything unusual that day."

Mike was relieved that this was out in the open now and that Madeline's justifiable anger had been short-lived. He was still working on his humble apology when his phone alerted him to a new text.

"Is that Conrad?" she asked.

Mike nodded as he skimmed through the reply. "He says to contact Jordan Crowley, the A.D.A. who handled the case. He included the contact info. I might as well get that ball rolling," he said as he copied the text and forwarded it to the number Conrad had given him.

"Okay, that's done," he said, setting his phone down. "I agree with what you said earlier. Let's go call on the Sheckles' neighbors. We don't really have any other leads at this point, and the more time that lapses, the less they'll remember."

"I'll get my bag," Madeline said as she rose from Mike's chair. As she rounded his desk, he intercepted her, pulling her gently to him.

"Do you forgive me?" he asked.

Madeline looked up at him, the last trace of irritation ebbing away as she noted the sadness in his eyes. "There's nothing to forgive. I know you hate Steven as much as I do. I think you showed a lot of strength and compassion by consenting to meet with him. I don't know if I could've done the same."

"Well…I hope you never do," Mike said, rearing back to make it clear how he felt about her having any contact with Ridley.

Madeline let out a dismissive snort as she detached from his embrace. "Don't worry. If he ever has another one of these cases for us to look at, *you* will have to deal with him. Hell will definitely have to freeze over before I'll even look at that man again." She started out the door, then turned around to add, "And just for the record, I still don't believe he's capable of good deeds. I don't trust him as far as I can spit, and I'm really only consenting to looking at this case in the hopes of unmasking his ulterior motives, whatever they might be."

Mike recoiled slightly at the cold determination on his partner's beautiful face. One thing he never wanted to do was get on her bad side.

SEVEN

It was mid-morning when Mike and Madeline pulled up in front of the Sheckle residence. Mike held the cardboard box containing the Sheckles' financial records while Madeline rang the bell. They had made copies of everything they needed for the file, but they wanted to hang on to the box containing Andrew's memorabilia for the time being. Natalie was home between her early morning and afternoon classes, so the timing was good.

Whereas Natalie had been tense and emotional during their initial meeting, the look in her brown eyes as she greeted them was more resigned, hinting at the acceptance of the pain that would reside in her heart from now on. Madeline figured there was some comfort in hiring them to find out what really happened that horrible day.

Mike carried the box in and placed it in the family room while Madeline let Natalie know they would be canvassing the neighborhood.

"We'll be in touch again soon," she promised as Mike returned. Natalie managed a tight smile of gratitude and a weak "thank you" as she slowly closed the door. A silent communication passed between the detectives before they headed down to the sidewalk, shoring up their resolve to do what they could for their client.

They had decided on a plan of attack on the drive over: they would start with any homes that had vehicles either out front or on the driveway. That might be their best hope of finding people at home during that hour on a weekday.

The neighbors most likely to have seen anything were the two flanking the Sheckle residence and the three neighbors across the street. Of those five homes, there were vehicles on two driveways. They decided to start with the house directly across the street, which had the best view of the Sheckle's driveway.

After Mike knocked on the door, they stood waiting, their ears straining to pick up any indication someone was home. The muffled sound of a female voice grew louder just before the door opened. A woman in her late forties came into view as she awkwardly tried to open the door with a cell phone held up to her ear while restraining a powerful natural phenomenon in raging puppy-hood. Hardly what you'd call a watchdog, the chocolate lab was wriggling with all his might to break free and greet the visitors with aggressive, sloppy kisses.

"Dabney! Stop that! Heel!" the woman called out ineffectually. Seeing that all was lost, she ended her call so she could reel her wiggly beast back into the house.

"I'm sorry about that," she said, corralling the compulsive kisser. "Let me just put him up," she said as she began to drag him down the hallway. A door shut and loud scratching began immediately. The woman returned out of breath, smoothing back a lock of shoulder-length brown hair.

"Hope we didn't catch you at a bad time," Madeline said with a solicitous smile.

"No, it's fine. I don't know if there'll be a good time until he hits his second birthday," she said with a laugh. "How can I help you?"

"I'm Madeline Dawkins, and this is my partner, Mike Delaney." Madeline handed her their generic MDPI card that listed both their names and contact info. "Your neighbor, Natalie Sheckle, has hired us to look into the circumstances surrounding her husband's death."

A pall as dramatic as a solar eclipse fell across the woman's features. It took a few beats before her thoughts came back to the situation at hand.

"I'm sorry. Please come in." She shut the door behind them and led them to a large, sunny room toward the rear of the house, away from the whimpering and door thrashing. No words were exchanged until after she motioned for them to take a seat.

"Can I get you something to drink?"

"No, thank you," Mike replied. "We don't want to take up too much of your time. We'd just like to ask you if there's anything you can remember about August tenth, the day Natalie Sheckle discovered her husband dead." Mike pulled a small note pad from his shirt pocket. "I guess I should start with your name," he added with a smile.

"Oh, sorry… I'm Jill Smalls."

"Were you home when Natalie found Andrew?" Madeline asked.

"Yes, I was. I will never forget it," Jill said. "At first, I didn't know what I was hearing. It almost sounded like the screech of a train in the distance. Then, when I heard it again, I realized it was a woman screaming. It was so frightening. I remember I got painful chills all over." Jill shuddered and rubbed her arms up and down as if physically reliving the moment.

"Could you tell where the screams were coming from?" Madeline prompted.

"I could tell they were coming from the other side of the street," Jill said as she motioned with her head toward the Sheckles' property.

"Did you go check it out?" Mike asked.

"I did after the second shriek. I remember I grabbed my phone first. I was ready to call the police. For all I knew, there could've been a robbery in progress, or something worse." Jill paused for a moment as she thought back. "When I got over there, I found Natalie crying hysterically in her front room as she tried to explain what happened to the 9-1-1 operator. Fortunately, we're only about a couple miles from the sheriff's office. There were three vehicles here in less than five minutes. In the meantime, all I could get out of Natalie was that Andrew was dead. It wasn't until later in the evening that we got the details of what happened."

"Did you hear or see anything prior to Natalie's screams?" Madeline asked. Jill shook her head.

"Did any of your other neighbors see or hear anything that you didn't?"

"Not that I'm aware of. When something like this happens, it shakes everything up. Everyone around here pretty much keeps to themselves most of the time. We're all friendly, but not very chummy, if you know what I mean. But during all the ruckus, I spoke to neighbors I hadn't talked to in years. Everyone was really shocked and heartbroken for Natalie. I mean, how tragic—first her son, then her husband. I don't know how she keeps going."

"Do you recall seeing anyone at the Sheckles' house that day?"

"No," Jill said, shaking her head resolutely.

"How about anyone on your street that day who you normally don't see?"

"Honestly, I just don't remember. I didn't remember anyone when the police questioned me, and unfortunately I still don't."

"We understand. If you do happen to think of anything about that day that might have bearing on this case, no matter how minor or insignificant it might seem, please give us a call," Madeline said before signaling to Mike that it was time to move on.

"I will, I promise," Jill said as she fell in step with the detectives.

"Thank you for your time. You've been a big help," Mike said as they stepped out on the front walkway.

"I wish I had more to tell you. Good luck."

They were going to need a whole lot of luck, and he wasn't feeling anywhere close to lucky.

No one home in the neighboring houses could remember seeing or hearing anything unusual on the day Andrew Sheckle's life ended. The owners of the houses to the left and behind the Sheckle property were at work when Natalie made her horrifying discovery. The lucky break Mike and Madeline had been hoping for probably wasn't going to come from the neighbors.

They had just gotten back to the Audi when Mike received a text.

"The A.D.A. who handled the Bartholomew case can speak to us during his lunch break," he informed Madeline. He handed her his phone while he started the engine. "Can you let him know that works for us?"

"Sure," Madeline said, already tapping out a reply. "Since we're going to be in the neighborhood, maybe we should pick up some lunch at Anacapa Deli on the way."

"Good idea," Mike said as the text left with a whoosh.

"Tell me what you want, and I'll phone it in."

"You make a pretty good assistant, you know that?" Mike joked, earning himself a sock on the arm. "Ow. I guess I'd forgotten how powerful your strikes are." He massaged his right bicep as he peered over at her.

Madeline didn't even bother to look up at him, though her lips were curved in a sly smile. "Hi, yes—I'd like to place an order to go…"

The building that housed the District Attorney's office on Santa Barbara Street was relatively quiet at that time of the day. They found A.D.A. Brian Digiorno eating a sandwich from a Styrofoam container, working during his lunch hour the way many in his profession did. Too many criminals and not enough hours in the week.

Madeline's foresight in bringing their own bag lunch was appreciated by Digiorno, making him smile for the first time all day.

"Mind if we join you?" Mike asked as he set the brown bag containing their to-go order on the corner of the desk.

"Be my guests," Digiorno said after wiping the mustard from the corner of his mouth. "Just pull up a couple chairs."

Mike rearranged the furniture while Madeline introduced herself. Brian rose to his feet, momentarily mesmerized by the local legend standing before him.

"Oh wow...I've heard your name a lot over the years," he said as he took her proffered hand self-consciously in his.

"I don't doubt that," Madeline said with a laugh. When Brian continued to stare at her absently, she thanked him for seeing them.

"Oh sure, no problem," he replied as he sat back down and reached for the Bartholomew file. "Here you go," he said, waving it back and forth, unsure who to give it to. As Mike had already started in on his sandwich, Madeline took the file. "I hope you don't mind if I keep eating. I've got to be across the street in half an hour."

"Not at all. Please go ahead," Madeline said as she read up on the case against Lindsay Bartholomew. "I understand the victim, Nick Bartholomew, was killed in a tractor accident." Brian nodded as he worked to clear his mouth. "I'm curious why the D.A.'s office went after a murder charge."

After taking a drink of his soda, Brian said, "This case was really driven by the victim's children. I can't think of their names off the top of my head..." he said, fingers tapping his temple as tried to call up the information.

Madeline searched the file. "Sean and Vanessa," she supplied.

"Yeah. That's right. I don't know how I could forget," he said, rolling his eyes. "The whole case stemmed from their fervent belief their stepmom deliberately killed their dad so she could get at his fortune. They were probably afraid she'd find a way to cut them out of their inheritance."

Madeline regarded the A.D.A. thoughtfully as she chewed a bite of salad. "Surely there was evidence of the defendant's culpability."

Brian gave them a knowing smirk. "If it walks like a duck…"

"What exactly are you saying?" Mike asked.

"The kids were on this case from the get-go. They hounded my boss every day. It basically became a situation where the D.A.'s office had to pursue it." Sensing their confusion, he added, "They got a sworn statement from the tractor repair guy in which he claims he made it very clear that the tractor wasn't safe to be ridden until the part was replaced. He swears he told Mrs. Bartholomew that in no uncertain terms. She doesn't tell her husband, he gets on the tractor, it goes haywire, he's thrown off and gets caught up in it…" Brian shook his head, a squeamish look on his face. "I know. It's quite the visual."

"And Mrs. Bartholomew? What was her story?"

"According to Mrs. Bartholomew, she left a note on the kitchen counter, next to a freshly baked pie, warning her husband not to use the tractor because it hadn't been fixed yet. She then went out to run errands and pick up her daughter at school. When she got back two hours later, she was passed by an ambulance coming down her road. She didn't find out what had happened until she reached the house and was greeted by sheriff's deputies."

"So…no note was found…"

"That's right," Brian replied after swallowing a bite of his sandwich.

"Not on his person, not in the trash? Not anywhere on the property?" Madeline quizzed him.

"Nowhere."

"That seems a little curious on the face of it. If Lindsay's goal was to kill her husband to get at his fortune, seems like she would've figured out a way for the note to surface to exonerate herself," Madeline speculated.

"You're right, though to me, the fact that she didn't do that also calls into question whether she actually planned to harm him. But that kind of conjecture is not part of my job description," Brian reasoned.

Madeline eyed him thoughtfully as she chewed.

"In any event, I still don't understand why she was found guilty of murder. If a note had been found saying the tractor had been fixed and was safe to use, then I could see how a case could be made against her. Surely, if she simply forgot to leave a note, then manslaughter, or at least negligent homicide would be on the table."

"In theory, you're right. But like I said, Bartholomew's children put a lot of pressure on the D.A. According to their separate sworn testimonies, they had both been in the kitchen of the main house when their father got home, and there was no note on the counter or anywhere else. The daughter's theory was Lindsay was having an affair with one of the ranch hands. She claimed to have witnessed them kissing in the barn prior to Nick's death. She maintained this was a case of cold-blooded, premeditated murder."

"That sounds like unfounded conjecture to me," Madeline said skeptically.

"Hey, I'm not saying I believed it, and I'm not the one who gets to decide who to prosecute," he said defensively.

"I meant no offense," Madeline said evenly, "but surely a woman of means can afford good legal representation."

A tight smile crept onto Brian's face. "Yeah, well, that's where the case really got weird."

"How so?" Mike asked.

"Mrs. Bartholomew started out with a powerhouse attorney from L.A. The story was, all the topnotch local firms were conflicted-out because the deceased man's family had used them at one time or another. Anyway, the kids did an end-run and managed to freeze her access to any of the joint accounts. And since she didn't have any accounts or other assets in her name, she lost her high-dollar attorney and had to go with a public defender."

Brian leaned back in his chair, eyeing each P.I. in turn. "I'm not implying there was anything wrong with that—in fact, I think she lucked out with the one she got, but the firm the kids retained pursued this case with what I'd call 'uncommon zeal.' I prosecuted the case for the state, but I was nowhere as brutal as they were."

"I don't understand. If you were prosecuting for the County and a public defender was representing the accused, why did Bartholomew's kids need to hire a law firm, and how did they manage to bar access to the defendant's own accounts?" Madeline asked.

"They immediately filed a civil suit for their father's wrongful death. That case went through the system much faster and resulted in the defendant losing any right to her late-husband's estate."

Mike and Madeline both reared back and shot a look at each other. Mike could tell she was starting to feel sympathetic toward the prisoner. This case had all the hallmarks of a nightmare come true, for more than one party.

"How old are these other children, Sean and Vanessa?" Madeline asked.

"They were twenty-six and twenty-two at the time of the accident," Mike replied as he studied the file. "So, they're twenty-eight and twenty-four now."

"Still living at home with dad," Madeline mused. "And how old is Lindsay?"

Mike consulted the file again. "Born July fourteenth, 1986. She's thirty-two now, so she would've been thirty when Nick was killed—twenty-seven when they got married in May of 2014."

Madeline's eyes grew wide in appreciation of the strained dynamic in the Bartholomew household. She could hardly hold back her astonishment as she confirmed what this meant.

"So, Nick Bartholomew married a woman who was only four years older than his son."

Brian nodded, his mouth pursed to preempt his own commentary.

"So, the daughter Mrs. Bartholomew was picking up at school was not Mr. Bartholomew's biological daughter…" Madeline speculated.

"That's right," Brian confirmed.

After studying him a moment longer, she gave Mike the signal they had gotten what they needed. They stood and thanked the A.D.A. for his time.

"Happy to help," Brian said, getting to his feet. "For what it's worth, I always like to see justice done, regardless of who prevails. If you can find a way to overturn the ruling, that'd be fine by me."

"Do you believe Mrs. Bartholomew is innocent?" Madeline asked, putting the A.D.A. on the spot.

"I'm not the one who gets to make judgment calls. I'm paid to prosecute the files that come across my desk," was Brian's carefully tailored response.

"Well, thanks again," Madeline said, keeping her focus on him until he started fidgeting with the files on his desk.

"Sure," Brian said self-consciously. As Mike and Madeline headed out the door, he added, "While you're in the neighborhood, you might want to see if you can have a word with Jim Hofstetler at the public defender's office across the street. He's stretched just as thin as the rest of us, but he might be able to give you a few minutes of his time. He'd have better insight into why Mrs. Bartholomew held firm to her innocent plea instead of taking a deal."

"Thanks. We'll do that," Mike said.

EIGHT

The welcome they received from the public defender who'd represented Lindsay Bartholomew at her homicide trial was not nearly as cordial as the one they'd received across the street. Jim Hofstetler was engaged in a rather acrimonious conversation when Mike rapped on the door jamb. The attorney signaled with an upheld hand to *hang on, be patient* while he brought the call to an abrupt end.

"Yes?" he barked as he hung up the phone.

"Mike Delaney and Madeline Dawkins of MDPI. We'd like to ask a few questions, if you've got a minute."

"If I had a minute for every time someone said that to me, I'd be on a ten-week vacation right now," the P.D. replied, not even bothering to make eye contact with them as he patted his smothered desk in search of his cell phone.

"We're here on a mercy mission on behalf of a woman you defended two years ago on a murder charge," Madeline said, getting a reaction right away in the form of a scrutinizing stare. "Our services have been engaged to look into Lindsay Bartholomew's case, see if she's been wrongly convicted," she clarified.

The name worked like an incantation. The sullen, reproachful stare softened into one of regret. Hofstetler's shoulders sagged along with this countenance. With a defeated sigh, he motioned for them to have a seat.

Madeline returned the favor by getting straight to the point. "According to our source, the warden at the prison where she's incarcerated believes she may be innocent of the crime for which she was convicted. In your opinion—strictly off the record—is Lindsay guilty of killing her husband, Nick Bartholomew?"

Hofstetler's eyes roved around his desk before glancing at his uninvited visitors.

"You realize I'm damned either way I answer your question. No, I didn't believe at the time of the trial that she killed her husband, and I still don't. Do I regret that I wasn't able to offer a better defense? Yeah, I do." Hofstetler let his statement hang in the air as he thought back to that case. "I also believe we could've had a better outcome if I'd had a little cooperation from the defendant."

"What does that mean? Are you suggesting she sabotaged her own defense?"

Hofstetler grunted his disapproval of Mike's insinuation. "I gave Mrs. Bartholomew competent legal representation, regardless of the circumstances," he huffed. "The prosecution had a better hand with two eye witnesses who swore up and down the defendant deliberately endangered her husband's life. She didn't help matters by refusing to plead down. She naively believed the jury would see she was telling the truth. And unfortunately, she had a little bit of a credibility issue."

"Why is that?"

"Because she's young, beautiful and guileless enough to believe that righteousness would prevail. We maintained Mrs. Bartholomew left a note instructing her husband not to use the tractor until a part was replaced, but there were two witnesses for the prosecution who swore under oath there was no note. No note when Mr. Bartholomew came into the kitchen and ate a slice of pie before taking that fateful tractor ride."

"And Mr. Bartholomew's children were supposedly present when he ate the pie," Madeline offered for confirmation.

"Naturally. Classic he said, she said. Except in this case there were two witnesses corroborating each other's statement."

"How about the allegations that Bartholomew's kids made about Lindsey fooling around with ranch hands?" Mike asked.

"Another convenient statement that couldn't be proven one way or the other. To be honest, I think that was the most damaging aspect of the trial."

"Did Lindsay deny having the affair?" Madeline asked.

"Of course she did. But like any accusation, once it was out there, it stuck in the minds of the jury."

"Did you put the ranch hand on the witness stand?"

"I would've, but he left town week of the accident."

"That's curious," Mike said.

"Very."

"I'm going to guess you had no luck tracking him down," Madeline ventured.

Hofstetler grunted his answer. "That kind of investigation takes money. People don't end up at the Public Defender Office out of choice. It's the only recourse for indigents."

"So, you're telling us that being the widow of a wealthy man didn't afford Mrs. Bartholomew the option of putting up a rigorous defense…?" Madeline offered, mostly to confirm what they'd been told by Brian Digiorno.

"I'm telling you…first of all, how do I know that you have the authorization from Mrs. Bartholomew to discuss this case?" the public defender asked, suddenly growing suspicious of the line of questions being thrown at him.

Madeline turned to Mike, who was already flipping through the file for the authorization form bearing Lindsay Bartholomew's signature. He pulled it out and handed it over to Hofstetler.

"We were contacted by a newly formed government offshoot of the California Department of Corrections that is working to rehabilitate prison inmates so they can assimilate back into society once they've served their sentences. We're just looking into this case, pro bono, to see if there's any validity to the warden's assertion," Mike said, though he could sense his words were being met with distrust and/or disdain. "We're just a couple of private investigators who'd like to help if there's any reason to believe this woman may be innocent."

Hofstetler let out a strained sigh and leaned forward, forearms resting on his desk as he eyed Mike and Madeline with open frankness.

"Look, I know who you are," he said, looking directly at Madeline, making her stiffen with apprehension. "I know all about what that monster of an ex-husband did to you. I can appreciate that you empathize with Ms. Bartholomew, and I applaud you wanting to help her. But there's little I can do."

"And we can appreciate how busy you are. We're starting from scratch here. Anything you can share with us will help us fit the pieces together, see what's missing and where we need to go from there," Mike said.

Hofstetler sucked in a deep breath as he leaned back in his chair. He let it out in a gust of stale coffee breath and defeat as he pushed himself up out of his chair.

"I need some air," he said, motioning with a wag of his head for his visitors to follow him. He remained silent until they pushed through the doors that opened out to the grassy expanse surrounding the Spanish Colonial Revival courthouse. Coming to a halt on a sun-dappled patch of lawn about twenty feet from the building, Hofstetler turned to face them.

"My opinion, for what it's worth…Lindsay wasn't the one who sabotaged Nick Bartholomew. I couldn't prove that with the limited resources at my disposal. His kids wasted no time in hiring a high-profile local firm with huge clout to make sure Lindsay didn't have access to Nick's fortune. They took advantage of a clause in the prenup that stripped her of any claim she had to the estate. They don't even give a damn about their adopted sister, who's now been separated from both parents. It pains me that a young mother is wasting away in prison for something she didn't do, while her child grows up without her."

Hofstetler sighed as his eyes traveled up to the clock tower, as if truth and righteousness could be found at that lofty height.

"We may never know what happened that day, but my gut feeling from the moment I met Lindsay is that she's innocent. She mourned the loss of her husband and was nearly paralyzed with grief when they separated her from her child. For someone who's used to riding her horse every day, the confinement has to be soul-crushing."

Both P.I.s started to query him at the same time.

"That's all I'm going to say," he preempted them. "I read the papers. I know you two have a talent for finding the truth. Do your digging. Find the motive. Unravel it from there. If you come up with anything on your own significant enough to reopen the case, you can email me," he said as he took a bent business card out of a worn leather wallet and offered it to Madeline.

"Thank you for this. And for your time," she said as he headed back toward the courthouse. The P.D. gave a half-hearted backhanded wave without turning around.

NINE

"What's your take so far?" Mike asked cautiously as they walked toward their office, regarding her askance, half-afraid to hear her response. He couldn't tell if she had been sufficiently intrigued by the case to forgive him for meeting with Steven behind her back.

"You know me—I naturally gravitate to the underdog." If the circumstances hadn't been so harsh, she might've laughed at her own comment. True, after what she'd been through, it was almost an automatic reflex to side with anyone who'd been treated unjustly, at least until it could be proven otherwise.

"So…does that mean we are fully on board with this case?"

Madeline took a moment to reflect on what they had learned so far. It seemed almost farfetched that a woman could be convicted of murder under such circumstances.

"I feel like we're not getting the whole picture here," she said at last.

"I'm sure we're not. Got any ideas on how to remedy that?"

"If we commit to this, it will be essential to speak with Lindsay," she said as she tried to envision the steps that would require. She had only a vague idea where Chowchilla was; she wasn't even sure what county it was in. It had to be hundreds of miles from Santa Barbara.

Mike was reluctant to offer an easy solution to the logistical challenge of getting to the prison. He knew she'd be galled to learn that a private jet was available to fly them up to Merced Regional Airport whenever they wanted, courtesy of Steven Ridley. His stomach tightened with apprehension as he regretted not giving her full disclosure sooner. Now she would be irritated with him all over again.

Picking up on Mike's reticence, Madeline came to a slow halt in the middle of the sidewalk. Mike steeled himself and turned around to face the music.

"What are you not telling me?" she asked.

Mike knew better than to play dumb or innocent.

"If we decide to take this case, we've got a way to get up there. And back. Quickly."

"How?"

Mike scanned the faces of passersby with the weak hope of running into an acquaintance as a means of sidestepping her question. His stalling was not helping the situation. Madeline crossed her arms, a clear sign that he was trying her patience.

"How?" she reiterated with emphasis.

"Private plane. With enough notice, we could be picked up at our airport and be there in under an hour."

Mike watched Madeline's features as she mentally dissected his response. It didn't take long for her to surmise that Steven was somehow involved. And just as Madeline had the ability to tap into his thoughts, their twenty-plus-year relationship allowed Mike to do the same with hers.

"Getting within thirty miles of you would violate the terms of Ridley's parole, so you can be assured this is not some kind of a trap. But one of the perks to his new role is having a plane at his disposal so he can visit the various facilities in the State's prison system. I understand how repulsive that visual is, but it sure helps us with the logistics of this case."

"That's assuming the big shot isn't using it himself."

"One way to find out," Mike countered as he reached for his cell phone.

The very idea of Mike having Steven's phone number made Madeline's jaws clench in anger. The man shouldn't even have access to a cell phone; he should still be locked in Lompoc Federal Correctional Institution, serving out his thirty-year sentence. The fact that he had access to a phone at all was an affront to her and everyone else who had their life torpedoed by his treacherous schemes. Having a private plane at his disposal was beyond the pale.

Is there any such thing as justice in this world? she wondered.

"We can—"

"Just do it, and let's get this over with," she said as she turned back in the direction they'd just come from.

"Where are you going?" Mike called out, conflicting imperatives competing for his attention.

"Just make the call, see if that idea is even feasible. But before I agree to anything, I need to have a face to face with Conrad," Madeline said as she headed for the District Attorney's Office.

Mike finished the text and hit send. "Hang on—I'm coming with you!" he called out as his partner crossed the street on a yellow light. It was clear she wasn't over his perceived betrayal yet, nor could he blame her. *This woman better be innocent*, he thought as he sprinted in front of oncoming traffic.

They caught up with Conrad Adams as he was exiting the courtroom, cell phone pressed to his ear as he wielded his over-burdened briefcase to clear a path to the exit. They fell in step, flanking him like a security detail until he came to a halt on the walkway outside the courthouse.

"What's up?" he asked distractedly as he ended the call.

"We'd like to ask you a few questions," Madeline said.

"Walk with me. I've got a meeting in five minutes." They continued on in silence until Conrad had a chance to scan through his messages.

"Is this in regards to Natalie Sheckle?" he asked as they walked through the courthouse grounds to Santa Barbara Street.

"No, it has to do with a case your office prosecuted in 2017. Bartholomew, Lindsay. She was convicted of premeditated murder for her husband's death by tractor," Madeline said as Conrad stopped just before they reached the sidewalk. The look on his face made it clear he had very distinct memories of that case, none of them pleasant.

"What about it?" he asked as he resumed his pace.

"We've been contacted to look into the circumstances surrounding this case on behalf of the defendant."

"To what end?" he asked, already on the defensive. They had reached the curb and had to yield to traffic surging up Santa Barbara Street.

"We're not trying to step on your toes, Conrad," Mike offered diplomatically, "but it is a rather strange case, on the face of it."

Conrad's contemptuous snort refuted that opinion. The last of the cars passed, giving them a chance to jaywalk. The detectives kept pace as the D.A. strode into the street.

"It may *seem* strange to you, but I can assure you it seems cold and calculating to the victim's children."

"That's if you believe their version. Who's to say there isn't a third version that would support reasonable doubt?" Mike countered.

"It was up to the Public Defender's Office to make that case," Conrad said flatly as he came to an abrupt stop outside his building. "If you want to second-guess someone's motivation, check with whoever handled her defense. Ask them why they didn't convince her to take a plea deal. We came all the way down to involuntary manslaughter, which was a gift. I stood to take a hell of a lot of heat from the victim's family because of that very generous offer, but Mrs. Bartholomew refused it."

"We just spoke with Jim Hofstetler," Madeline said in a tone she hoped would ratchet down the animosity emanating from the District Attorney. Never in their four-year acquaintance had she seen him so irritable. It made her wonder if their timing was bad, or if there was more to this case than anyone had revealed so far. "He claims Mrs. Bartholomew was dead set on clearing her name. If it were me, I would've wanted to do the same."

Conrad exhaled a gust of pent up frustrations, looking away for a moment as he composed himself.

"Look, I'm sorry if I come across as a heartless S.O.B. here, but I've got a nightmare of a case on my hands right now, and to be honest, I do feel a pang of regret when it comes to how the Bartholomew verdict came down. She's a young woman, a mother. I get that. If she'd only met us halfway, she could've been back with her daughter in under two years. Now she's serving a twenty-year sentence. In my opinion, no one got justice."

A visible change settled over Madeline's features as if something fundamental to her perception of this case had just been revealed.

"Thank you, Conrad. I appreciate you telling us that," she said. "Getting your perspective helps us a lot."

The D.A. shifted uneasily as he regarded Madeline and Mike in turn, trying to read the subtext. He wasn't the only one curious as to the change in her tone, but Mike held on to his poker face.

"If you feel conflicted by your role in the Bartholomew tragedy, then I feel there's probably room for doubt. And I don't see that it will do any harm to just take an unbiased look into the circumstances surrounding Mr. Bartholomew's death. If we come up with nothing new, the only thing lost is our time."

Pedestrian flow caused the trio to step out of the main thoroughfare, giving all three a chance to relinquish the tension that had gripped them during their debate. Principles were a luxury not everybody could afford to defend. Or in the case against Lindsay Bartholomew, principles had cost her everything.

"Thanks for giving us your time and your honest opinion," Mike said as he held out his hand to the D.A.

"If you do find anything revelatory to the guilt or innocence of Mrs. Bartholomew, I'd like you to share it with me," he said as he gave Mike's hand a shake. There was a hint of détente in Conrad's tone that made Madeline smile.

"Don't worry, Conrad—we'll be sure to."

TEN

A cold chill that had nothing to do with the air conditioning descended on Madeline as soon as she stepped inside the Falcon 900XL. The elegance of the interior hit her like a slap in the face. Even the exterior of the jet was gorgeous; the graceful lines and the high, proud tail reminded her of an enormous, sleek bird. Despite the grandeur, being inside it caused a prickling sensation not unlike fear to wash through her limbs, putting her on edge, alert and distrusting.

"Welcome aboard," one of the two captains said, his smile broad and his manner easy-going. A man in his late forties, he came across as being quite happy with his career choice. Madeline forced a smile for his sake, though all the warning bells were going off in her head. The message she was receiving cautioned her to beware of ex-husbands offering favors.

"Thank you," she managed before venturing hesitantly farther into the cabin.

"Sit anywhere you like," he said breezily. "You two have the whole plane to yourselves."

Mike followed Madeline in, stopping briefly to shake hands with the captains.

"How long is the flight?" he asked.

"Forty minutes from takeoff."

Madeline hadn't made up her mind where to park herself when Mike caught up with her.

"Hard to decide where to sit," he said with a happy smile. Madeline ignored his attempt to play up the good points of what they were embarking on. She lowered herself tentatively into one of the white leather club chairs, looking anything but comfortable.

"You could grab a quick nap if you wanted to," he joked, extending his hand toward the bed made up toward the rear of the plane. One look at her told him his levity wasn't appreciated. He let his arm fall back to his side and chose to sit across the aisle from her, letting his eyes wander anywhere but at her.

Mike didn't need Madeline to tell him what had her so on edge; it was written all over her face. The way her eyes flitted around the posh interior while her hands clutched her biceps told him she was exercising every bit of her self-control, her guard up, as if afraid Steven would pop out of one of the storage compartments any second. The air between them fairly sparked with tension. Madeline looked about as comfortable as a cat in a bubble bath. Self-recriminations circled through Mike's head, slaying any justification he might come up with for ever thinking this idea had merit.

"We're going to be taxiing out in a few minutes," the other captain said as he came over to where they were seated. "We don't have an attendant on this flight, but you're welcome to help yourself to any of the refreshments in the galley once we hit our cruising altitude. Buckle up for takeoff."

"Are you furious with me?" Mike asked once the captain was out of sight.

Madeline let out a long sigh. The powerful engines roared to life, producing acoustic vibrations throughout the aircraft. The captain announced they had been cleared for takeoff.

The jet glided forward like a Doberman straining on its leash, then made a left turn onto the airstrip while a montage of horrible memories from her ordeal with Steven flashed through Madeline's mind, flickering images accompanied by the ghosts of feelings of confusion, alarm, mortification and abject terror. It was all she could do to stay seated as her teeth clenched the fleshy insides of her mouth and her fingernails threatened to draw blood from her hands.

What seemed like endless seconds passed before she was able to calm herself. "I'm not mad at you," she said at length, her gaze meeting Mike's briefly before she turned to look out her window. Palm trees and mountain peaks flickered past them like a sped-up travel advertisement. After several beats, she turned back to him and said, "I can't decide if I'm angrier with Steven or myself for letting him get to me."

The Falcon thundered down the runway with such force it took their breath away. Adrenaline sped through them like they were on a rollercoaster ride, and begrudging smiles managed to unseat tight-lipped frowns. The engines surged with palpable force, making the interior of the plane quake until they were airborne. A couple minutes passed before Madeline's feelings crystalized.

"Whenever I think of how Steven sabotaged my life when his Ponzi schemes blew up on him—after all those years of being a dutiful, supportive wife—it brings up such feelings of powerlessness. It makes me doubt myself. And now I feel like I've been sucked back into that arena where he's pulling the strings again, watching us perform for his own amusement and personal gain, like he's the puppet-master, back in his glory."

Mike winced at her words, feeling ashamed for ever letting himself be baited by Ridley. If he hadn't been seduced by his lust for revenge, he wouldn't have gone anywhere near that sociopath. The whole drive up to Lompoc had been spent vacillating between thoughts of turning around and ripping him limb from limb. In the end, all he had managed to do was thrust Madeline back into his orbit.

"I'll tell the pilots to take us back," Mike said as he rose up from his seat.

"No," Madeline said adamantly as she motioned for him to sit down. "If we did that, I'd be letting Steven know I couldn't stand up to his power, that I had been intimidated by him and had lost my nerve." She smiled wanly at Mike's wounded expression.

"We're going to see if this woman is worthy of our help. If we come away thinking that she was unjustly convicted, then we'll do what we can to find the truth about her husband's death. If not, we wash our hands of it. Either way, we never need to be in contact with Steven again. He's nothing but a paper tiger, whether he realizes it or not."

Madeline gave Mike a half-hearted smile that she hoped would ease his sense of guilt. Without speaking, she managed to remind him of their code of ethics and their mutual commitment to righting injustice wherever they found it in the course of their investigations. In this case, she seemed to be saying Steven Ridley was merely the errand boy.

"I wonder who actually owns this bird," she mused, shifting out of her introspective mood.

"That reminds me," Mike said, lifting his phone out of his shirt pocket. "I took a photo of the plane's N number. I'm going to send it to Samir and have him run a check on it, see what we can learn about the owner. I think it might be interesting to see who Steven's new benefactors are."

The devilish look on Mike's face was contagious. Madeline found herself smiling at the thought of using their investigative tools to dive into Steven's saintly new persona. This served as a reminder that their profession and their standing in their community gave them a much stronger hand and greater credibility than that of a paroled swindler. She realized now she had let her fear of Steven put her back into the role of victim, playing defense, something she had vowed would never happen again.

The Falcon turned away from the coastline and headed inland, high and fast, as its ultra-sleek design and name would suggest. Madeline leaned back in her seat, her thoughts turning to the woman they were heading to see. There was a kinship between them in that they had both lived in a rarified environment before their lives imploded. They had both experienced great comfort and had been married to wealthy men.

In her case it had all been an illusion, propped up by lies and other people's money. It struck her as ironic that the man who had destroyed her own life was now advocating to save Lindsay Bartholomew's. Of course, his intervention was self-serving in that it would put another feather in his cap if they succeeded. A caption blazed in her mind's eye below a smarmy photo of her conniving ex:

Steven Ridley, champion of the unjustly convicted.

Revolting. The kind of thing that might inspire a reality TV series.

To put him out of her mind, she got busy making notes to herself, questions she was hoping Lindsay Bartholomew could answer. Her side of the story was important, but it would be crucial to find another plausible explanation for her husband's death, since clearly her account of the events wasn't credible enough to convince a jury.

What they would need to come up with was a list of everyone involved with the ranch and anyone who had access to the property during that time. They would also need to get the lay of the land. With that size property of varying topography, it would be possible for someone to be on the ranch without anyone's knowledge.

It really was no wonder that Bartholomew's children had gone after Lindsay so vigorously. Losing a loved one under such circumstances would seem horribly unfair. In their minds, *someone* should be made to pay. There was also the future of the ranch to consider, plus any other holdings Nick had in his estate. They would also need to know if there had been any disputes or disagreements with anyone outside the family compound.

There was so much they needed to find out. And something told her Lindsay Bartholomew wouldn't have all the answers.

ELEVEN

The air inside the empty visitors' room was every bit as cold as outside, only artificially so, heavy with whiffs of cleaning solvents and regrets. The twenty-foot-square room held six rectangular tables, each with four metal chairs that served to amplify the cold as Madeline and Mike took a seat and waited for Lindsay Bartholomew to be shown in. As this meeting had been granted outside normal visiting hours, they would have the entire space to themselves. If there was any plus to the situation, Madeline figured that was it.

The backsides of both detectives had nearly grown numb from the frigid seats by the time the prisoner was brought in. They stood to greet Lindsay, who was led in without any restraints. The guard let the visitors know they had been given twenty minutes to interview the prisoner.

Nearly two years of incarceration had not stripped Lindsay Bartholomew of her looks. She was tall and slender, with perfect posture and a natural grace few people are born with. In spite of serving a twenty-year sentence, her comportment gave no hint that she had succumbed to self-pity. Self-torment, maybe. But she was definitely nobody's victim. Standing across from them in a prison uniform comprised of a baggy light blue pullover top and navy pants, she managed to come across focused and strong.

Madeline broke the awkward silence by offering her hand. "Hi, Lindsay. I'm Madeline Dawkins and this is my partner, Mike Delaney."

"Hi," Lindsay said, revealing naturally white, perfectly straight teeth. Even without a trace of makeup, she was still beautiful. She shook hands with both P.I.s before they all sat down. "I just want to thank you both for coming all this way to see me. I don't know if there's anything you can do to help me, but I sure appreciate you taking the time to try."

"We're glad to help, if we can," Mike said.

Lindsay shifted in her seat as she tried to read her visitors' true intent.

"I have to ask—does this mean you believe I'm innocent of killing my husband?"

"It means we're keeping an open mind," Madeline replied as she held Lindsay's gaze. Her words, though spoken impartially, seemed to steal a measure of Lindsay's hope.

"We are certainly willing to investigate what happened on the day of your husband's death, see if there's anything new we can uncover," Mike offered.

"How can you do that? I mean, how do you go back in time? How can you see what really went on that day over two years ago?"

"All we can do is gather every bit of information we can find and see if any of it leads us to a better understanding of the events that occurred," Madeline said.

Lindsay drew in a deep breath and let it seep out, resigning herself to the help of strangers, a proposition that carried no guarantees.

"All the facts have to be assembled in order to see the whole picture, like a jigsaw puzzle."

"I understand," she said stoically. "What do you need from me?"

"We'd like you to tell us everything you can recall about that day, before and after Nick's accident," Madeline said. "We need to know anything and everything, no matter how insignificant it might seem to you. With your permission, we'd like to record this interview, for our use only. Whatever is said in this room will remain private and confidential."

Madeline waited until she received Lindsay's consent to turn on the recording device. For the record, she stated the names of everyone present, the location, date and time of the interview, then Mike took the lead.

"Lindsay, please take us through that day from the time you got up," he suggested.

"All right. Um, well…I got up around 6:30, like I usually did, and made breakfast for Joni, my daughter."

"Was Nick up already?"

"Yes. He always got up earlier, usually around 5:30. He often went surfing first thing in the morning. He loved being out in the water at sunrise." Madeline began to make notes, and Mike nodded for Lindsay to continue. "I was making some oatmeal when Nick came into the kitchen through the back door. He was a little out of sorts because there was something wrong with the tractor. He called the repair guy from the kitchen phone. He could only come out around noon, but Nick had an appointment in Santa Barbara and couldn't make it back in time, so I said I could be there when he came."

"Was there anyone else on the property when the repairman came?"

"Yes. There are always people on the ranch. There are several houses in addition to the main house, three just for the families of the key employees—the ranch manager, who oversees the livestock, the housekeeper, and Eduardo. He and his staff oversee the avocado and citrus crops and the vegetable garden. Nick's kids, Vanessa and Sean, each have their own homes, though they often hung out at the main house, mostly to keep tabs on me, I think."

"What makes you say that?" Mike asked.

Lindsay let out a resigned sigh and leaned back in her chair. Looking as though she was about to make a confession, she straightened up, hands tucked out of sight.

"I assume you don't know my history with Nick's family…" After receiving her answer, she took a deep breath and forged on.

"I met Vanessa three years before Nick and I got married. She started taking riding lessons from me at the stables where I boarded my horse in Hope Ranch. She had been a very enthusiastic English rider since she was ten, but she wanted to start competing in rodeo events, like barrel racing and team penning. I've always been a western rider, and I started competing around the state when I was fifteen. Where I boarded was only about a fifteen-minute drive from Rancho Vista Encantada, which is considered close when you're out on that stretch of the coast. Vanessa had just turned sixteen, so she was able to trailer her horse down for lessons three times a week. Sometimes Nick would show up to watch her."

Lindsay shifted in her hard chair in search of comfort, not only for her body, but with the past.

"I knew almost from the beginning there was something between Nick and me. I felt an almost electrical charge whenever he showed up. At first, I could tell Vanessa thought it was cool—her dad hitting it off with her trainer. I don't think she thought for a second there was any kind of physical or emotional attraction there. And I certainly wasn't angling for something like that. I mean, he was married and the father of one of my students, and twenty-two years older than me."

Resting her forearms on her thighs, leaning in toward the table as if searching for the words or the courage to explain how her life had gone so sideways, Lindsay drew in another deep breath and continued.

"In Vanessa's senior year in high school, Nick filed for divorce. What a bomb that was. I heard about it first from Vanessa, whose world just blew apart. To be honest, I was in a kind of limbo where I didn't know which way to turn. Vanessa and I continued our lessons, but her mind and heart weren't in it. She was so distressed, she couldn't concentrate. The lessons had become more like counseling sessions. Her mom moved out—she was asked to leave, and that was a whole other drama. Nick started showing up in Hope Ranch while I was there alone. I guess he needed someone outside the family he could confide in. I felt really torn. Vanessa was like a little sister to me, but I never felt as happy or relaxed around a man as I did with Nick.

"Of course, we were asking for trouble by not defining our relationship. We just kept finding more ways to spend time together, without Vanessa. It was inevitable that she was going to find out. We should've addressed our feelings for each other and made a plan *before* word got around. I can't tell you how many times I've beat myself up about that."

"How long after Nick and his wife separated did you two make your relationship official?" Madeline asked.

"We waited until the divorce was final, which took a little longer because of the circumstances."

"Because of the division of assets?" Mike asked.

Lindsay wagged her head ambiguously. "There were a couple times when I thought Nick was going to go back to Patricia for Vanessa's sake."

"How did Nick's son take the break up and your relationship with his dad?" Madeline asked.

"It's hard to say. Sean's four years older than Vanessa, and he was already out of the house, traveling the world as a professional surfer. I think he felt like he'd already moved on from his family."

"But he has his own place on the ranch?" Mike queried.

"Yeah, he came back after Nick and I had been married for about a year.

I wouldn't say he was especially welcoming to me, but he was pretty detached from the whole thing. He was all about waves and chicks. He had plenty of funds at his disposal, most of which he earned on the pro surfing circuit. Independent and aloof is a good way to describe him."

"Did you move to the ranch before or after you and Nick married?" Madeline asked.

"After."

"Your daughter is from a previous marriage?" Mike asked.

"I had never been married before Nick," Lindsay said as she shifted uncomfortably away from the question. After a moment of strained silence, she added, "Lindsay's biological father raped me. I decided to keep the baby instead of putting her up for adoption."

It was the P.I.s' turn to shift in their seats. There were a lot of complexities to this story, and they were only five minutes into their visiting allowance.

"Did Nick adopt your daughter?" Madeline asked.

"Yes, right after we were married. I was really touched that he wanted to do that."

"Did that create a further strain on the household dynamics?"

Lindsay's head rocked equivocally. "Probably. It's hard to tell. Vanessa pretty much hated me by then, and Sean was so oblivious, I'm not sure anything going on in our lives penetrated his sphere."

"Okay, going back to that day, when the repairman came to look at the tractor..." Madeline redirected her.

"I showed him where it was and went back to the house to make a pie. I had some blackberries Eduardo had picked for me. I was just taking the pie out of the oven when the repairman knocked on the back door. The problem was bigger than he first suspected. He had fixed one thing only to find out one of the gears was completely stripped and another part needed to be replaced. He said it would take three or four days to get the parts he needed. He made it absolutely clear the tractor couldn't be ridden until the parts were replaced. I had to go into town to do some shopping and pick up Joni, so I left a note on the counter for Nick—right next to the pie—telling him the tractor hadn't been fixed and couldn't be ridden until the new parts were put in. I knew he'd find it because he couldn't resist my pies."

This last remark triggered painful spasms of loss as fond memories tore at her heart. She sniffed and looked away until she could regain her composure.

"It just seemed like the most logical place to leave it. You can't imagine how many times I've regretted that decision, yet when I run through that scenario—which I do every single day—I still come back to the fact that the note didn't walk off by itself. Someone had to have taken it. I don't see any other way it could've happened."

This description of events was consistent with what the detectives had been told already. Consistency was considered a bonus in their line of work, unless it was the practiced kind of consistency.

"What exactly was the tractor used for?" Madeline asked.

A bittersweet smile flickered across Lindsay's features before leaving her with a haunted look in her light blue eyes.

"Nick had two acres planted in vegetables, herbs and berries, which was great, living so far from the nearest grocery store. He wanted to turn the soil so he could start planting the summer's crop. He also used it to prepare the ten acres of land that he'd made available for Vanessa's vines." When the detectives looked at her quizzically, she elaborated.

"After her parents' marriage fell apart, Vanessa went to UC Davis to study wine making. Allowing her to start her own vineyard was Nick's way of making amends for the break-up of her family."

The expression on Lindsay's face was a mix of regret and longing. Speaking of her past highlighted everything she'd once had and lost. Madeline watched as a new thought disturbed her features, bringing a latent memory to the surface.

"What is it?" Madeline asked. "Did you just remember something?"

Lindsay remained mute for a few beats while her thoughts crystalized. "It's nothing. I don't know what made me think of it, but I just flashed on a big blow-out between Nick and Vanessa. Not that it's relevant to his death or anything."

"Why don't you tell us about it?" Madeline prompted.

"It was after they planted five acres in chardonnay grapes. Nick had conceded to Vanessa's pestering, though he wasn't very keen on it. But five acres wasn't enough for her. She wanted another five so she could plant pinot noir grapes. But the thing that really ticked Nick off was when she told him she'd inquired about getting permission to have a tasting room open to the public in exchange for giving up half the ranch to the Land Trust. Nick hit the roof. I didn't even know he was capable of that kind of anger."

"Did that change the relationship between Nick and Vanessa?" Madeline asked.

"They were at odds for a while, but I didn't think it caused a permanent rift between them."

"Who else was in the house when you left to pick up your daughter?" Mike asked, steering the conversation back to the day of the accident.

"No one."

"What about the housekeeper? Was she working that day?" Madeline asked.

"Yolanda had been there, but she left at noon on Wednesdays and Saturdays."

"And you saw no one else at the house or close by?" he pressed.

"I didn't. If I had, I would've made sure to tell them about the tractor, too."

"And you felt comfortable with just leaving a note on the counter?" Mike asked. "I'm not trying to play Monday morning quarterback here, but I'm curious why you didn't call Nick or send him a text to let him know the tractor hadn't been repaired."

Madeline looked up from her notetaking to gauge Lindsay's response. She was curious to see how Mike's persistent questioning and skeptical tone were being received. She could tell Lindsay wasn't particularly comfortable, but she didn't look flustered or defensive. She had probably been down this road numerous times, not only with attorneys, but with her own conscience.

"Nick was not big on using his cell phone. I had learned the hard way that most of the time it was either turned off or the battery was dead. He said he only carried it for emergencies, but the truth was it probably wouldn't have had a charge if he ever did need to use it."

It ran through both detectives' minds that the best scenario under those circumstances would've been to tape a note on the tractor seat, that way nobody would've touched it. They also imagined Lindsay would've given anything to undo that oversight. Then again, if someone had deliberately wanted to sabotage Nick and/or Lindsay, that might not have made any difference.

"What was your reaction when Vanessa and Sean insisted there'd been no note on the counter?" Madeline asked.

"At first I thought it had either been thrown away by accident or overlooked during all the commotion. I even insisted they look in Nick's pockets to see if he'd taken it with him when he went to check out the tractor. But mostly, I was really beyond rational thought. I just couldn't get my head around what had happened… I couldn't believe Nick was gone. I couldn't really even concentrate on all the other drama. All I could think about was that my husband was dead, and I was never going to see him again."

"Who was the first to suggest you deliberately withheld the information about the tractor being unsafe?"

Lindsay inhaled a deep a breath, releasing it with a sigh of resignation.

"Vanessa."

With the bad blood between them, it didn't come as a surprise that Nick's daughter would turn on Lindsay, just to have a convenient place to park her rage and grief.

"She completely lost it and started screaming at the sheriff's deputies that it was my fault her father was dead. That just devastated me. They showed up the next day and asked me to come to the station with them to get the events of the previous day on record."

"Did you ask for an attorney to be present?" Mike asked.

"No. I didn't think I needed one. I stupidly thought they could see that Vanessa had become unhinged by her father's death. I believed them when they said it was only a formality."

"Did they arrest you for Nick's death when you went in voluntarily?" Mike asked.

"No, but I was very unnerved by the way they were questioning me. It felt really aggressive, like they knew something and were trying to catch me in a lie."

"Did they?" Madeline asked.

"No," Lindsay said matter-of-factly. "Everything I told them was the truth. But I was shaken up. I was a nervous wreck all the way back to the ranch. When I got home, I called one of Nick's closest friends and told him I needed help. Brad's the one who eventually got me in touch with the law firm down in L.A. If he hadn't done that, I would've probably been sitting in the county jail cell a lot earlier. At least I had a few months to sort out what the future might hold for Joni and me."

"Before we came up here, we spoke with the A.D.A. who prosecuted your case and the Public Defender assigned to your defense," Mike told her. Lindsay didn't say anything, but he could sense how just thinking about those two individuals caused her anxiety to increase. "They both said your stepchildren fueled the D.A.'s actions against you. We got the impression they were hoping you'd plead down to a lesser charge."

"How could I do that?" Lindsay's voice rose with indignation. "I did not orchestrate my husband's 'accidental' death," she fairly spat. "My only chance at setting the record straight and clearing my name was to fight the bogus charge." Her hands came to rest on the table, folded together as if in earnest prayer. "How could I do anything but maintain my innocence? How could I expect my daughter to be okay with me admitting to having anything to do with Nick's death? My only hope was to fight and pray that somehow the jury would see that I loved my husband and would've never done anything that would put him in harm's way."

The tension arising from Lindsay's impromptu testimony was palpable. As Mike and Madeline absorbed the force of her words, they both were persuaded to believe her version of events. Whatever actually happened that day, they were willing to consider someone had intentionally sought retribution of some sort.

But there seemed to be no halfway here: either there was a note warning Nick the tractor was unsafe, or there wasn't. If someone had taken or destroyed the note without considering the consequences, wouldn't his or her conscience demand the truth be told for the sake of the two lives that would be ruined if Lindsay was wrongly convicted? It was hard not to imagine that the strain of such a secret would fester to the point of poisoning that person's life. Then again, sociopaths walk away from the mayhem they create without a moment of regret.

The only thing Madeline or Mike could be certain of was that somewhere out there, someone knew the truth of what really happened that day. The trick would be finding out who that someone was.

TWELVE

Mike and Madeline silently processed their conversation with Lindsay Bartholomew during the ride back to Macready Field, hoping insight and inspiration would strike them at some point.

They had left Lindsay with the impression they would start an investigation into the events leading up to Nick's death, but where to begin? A cold case with any tangible evidence gone at this point didn't leave them a lot to work with. Besides, the *lack* of evidence was the crux of Lindsay's perceived guilt. What they really needed was a chance to speak with the members of Nick's family and anyone who lived on the ranch at the time of the accident. A tall order, considering any emissary from Lindsay's camp would be treated with suspicion and hostility.

As they boarded the plane, Mike stopped for a moment to confer with the captains while Madeline went back to her previous seat and got to work. She wanted to send an email to Samir before they were cleared for takeoff, but her resentment toward her conniving ex-husband prompted her to first see if Samir had gotten her the info she'd requested prior to their visit with Lindsay.

Though she wasn't a complete stranger to lavish lifestyles, the attachment Samir had sent made Madeline's jaw drop in shock, which was quickly followed by disgust. Shock at the price tag for the fancy ride she was traveling in, and disgust that after all the truly despicable crimes Steven had committed, he was privileged to fly around the state in a forty-five-million-dollar jet.

Laughter alerted her to the fact that Mike had ended his brief conversation with the pilots and was headed back to join her. She closed the attachment and began a new email to Samir. She was absorbed in her task when Mike settled into the seat across from her. Just by the vibe he was putting out, she could tell he was feeling rather smug about something.

"What canary have you swallowed?" she asked as she sent the email into cyberspace.

"Oh, nothing," Mike demurred, wiping the smile off his face. When Madeline continued to stare at him, he fessed up. "I asked the pilots if they could fly over the stretch of the coast where the Bartholomew ranch sits. Unfortunately, that section of the coast is designated as a 'Restricted Area,' due to the proximity to Vandenberg Air Force Base. It was worth a try."

Madeline was still regarding him with a look he couldn't quite interpret. Mike's explanation didn't really answer her question, but she let it slide in favor of getting down to business.

"If we take on this case, our main challenge will be getting physical access to the property where the accident happened." With that thought hovering between them, her attention shifted to the view of the northern San Joaquin Valley as the jet began to gain speed for takeoff.

Mike followed her example, hoping the answer to that quandary could be found in the scenery whisking past the windows. After being instilled with the conviction that an innocent woman was sitting in prison for a crime she hadn't committed, the reality of what they were up against took most of the wind from his sails. The delicate, absentminded tapping of Madeline's nails on her tablet as she stared out the window told him her mind was whirring like a mainframe computer as it shifted through their options and obstacles.

"We need a lead on the Sheckle case," she said.

"The Sheckle case?" Mike asked, wondering if she'd misspoken.

"Yes. What we really need is some inside help. There's no chance in hell the Bartholomew children are going to give us access to Rancho Vista Encantada, not without some major lobbying on our behalf. Which is why we need Conrad's help."

Mike sat there, his expression mirroring his confusion as he tried to follow Madeline's line of thinking. "Quid pro quo?"

"Yes. I don't see anything wrong with it—do you?"

Mike shifted in his seat. "No, I guess not. We're doing him a favor by investigating Natalie Sheckle's claim. That's just as much of a longshot as Lindsay Bartholomew's claim of innocence."

"Two women in a world of misery, both widowed by circumstances that haven't been sufficiently explained," Madeline added, her tone somber. "But Conrad is going to be an obstacle to getting the access we need unless we can barter with him."

"I getcha," Mike said as he leaned back against the leather seat. "So…the question is how to get a break in the Sheckle case… Got any bright ideas?"

"No…not yet," she said with a heavy sigh. "I've got Samir looking into a couple of things that struck me as odd, but it's going to take time and leg work to see if anything comes of it. But the Bartholomew case is more urgent, as far as I'm concerned. Every minute Lindsay languishes in that prison is precious time lost for her and her daughter."

"I agree," Mike was quick to answer.

"So, maybe we just take our 'efforts in progress' to Conrad and vaguely explain that one hand needs to wash the other here."

Mike responded with a light laugh, taking delight in being back in the thick of the action with his partner and two unusual, nearly hopeless cases. His joy was dampened somewhat as he recalled how close he'd been to losing her four months earlier. Seeing how pleased she was at having two challenging cases to focus on, he banished the thought and grinned right back at her. It was hard to imagine anything being impossible when there was so much going in their favor. Together, anything seemed possible.

Though they couldn't fly over Gaviota because of the protected airspace, they were still able to catch the sunset along the coast as they came in for a landing. The sun had touched the horizon and was sinking rapidly, shrinking to a puddle before its brilliant orange fire disappeared altogether.

To live out on the Gaviota Coast in such isolated natural beauty, away from the hubbub of daily life that existed just fifteen miles south on the 101, was a delicious fantasy not many could afford, or actually cope with. Being secluded like that wasn't for everyone, but it made Mike wonder if he should look into buying a parcel up in Hollister Ranch before the price was totally out of his reach.

Madeline's thoughts were also on the Gaviota Coast as they approached

Santa Barbara Airport, though from a different perspective. She kept imagining what life had been like for the Bartholomew household before tragedy struck. All the beauty and all the joy-filled moments that had been shared between Lindsay and Nick Bartholomew were but synapses in time, a brief spell of love and contentment, shattered by a horrible accident. Or perhaps a calculated, spur of the moment decision by someone to end a life and a marriage still in its infancy. The big question was who, followed by the lesser question of why. If she could figure out either one of those answers, that would lead her to the other.

"I'm sending Conrad a text," Madeline said as they banked over the ocean and headed toward the Santa Barbara Airport. The lights of civilization were already flickering on in advance of the darkness that would quickly put an end to the short November day. "Maybe we'll catch him in a better mood now that it's almost cocktail time," she added as the text whooshed away.

Mike smiled, arms crossed contentedly as he studied his partner. He knew it was unseemly to appear so unbothered after meeting with a young woman stuck in a hell she couldn't understand, but he found it impossible not savor this fine moment. Madeline was healed and back in her element. He was with the only woman he'd ever loved. What more pleasure could he possibly hope to snare in his time on earth?

If there was one thing he'd learned after the ordeal he'd been through to free his cousin's girlfriend and her sister, it was to seize every good moment and every chance for real love, because you're only going to get so many.

The unexpectedly fast reply to Madeline's text brought Mike out of his introspection.

"He says to meet him at The Dolphin for a drink. He's headed there right now for a quick debrief with one of his A.D.A.'s. The timing looks like it might be perfect," Madeline said as she answered the text without consulting her partner.

"Aren't you tired?" Mike asked. The flight had relaxed him to the point of having no desire to move a muscle.

"I'm fine," Madeline said as she checked her appearance in her compact mirror. She smiled to inspect her teeth—a sight Mike found beyond endearing—then applied a fresh coat of lipstick before calling it good enough. "You look a little tired," she noted as she eyed him up and down while stashing her beauty aids.

"I'm fine. Just relaxed."

One of the captains called out to advise them of their imminent landing. They buckled up, preoccupied with all that had happened in this eventful day, one that wasn't even over yet.

"What's our plan of attack?" Mike asked.

"With Conrad?" Mike nodded. Madeline took a moment to come up with one. "We're going to have to do extensive digging to uncover anything that might lead us to Andrew's assailant, if in fact there is one. We will pursue the case until we've exhausted every possible lead or line of inquiry. In return, we need him to get us access to the Bartholomew ranch." Madeline shrugged her shoulders. "That seems reasonable enough, don't you think?"

Mike let out a bark of a laugh and shook his head. "I'll let you do the talking."

Madeline chose not to respond. She had no problem speaking her mind, especially not to Conrad. Over the last four years, MDPI had been involved in some of the most high-profile cases Santa Barbara County had ever seen. She and Conrad were almost like an old married couple; they knew where all the bodies were buried, literally and figuratively.

~~~

"I don't know what makes you think Bartholomew's kids would speak to anyone trying to help their father's killer get out of prison," Conrad said with indignant astonishment, "let alone give you access to their ranch."

Mike took his cues from Madeline, who sat serenely in the chair next to him, eyeing Conrad with confident neutrality. He could tell Conrad found her composure unsettling, as anyone would who'd witnessed Madeline's uncanny ability to assess people and solve crimes. Mike almost felt sorry for the D.A. He wouldn't want to be in his shoes, responsible for prosecuting cases and dispensing justice. Nobody could get it right all the time.

That's the beauty of our profession—we get to keep digging until we find the truth, Mike thought before fastening on to Madeline's reply.

"I don't know that it has to be viewed as an antagonistic situation, Conrad. After all, wouldn't Nick Bartholomew's children be disserved if the real perpetrator was still roaming free? There may have been bad blood between Nick's kids and Lindsay, but they've all been adversely affected by Nick's death. Unity can be forged from those kinds of circumstances. And then maybe some kind of healing can begin, for all of them, including Lindsay and her little girl."

The mention of the child Nick Bartholomew thought enough of to adopt took the starch out of Conrad's automatic reflex to defend his decisions. Sensing she'd found a vulnerable spot, Madeline continued to make her case.

"I think we can all agree that if Bartholomew's kids hadn't succeeded in stripping Lindsay of her portion of Nick's estate, the L.A. firm defending her would've never allowed for a murder conviction. They would have paraded everyone Lindsay had ever known past the jury until they were all convinced she wouldn't harm a fly, let alone the man she loved, and then you would've been looking at an acquittal."

Madeline could tell by Conrad's stiffening posture that she'd hit a nerve and was very close to offending him, losing his cooperation altogether. But instead of dialing back the rhetoric, she pressed on.

"I almost can't work 'Lindsay Bartholomew' and 'malice' into the same sentence, yet your office managed to get her convicted on first degree murder."

"She could've taken the plea offer," Conrad fired back just as a cocktail waitress brought a scotch for Madeline and a tonic with lime for Mike.

The brief exchange of money for beverages gave the occupants of the table a chance to ditch the aggressive tone of their discussion. Playing the moderator, Mike tried to lead them down a less combative path.

"I can understand how important it was for Lindsay to reject the plea your office offered in exchange for a confession. If I had been in her shoes, I know I would've held on to my integrity and fought to clear my name, if for no other reason than for the sake of my loved ones. I don't hold myself out as a human lie detector, but I found it difficult to believe she would sabotage her husband in either a fit of spite or coldblooded premeditation."

Conrad threw back the last of his martini and handed the empty glass to the waitress as she passed by on the way to the bar. "Another?" she asked, to which Conrad nodded before returning his attention to the detectives.

"Is there really anything wrong with us taking an unbiased look into what went on the day Nick Bartholomew had his accident?" Madeline asked, her tone neutral and her gaze frank.

"I don't see anything wrong with you snooping around on Lindsay's behalf, but I don't like being dragged into it," Conrad countered.

Madeline had to make a conscious effort not to smile. "In the four-plus years we've known each other, we've managed to be respectful and work together, regardless of our personal or professional positions. When you brought us the Sheckle case, we took it on without hesitation." Conrad tried to interject, but Madeline didn't yield. "This looks to be a clear case of suicide, but you were persuaded by Natalie Sheckle that her husband would never take his own life. Now, we're pretty much in the same boat with Lindsay Bartholomew. The point is, all we have to go on at this juncture is our gut-level readings. We believe both cases deserve a closer, perhaps less biased look. That's all we're after here."

The waitress set Conrad's second martini down and made eye contact with his guests to see if they needed anything. Mike and Madeline shook their heads. Conrad stared down into his drink for a moment before taking a thoughtful swig.

"I can't conceive of a way to convince Bartholomew's kids to let you on the property," he said at length. "If I even suggest to them that you want to snoop around the ranch on Lindsay's behalf, they'd flip out, and rightly so. In their minds, justice has been served. And let's not forget that they've lost the father they loved. Anyone coming to them from Lindsay's camp will get nothing but grief for their efforts."

Mike felt the hope they had on the plane evaporate. He couldn't blame Conrad for not wanting to help, and he found it hard to argue against the point he just made. But Madeline didn't see defeat; she just read the cue for using a different strategy.

"I don't doubt that one bit, especially after they went to such lengths to strip Lindsay of her rights as one of Nick's heirs. So, let's approach this from a different angle. Give us access to all the evidence the sheriff's department collected that allowed your office to bring charges against Lindsay." Conrad balked, but Madeline wouldn't back down. "If we can find any discrepancies, anything that would've allowed Lindsay to present a better case for her defense, *then* you talk to the Bartholomew heirs and let them know that new evidence has come to light and that MDPI wants to investigate to see if there's any valid reason to reopen the case."

Mike covered his mouth and feigned a cough to keep from laughing out loud. Madeline never ceased to amaze him. It seemed as though her powers of observation and reasoning had grown even stronger since she came out of her coma. Maybe that downtime allowed her mind to reflect on all she had been through in her life, recalibrating all that data into a more streamlined, efficient bank of knowledge. Or maybe she just grew smarter every day. Either way, she was a force to be reckoned with.

"What is it you're after, exactly?" Conrad asked, already looking defeated by Madeline's determination.

"A list of everyone the deputies spoke to, surveillance tapes from the ranch—if there were any, a list of the physical evidence seized, access to the taped interviews with Lindsay. Make that everyone they interviewed after the accident," Madeline amended, pausing to see if she could think of anything else. "That will get us started," she hedged.

"Christ. Send me an email, and I'll get what you need. What's tomorrow… Friday? Okay, I'll make sure you get it before the weekend."

Madeline wanted to press him for first thing in the morning, but decided to accept the terms graciously. There might be more she needed down the road, so she didn't want to use up all her bargaining power.

"In return, I expect you to conduct a thorough investigation into Andrew Sheckle's death. Ideally, an alternate theory for his demise or a compelling reason for him to take his own life." This mandate seemed to square things in Conrad's mind. He gulped down the rest of his drink and pushed away from the table.

"I've got to go. I've got an event I have to attend in an hour," he said after getting the bad news from his watch. He stood and reached into his pocket.

"We've got this," Mike said, signaling to the waitress for the tab. Conrad nodded his thanks, then bent down to retrieve his bulging briefcase. He bid them goodbye and began to make his way past the bodies that had accumulated around the barstools, blocking passage, requiring him to use physical contact to clear the way.

Madeline and Mike watched Conrad disappear in the crowd before analyzing what exactly they had achieved.

"So now we have to pull a rabbit out of our hat," Mike said.

"Two rabbits."

"Right. Two rabbits." Mike watched as Madeline took a contemplative sip of her scotch, experiencing an unexpected feeling of envy for the comfort alcohol used to provide him. He drank his tonic water, doing his best to find something akin to fortitude in it. "Got any clever plan of attack up your sleeves?"

Madeline pulled her tablet out of her bag and checked her emails. Finding Samir's reply with attachments brought a smile to her face. She tapped out an answer as she clued her partner in on what it said.

"Samir has the info I requested while we were on the plane. I told him to bring it by. Hope you don't mind."

"I don't mind. What kind of information?" he asked as he shifted in his seat and leaned back, arms crossed in a challenging manner. He was merely curious to hear what other brilliant ideas had been hatching in that pretty head of hers.

"Just public documents," she replied vaguely. She studied Mike's bemused expression for a second before something else caught her attention. "That was quick."

Mike turned to see what had her smiling. He let out an amused laugh and straightened in his chair as Samir squeezed his way through the throng. As the bodies continued to accumulate inside the bar portion of the eatery, the noise level had risen along with the head count. Spotting his bosses, Samir's face broke into an irrepressible smile. He made it to their table and stood grinning with indefatigable good humor.

"You must've been hiding in the bushes," Madeline remarked as Mike scooted the chair vacated by Conrad toward Samir with his foot.

"You said this is where you were meeting the D.A., so I just waited," Samir admitted, beaming like he was in the company of royalty.

"Sit," Madeline finally said, to which Samir eagerly complied. The cocktail waitress was on him immediately.

"I'll have a beer," Samir happily informed her. Such a generic request prompted her to point to the list of thirty craft beers on tap written on the chalkboard next to the bar. Mike made a suggestion based on the one listing the lowest alcohol content, being that it wasn't quite the weekend yet. Samir looked thrilled that his boss had ordered for him.

If only everyone were so easygoing, Mike thought wistfully as Madeline seized the file Samir slid over to her side of the table.

"What did you find?" Mike asked Samir as Madeline read through the data he had culled from various sources on the Internet.

"Well…"

"This is interesting," Madeline cut in. She glanced up at Mike, her eyes full of unexpected pleasure. "In February of this year, Rancho Vista Encantada received permission to engage in a 'for profit' venture on site—meaning open to the public—in exchange for deeding half of the ranch to the Land Trust in perpetuity."

Madeline recalled what Lindsay had said about Nick's love affair with that impressive hunk of ocean-view land. The 2,400 acres belonging to Nick Bartholomew and his heirs before his death were now a mere twelve-hundred, still plenty enough land to act as a buffer from the outside world. But according to Lindsay, selling what had been in the Bartholomew family for generations was something Nick had been adamantly against. Lindsay had given no indication of knowing what her stepchildren had done with the family legacy. She had been cut off from her former life so thoroughly, it was almost like it never existed.

"Check out the next page," Samir prompted her. He was brimming with pride and expectation. The waitress appeared and set his beer on a paper napkin before dashing off. Samir followed her with his eyes before eagerly taking a healthy gulp of his reward for a job well done. He turned his focus back to Madeline, who looked quite pleased with what he'd found.

"What is it?" Mike asked. He recognized that look, that *now we're getting somewhere* look. She was too absorbed in what she was reading to answer, but he could tell whatever Samir had unearthed had to be significant.

"Excellent job, Samir."

Samir was beaming with pride. He was so thrilled at having been charged with more investigative work. It made him feel like he was really part of the team now, instead of just being office support. He had taken that role in the beginning to get his foot in the door, and while Madeline had been recovering from the gunshot wound, coma and the subsequent paralysis, Mike had relied on him to do a lot more of the nuts and bolts detective work, letting him use the knowledge he'd picked up while in the police academy.

"Thanks, Boss—I mean Madeline!" he stammered, earning a laugh from his employers. "Sorry, that just slipped out."

"That's all right, Samir. At this moment, I'm quite proud to be your boss."

"Is anyone going to share the good news with me?" Mike asked, his tone a little testy.

Madeline slid over the screenshot Samir had taken of an announcement regarding the new enterprise at Rancho Vista Encantada.

"'Bartholomew Vineyards. Tasting room for local winery…fresh produce… now open to the public.'" Mike smiled. "Well, how about that? Looks like we lucked out here."

Madeline retrieved the announcement to study it further. "'Open daily from 10am to 5pm.' That's where we're heading tomorrow."

Mike tugged the piece of paper back to study the details. "Where did you find this?" he asked Samir.

"I did a search on the name of the ranch and found an article about the business in a back issue of *Santa Barbara Today*," he said, motioning for Madeline to look in the file. "I got this hunch to go through the whole issue, just in case they had run an ad for the place, which businesses will sometimes do to capitalize on the publicity."

"You've got good instincts," Mike commended Samir, making his dark complexion glow with pride.

Madeline leaned toward her companions and raised her voice to be heard over the din as she read from the article.

"'It was my father's dream to open our ranch to the public in order to share the bounty the Bartholomew family has been so privileged to enjoy for more than a century,' Vanessa Bartholomew told us as we toured the new commercial venture on the ranch that offers fresh produce, a wine tasting room and a gift shop. 'We're thrilled to announce that our first vintage of Rancho V E chardonnay is now available. This is a true boutique wine, coming from our first ten-acre vineyard, so quantities are limited…'"

Madeline's voice trailed off as she scanned through the rest of the article. "'Our operation is still in its infancy, but we've got big plans for the future. We've just planted another twenty-acres in chardonnay and pinot noir grapes and are very excited about the expansion. We will continue to showcase other local vintners in addition to our own wines, so be sure to drop by and support our local businesses,' Ms. Bartholomew added."

Madeline let the page fall back into the file, while her thoughts ran in several directions. She was so glad they'd had a chance to meet with Lindsay face to face. It gave them context in which to insert all this new information. What Lindsay had said about Nick's reluctance to put in a vineyard colored Vanessa Bartholomew's actions as being rather opportunistic. Opportunistic to the point of being suspicious. Nick dies, Vanessa wastes no time in making her dream a reality.

One look at Mike told her she wasn't the only one who found the new venture on the Bartholomew ranch questionable. She was anxious to get back to the office so they could start plotting all they'd discovered on the boards to allow them to better connect the dots. She was just about to suggest that to Mike when an electrical current of pain ran from the middle of her back all the way to her left foot, a clear signal that she'd pushed herself too far for one day.

"You okay?" Mike asked discreetly, recognizing the subtle cringe.

"I'm fine," Madeline said, though they both knew she wasn't.

"Great work, Samir," Mike said as he stood up to leave. "Why don't you order yourself something to eat," he added as Samir eyed the cash Mike tossed onto the table, which was obviously way more than they could've spent on a few drinks. Turning to Madeline, he picked up the folder in one hand while helping her out of the chair with the other.

"Thanks, Samir—you've done a terrific job," Madeline said as she tried to disguise her mincing steps.

"There's more in the file," Samir happily informed them, anxious to make sure they didn't overlook anything.

"We'll check it out," Mike said as he shepherded Madeline around the table and toward the exit.

Even Samir could tell by now that Madeline was experiencing a setback. He flashed a look of concern at Mike as she walked past him. Mike's unspoken reply told him that she just needed to get flat for a while. Still, Samir couldn't help feeling anxious about Madeline's condition. In some corner of his mind, he would always feel responsible for what had happened.

Samir's gloomy funk was dispelled when a long-legged blonde leaned down to ask if she and her friend could join him, her sidelong glance pointing out the shortage of available seats. It took two whole seconds for him to jump up and motion for them to have a seat. The wad of cash Mike had left would certainly cover a few drinks and a couple appetizers. Samir smiled at being rewarded for a good bit of detective work. It didn't even matter that he couldn't hear a word his new companions said. He just sat there and grinned for all he was worth.

THIRTEEN

Mike assumed Madeline would want the comfort of her own bed after their intense day, but she set him straight once they turned in the direction of her house.

"Do you mind if I crash at your place tonight?" she asked, her head lolling toward him, a clear sign she was wiped out.

"No, not at all," he said with a happy grin.

"I've been cooped up at my place for so long, I can't stand the thought of being back there after my newfound freedom," Madeline said, her smile matching Mike's before some other thought disturbed her peace of mind.

Mike watched her surreptitiously as he piloted them over the hill on Carrillo and swooped down onto the Mesa, trying to take a reading on her physical and emotional state. He sensed earlier that she'd been extremely uncomfortable flying around in the same plane Steven Ridley used when conducting his self-serving business on behalf of the California Department of Corrections and Rehabilitation.

By the look on her face, he guessed she was reliving that galling experience. It had to have been an affront to her sense of justice to see Steven acting the bigshot once again, after what he'd done to her and dozens of others. It was a cruel twist of fate that he managed to land on his feet again after only serving four years of his prison sentence. What made the affront worse was Mike's involvement in that emotional ambush.

"Are you hungry?" he asked, extending the only olive branch he could come up with.

"I could eat," Madeline said without much enthusiasm. "I'm sure I'll feel better once you pour me a glass of wine and massage my shoulders." She flashed him a teasing smile.

"I'd be delighted to pour you a glass of wine, massage any part of you, and even make you my famous linguine carbonara."

When Madeline turned to look out the window after giving him a wan smile, Mike's fears were confirmed. Problem was, any reference to Ridley would only further dampen her mood. He was trying to find another inroad that would lead them back to her sleazy ex so he could somehow apologize again without seeming to do so, but Madeline beat him to the punch.

"I don't regret our involvement in the Bartholomew case—at all—but I can't help feeling like Steven's playing me—*us*. I know how that sick bastard's mind works. He actually takes great delight in being the puppet-master. And I can guarantee you he's never done a single thing in his life that wasn't motivated by self-interest."

Madeline glanced over at Mike before continuing. "Knowing that leads me to wonder what his big plan is, his long game. I don't believe for a second that he's been reformed, found God, grown a conscience, or whatever. Steven Ambrose Ridley doesn't do anything unless it benefits him somehow. And I'll be damned if he's going to use us to achieve some self-serving goal."

Mike sucked down a deep breath before giving her the reply she seemed to be waiting for. "So, the question is, how do we pursue the Bartholomew case without furthering Ridley's cause?"

Madeline shook her head and turned to stare out the window. Was this case just about Steven building his own clout, establishing a reputation for himself with the state government officials? It certainly fit his M.O., and she had no qualms believing the worst about him.

Mike didn't have any handy reassurances to offer. Ridley would always be an untrustworthy wildcard, as far as he was concerned. Madeline shifted in the seat to face him, as if she were trying to read his mind, or trying to get him to read hers.

"I guess the only way to find out if Steven is trying to pull a fast one here is to do a deep dive on the Bartholomew case," she said. "We'll just take this on without any preconceived notions of guilt or innocence and see where it leads us. We have no vested interest in this case or the people involved. Instead of approaching this as advocating for the underdog, we'll just remain neutral. Conrad's going to give us access to the evidence, and we'll just be nosy-bodies."

Mike nodded in agreement. "I like that idea. For one thing, it takes the burden of Lindsay's predicament off us. We will dig and dig until we have a clearer picture—one way or the other—if for no other reason than to satisfy our own curiosity."

"Exactly. And I think we'll be less prone to overlook incriminating evidence that way. For all we know, Lindsay Bartholomew could be the schemer her stepchildren think she is."

"That's entirely possible. And the whole thing about a mother rotting in prison while her daughter is farmed out to strangers could be a convenient spin for getting someone to champion her cause."

"That's right," Madeline agreed as she sat back and took a deep breath. She could already feel the tension start to slip away now that she had effectively taken Steven out of the equation.

But instead of putting him out of her mind, she relegated him to the fringes. She'd learned the hard way how dangerous it was to dismiss him outright. Now that he had been liberated from prison, she had to consider him a real threat to her and anyone connected to her.

After Mike made good on his offer of loosening the knotted muscles in her back and shoulders, he set about making her favorite pasta dish. As the pancetta sizzled in the frying pan and the water was brought to a boil for the linguine, Madeline used one of Mike's notebooks to plan the next day's strategy. She took a seat on one of the chairs facing out toward Santa Barbara's curving coastline.

Mike stood at the kitchen island of his Shoreline Drive 1960s bungalow, keeping an eye on Madeline as he assembled the ingredients. There was so much history between them, both good and bad. She had saved his life by guilting him into rehab nine years earlier. He'd been on some sort of crusade to destroy himself ever since she broke up with him. From this point in time, he couldn't remember what had been so appealing about a life centered around drugs and alcohol, except for the fact that they dulled his senses to the loss of his one great love.

How ironic that the woman who'd spawned such self-loathing was the one who forced him to take a hard look at himself. Her courage continued to inspire him, not only to live a substance-free life, but to make the most of every day he was given. Those days that included being in her company were a gift he never lost sight of.

Once Mike had the pasta in the water and the timer set, he wandered over to where she sat to peer over her shoulder. He was surprised to find she was focusing on the Sheckle case after all their talk about the Bartholomew conundrum.

"I'm putting down some possible lines of inquiry before I get too distracted. We owe Conrad for getting us what we need on the Bartholomew case. Problem is, we don't have anything concrete to work with yet."

Mike took the pad and plopped down in the club chair next to hers to read her notes.

- *Contact Andrew's employee – find out why he was home in the middle of the day*
- *Have Samir do an extensive review of all bank accounts to find any anomalies: one-off payments, cash withdrawals, etc.*
- *Review all credit card purchases*
- *Canvas neighborhood again. Somebody may have heard or seen something – if not that day, maybe another day*
- *Check cell phone history for any names from his past. Cross-reference school yearbooks*
- *Review frame shop's books. Cross-reference customers to past friendships*

"It's not a lot, but it'll get us started," Madeline said as Mike handed the pad back to her and went to turn off the timer and drain the pasta.

"There's got to be a trail somewhere. Somebody's got to know something. There's someone out there who wanted Andrew dead and wanted to make it look like a suicide. The big question is why."

"It's always 'why,'" Madeline agreed as she abandoned her notetaking to see what was making her mouth water. Her stomach grumbled at having gone so long without food. She got up from her too-comfy perch and went over to watch Mike at work, cutting off a thin slice of parmesan cheese to appease her hunger.

"Okay…what would drive a person to kill someone and make it look like a suicide?" she asked.

"Off the top of my head, I'd say money."

"I know. That's a fairly common motive. And in this case, that would point directly at Natalie. But she appeared to have known about the two-year suicide exclusion," Madeline mused.

"True. But we don't know that for certain. Maybe just proving—like we already have—that the body was moved to make it look like a suicide would be enough to satisfy the insurance company that Andrew was murdered…?" Mike suggested.

"That would be fairly convoluted and risky, don't you think? I mean, why go to the trouble of making a murder look like suicide, which isn't covered, then have to convince law enforcement it was murder after all?" Madeline shook her head as if that kind of twisted thinking was beyond her current mental state. "Can you think of any other scenario that would fit?"

"Not at the moment," Mike replied as he plopped the drained linguini into the saucepan and stirred it around with the pancetta, egg yolks, garlic and cheese and turned up the heat for a couple of minutes. "Ready for that glass of wine?"

"I certainly am," Madeline said, happy to call an end to the day. Her brain needed a little downtime to process everything they'd learned about their two new cases. Two dead husbands. One wife in prison, the other faced with having to give up her home and all the memories attached to it. Both stripped of the loving relationships they'd once had.

It was no wonder Madeline could relate to their predicaments so well; she had also lost her home and the man she loved—not through death, but through a devious scheme orchestrated by the very man who now sought their services on behalf of one of the widows.

"What is it? You look like you're in a trance."

"Oh, nothing. I was just thinking about the masks we all wear and the complexities lying just beneath the surface."

Mike gave her a knowing smirk, understanding her trepidation about delving into the murky waters of other people's problems. Their line of work exposed them to all sorts of unseemly realities, and it was hard not to feel a little sullied by each case. They always managed to brush off the grime and grit once the cases were closed, but it was impossible to un-know something. Both of the cases they'd been working on when she got shot would haunt the recesses of their minds for the rest of their days.

Though it was hard to see anything overtly sinister on the surface of the Sheckle and Bartholomew cases, he knew that would change once they began digging in earnest.

"What's our game plan for tomorrow?" he asked as he set two bowls of sinfully rich pasta on the table.

The question went unanswered while Madeline bathed her senses in the dish in front of her. She didn't respond until she had taken a huge mouthful and washed it down with a healthy swig of Barolo. Though she could never be accused of being unladylike, the way she seized upon her dinner was rather out of character.

"*Oh my God*, this is unreal," she said, favoring Mike with a messy, enraptured smile.

"I'm glad you're enjoying it."

"That's an understatement. But to answer your question, after we plot out our two cases on the boards so we can get a handle on exactly what we know so far, I say we head up to Rancho Vista Encantada, have ourselves a little look around."

"I agree."

"Maybe on our way up, we can stop at Andrew's frame shop and have a word with his former employee."

"Great minds do think alike," Mike said, clinking his glass of sparkling water against Madeline's wine, earning himself one of those smiles that made him light up inside. "To solving our two new cases," he offered as a toast.

"Hopefully they won't be quite as dramatic as the last two," Madeline amended.

"I seriously doubt we'll be shot or beaten half to death," Mike said, earning a stern look from his partner.

"Don't tempt fate. Nothing is ever as it appears on the surface," she warned, her expression clouding for a moment before she dove back into her pasta with gusto.

FOURTEEN

Mike and Madeline had already gotten what they knew so far about their two new cases tacked up on separate boards by the time their employees filed into the office. Though they had come up with more insights as they began piecing timelines and circumstances together, the collages left them with more questions than answers.

"Good morning, Samir," Madeline greeted her somewhat disconcerted employee as he came into the conference room and surveyed all that had happened in his absence.

"Good morning," he answered, stowing his pack under the long conference table.

"Sorry for commandeering your 'office,'" she said, using air quotes to acknowledge that his nomad status was something they needed to rectify. Though she knew there was an issue regarding desk space because of the new hires, the office had just been expanded right before her unscheduled leave of absence. She had no handy solution to the downside of increased commerce, other than for the investigative side of operations to float as needed. They would just have to make do until they could come up for air to think about practical matters.

"No problem," Samir replied, his hands deep in his pockets as he moved closer to the boards to scrutinize what they'd discovered so far.

"This just came for you," Sydney said as she placed the manila envelope on the end of the conference table and made herself scarce. Samir watched her hasty retreat, sensing how intimidating this aspect of their operations was for someone not initiated in resolving the seamier issues in life. He also detected an undercurrent of curiosity, the pull of the sometimes-baffling process of unearthing the truth. It quickly crossed his mind that perhaps he could offer private tutoring to help demystify the business during off-hours.

As Madeline was closest, she opened the package the D.A. had sent over and spread the contents out on the table. In addition to the ambulance, two squad cars responded to the emergency at the Bartholomew ranch. The sheriff's deputies were first on the scene and took photos once they determined Nick was already beyond help. Though she wasn't especially squeamish, she hadn't been prepared for the extent of Nick's injuries. He had bled out quickly due to the severing of his femoral artery when his right leg was crushed by the tractor. More photos showed the aftermath from various angles.

Having seen enough evidence of Nick's tragic demise, she turned to the written report. She scanned through it quickly before handing it to Mike. The pertinent information read as they had expected: Male, 52 years of age, fatally injured while operating a tractor. No witnesses to the event. Victim was deceased when the deputies arrived. Body was transported to the Santa Barbara Coroner's Office for the postmortem.

Underneath all the paperwork was a memory stick inside a clear plastic pouch labeled "Recorded Interviews with Bartholomew household." Madeline held it up for Mike to see before heading into his office. Mike was quick to follow suit. He turned to Samir, motioning with a wag of his head to join them, before disappearing through the doorway. Samir was only too happy to comply.

Madeline slipped the thumb drive into the USB port on Mike's laptop and turned it so the men could see the screen from where they were seated. A list of files beginning with "Interview with L. Bartholomew" appeared on the screen, followed by six other names, presumably people associated with the ranch.

After double-clicking on the first file, Madeline scooted Mike's chair over next to him and took a seat as the interview process got underway. One of the deputies started by giving the names of everyone present in the room, plus the date, time and location. The P.I.s had no trouble recognizing Lindsay, though the time spent in prison had taken some of her former vitality. The subsequent two years of mourning and imprisonment had stripped her of the healthy glow that a life lived in sunshine, fresh air and happiness had bestowed on her. She appeared understandably shaken, her gaze fixed on something no one else could see.

Since this was the first informal interview after the discovery of Nick Bartholomew's mortally wounded body, there was no one present to protect Lindsay from self-incrimination. Madeline paused the recording and pressed the intercom button to let Sydney know they were not to be disturbed. Taking her cue, Mike closed the office door with a backward stretch of his arm, then nodded to Madeline to resume the tape.

After stating her name, address and relationship to the deceased, she seemed to have difficulty staying focused on the questions being asked of her. Five minutes into the interview, one of the deputies asked if she was all right. She answered by bursting into tears. The recording was paused and restarted when Lindsay had gotten her emotions under control.

Madeline carefully scrutinized the behavior of the three people in the video. Though visibly shaken, Lindsay came across quite different from the woman they had met the day before. Even the way she sat in the chair across from the sheriff's deputies with natural poise contrasted sharply with the woman she had become—dejected, baffled and running out of hope.

Lindsay was prompted to reiterate what she had told the deputies the day of the accident, specifically, the events that transpired prior to her leaving the property at midday. There was very little difference in what Lindsay said on record that day compared to what she had told Mike and Madeline when they visited her in prison.

Madeline chalked up a mental point in Lindsay's favor for her summation of events not coming across as a well-rehearsed speech. This was a scene from her life that had been revisited countless times—silently as well as vocally—since that terrible day over two years ago. It could easily have become something of a mantra, except for the fact that the pain and disbelief in Lindsay's recollections remained just as raw and haunting now as they were immediately after the tragedy.

The interview had all the hallmarks of a perfunctory task, from the deputies' point of view. They covered all the normal questions that would arise from a calamity of this nature. Everything had been asked and answered in less than ten minutes. The interview concluded in the customary fashion.

Madeline shot a look at Mike before clicking on the next file labeled V. Bartholomew. Whereas Lindsay's grief clung to her like a wet shroud, Vanessa

Bartholomew's grief manifested itself as a scorching wrath. She had little use for the questions put to her, launching into her own barrage of accusations and demands for her stepmother's arrest.

Though the deputies were trying to keep the interview as civil as possible, treating the grieving daughter with respect and patient calm, Vanessa wasn't about to let up until she had completely vented her spleen. They wisely sat back and let her spew until she got to the point where all that was left was raw sorrow. The recording stopped just after she lost her struggle for self-control and started up again three minutes later.

"*Please just walk us through your actions and observations on the afternoon of April 21st, starting from the time you last saw your father before the accident,*" one of the deputies prompted. The camera caught Vanessa's scowl at the word "accident," but she swallowed her bitterness long enough to reply.

"*I was looking for my dad because I needed to ask him about an order he had placed for fertilizer. I thought he'd be by the barn, but when I couldn't find him there, I went to the house. My brother Sean came in through the front door as I was coming in through the kitchen door. He said he hadn't seen Dad either, but his truck was out front, so we knew he had to be around somewhere. I checked the rest of the house, but there was no sign of him. When I went to the kitchen to ask Sean when he had last spoken to our dad, he was about to eat the pie right out of the tin.*"

"*The pie your stepmother had made…?*"

"*Yeah, that pie,*" Vanessa shot back, her voice laced with venom. "*I got it away from him and cut a big slice so he wouldn't make a mess of the whole thing. The point is, I can tell you with absolute certainty there was no note on the counter, or anywhere else. Lindsay was lying about that. And obviously my dad hadn't seen any note, because when he came inside the house a few minutes later, he told me he was going to start plowing the field as soon as he had some lunch. You need to ask Lindsay why she lied about leaving him a note. Once you start digging around, you're going to find out she was having an affair with one of the ranch hands, a guy named Seth Arnold. Lindsay knew exactly what she was doing. If she'd said she meant to leave a note and forgot, that'd be one thing. What really happened is she seized the opportunity to become a rich widow. She never cared about my dad. She was only ever after his money.*"

"*Where were you at the time of your father's accident?*"

"*I was at my house. I didn't know anything had happened until I heard the sirens. I never heard sirens up at the house before. It made my blood run cold. I don't know why, but my first thought was my dad and the tractor.*" There was a muffled sound as Vanessa battled back tears. "*I wish I'd never introduced him to her. I wish I'd never taken riding lessons from her in the first place. If only I could undo that, my dad would still be alive.*"

Madeline paused the video and looked over to Mike for his reaction. Leaning back in his chair with his arms crossed, a cynical grin and arched brows telegraphed his opinion.

"Well, Lindsay wasn't exaggerating about Vanessa's attitude toward her," he said as he uncrossed his arms and sat forward. "This is the day after the accident. Vanessa was already waging a campaign against her stepmom and former trainer. With Sean backing up her testimony, it's no wonder they brought Lindsay in for a second interview, and ultimately arrested her."

Madeline nodded her agreement and clicked on the third interview. It was Sean Bartholomew's turn to give evidence. Unlike his sister, his manner was subdued. He managed to answer the questions put to him without taking offense or mounting a case against his stepmother. His recollection of the events prior to his father's accident mirrored Vanessa's, minus the acrimony and accusations.

The fourth statement was given by Yolanda Cisneros. She was asked to state her relationship to the family, the number of years she'd been in the Bartholomew's employ, and her actions on the day of Nick Bartholomew's death. Ms. Cisneros was the only interviewee so far to appear nervous or apprehensive.

"*When was the last time you saw your employer, Nick Bartholomew, alive?*"

Though the question was put to the housekeeper in a neutral, strictly professional tone, Yolanda recoiled at the raw reality now facing the Bartholomew household.

"*Please answer the question, Ms. Cisneros,*" one of the deputies prompted.

"*I saw him that morning while I was cleaning up the kitchen. I leave at noon on Wednesdays and Saturdays, and I have Sundays off,*" she added in the spirit of full disclosure.

"*And you did not see him after that?*"

"*No, sir,*" Yolanda said with a shake of her head.

"Were you there when the tractor repairman came?"

"Yes. I saw him pull up to the house as I was leaving."

"Did you speak to him?"

"No, sir."

"Did you hear the repairman tell Lindsay Bartholomew the tractor was unsafe and couldn't be ridden?"

"No, sir," Yolanda answered with a vigorous shake of her head.

"When did you come back to your employer's house?"

"I went back up to the main house when I heard all the sirens."

"And you live in one of the dwellings on the Bartholomew ranch, is that right?"

"Yes, sir."

"Did you see anyone else up at the main house before you left at noon?"

"I saw Vanessa in the morning. She came by looking for her father." This recollection caused the housekeeper to choke up. Her body began to quake as she forced down sobs of grief. A box of tissues was pushed across the table toward her. She kept her eyes downcast as she reached for one and blotted the tears streaming down her face. When she seemed to have her emotions under control, one final question was put to her.

"Is there anything else you can tell us about that day? Anything else out of the ordinary?"

Yolanda shook her head. The deputy pressed her for a verbal reply, to which she answered *"no sir."*

The next three interviews were of other employees on the ranch: the stable hand named Jerry Ringwald; Lester Prinz, ranch foreman/crop supervisor; Smith Green, the foreman's assistant.

The seventh file on the memory stick was of Lindsay's second recorded statement, taken two days after the first. Lindsay was dry-eyed and more alert this time around, though a part of her seemed to shut down as she responded. When the questions became nuanced versions of what had previously been asked and answered, Lindsay became wary, pointedly demanding to know why she had been brought in again after having given her statement twice already. She wasn't snippy or rude, merely perplexed, her emotions still very raw and her heart still grieving for her loss.

"*Look...I know you're just doing your job, but I've already answered these questions, here and up at the ranch. Asking me again isn't going to bring Nick back. It's not like I left him somewhere and forgot about it. He's dead! We can go over what happened that day a hundred times, but my story's not going to change and Nick's death is never going to make any sense,*" Lindsay said, her voice raw with emotion as she lost her composure and wretched sobs shook her body.

The recording was paused. When it resumed, Lindsay had pulled herself together somewhat, but it was clear that she was starting to resent what she was being put through. As a matter of pride, she kept her answers brief and her emotions in check until the interview was brought to a conclusion.

Madeline replayed Lindsay's second voluntary visit to the sheriff's office. What she was paying specific attention to was Lindsay's manner, the way she conducted herself and the way she answered the questions. She scrutinized Lindsay's body language, facial expressions and tone of voice as well as her replies.

Madeline stopped the video prior to the official ending of the interview, remaining silent as she analyzed everything they'd learned about this case and how it jibed with her impression of the woman they'd met with the day before.

"You look like something's bothering you," Mike said at length.

Madeline pushed away from his desk. "Everything about this case bothers me," she said as she disappeared through the doorway.

Mike gave Samir a look shared by men in the trenches when they know the sudden quiet can't be trusted, then they both followed her back to the conference room. Knowing her audience was behind her without needing to turn around, Madeline gave voice to what had gotten her hackles up.

"Obviously, somebody is lying about the note Lindsay Bartholomew said she left for her husband. Now, assuming Nick didn't burn or eat or otherwise dispose of it, there can only be two possibilities regarding the note. Either it existed or it didn't. Either Lindsay wrote it and someone took it and-or destroyed it, or she didn't leave one. She could've *planned* to write it and forgot, but I think if that had been the case, her response to Nick's death would've been laden with guilt. So, if she lied and continues to lie about having written it, then *not* leaving a note as she had been instructed to do was intentional and premeditated."

Turning her attention away from the case board, she said, "What we need to determine is motive. Let's assume that Lindsay wrote the note. What would motivate someone to take the note off of the counter?" She let that question hang in the air for a moment as they all envisioned such a scenario.

"I suppose either Sean or Vanessa could've found the note and held on to it with the intention of giving it to Nick, then forgot. If that were the case, I could imagine them being too shocked, devastated and-or ashamed to admit their mistake. Having Lindsay—someone Vanessa saw as a traitor and an interloper—take the fall for that mistake might have been a convenient way to hide his or her own culpability." Madeline gave Mike and Samir a knowing look before continuing to speculate.

"According to Vanessa's statement, Sean was in the kitchen while she went to check the rest of the house. For argument's sake, it would've been easy for him to stick the note in his pocket, with the objective of going to look for Nick. But then he sees the freshly baked pie and dives in. Vanessa comes back to the kitchen, sees the mess he's making. She jumps in and cuts it, further distracting him. Nick shows up, the conversation goes to other matters. Sean forgets all about the note in his pocket. Nick goes out to do the tractor work he promised Vanessa he'd do. Tragedy strikes."

"I can easily see that happening," Mike said.

"Me too," Samir piped up, his hands tucked up under his crossed arms, slightly self-conscious but excited to be included in the confab.

"Sean knows Vanessa hates Lindsay for splitting up her parents," Mike agrees. "His father's dead, and nothing's going to bring him back. It's a tragedy, but will him admitting he forgot to give his dad the note change anything? No. It's only going to create more heartache for the family. Vanessa believes Sean's version of events because she was there in the kitchen with him. That's why she was practically frothing at the mouth during the interview. And if that was the way it really all played out, is Sean going to admit to being at fault for his father's death?"

"And let Lindsay inherit a portion of Nick's estate?" Madeline added. "Like you said, Vanessa was pretty worked up during her interview. She wanted blood. She wanted someone to pay for what happened. But her unhappiness began with her parents' divorce. I'm not a psychologist, but I didn't really see a lot of grief there. I saw a lot of anger."

"I'm not saying I don't agree with you," Mike said, "but grief manifests itself in different ways at different times, depending on the person."

"True. And so does guilt," Madeline said. "Some people have a hard time taking the blame for their own mistakes. And in this case, if Sean *did* pocket the note and is responsible for Nick's death, then he'd have to admit that to his sister. That would be a very painful, difficult thing to do. And if Lindsay is there to take the fall, so much the better. She didn't belong there to start with. Taking her out of the equation settles the score as far as Sean and-or Vanessa are concerned."

Mike groaned as he shifted his weight against the wall.

"I'm just speculating," Madeline qualified, crossing her arms in front of her. Samir looked from her to Mike, gauging their mindsets as he processed his own opinions.

"Is Lindsay's version of events more believable than Sean's or Vanessa's?" he asked, earning himself rather surprised glances from his two bosses.

"I was inclined to believe her," Mike said. Madeline let a beat pass before nodding her tentative agreement.

"I'll say that I didn't *disbelieve* her," she hedged. "Let's just say the jury's still out. What's your opinion?" she asked, putting Samir on the spot.

"She seemed authentically devastated to me."

"She could still come across that way if she'd been responsible for her husband's death," Madeline countered, hiding her pleasure at seeing Samir join in their brainstorming process.

"True," Samir agreed. The room went silent as the three pondered the various possible versions of what led up to Nick Bartholomew's death.

"What's our next move?" Mike asked.

"I think it's time for a trip up to Rancho Vista Encantada," she said as she picked up the article Samir had found about Vanessa Bartholomew's winery. "But we said we wanted to stop by the frame shop to speak with Natalie Sheckle's employee first."

"Yep. I still think that's a good way to do it," Mike agreed.

"Samir, mind holding the fort while we're gone?" Madeline asked, not wanting him to feel like his status had only been temporarily elevated.

"Oh sure—I'm mean, no, I don't mind!" Samir replied, his mood verging on buoyant.

"Great," Mike said as he fell in step behind Madeline, leaving their protégé basking in pride.

"I need to grab my bag," Madeline said as she headed into her office. As she was reaching for her tote, she saw an email come in. She was leaning toward her computer screen to read it when Samir appeared at the threshold. She gave him an inquiring look, to which he answered by inching his way in, hands back in his pockets, his head at an angle as if he were half afraid of meeting Madeline's gaze head on.

"What is it, Samir?" she asked, dividing her attention between him and the email.

"I just want to thank you for letting me be part of the team. I know I wasn't the best assistant you ever had, but I sure do enjoy being able to use the skills I learned at the academy. I hope I can be worthy of the chance you're giving me."

Madeline had to fight back a smile. "You seem to have a natural aptitude for investigative work, Samir. We're glad to have you on board," she said as she slung her bag over her shoulder. "Feel free to use my desk while we're out."

She could feel the radiance of Samir's broad smile on her back as she passed though the doorway, igniting a smile of her own. It felt so good to be back in her element, physically whole again, with her psyche on the mend.

FIFTEEN

The detectives reached The Frame Job at a quarter past ten. Madeline had sent Natalie Sheckle a text asking her to give her employee a heads up about them coming, to avoid a delay and to confirm it was okay to talk to her. Natalie texted back as they pulled into the parking lot. They'd need to speak to Evie Brunswick, and she was expecting them.

There were only two people inside the shop when they walked in: a woman in her thirties with a wild thatch of dyed red hair, the garish hue of a child's crayon, and a gray-haired man behind the long work table toward the back. The woman was flipping through an index box of orders as she chatted with her coworker, who was in the process of measuring a piece of wood for a custom frame. Their amiable conversation halted as the detectives crossed over the threshold.

"Hello," Evie offered tentatively, trying to determine if they were customers or the private investigators Natalie had warned her about. By the looks of them, they didn't fit either category. "Can I help you?"

"Evie?" Mike enquired.

"That would be me," she replied as she came around the counter. Her ensemble was every bit as loud as her hair color and appeared to be an amalgamation of thrift store finds. She seemed hyper-alert and a tad cautious as she made her own appraisal of the tall, well put together blond surfer dude and his decidedly glamorous partner.

"Natalie said you'd be expecting us," Mike offered as he produced his P.I. identification for her perusal, indicating Madeline as his partner with a side nod in her direction. Her license was also in her jacket pocket if she needed it, though she figured rightly that Evie would be satisfied with Mike's credentials.

Not surprisingly, most people they encountered out in the field were drawn to Mike's presence, since they were more comfortable with a man being in the role of private investigator. Besides, Mike would receive that kind of deference if he'd been selling vacuum cleaners door to door, especially from the fairer sex.

"Is there somewhere we can talk?" he asked as he stowed his ID back in his pocket.

Evie motioned with a wag of her head to follow her to the back room. "Holler if anyone comes in," she said to her coworker before entering the storeroom, an area about the same size as the showroom, though more congested due to the large work table, racks of materials and finished orders wrapped in brown paper that took up most of the space.

"Sorry, this place is a mess," Evie said as she gave up the hope of finding a spot that seemed appropriate for a meeting of this nature.

"No problem. We'll be brief. We just have a few questions," Mike assured her.

"Fire away," Evie said, wincing at her choice of words as they left her lips. Mike pretended not to notice.

"You were here on August tenth, the day Andrew died..." he offered for confirmation. Evie nodded her head while her arms closed protectively around her. "We've been told Andrew left here around two o'clock that day and that was the last time you saw him. Did he say where he was headed?"

"No," Evie said curtly with a sad shake of her head.

"Did his departure strike you as unusual?"

"A little," Evie admitted, shifting on her feet, her eyes sweeping over to Madeline just to have a diversion from Mike's penetrating gaze. "He'd already taken lunch at twelve and was back at quarter to one. So yeah, it was out of the ordinary for him to leave in the middle of his work, but it didn't strike me as *suspicious* or *ominous*." Judging by her body language, reexamining the events of that day brought up feelings of loss, shock, and remorse. There were always a lot of "if onlys" in the aftermath of a tragedy.

"Can you recall anything he said or did prior to leaving?" Mike asked.

Evie bit her lip, her gaze straying as she mentally scanned the memories that filtered to the forefront of her mind. "I remember asking him about an order... Someone had just called to see if it was ready...yeah, that's right."

Looking Mike directly in the eye, she elaborated as the memory gelled.

"It wasn't supposed to be ready until the next day, but he had gotten it done early." Evie fell silent, her eyes drifting again. "He had picked up the parcel and was about to hand it over to me when his phone chimed. It seemed like he was expecting the text, 'cause he left me standing there, you know, like this." Evie demonstrated with outstretched hands. "I remember now thinking it was bad news or something because of the look on his face when he read the message. I almost asked him if there was something wrong, but then he handed me the parcel, and that was it."

"And he didn't say anything to you, about the message or why he was leaving? No mention of having an appointment elsewhere—with a doctor or a client?" Madeline asked.

"No," Evie replied, her head oscillating from side to side, her eyes closed. "I took the order up to the front and called the woman back to let her know she could pick it up anytime. I could see his car drive by from where I was standing, and I remember having this…feeling…nothing that I could really get a handle on, but just this weird sort of vibe, like something bad was about to happen."

"Like a premonition?" Mike offered, to which Evie shrugged. "Did he say anything before he left?"

"No," Evie replied, her lips pursed as she shook her tousled 'do.

"Was it your sense that the text message triggered his departure?"

Evie considered the question for a moment. "Yeah, I guess at the time that's what I thought."

"Had you noticed any mood swings in Andrew in the weeks leading up to his death?" Mike continued.

Evie emitted a groan that managed to imply both sorrow and regret, a sound that called to mind the pain of not being able to rewind the past, to intervene before disaster struck.

"Andrew just wasn't the same after he lost his little boy," Evie said, her eyelids fluttering as if holding eye contact during such a discussion would expose just how raw her feelings on the subject still were. After drawing a deep breath, she elaborated. "I know he did his best to stay strong for Natalie's sake, but his heart was broken from the loss. People say that it just takes time for the heart to mend after something like this, but sometimes the pain is just too heavy to bear."

Madeline let a beat pass before she asked, "What do you think of Natalie's conviction that Andrew didn't commit suicide? What's your gut-level feeling?"

The camouflage of hair, makeup and startling attire lost some of its potency as Evie grappled with the tragedy that had befallen her employers. "If it were *me* instead of Natalie, I'm not sure I would be able to live with the pain that my husband deserted me when I needed his emotional support most. So, yeah, I get what she's going through. Denial's the first phase of grief, followed by anger, bargaining, depression and acceptance. I've read about all that. Maybe she just needs to go through this to get to that final stage," Evie offered with a shrug, forcing her lips into tentative smile.

The trio stood silently for a moment as if to give the fourth presence in the storeroom—Sheckle family grief—its due.

"Thank you for your time," Mike said as he held out his MDPI card. "If anything occurs to you that might have bearing on Andrew's state of mind or the events leading up to his death, please let us know."

Evie nodded her goodbye to the P.I.s, taking a moment to compose herself before rejoining her coworker. Revisiting that horrible day made her realize she wasn't immune to the raw feelings of grief stemming from the violent death of the man she'd worked closely with for almost six years. She blinked back the beginnings of tears and drew in a couple ragged breaths before shoving the past behind her again.

SIXTEEN

As a consequence of being located on the pristine Gaviota Coast, signage for the new Bartholomew enterprise had been kept to a minimum so as not to detract from the natural beauty and ruralness along the scenic highway. The marker for this new establishment was so low-key, Mike and Madeline nearly missed the driveway for Bartholomew Wines & Produce.

They pulled off 101 and passed through the wooden gates left open to suggest they had come during business hours. The gravel drive meandered past specimen olive trees still in their crates—presumably to control their growth—and dwarf lemon trees, heavy with fruit. Madeline rolled down her window and inhaled the heady fragrance as she estimated what all these improvements must've cost.

The gravel drive ended at a parking area delineated by railroad ties and more olive trees, though these had been planted as a border to conceal the view of the areas not open to the public. At eleven o'clock on a non-holiday Friday morning, the detectives were surprised to find they weren't the only visitors. They took the last of six spots next to the building and got out to survey the surroundings.

Wine barrels cut in half and used as planters flanked the entrance to the rustic structure made from rusted corrugated metal and distressed beams. The largest red mandevilla blooms Madeline had ever seen sprawled across weathered trellises. Lush winter honeysuckle vines covered the split-rail fence that flanked the structure on both sides, sweetening the air and attracting bees. The warm flagstone apron surrounding the entrance, beyond the reach of ocean breezes, was about as welcoming a spot as could be found on a brisk November morning. Madeline took one last deep breath before going inside to see what the Bartholomew heirs had been up to since their father's tragic demise.

The rustic theme continued through the interior of the gift shop, which showcased everything from Santa Barbara County wines to fresh baked goods, honey, produce, nuts and assorted souvenirs, some with the Rancho Vista Encantada logo. One couple was headed out with a case of wine as Madeline and Mike entered. A group of three women hovered around the various displays like delighted bees, oohing and ahhing, touching and smelling. A few other patrons roamed around, seemingly content to just look, sniff and smile.

The sole employee on duty, a tall, slim, eager-to-please fellow in his mid-twenties, was talking up the ranch's signature wine to a young couple, while casually ringing up another purchase. The whole scene was not uncommon for the more rural areas of North Santa Barbara County, but highly novel for this sparsely populated stretch of the coast.

The fact that all this had come together in the two-plus years since Nick Bartholomew's death had Madeline's radar squawking like a Geiger counter. Building and business permits anywhere in the county required an inordinate amount of time, patience and money, as dedication to preserving what made the county so special caused an overabundance of scrutiny. It could take years just to have a project okayed by the Planning Commission alone. And yet, here stood an enterprise that was already up and running on a large parcel of land that had only recently been cut by half in exchange for the rights to set up a commercial enterprise just off the coastal highway. It must've taken quite a concerted effort and special handling to accomplish something like this so quickly.

"Let me know if I can answer any questions."

Sensing Madeline's preoccupation, Mike was the one to respond to the greeting called out from behind the counter.

"Thanks. We're just going to have a look around."

"Please do!"

Madeline set off on a short tour of the gift shop, which opened into an elaborately finished tasting room. Instead of continuing on with the homey tin siding used in the gift shop, the walls and floor of the room reserved for tasting events were made of cut stone, creating a space that was noticeably richer in appearance and cooler by several degrees.

Tables fashioned from industrial-size spools anchored the corners, while a long table made of a single piece of wood from a once-towering eucalyptus tree took center stage. Wooden crates of wine were stacked halfway up the back wall. Dramatic black and white photos of vineyards and harvests accented the rest of the wall space.

All this generous use of money made Madeline wary. Her instincts were telling her this scene was all wrong, especially when juxtaposed with the visiting room at the women's prison in Chowchilla. Past injustices from Madeline's own life caused a visceral reaction to what had transpired on Rancho Vista Encantada since the departure of Nick Bartholomew and his second wife. None of what she'd seen so far felt kosher to her. It made the removal of Nick and Lindsay seem awfully convenient, especially in light of Nick's stance on safeguarding the ranch for future generations.

"You okay?" Mike asked quietly as he came up next to her, breaking through her thoughts.

"Yes, I'm fine," she replied as she picked up a book from the display in front of her as a prop.

"You look like something's got you spooked," he whispered. Madeline glanced over at him but made no reply as her eyes shifted to the scene around them, landing on the employee. Having seen Sean Bartholomew on the taped interviews, she knew this was not him. It made her wonder if this guy was Vanessa's love interest or just staff.

"I'll tell you later," she said as a few more customers said their farewells and walked out of the shop, leaving the group of three women and them as targets for salesmanship.

"*A Vintage to Die For,*" Madeline read from the cover of the book in her hands. "A Beaujolais Jones Detective Mystery," she said with an amused chuckle.

One of the women from the trio intercepted the employee who was on his way over to her and Mike. Madeline set the book down, taking one final look at the display.

"Maybe that's what we should do when we retire—write novels based loosely on some of our cases," she joked, getting a reluctant smile out of Mike.

"Not a bad idea. It would be a lot safer," he said with a laugh. "At least they'd be authentic and factual."

"If you have any questions about our products or our wine, just let me know," the salesman said as he appeared on the other side of the book display.

"We were passing by and saw the sign. We didn't even know this was here," Madeline said.

"Well, we're glad you stopped by. My name's Luke, if you need anything."

"How long has this shop been open?" Mike asked.

"About four months now."

"It sure is a charming place," Madeline said. "I like how you also have fresh produce and soaps and other gift items." Seizing the opportunity to get some truthful answers, she picked up a bottle of wine from a neighboring display. "Is this Rancho VE wine made just for your shop?"

"Actually, the grapes are grown and pressed right here on the ranch," Luke said. "I can give you a taste, if you like…"

"Oh, thanks…it's a little early for us," Madeline said with a grateful smile. "But maybe you can tell me a little bit of the history behind this ranch."

"Oh, sure. It's been in the same family for over a hundred and twenty years. It was a part of an original land grant rancho that was divided over time, with some of the parcels being sold off. The parcel we're standing on—which is twelve-hundred acres—used to be double that, but the owners recently put half of it in the Land Trust for preservation and public use. In exchange, they were given the rights to open this tasting room and sell their crops directly to the public—the avocados, lemons, oranges and eggs, along with their Rancho Vista Encantada wines."

"I didn't realize wine grapes would do well so close to the coast," Madeline ventured.

"I know, right? But actually, there are some varietals that do really well with cool, foggy conditions."

Sensing they were in for a sales spiel that could go on way too long, Mike threw out another question to divert the conversation.

"Who actually owns this ranch and this…enterprise?"

"The Bartholomew family," Luke said with a fair measure of authority, nodding his head as if that should explain everything.

"Something just clicked in my brain…" Madeline said, tagging on to Mike's line of discovery. "I remember there was a trial…? Uh…something about a *murder* maybe…? I think the *wife* was found guilty…? Was that *this* family?" she asked, feigning ignorance.

"Yes, unfortunately that was this family," Luke said, his lips pursing tightly.

"Oh, that's too bad," Madeline sympathized, her expression contrite.

"Well, on the upside, it looks like the family has carried on," Mike offered, providing a spin Luke could work with.

"That's right. And that's the important thing. Even though the family has lost so much, they have come together and created a legacy their father would be proud of."

"But it seems like that tragedy happened not that long ago…maybe only a couple years ago. How did they get this kind of thing approved and built so quickly?" Madeline asked.

"I couldn't tell you," Luke said with a shrug. "That happened before I was brought on."

"I see…" Madeline said.

"Excuse me…?" one of the three ladies interrupted. "Do you have any more of these?" she asked, holding up a tea towel with a vintage rendering of a crate of lemons in the foreground and the Gaviota Coast as the backdrop.

"Thank you for your time," Mike said, touching Madeline's arm as to move them along.

"Yes, thank you so much," she said. "Is it all right if we just look around outside?"

"Oh sure. Please feel free to explore all the way to the metal gate."

"Great, thanks a lot," Mike said with a wave as he guided Madeline out the door. "Well, that was interesting."

"Yes. Interesting, but not very informative."

"Well, we know Nick Bartholomew's heirs managed to forge a future for themselves rather quickly after his death," Mike said as he took in the artfully staged trappings. Madeline didn't reply; she was already putting distance between herself and the gift shop, heading out of the parking area to the road that continued its climb into parts of the ranch off-limits to the public.

By the time he caught up with her, the metal gate signifying the boundary to the private part of the ranch was within sight. Judging by her deliberate pace, Madeline wasn't content to abide by such limitations. As she slowed to survey the obstacle, the low purr of a golf cart grew closer. Mike was already working on an excuse for both of them when the cart came to a halt beside him. He cleared his throat as he turned to face the middle-aged Latina at the wheel.

Madeline, playing it cool, looked positively delighted by the arrival of a family insider. Before any discouraging words were uttered, she was on the woman like a heat-seeking missile.

"Hi there!" she called out enthusiastically as she picked her way daintily down the bumpy road toward the new arrival. "Do you live here?" she asked, her smile conveying her pleasure at encountering one of the fortunate few who had access to such a place. Baffled by Madeline's exuberant reception, the woman was temporarily at a loss for words.

"Excuse me for being so forward," Madeline said, a hand to her chest in a gesture of apology. "We've just been inside the gift shop and winery and we're just absolutely *enchanted* by this lovely place!" She paused to let her spiel settle in, reading the shift in attitude of the woman she guessed was part of the staff. Judging by her age and the videotaped interviews, Madeline had her pegged as the housekeeper. "We just got a little background on the ranch and the winery from Luke," she offered as credentials, gesturing toward the tasting room. "What a fabulous place to work! Have you been here long?"

To Mike's astonishment, the woman on the golf cart did not clam up or immediately send them packing. Though she didn't turn off the engine, she did relax her posture, obviously warming to Madeline's affected charm. It was apparent the woman did feel very privileged to live in such an idyllic environment.

"I have been here for twenty-three years next month," Yolanda Cisneros replied with obvious pride. Madeline reacted to this disclosure with just the right level of amazement to seem authentic.

"You must feel so blessed," she said, to which Ms. Cisneros answered with a shy smile and a solemn nodding of her head.

"I am very lucky."

"Do you actually *live* here on the ranch?" Madeline asked, her expression conveying her awe at such a concept.

The housekeeper's nod was full of pride and gratitude.

"So, you're practically part of the family!" Madeline gushed.

"Yes, the Bartholomews are like family to me," Yolanda agreed.

"So, you were here when Lindsay and her daughter lived here," Madeline said in the same unthreatening tone, even though her statement revealed her familiarity with the family and their tribulations, which was at odds with the pretense of ignorance. Sensing the housekeeper's shift from ease to trepidation, Madeline switched gears.

"I understand that you were very fond of little Joni," Madeline pressed on, "and Lindsay, for that matter." When the faltering smile on Yolanda's face sank into a frown of distrust and dislike, Madeline edged closer, wrapping her hand on the metal bar that supported the top of the golf cart, fixing the woman with earnest compassion in her eyes.

"We visited Lindsay at the prison yesterday," she said, watching the housekeeper's reaction carefully, judging by each nuance of her expression and body language that she was torn between loyalty and compassion. "My partner and I have taken on her case because we feel there was a rush to convict Lindsay from the start. We'd just like to ask you a few questions. We don't have an agenda, but we feel that little Joni Bartholomew deserves to know if her mother has been framed for the death of her adoptive father."

Mike observed this conversation as he hung back, keeping a respectful distance while Madeline made their case on Lindsay's behalf. Sensing the housekeeper was teetering and could go either way, he added his support to Madeline's argument.

"Even the warden at the prison where Lindsay is incarcerated has doubts about her guilt, as does her public defender and the prosecuting A.D.A.," he said. "We're not picking sides here, but we believe there's enough doubt to warrant a deeper look into what really went on that day. Anything you tell us will be strictly off the record," he said as he took a business card from his wallet and handed it to the housekeeper.

"Is there somewhere we can talk for a few minutes?" Madeline asked. "We promise we will not share anything you tell us if our investigation doesn't uncover evidence that exonerates Lindsay," she added, the earnest plea in her eyes upping the persuasion of their appeal. "For Joni's sake?" she added, giving the housekeeper's conscience a nudge toward doing what her heart felt was right.

Madeline watched intently as Yolanda shifted in preparation of continuing up the hill. "Are you really willing to live under this cloud for the rest of your life? Whatever happened that day, we don't believe you had anything to do with it. But justice hasn't been served if the wrong person has been sent to prison," she said, her eyes locked on the housekeeper's long enough for the woman's resolve to falter.

Mike and Madeline followed Yolanda across the highway to the house that came with her employment package. It wasn't hard to understand her reluctance to speak out of turn about the very people who made this enviable lifestyle possible. Located on the coastal side of the 101, with a generous view of the ocean from the front porch, the hacienda-style structure had a very homey, authentic feel to it. Not surprisingly, it was kept in immaculate condition.

They had taken the housekeeper up on her offer of coffee, sensing the woman's need for a little more time to fortify her resolve. Sitting at the round table in the area off to the side of the kitchen, they had a view out the French doors to a small patio flanked by fruit trees, with a fountain in the center that probably hadn't seen water since the prolonged drought had begun.

Their position also afforded them a glimpse of the living room and the hallway leading to what they assumed were the bedrooms and bathroom. Though the house was modest, it was not hard to understand where Yolanda's loyalty lay, or why. With a perk like this, someone would have to think long and hard before going against the interests of his or her employers.

"Cream or sugar?" Yolanda asked as she set a tray with three mugs of steaming coffee on the table and handed two of them to her guests. Both declined the condiments, preferring to drink theirs black.

"Good coffee," Mike said with genuine appreciation as he set his mug down and smiled his thanks.

"We're grateful for your willingness to talk with us," Madeline said after dutifully taking a sip of the coffee she didn't want or need. With the memory of Lindsay Bartholomew confined to a prison cell haunting her thoughts, she got right to the point.

"During your video-recorded interview with the sheriff's deputies, you stated you left the main house at noon on the day of Nick's death, as you did every Wednesday, and that was the same time the tractor repairman showed up." Yolanda verified this fact with a solemn nod, drawing a deep, shuddering breath. "So, you weren't there when the repairman informed Lindsay the tractor was unsafe to ride." This was met with a resolute shake of her head. "You didn't see a note, because the repairman hadn't inspected the tractor yet."

"That's right."

"And you didn't see a pie, either."

"No."

"Because Lindsay hadn't started on it yet…" Yolanda nodded. "And you weren't at the house when Lindsay left to do errands and pick up Joni…"

"No."

"And you weren't up at the main house when Nick had the tractor accident."

Yolanda shook her head again as she dabbed at the corners of her eyes.

"I'm sorry to ask you these questions, Yolanda, but I want to make sure we have all the facts straight. When did you find out about the accident?"

"It was about two-thirty. I heard a lot of sirens on the highway, but they didn't sound like they were continuing up 101. I called the foreman to see if he knew what was going on. He said Nick had an accident on the tractor. I could tell by the sound of his voice it was bad."

Neither detective spoke for a moment to let Yolanda gather her composure.

"You heard multiple sirens, around the same time?" Mike asked. Yolanda nodded. "So, the sheriff's department had already been called?" Yolanda shrugged.

"I don't know who called them or when, but the sirens were only about five minutes apart. Three sets of them."

"What did you do then?" Madeline asked.

"I got in my car and drove over to the main house."

"When you got up there, were any emergency responders still there?" Madeline inquired.

"The paramedics had just shut the doors of the ambulance when I pulled up to the house. There were also two sheriff's vehicles."

"Who else was there?"

Yolanda's eyes drifted as she sought to recall all the faces present during that life-altering moment. "Sean and Vanessa were there. Vanessa was hysterical. Sean was trying to hug her, calm her down. They hadn't been close for a

long time, but I remember thinking that tragedies can bring families together."
Yolanda stared down at her hands as more images from that horrible day passed
before her mind's eye.

"Lester and Smith and Jerry were there. Lester—he's the foreman—he was
speaking to one of the deputies. Smith and Jerry were standing closer to where
I parked, so I asked them what was going on." With her focus coming back to
the present, Yolanda looked back and forth between Mike and Madeline. "I
knew without even being told that Nick was already dead. You know how you
can't put something together in your mind, but inside," Yolanda said as she
patted her chest, "inside, you *know*. If Nick was still alive, Vanessa would've
been in the ambulance with him. Sean, too.

"Were there any others present?"

Yolanda scanned her memories carefully and shook her head.

"What was your reaction to Lindsay's arrest?" Of all the questions put to
her, this was the one that got the most animated response.

"I couldn't believe it. I thought there's no way Lindsay would put her husband in danger. No way. She loved that man, very much. Anyone could see
that." Yolanda said as she pointed to her eyes with emphasis. "I have to confess
that in the beginning, I didn't like Lindsay because of how hurt Vanessa was by
her parents' divorce. She blamed Lindsay, so I blamed her, too."

"What changed your mind?" Mike asked.

"The way she and Nick were together, and the way she treated her little girl.
She was a good mom. And she'd always been nice to me, even though I think
she knew I resented her for what had happened between Nick and Patricia. But
she never ordered me around or treated me like I was just an employee. Plus,
no one could deny that Nick and Lindsay were really in love."

"Except Vanessa," Madeline offered.

"Except Vanessa," Yolanda echoed with a sad nod of her head.

"Would you say Vanessa resented her father for divorcing Patricia and
marrying Lindsay?" Mike asked.

Yolanda wagged her head equivocally. "I don't know what to say about
that. I know it takes two people to have a relationship, and Nick tried hard to
make it up to Vanessa. He gave her everything she ever asked for. Well, almost

everything. Eventually, things got better between them." Yolanda managed a wan smile as she reflected on the past.

"After Vanessa graduated from college, Nick had a new house built for her so she could live on the ranch and still have her privacy. It's a beautiful house, bigger than the one Sean lives in. Nicer, too. It seemed like Vanessa stopped hating Lindsay so much after she moved back here. But since the accident, it's been worse than ever. She still carries that anger around with her, which is bad. It will only poison her."

"Did you witness or hear about any disagreements between Nick and anyone here on the ranch, or anywhere else?" Madeline asked.

Yolanda pursed her lips, her head shaking from side to side. "Everyone loved Nick. He was a good man. Very generous, good sense of humor, respect-ful, kind. I've never known anyone like him."

"In Vanessa's statement at the sheriff's office, she accused Lindsay of having an affair with someone named Seth Arnold," Madeline said. When Yolanda offered nothing more than a blank stare, she tried to jog her memory. "He was one of the ranch hands."

"That name doesn't sound familiar. You'd have to ask Lester, the foreman. Guys come and go around here all the time," Yolanda said with a shrug.

"To your knowledge, was there anyone else on the ranch that morning who wasn't normally there?" Mike asked.

"Not that I know of."

The detectives glanced at each other to see if they could think of anything else to ask the housekeeper.

"Sorry for the ambush, Yolanda. This has helped us get a better idea of what we're dealing with," Madeline said as she and Mike stood up. "I'd like to get your phone number, in case we have any other questions."

"Okay. I'll write it down for you," Yolanda said as she rose up slowly and went in search of a pen and paper. "Do you think you can help Lindsay?" Yolanda asked as she came back to where the detectives were standing.

"Hopefully, we can find out who's telling the truth and who isn't," Mike replied, purposely keeping his answer vague. Yolanda acknowledged the distinc-tion between what was asked and how it was answered. Whichever way this investigation fell, it wasn't going to bring Nick back or undo all the heartache of the last two-plus years.

"I hope you can reunite that little girl with her mommy," Yolanda said, seeing that as the only potential upside at this point in time.

Madeline asked Yolanda to call them if she could think of anything else that might help them figure out what really happened the day Nick died. They left her standing on the threshold, MDPI card in hand, her heart heavy with sorrow, trying to foster the hope that something good could come out of this investigation.

SEVENTEEN

"So, where to now?" Mike asked as he guided the Audi out of Yolanda's driveway.

"I think we should do a little reconnoitering on this side of the property while we have the chance," Madeline replied while her fingers tapped away at her cell phone. "Just to get the lay of the land," she added, though Mike knew curiosity was really the motivation. It wasn't every day outsiders got a peek at such a rarified existence.

"Not a bad idea," Mike agreed as he turned left, heading farther away from the highway, in the direction of the beach.

It was impossible not to be awed by the landscape they traversed as they headed south. Grassy fields, brought back to life thanks to a few recent rain showers, flowed toward the slate blue Pacific that was now stretched out in front of them.

Even with gray clouds overhead, the visibility was phenomenal, the view truncated only by the stands of tall trees that proclaimed the original borders of Rancho Vista Encantada on either side. An unofficial-looking barbed wire fence could be seen in the distance, running parallel to the road they were on. Madeline figured it was most likely the new boundary line between what the Bartholomew family still owned and what was given away in trade for the commercial rights.

Staring straight at them from the ocean was Santa Rosa Island, a sight only occasionally visible from Santa Barbara. To their right squatted San Miguel, and to the far left sprawled Santa Cruz, the largest of the Channel Islands, appearing bigger from this vantage point due to its proximity to the coastline.

"Wow," Madeline said as the Audi slowed. Spotting a dirt patch large enough for several vehicles, Mike pulled over and cut the engine. Without exchanging a word, the detectives got out and gravitated to the edge for a look down at the shore. A stiff breeze several degrees cooler in their exposed location sent their hair swirling.

"Should we go down?" Mike suggested as his partner tried unsuccessfully to corral the burnished gold locks creating a hair funnel around her head.

"Sure," she said, figuring rightly it would be less blustery once they were down on the sand, sheltered by the cliffs. She followed Mike's lead down the crumbling asphalt path that was wide enough for a vehicle, though she wasn't keen on the thought of driving it, in either direction.

"How cool is this?" Mike asked as she came alongside him on what was left of the paved apron.

"Not surprising Sean grew up to be a world-class surfer," Madeline remarked after filling her lungs with the cold, briny air. Inching to the edge of the pad in her decidedly unbeachy heels, she scanned the coastline in both directions.

Mike joined her, though his eyes were riveted to the ten-foot swells breaking every eight seconds, by his reckoning. An unrealistic vision of selling off all his assets in exchange for a lifestyle like this got his heart and mind racing. He would give up everything for a sliver of this kind of paradise.

"Looks like a cabana over there," Madeline said, breaking through her partner's fantasy, hoping he'd take the bait and go check it out.

"Oh…yeah, it does. Think I should have a look?"

"I do. My guess is it's not occupied."

"No, probably just used for beach gatherings," he said as he slipped off his shoes. After he rolled up the cuffs of his pants, he set off in sand deep enough to swallow his feet.

Madeline rubbed her shivering arms before figuring she could get out of the wind if she went a few feet up the path. Once protected by the rutted face of the earthen corridor, she surveyed the view again, imagining what life had been like for Lindsay and her daughter. A dream come true that had dissolved into a nightmare.

"I wonder if they'd let me rent that," Mike said as he hit the pad and began his ascent up, shoes in hand. Madeline's dismissive laugh conveyed her doubts.

"What does it look like inside?"

Mike let out a wistful sigh, shaking his head in wonder. "It's the ideal hideaway. It's more like a small cottage than a cabana," he said as Madeline fell into step with him. "There's a full-on kitchen—small, but totally serviceable, with an island and bar stools. Good size table. Looks like they could seat eight, easily. Probably squeeze in a couple more. A big sofa, which I'm guessing pulls out into a bed. A couple comfy chairs...a bookcase..." Madeline looked over at him in mild disbelief. "I'm not kidding. And I couldn't really see into it, but looks like it has a full bathroom and some kind of large storage closet."

"Wow."

"I know. That's all I could say."

Mike shook his head, his thoughts a mix of longing and compassion. Nick Bartholomew was the kind of guy he could easily relate to. Half a generation older, but otherwise kindred spirits, both enjoying the fruits of their predecessors' efforts. Both in love with the sea and coastal living. Whereas this case had initially felt like an albatross he'd wrapped around his own neck, causing him a great deal of consternation and regret, he now felt invested in getting to the truth about Nick's accidental death, as if they'd become connected somehow.

"Where to now?" he asked as they simultaneously reached for the door handles, anxious to flee the persistent, bone-chilling wind.

"The office," Madeline replied once she was ensconced in the passenger seat. "I think we need to assimilate everything we've learned today, see how it all fits together and where all of it leads us." She reached for her phone and began an email as Mike wiped off his feet and put on his shoes.

Mike got in and started the car while Madeline remained focused on her phone. Her level of concentration told Mike she was working on an idea that she hadn't yet shared with him. He held his curiosity in check until the unavoidable turns and bumps in the road made her take a pause.

"Looks like something's got your wheels spinning," he said, prying without seeming to pry. Madeline resumed her task long enough to finish the email and send it on its way. She sat back, her eyes looking straight ahead, her mind clearly elsewhere. Mike had given up on her sharing her thoughts when she abruptly answered him.

"I just sent Julia Cummings a message, a tip-off, really." This disclosure seemed to be sufficient as far as she was concerned, but it did nothing to enlighten her partner.

"A tip-off? What kind of tip-off?"

"I told her about our visit to Bartholomew Wines and Produce, the unique new venture on the Gaviota coast. I also told her I'd be passing this tip on to the other local news outlets if she wasn't interested." Madeline's gloating was interrupted by the pinging of a new text message.

"She took the bait. She's salivating," Madeline reported happily. "She's going to try to set something up for tomorrow."

"I guess I'm just being dense here," Mike said as he gave her a sidelong glance, trying not to let her smugness get the best of him. "This makes you happy, why exactly?"

"In exchange for my tip-off, Julia has agreed to let me tag along with her as part of her crew. I made that part of the deal."

"Why couldn't she just do the piece without you?" Mike asked, sure Madeline was keeping something from him.

"Let's just say I convinced her I had additional background on the family that I would also pass on to whomever did this piece."

"Did you tell her we were reinvestigating Nick's death?" he asked, taken aback by her cavalier attitude. Madeline laughed at his worried expression.

"No. I didn't tell her anything about that. I will, however, keep my part of the bargain after we conclude our investigation."

"But what if we don't find anything that exonerates Lindsay?"

Madeline shrugged. "Then I simply tell her we took on the case *pro bono* as a favor, but it was a nonstarter."

"And if we do find that someone framed Lindsay for her husband's murder...?"

Madeline shrugged again, her smile conveying her lack of concern.

"I don't see either scenario being an issue for us. I will honor my word if we find out Lindsay is in fact innocent. The way it boils down, either Lindsay left a note for Nick or she didn't. If she didn't leave a note and lied about it, she created the situation she's now in. If she did leave one, then someone deliberately took it. If that's the case, that someone effectively caused Nick's death while framing Lindsay. Maybe the act was merely spiteful, and whoever took the note didn't think the consequences all the way through. But by not coming forward after Lindsay's arrest, that created another layer of guilt. The point is, whoever it was had to be a regular fixture on the property—either a family member or one of the employees. Getting on the ranch and getting a look at who has access is critical."

"I totally agree with your logic, but…" Mike conceded as Madeline's phone pinged again, ending the discussion.

"Good thing we're heading back to the office," she huffed.

"What's going on?"

"The Chrysalis event is next weekend and the company liaison has just thrown us a curve. Mind if I make a call? I'm sure Lauren will be in a tizzy when she reads this," Madeline said, already placing the call.

Mike could hear her assistant's panicked bleating even though the conversation wasn't coming through the Audi's speakers. He listened for long enough to learn Madeline had already thought of a workable solution, then turned his thoughts inward as they left the unspoiled paradise of Gaviota and entered the outskirts of Goleta.

A quick check of his instincts told him that Madeline's plan for infiltrating the Bartholomew compound was a good one. Without deeper probing of the occupants on the ranch, they would have no effective way of discerning what really happened the day of Nick's accident.

His only regret was not being with her when she did her snooping. But he knew better than to voice his concerns, especially after she'd been sidelined for months. If he hadn't already set up inspections of his two apartment complexes in L.A. with his onsite managers, he would've been tempted to bail on his cousin's bachelor party and go with her.

"Everything okay?" he asked as Madeline ended her powwow with Lauren.

"It's going to work out fine. It's just a bit of a scramble, since it's a Friday. I'll make a few calls once we're back in the office, then you and I can do a little brainstorming," she said with a satisfied smile, a sight that made Mike's heart swell with joy. Madeline savored the moment, then got back to her emails while her chauffer ferried them along.

EIGHTEEN

Mike opened his eyes to a crack of light peeking through his plantation shutters. He reached for his cell phone slowly, careful not to rock the bed. He guesstimated it was just after six a.m. and overcast, judging by the quality of the light. The time on his phone read 6:06. He carefully peeled back the duvet and moved his weight slowly off the bed, looking over his right shoulder to make sure he hadn't woken Madeline. Her back was turned, but she made no movement except for the barely perceptible rise and fall of her ribcage as she breathed in and exhaled.

Madeline kept her eyes closed until she heard Mike's cautious footsteps in the hallway. She remained still until the showerhead sputtered, its spray pelting softly against the glass enclosure. She rolled onto her back, a smile on her face as she stretched and luxuriated in the coolness of the sheets on Mike's side of the bed, letting thoughts populate of their own free will until she decided to focus on mental preparations for the day ahead.

"I'm so in love with you, baby ~ can't tell night from day. So in love with you, baby ~ you just take my breath away," Mike sang in a hushed falsetto, as if he were mimicking Diana Ross, assuming the closed door and the sound of the water bouncing off the hard surfaces would cancel out his enraptured singing.

"Not a day goes by I don't thank my lucky stars for you," he crooned in a deep bass, *à la* Barry White as he answered his female counterpart.

Madeline giggled softly, torn between keeping up the sleep charade and joining him, but unaccustomed laziness won out. She was still distracted by the thoughts that had awoken her shortly after five—insights, nagging inconsistencies and concerns about that perennial spook, Steven Ridley. Even though she constantly reminded herself that she had bested him years ago, his liberated status chafed like ill-fitting shoes.

No matter how Zen she tried to be about his very premature release from prison, she could never get past how undeserving he was of his newfound freedom. And in rare moments like this, when her guard was down, she experienced pangs of fear. For all his talk of spiritual metamorphosis, she knew in her gut he was the master of the long game and never one to let a perceived slight go unanswered. The nagging question was, did his freedom put her at risk?

With effort, she tuned out the static in her brain and enjoyed the rest of Mike's impromptu serenade until the water shut off. She listened as she imagined him reaching for the towel and drying off. She rolled onto her right side just before the squeak of the door handle and closed her eyes, detecting the soft patter of bare feet as Mike peeked over the end of the bed at her.

"Good morning," he offered, giving her left foot a playful wag with his free hand.

"Good morning," she smiled back.

"Looks like you slept well."

"I did," she purred.

"I think I'm going to reschedule the inspections until next weekend. We have to be down there for the wedding anyway, so it doesn't really matter."

"True, but you still have the bachelor party to attend. You thought it made more sense to knock them out at the same time," she reminded him.

"Yeah, but I'm thinking about bailing on that, too."

"What?" she said, sitting bolt upright. "You can't do that. Jesse's counting on you being there. If it wasn't for you, this wedding wouldn't be happening."

"I know that, but—"

"Those sisters owe you their lives, and Jesse feels so deeply indebted to you," Madeline argued as she slid out of bed and pulled her cashmere robe on.

"We'll be there for the wedding," Mike argued.

"I know Jesse would be very hurt if you didn't go to his bachelor party," she maintained, arms crossed adamantly, giving her partner no wiggle room. "Are you worried about leaving me alone? Is that it?" She knew as soon as the words left her mouth she'd hit on the real reason for his sudden change of heart.

"No," he said, attempting a convincing posture in response to her confrontational body language. "We've got two difficult cases on our hands, if you recall, both of which are time sensitive."

"Ha, ha, ha," Madeline retorted sarcastically. "Nick Bartholomew and

Andrew Sheckle can't get any deader than they already are, and the plan I've set into motion regarding Lindsay's case doesn't include you anyway. So don't try to use either of those as an excuse not to do your familial duty." She continued to glare at him defiantly until he grudgingly conceded her point.

"But I will worry about you," he promised as he followed her out of the bedroom.

"Please don't," she answered over her shoulder as she pulled two mugs down from the cupboard and set them next to the coffeemaker. "I will be Julia's constant shadow. No one's going to have an opportunity to get me alone, even if they figured out who I am and what I'm up to. Besides, no one in the Bartholomew household is even aware that we're looking into Nick's death."

"Yolanda knows," Mike rebutted as he took the proffered cup of coffee. Madeline conceded his point with a reluctant nod as she leaned back against the counter, letting her coffee cool enough to drink it without scorching her tongue.

"So, the question is, where do Yolanda's loyalties lie?" she asked as they gravitated over to the front windows to take in the view of the sun rising over the coastline to the east. An artful smattering of clouds provided a technicolor lightshow in every conceivable shade of pink, orange and red, coloring the sky and water in an awe-inspiring reminder of why they lived in Santa Barbara and how fortunate they were.

"My hope rests on Yolanda being loyal to her employer's memory," Madeline said, answering her own question. "I also think she's quite conflicted by Joni's separation from her mother. If we've got any hope of her keeping quiet about our investigation, I think it's her lingering sense that Lindsay is a good person and was a loving wife and mother. Hopefully, that will buy us enough time to figure out what really happened that day."

Mike let a sigh seep out as he nodded his head in solidarity with her hope. He slipped his arm around her and planted a kiss on the top of her head. She returned the sideways hug while her mind continued to grapple with the cluster of known facts and nagging questions. She intentionally put her thoughts on pause and brought her attention back to Mike.

"When are you taking off?"

"Pretty soon, I guess, since my company's not wanted or needed."

Madeline suppressed a laugh and bestowed a kiss on his cheek.

"You know you always enjoy visiting your assets," she teased him, "and I'm sure you will find a convenient pretext for leaving the bachelor party early."

"That's a guarantee," he said before extracting a real kiss and moving on with his day, the mantra *get it done and get it over with* giving him the discipline he needed to refrain from ravishing his partner from head to toe.

Madeline smiled at his retreating figure, feeling his desire for her and the stirrings of her own. She soaked up the warmth of his love a moment longer, then focused on her game plan for the day.

~~~

Madeline's first stop was her house to pick up a few items to take to Mike's later. As she rounded the hood of his old Mercedes and headed up the front walk, she got an irritating reminder of one reason she enjoyed staying at his place so much, courtesy of the collection of blue doggie poop bags that littered her front lawn. Even if she hadn't had a long history of this kind of aggravation from her nasty neighbor to the east, the location of the bags alone made it plainly obvious where they'd come from, as the front of her property was shielded by a copse of fifteen-foot scheffleras.

During the four months of her hospitalization and recovery at home, she hadn't been aware of any such cowardly acts, but for all she knew, Mike had managed to shelter her from such childish pranks with his daily presence. She had actually convinced herself that Mike had had a little man-to-man "chat" with him, wherein Dodgy Doug would've seen the error of his ways. Now she knew otherwise. She wouldn't be surprised if he was watching from his upstairs window, waiting for her discovery.

She'd only been gone a day, yet there were four of these disgusting reminders of what a spiteful, obnoxious menace her next door neighbor was. Since he only had one dog, she had to wonder if he collected these from around the neighborhood or just saved them up for a more impressive attack once the coast was clear.

Fuming and resisting the urge to bang on his door and confront the pesky weasel, she took out her phone and snapped a photo of the outrage. What she planned to do with it was still up in the air. But she knew she had reached the end of her tolerance. It galled her to think that she had actually been protecting the jerk all this time. If Mike had any idea of all the petty ways Doug showed his disrespect for her, he'd pulverize the guy, which wouldn't do either of them any good in the long run.

What was most annoying about this childish display was the lack of justifiable cause. Madeline had come to the conclusion the disgruntled fifty-something was suffering from inherent insecurity mixed with a God complex, causing him to resent anyone who managed to live their life without his expressed approval. Maybe he didn't like the fact that she had made a mark of sorts on this town—despite her salacious past—but didn't have the time or inclination to suck up to him. Maybe he didn't like the fact that she wasn't married and had a boyfriend who often stayed the night. Or maybe he held a grudge because he so wanted to believe the worst of her after that sick video of her rape went viral.

All she knew for certain was his small acts of aggression—spraying her freshly-cleaned windows with his hose, peeping at her from his upstairs window when she took her work out to the back deck, stealing her Sunday edition of the *L.A. Times*, repeatedly banging his trash can lids down in rapid succession for no other reason than to startle or annoy her—had gone on too long. At this point, she didn't care what kind of unflattering tales he'd try to disseminate around the neighborhood or what form his disdain would take next. If he was intent on being a cowardly pest, he was about to get a taste of his own medicine.

After depositing her tote on her front porch, she crossed the lawn and began collecting the poop bags with the intent of hurling them back where they'd come from. But as she raised her hand to lob the first poop bomb over the eight-foot Eugenia hedge, anticipating the satisfying *thwap* it would make as it hit the side of her neighbor's house, she checked her anger and dropped her arm. The only thing worse than being hounded by a petty, cowardly chump like Smug Doug was to descend to his level. She wanted to put an end to this unwarranted assault, but retaliating in kind would only keep it going.

Frustrated and still fuming at the affront, she took the offending bags to the other side of her driveway and deposited them in the trash can. Somehow, someway, she was going to put a stop to this petty hostility in a manner that would make her point without backfiring on her.

After disarming her alarm, she flipped through her mail as she made her way to her bedroom. She grabbed an overnight bag and began filling it with a few things she wanted to take to Mike's later, then stripped out of yesterday's clothes. She picked out a pair of black slacks and paired it with a loose gray sweater and a pair of flats. The result was suitably dull. She then took down a round box from the top of her closet and removed three wigs. Standing in front of her full-length mirror, she debated which one was right for the day's assignment: the shoulder-length brunette, the platinum bob, or the long auburn curls.

Deciding it would be better to blend in than to stand out, she chose the brunette number. She removed her jewelry and toned down her lipstick, then twisted and fastened her hair closely to her scalp. Once the wig was in place, she rooted around in her accessories drawer until she found a pair of black-rimmed glasses, their lenses not good for anything but show.

She put them on and laughed at her reflection. No one would give her a second look, which is exactly what she wanted. As an afterthought, she sent Julia Cummings a text suggesting where they should meet prior to heading up to the Bartholomew ranch.

Before the rendezvous with Julia, she wanted to stop by the Sheckle residence. Their visit to the frame shop had brought up questions she wanted to put to Natalie, but she was torn between calling to make sure Natalie was home and keeping it spontaneous. She was troubled by Evie's recollection of the text Andrew received prior to his sudden departure, a text that clearly upset him. According to his phone, the only texts or calls he'd received were several hours before his death, which begged the questions who sent him the text and who deleted it. After deliberating, she decided the best strategy was to show up unannounced.

She gathered up everything she needed before arming the alarm. Once outside, she locked the door and made her way to the Mercedes. She had just unloaded her stuff on the passenger's seat and was heading for the driver's side when a backwards glance at her front yard got her to thinking about installing surveillance cameras so she could catch Dodgy Doug in the act. As she added that chore to her mental to-do list, she realized that had already been seen to by Mike. If she could find where he'd mounted the cameras, she could adjust them so they caught the action on the east side of the property.

Figuring Mike would want to focus on the driveway and the path leading to the front door, she started checking in the bed with the scheffleras that bordered the sidewalk. It took some careful searching, but she finally found the two very discreet cameras. She repositioned them to capture the view she wanted. Knowing Mike, these wireless gadgets were probably equipped with night vision capabilities. She smiled at this fortuitous turn of events and got on with her day, looking forward to seeing what Dubious Doug's next move would be.

She hadn't yet reached the driver's side door of Mike's Mercedes when the obvious flaw with her plan hit her. Mike would be the one to see what was going on, not her. She stood there for a moment as she debated whether or not to put the cameras back to their original position. Having Mike alerted to her neighbor's bad behavior might blow the situation up in the worst possible way, with Mike getting arrested for battery.

No, she thought as she started back through her front yard, *I don't want this to be Mike's problem. I'll just have to figure out another way to deal with that creep.*

But dealing with pests would have to take a backseat to solving the mystery of the two dead husbands. With that sobering thought, she retraced her steps while she willed her brain to concentrate.

The drive to Natalie's hadn't yielded any new insights into Andrew's death, merely more questions. She had already turned onto Natalie's street when she remembered her disguise. The simple fix was to ditch the glasses, remove the wig and let her hair down, which she would have to do after she pulled over. Unfortunately, there were a lot more vehicles parked along the street than she'd seen there before. In fact, all the curb space on both sides of the street was taken in a half-block stretch, with the Sheckle property being somewhere in the middle.

Puzzled and still speculating whether the congestion was due to college kids home early for the Thanksgiving holiday or a backyard wedding, she was forced to drive past her target. Continuing her slow passage with no spaces in sight, she glanced over at Natalie's house as she crept by, wondering if she should just park on the driveway.

She slowed and was about to back up and turn onto Natalie's driveway when her eye caught movement on Natalie's front porch. She sat there, mouth agape as she regarded a scene that shed a whole new light on the grieving widow. Reflexively, she shifted into drive and goosed the accelerator enough to get out of sight, pulling over at the first available spot farther up the street. She sat there a moment, stunned.

As her heart beat wildly, her mind entertained lame, unconvincing excuses for why Natalie Sheckle would be kissing a man goodbye on her front porch at eight-forty on a Saturday morning. What she'd seen was no affectionate peck on the cheek. Regardless of the brevity of her glimpse, she'd had a direct line of sight to Natalie's front walkway. There was no doubt in her mind that the grieving widow was participating in the kind of kiss not shared with a relative or close friend. Though she'd only gotten a brief look, there was no mistaking the caressing hands of both participants. She also got the distinct impression of this being a stolen moment, one more reassuring kiss to confirm their intentions. *A lovers' pact?*

What the hell?

Her own physical reaction to what she'd seen confirmed her instincts: there was definitely something wrong with the scene she'd just witnessed.

Why would a widow who was already involved with another man be so invested in proving her late husband had been murdered?

What she'd just observed made her question everything Natalie had told them, and it put her insistence that Andrew didn't kill himself in a completely different light. What if Andrew had witnessed what she'd just witnessed? What if he came across a text or a voicemail from Natalie's mystery man? Or what if the text he received the day of his death was sent by a concerned neighbor? What if the idea of Natalie having an affair was simply too much heartache for him to bear after the loss of his only child?

Madeline's speculations were cut short as she caught a glimpse in her sideview mirror of the lean, dark-haired man as he briskly crossed the sidewalk, head down as if consciously keeping a low-profile. She watched his lanky frame as he ducked down and disappeared inside a parked car. Within seconds, the sleek, dark, muscle car pulled away from the curb, cutting off a car in the process. She had to wait until both cars passed her before she could follow suit.

Though having a shield between her and the target had its advantages, she really needed to get a look at the license plate. She had to at least determine the make and model of the car and get a partial plate number or she'd have no way of finding out who it was registered to.

"Come on, come on, come on," she muttered under her breath as the subject's car yielded to oncoming traffic before it could make a left turn onto the main thoroughfare. The car ahead of her also had its left turn indicator on. She inched along with the two cars as if they were attached.

The light changed to yellow. She knew she wouldn't make it through the intersection unless she blatantly ran the red light, so she hung back slightly as the two cars in front of her moved in sync. At least she would get a better side visual of the one she was after. Though she couldn't see the make, she committed its silhouette to memory. A two-door, late-model American muscle car, graphite gray, with darkly tinted windows and matte anthracite rims. Distinctive, in a decidedly masculine way. It seemed safe to assume a fair amount of the driver's ego was tied up in his macho ride. She was willing to bet it was his prize possession. She'd also put money on him being a renter as opposed to a home owner, using as much flash as he could afford where more people were likely to see it.

The traffic on the main artery was backed up, so she still had a hope of catching up enough to follow at a safe distance, if the lights worked in her favor. It didn't take long for that rosy hope to fade. The light on Patterson changed, and all the cars made it through the intersection before she got the green light again. Even stomping the gas pedal didn't give her enough time to reach the next intersection before that light turned red.

"Damn," she muttered, her hands clutching the wheel tightly enough to whiten her knuckles. Now all she had to go on was an overwhelming apprehension that MDPI was being played.

The abrasive trill of a car horn startled her back to the present. Her foot overcompensated, pressing down hard on the accelerator and jolting the heavy old car through the intersection. She earned another honk of protest as she made a hasty lane change to get on the Northbound 101 on-ramp.

She arrived at the rendezvous spot earlier than anticipated, giving her time to puzzle over the Sheckle case. She and Mike had readily accepted the referral because it had been brought to them by the D.A., the spin being he was trying to help out a grieving widow. But maybe it had never been Natalie's intention to hire a P.I. firm; maybe she had only been trying to get the D.A.'s help in changing the findings of Andrew's death from suicide to murder, after discovering the suicide clause in Andrew's life insurance policy was still in effect. She could've gone along with the charade simply in hopes of persuading MDPI that Andrew would never take his own life, therefore his death had to have been by someone else's hand.

But how would they have proven it was murder if it wasn't?

Maybe Natalie backed herself into a corner when she went to see the D.A. Maybe she never expected him to send a couple private investigators her way.

Madeline mulled this over for a moment, but dismissed that line of reasoning. All Natalie had to do was decline their services. Instead, she had turned Andrew's personal effects over to them without hesitation. Something else was going on here.

Theories and hypotheses assailed her from all sides. Maybe Andrew had discovered that Natalie was having an affair and killed himself out of pure despair. Maybe Natalie purposely botched up the scene in the bedroom to make it look like murder, eliciting the help of her lover to create a scene they hoped would support a suspicious death investigation. But they'd have to be careful that it didn't point back to them...

With her gaze going inward, she played a scene in her mind of the lovers trying to make rushed decisions. If Natalie was cognizant of the two-year suicide exclusion still being in effect, then the knee-jerk reaction may have been to move the body and/or the chair to make it look like Andrew had been shot by someone else. The blood splatter would've been inconsistent with the positioning of the chair, but what did that prove? Did it point to murder, or did it point to a cover up? Or did it just play into a disclaimer from Natalie that she might have altered the scene as she reacted to finding her husband shot to death. Maybe admitting as much was one of the reasons law enforcement came to the conclusion the death was an act of suicide as opposed to homicide.

So many speculations only served to make her feel more confused. After checking the time, she took a deep breath and tried to project herself into the scene in the Sheckle master bedroom that day.

"Okay..." she said out loud, needing the sound of her own voice to give credence to her thoughts, "according to Evie, Andrew got a disturbing text…a text that has since been deleted. He rushes home." Madeline's gaze went inward as she envisioned how Andrew had reacted. "He rushes home, catching Natalie with a man in their bed. Andrew's world blows apart. He's deranged with grief. All he can think about is ending his misery. So, he grabs a gun that he keeps hidden for protection, and he aims it at… Who does he aim it at? Himself? Natalie? The other man? Natalie claims that he would never touch a gun, but she could be lying…

"So, who sent the text? How come there's no text on his phone?" She grabbed a pad and a pen from her tote and began to make notes to herself.

Who sent the text?
What did the text say?
Who deleted it?
Where did the gun come from?
Was Natalie lying when she said Andrew didn't own a gun?
Check police report to confirm gun found/used was actually stolen

The fact that the gun recovered at the scene had supposedly been reported stolen years earlier nagged at her. Nothing she had learned about Andrew from his wife and his employee suggested he was the kind of person to possess a stolen handgun. The laws for gun purchases had become stringent enough that no reputable gun merchant would risk his or her license by engaging in such practices. Which brought her right back to where she'd started—hounded by speculations and no concrete proof to back them up.

Madeline sat as still as a statue, almost afraid to breathe. This was all wild conjecture, but a few concrete answers might actually lead them to a viable theory they hadn't yet considered.

"Okay," she said to herself, shifting restlessly in the driver's seat, "forget the provenance of the gun for a moment. Think about Natalie and this possible affair. What if a well-meaning or nosey neighbor alerted Andrew via text that there was a man at his house in the middle of the day? Andrew rushes home and finds his wife in bed with another man. He falls into his father's old recliner, utterly devastated. There's a gun…however *that* gets there…he points the gun at himself. Before Natalie or the other guy can intervene, he pulls the trigger."

Madeline shook her head absently. This theory was farfetched, but something along those lines was still a possibility. "But why was the chair moved away from the corner? Maybe the chair was moved afterwards to give more credence to the scenario that Andrew had taken his own life. The chair had meaning for him. Maybe…" After letting out a frustrated huff, she gave voice to further speculations.

"Okay… The gun goes off, and now whoever's there is afraid someone may have heard the gunshot. So, Natalie and her lover scramble. They pull the chair out of the corner, put Andrew in it, put the gun in his hand, wiping their prints off first. The guy sneaks off the property and vanishes. Natalie is supposed to report her husband has been shot dead, but she waits a few minutes, just in case someone has seen the guy leave. Since she doesn't hear sirens, she decides to leave and comes back after a reasonable length of time. She had to be convincing when she calls 9-1-1. She had to show real grief. She doesn't offer an opinion of what may have transpired. Her story is she came home and found him already dead…"

A rap on the passenger side window made Madeline jump. She glanced over to find Julia Cummings, who apparently found the scene amusing.

"Sorry. I thought I heard you talking on the phone, so I was just trying to get your attention," Julia said with a condescending smirk as Madeline emerged from the Mercedes, bags in hand. "I almost didn't recognize you in that getup, but figured it had to be you since this is the only vehicle here."

"I'm intentionally trying to conceal my identity," Madeline replied, her tone lacking its usual friendliness. For the sake of cooperation, she kept her opinion of Julia's own attire to herself, though the tightfitting, thigh-grazing, fluorescent orange dress looked as if she'd literally grown into it. *At least she had the decency to cover it with a blazer,* she thought, blinking reflexively at the garish hue.

Julia caught the flicker of disapproval on Madeline's features, but checked her irritation, deciding not to take offense, considering the circumstances. She was counting on finding out the real reason Madeline had gone to such lengths to gain access to the private areas of Rancho Vista Encantada.

"You're going to ride up with me in the Explorer," Julia said as Madeline came around the back of the Mercedes and fell in step with her.

Madeline was pleased to see the station had thought enough of this piece to put a film crew on it. Keeping Vanessa Bartholomew and company distracted while she got access to that side of the property had been her primary objective for suggesting this piece to Julia. Observing those who lived and worked on the ranch would give her better context for piecing together what happened the day of Nick's accident.

"I do appreciate you suggesting this piece, but I'm not going to forget about our deal," Julia said with a shrewd glint in her eyes as they got in the station's SUV.

"Don't worry, you'll get your story as soon as I'm at liberty to tell it."

"That sounds like preemptive stonewalling."

"I have no intention of reneging on our deal. I like the idea of having a reciprocal arrangement with you. I think it will serve us both much better than our previously adversarial roles," Madeline said as she closed the passenger side door of the Explorer. The van with the satellite dish and all the recording equipment followed them out of the otherwise deserted parking lot.

"I hope you don't intend to censor what I can and can't report on," Julia said with a fair amount of attitude as they merged onto the 101, heading north.

"I wouldn't dream of it. Besides, there are so many talking points, you'll run out of time before you run out of material," Madeline replied before ticking off all the possible lines of inquiry open to her. "You've got a new Santa Barbara County winery. A young female winemaker. An original land grant rancho that's been recently divided, half going into the Land Trust for preservation and public access, in exchange for commercial rights for the only retail business on the scenic Gaviota coast. Plus, there's Vanessa's brother, Sean Bartholomew, local surfing legend. What more could you ask for?"

"How about the bizarre, tragic death of the patriarch a couple years ago…?" Julia asked, eyeing Madeline suspiciously.

"I think I'd steer clear of that subject, if I were you," Madeline replied coolly, not taking the bait. "I don't imagine it would go over very well if Vanessa Bartholomew burst into tears on camera."

Julia shot her a reproachful look, stinging at the insinuation that she'd ever stoop so low for the sake of provocative film coverage. It would serve no one to alienate the subject. Besides, she would never be that shortsighted. It galled her that Madeline would condescend to her like that.

Madeline chose to ignore the bad vibes emanating from Julia. She sat back and enjoyed the scenery, not minding at all that the newswoman had given up on conversation.

It only took them twelve minutes to reach the gates at Rancho Vista Encantada. This time, she was ready for the low-key signage and alerted Julia in advance so they wouldn't miss the turnoff. Unlike the previous day, the clouds were harmless white affairs, layered and scattered about the sky, creating depth that hinted at the vastness of the atmosphere above them. From the opposite side of the same parking area where she and Mike parked the day before, they were able to see a peek of the ocean and the islands, darkened by the patch of clouds hovering above them, making them appear more mysterious and regal in shadow.

"Pretend you have a reason for being here," Julia said as she thrusted a clipboard at Madeline.

Madeline flicked through the printout of station memos official enough to pass as being relevant to the purpose for this visit. She dutifully hugged it to her chest and affected an attitude of being a necessary component to this interview.

They had only seconds to take in the view before they heard footfalls coming from behind as Vanessa Bartholomew crunched her way over the crushed granite. Madeline took a step backward, making herself virtually invisible while Julia slid fluidly into her accustomed role of local TV personality.

From her vantage point off to the side, Madeline was able to take the young winemaker's measure. Everything about Vanessa Bartholomew spoke of confidence: her tall stature, purposeful stride, erect posture. Keen intelligence flashed in her blue-green eyes. Her mane of straight blond hair and her natural good looks were an extra bonus when added to all the rest of her obvious gifts.

Dressed in elegant, understated attire of khaki slacks and dusky aqua silk blouse that clung to her willowy frame, she was a P.R. firm's dream client. There was no room for doubt; this young woman was a force to be reckoned with. No wonder the D.A. eventually felt compelled to prosecute Lindsay for murder. With a burning need for justice, Vanessa would've brought a determined force to her demands that Lindsay be held responsible for her father's death.

The young winemaker received the reporter as if she were a longtime friend. Though it struck Madeline as odd at first, she reminded herself that Julia was a well-known figure in Santa Barbara. People naturally gravitated to her, forgetting completely that the acquaintanceship was one-sided.

"I see you've got your crew," Vanessa surmised, offering Madeline a perfunctory "hi" as an aside before turning her thoughts to logistics. "So, I was thinking we could start up by the vineyards."

"That sounds great," Julia was quick to agree. "You just tell us where to go, then we'll set up and begin the interview. I'd love to see as much of your operations as possible. The more we can show, the more excited people will be about coming to check it out themselves. The views are spectacular, by the way." Julia sighed deeply after turning around to snatch another quick peek.

"Wait until you see the view from farther up," Vanessa teased as she turned and marched over to a bright red Kawasaki Mule.

"Should we just follow you?" Julia asked.

"Yes. I'll wait for you."

Madeline was impressed by the way Vanessa handled herself. She was the most confident, in-charge twenty-four-year-old she'd ever encountered. She may have been devastated by the grisly, premature death of her father, but that had not derailed her focus. Throwing herself into oenology may have been a means of dulling the pain of her parents' divorce, but it was clear she was determined to make a name for herself while keeping Rancho Vista Encantada a going concern. It could've been her way of paying tribute to her deceased father and all the Bartholomews who had come before him, though selling her brother on the concept of giving half the property away to get her winery must've taken some pretty big promises on her end.

"Are you ready?" Julia asked impatiently, breaking into Madeline's thoughts.

"Sorry. Couldn't take my eyes off the view," Madeline lied as she climbed inside the Explorer, her thoughts already on what they might find up at the Bartholomew compound.

NINETEEN

Myriad questions buzzed around Madeline's head as the procession headed up the compacted shale road that wove through gradually ascending hills. For starters, she wondered who all lived on this side of the ranch. Given the circumstances, she'd probably have to pump Yolanda for that kind of info, as that would likely not fall into the scope of the interview.

"Are you planning on shooting in the vineyards?"

"Yep," was Julia's tight-lipped reply.

"Did Vanessa give you any idea of how big the wine operation is in terms of employees?'

"They've got eight fulltime employees right now, but they're looking to take on more workers as they plant more grapes." Julia flashed her dark eyes over at Madeline briefly. "You getting what you want?"

"That remains to be seen," Madeline answered evasively before turning to look out the side window. She wasn't willing to share the fact this was merely a fishing expedition. At the moment, she didn't know exactly what she was looking for. She could only hope she'd recognize it when she came across it.

Once they reached their destination and everyone got out of their respective vehicles, the four crew members took in their surroundings with slack-jaw wonder. Rains in October and earlier that month had fostered wild grasses that obscured most of the dried brush, the ragged remnants from spring's volunteer offerings of fennel and mustard. From their eighteen-hundred-foot elevation, the view toward the ocean was almost startling. It seemed as though the rest of the Santa Barbara coastline had been miniaturized from this altitude. Conversely, the three visible Channel Islands loomed larger, now that more of each had been exposed by leveling the curvature of the earth. Their perceived closeness set Madeline's heart aflutter.

Contrasting with the rush of positive emotions, a flashback to the Chow-chilla Women's Prison made her heart contract. Thinking about Lindsay, a woman who had undoubtedly traversed this terrain on horseback numerous times while enjoying this very sight, made her feel queasy with dread. Though she knew better than to invest in a person's guilt or innocence until all the facts were known and all the lies disproved, she couldn't help seeing the parallel between her once-perfect life and Lindsay's. If Lindsay was in fact innocent, then perhaps she too could start again. That fledgling hope filled Madeline with a renewed sense of purpose.

Turning back to what the Bartholomew family had seen fit to add to this rural setting, Madeline was particularly keen on the two huge barns set back at a respectful distance. Barns held farm equipment, as in the type that had delivered a fatal blow to the former lord of the land. As her eyes panned the horizon, she discovered three smaller outbuildings in addition to the main house and what appeared to be two other dwellings in the distance

Breaking from her contemplation, she caught up with Vanessa and Julia as they prepared for the interview. With all the focus on those two, Madeline was able to edge away and do a little casual exploring on her own. She wandered away from the vineyard and took a peek inside the closest of the two barns. As she had suspected, it was filled with what you might find on any rural property, mostly farm equipment, including a tractor. She gave it a wide berth as she circled it, trying to envision what exactly had gone wrong with the machine and how Nick came to be caught under it, assuming it was the same vehicle. She shuddered at that gruesome visual. If it had been *her* loved one who was killed by the tractor, it would've been long gone.

She finished her inspection of the first barn, quickening her pace as she went to check out the other one about fifty yards to the north. She could tell as she got closer it was clearly a more recent fabrication. Aluminum siding stretched up a good twenty feet at the apex. The modern, barn-shaped structure housed rows of huge fermentation vats, tanks and barrels, and other winemaking equipment. The temperature inside was at least fifteen degrees colder, and there was a slight metallic smell to the fermenting wine that she could almost taste.

The sound of approaching voices from the other side of the far wall spurred her to make a hasty exit. She slipped outside and made it around the right side of the building and affected a casual stance with the clipboard to her chest as if what she'd been doing was essential in some way. Julia gave her a wary look as she, Vanessa and the crew came around the corner.

"I see you've found the fermentation tanks," Vanessa said as she sauntered purposefully past Madeline.

"Yes, I think we need to get some footage of that," Madeline bluffed, ignoring the perturbed vibes Vanessa was sending her way. She stepped out of everyone's path, then followed them inside, hanging in the background like her presence mattered. Julia telegraphed a warning to stay in her role and not annoy their hostess.

The next stop on the tour was the first vineyard Vanessa had planted.

"I came home from Davis after my first semester and insisted that I had to plant a vineyard," Vanessa said, laughing at the recollection while the cameras filmed her in a close up. "That was not an easy sell, I'll tell you," she added before falling into a slow walk with Julia, allowing the crew to capture acres of vines decked in their glorious fall hues of crimson, russet and amber.

"As a tribute and a thank you to my late father for indulging my *calling*," Vanessa said as she came to a halt and looked directly at Julia, "wines from this first vineyard carry the Nickolas label." Madeline noted her tight-lipped composure as she said her father's name. To Vanessa's credit, she quickly masked her feelings with a humble smile.

One of the cameramen closed in to catch Julia's reaction. "I'm sure that would make him very proud," she said, her voice hinting at the emotion behind the sentiment. "And this year marks your debut vintage..."

"Yes. The Nickolas 2018 pinot noir has been released and can now be purchased from our tasting room. It will also be available in other local wine shops by early spring."

"And your tasting room is quite unique because it's the only commercial venture on this stretch of the coast," Julia was pleased to add, feeding into her subject's agenda.

As the carefully choreographed banter continued, Madeline hung back far enough to study Nick's daughter in action without drawing any more attention to herself. The contrast between Lindsay's description of the horse-crazy teenager who took riding lessons from her and this very determined young trailblazer was noteworthy. Losing her innocence during the breakup of her parents' marriage had set Vanessa on the path to becoming self-reliant. With newfound convictions that life would only give her what she could grab with both hands, she managed to claim a part of the family ranch as her own. Madeline had to wonder what Sean thought of her seizing some the estate's acreage for her enterprises.

As if on cue, a light metallic late-model Ford truck loaded with all the bells and whistles sidled past. The driver was a bad-boy handsome surfer dude in his late twenties, with sun-streaked brown hair, still damp from a recent shower. Sean slowed slightly to take in the scene unfolding on his property. Madeline got the distinct impression he found the sight of his sister holding court with a news crew in attendance irksome, perhaps even ostentatious. He punctuated his scowl with lead-footed disdain, leaving a cloud of dust in his wake as his two right tires hit the dirt patch on the road's shoulder.

Madeline sidestepped the dust plume and turned her attention back to the vineyard just as everyone started walking in her direction, signaling time for another change of venue. While the two-man film crew got back into the van, Vanessa conferred with one of the ranch hands. This gave Julia the opportunity to fill Madeline in on what their next move would be.

"We're going to do a shoot down at the tasting room. Dave and Chuck are going to scout out possible shots while you and I get a quick private tour of the family compound," Julia confided in a hushed voice. She seemed downright giddy at the prospect.

Madeline smiled at this fortunate turn of events. "Nicely done," she commended her reluctant accomplice.

Having a visual of where the Bartholomews lived prior to Nick's death would make it easier to conjure up scenarios of what transpired that day. Ideally, those inspirations would dovetail with Lindsay's claims of having left a note for Nick that warned him not to use the tractor. And if she were really lucky, maybe she'd divine who took the note and why. It was a stretch, but it cost nothing to hope.

The red Kawasaki rumbled around the largest of the two barns and pulled up next to the visitors. Apparently, this was how Vanessa planned to show them the family residences. The options for seating presented a problem; the padded vinyl seat was wide enough to accommodate three, though whoever sat in the middle would have to straddle the gear shift.

"I'll ride in the back," Madeline offered after Julia silently made it known she was not risking bruised knees for the privilege of touring the Bartholomew compound. Madeline had no desire to get close enough for Vanessa Bartholomew to figure out she was disguising her appearance. That would surely trigger suspicions that might blow this whole line of investigation.

"There's enough room up here," Vanessa argued as she watched Madeline sum up the best way to hoist herself up into the high, shallow bed.

"I'll be fine back here," Madeline assured her as she used one of the burly tires to boost herself up over the side. Her shoes thudded against the corrugated metal as she sat down cross-legged with her back to the others.

"Ready?" Vanessa asked in an amused tone before shifting into drive. Even with her back turned, Madeline could tell Julia was enjoying her discomfort. Madeline lurched, swayed and bounced during the two-minute jaunt that ended abruptly in front of a charming single-story, hacienda-style home. Vanessa cut the engine so she could be heard without having to holler.

"This is the house my dad built for me after I graduated from Davis."

"I love it," Julia enthused. "It's the perfect size—not too big, not too small. The gardens are just gorgeous."

"Thanks. I was inspired by Ganna Walska's Lotusland, except I used only drought-tolerant plants and tried to stick to natives, though I did go kind of overboard on the cycads—not to the extent she did, but then again, I didn't have a million dollars' worth of jewels to sell," Vanessa said with a laugh.

She turned the key and took her foot off the brake, letting the Kawasaki idle past the gardens that led away from the house. Madeline noted how well-maintained the paths were, which suggested they had plenty of hands working on the ranch. She spotted several groupings of outdoor furniture, all expensive-looking, all in keeping with the minimalistic nature of the gardens. The whole thing was magazine-worthy and tastefully done.

After another short drive up a gradual incline, through rolling hills spotted with oaks and other native flora, the road leveled out. A much larger home surrounded by mature oaks, pepper trees and pines came into view. Madeline assumed this had been Lindsay's residence while Nick was alive.

Vanessa turned the Kawasaki off again as she explained that her great-grandfather had built the house in 1901, and pointed out the changes that had been made over the years. Madeline studied the classic Spanish Revival architecture with its whispers of an illustrious past. She could almost hear Julia's unspoken regret at not being able to get this on film.

"So much rich history on these land grant ranchos," she said wistfully. From Madeline's perch, she observed Vanessa's breezy acceptance of what had been her birthright.

"Yes, we are so blessed to have been the recipients of that land deal. Back then, with so much more land than inhabitants to work it, acquiring huge parcels outside of settled areas was kind of a gamble. Before there were cars, not many people wanted to be in such rural areas. Of course, that's all changed now. Ultimately, people with money want lots of land to themselves. Some of the neighboring ranches have sold for over a hundred million dollars."

Vanessa let that staggering figure absorb in her guests' minds as she surveyed her domain. As she reached for the key, Madeline sent an urgent telepathic message to Julia. Sensing it wasn't reaching its target, she risked overstepping her bounds.

"Who lives here now?" she asked. Both heads swiveled around in unison.

"I do," Vanessa answered matter-of-factly, generating a soft "oh" of confusion from Julia.

"I thought that first house was yours…"

"It was…I mean, *technically*, it still is, but my mother lives there now."

"Oh…I see," Julia commented, her head nodding placidly.

Sensing that Julia didn't really see at all, Vanessa clarified the situation. "After my father's death—which I'm really not okay talking about yet—my brother and I both felt better having our mom close by, for reasons I'm also not going to get into."

Madeline was glad the two in the front couldn't see her expression; the fact that Nick's first wife was back in residence on his family's land while his second wife now resided in prison was quite a revelation. How exactly that had any bearing on the events leading up to his death was unknown, and probably not even relevant. But still, it gave Madeline the impression of Lindsay Bartholomew's existence having been wiped away, plastered over, expunged.

"Oh sure, I totally understand. We have no desire to pry into your private life," Julia was quick to assure her.

Having made her boundaries perfectly clear, Vanessa fired up the Mule again.

"Since this has run longer than I expected, I think we should skip my brother's house and get down to the tasting room," she said as she hit the gas pedal and executed a quick U-turn that nearly tossed Madeline out of the back.

Once in the Explorer and following Vanessa back down to where they had started, Julia queried Madeline over the reasons behind this elaborate ruse.

"It's not really a ruse," Madeline argued. "You're here to tape a human interest story for KSBC."

"I know why *I'm* here. What I don't know is why you've gone to such lengths to get on this property."

"I told you I can't divulge that just yet." Trading distrusting glances, Madeline added, "Don't worry, there's nothing diabolical afoot. I've got bona fide reasons for needing a closer look at this family."

"It's Lindsay Bartholomew, isn't it?"

Madeline kept her expression completely neutral, giving away nothing.

"If I said no, would you believe me? Didn't think so," she said after meeting Julia's put-upon glare with one of her own. "Look, for the sake of future mutually beneficial collaborations, you're going to have to take me at my word. I can't divulge anything at this time."

Julia had little choice but to trust Madeline. She pulled the station's vehicle into one of the parking slots across from the gift shop-slash-produce market-slash-tasting room. Vanessa had beat them back down and was clearly impatient for them to get this piece wrapped up and on the air and the station's website as quickly as possible.

While Julia and company went about the business of setting up the next shoot with Vanessa, Madeline hung around the periphery, trying to be inconspicuous without missing a moment of the action. She watched as the two cameramen fussed with the lighting and sound, while Julia prepped Vanessa on the questions she'd be asking and what viewers would likely want to know about this exciting new enterprise on the Gaviota coast.

In addition to Madeline, there were a dozen or so visitors who were keen on observing the media coverage. Their interest added an air of excitement.

This was a hip and happening spot and they were hip and happening people for being on the cutting edge. Cell phones emerged, ready to record the action.

From her vantage point at the far end of the displays, Madeline tried to maintain a low profile, picking up bits of the conversations around her as Vanessa and Julia walked through their talking points. Out of the corner of her left eye, she caught a glimpse of a rather glamorously turned-out woman with stylishly cut hair in a shade only achieved by a canny colorist.

Rich gold with copper lowlights, Madeline thought as the attractive woman strode purposefully toward Vanessa. Above average height in her heeled boots, the woman gave Vanessa a quick, affectionate hug from the side, then ducked out of camera range.

"I'll be watching from right over there," the woman said as she touched her fingertips to her lips and blew a kiss to Vanessa.

This must be the first Mrs. Bartholomew, Madeline surmised, shifting slightly to the left to make room for her. It took a lot of self-control to not give this affable, effervescent woman a proper once over. *Patricia*, she mused. *I wonder if she reverted back to her maiden name…*

Sensing Madeline's covert attention, the woman turned and beamed a dazzling smile, broadcasting her unabashed pride.

"This is a big day for my daughter—her first significant media coverage," Patricia confided in a hushed voice.

"Oh, she's your daughter…? Congratulations to both of you," Madeline whispered back, aware that the dialog between Vanessa and Julia was now being recorded. With her radar on high alert, it took considerable willpower to stand there at such close range, when what she really wanted to do was stand back and size up the first Mrs. Bartholomew. She was forced to make do with reexamining what little Lindsay had said about Nick's first wife.

Talk about a twist of fate—make that a double twist, Madeline thought. *Nick leaves his first wife after meeting Lindsay, regardless of whether the split was a direct consequence of their meeting or not. Then Nick dies under a cloud of suspicion, for which Lindsay is sentenced to twenty years in prison. And now the jilted wife is back on the ranch, basking in her beautiful daughter's achievements, all of which were made possible by Nick's death.*

Madeline imagined that might sound like cosmic justice to some folks, whether it was deliberately engineered or just karmic payback. Though she felt more of an allegiance to Lindsay at this point, it was hard to miss the absolute joy and love exhibited by the woman standing next to her, a woman who didn't strike her as evil or dastardly in any respect, though she knew better than anyone how deceiving appearances could be.

That's the trouble with other people's divorces—it's sometimes hard to tell the good guys from the bad.

But no one was good or bad all the time, and often perception carried more weight than the actions themselves. Plus, it was difficult to accurately judge other people's marriages when you were examining them from such a remove.

While everyone in the gift shop watched on in respectful silence, Madeline traded places with a shorter spectator behind her. Once out of everyone's view, she was able to float in the background, taking in what was being said on camera while watching other observers, but mainly focusing her attention on Patricia Bartholomew.

"What would you say to those who question the quality of wines made from grapes grown on this stretch of unproven terrain, in these less than ideal conditions?" Julia asked.

"Try them!" Vanessa countered with a playful laugh. "Our wines speak for themselves," she added with a confident smile. "Just because wine grapes haven't been planted on this stretch of the coast before doesn't mean they can't be used to produce high quality wine. Consider all the different varietals used around the world, depending on soil and climate conditions. What my education at UC Davis taught me is to play with the elements and the varietals, find the most compatible stock for the soil and weather, and just try it. I'm over-simplifying here, because really the success of any vintage needs a lot of knowledge and a degree of luck. But experience combined with intuition and openness to new approaches are what California wines are all about."

The interview wrapped up with Julia thanking the maverick winemaker and encouraging everyone to check out the unique new establishment on the Gaviota Coast.

When Julia signaled to her cameramen that it was a wrap, hearty applause broke out from the enthusiastic spectators. Patricia Bartholomew was quick to give her beautiful daughter a congratulatory hug, then stood holding her hands as they savored what could be an important step in her career. From Madeline's standpoint, she could only see Vanessa's expression. It was a mix of triumph and humility, with maybe a dash of melancholy.

Or maybe guilt, she speculated as she studied one of her key suspects in Nick Bartholomew's death. She recalled what Lindsay said when they were interviewing her at the prison, how Vanessa's world blew apart when Nick filed for divorce, how she was so distressed, she couldn't concentrate. A traumatic event like that could have a profound effect on one's psyche, especially that of a teenage girl. What better way to settle the score with the two people she blamed for the quake that rocked her world? She had means, motive and opportunity. And she was thriving now that the biggest impediments standing between her desire to create her own winery on the family land were now permanently out of the way.

Bodies began milling about again, looking more intently at the wares on offer, evidently feeling the sincere desire to support this up-and-coming establishment with their buying power.

Madeline was buffeted from one vantage point to another as she continued to find herself blocking someone's view of the merchandise. She caught a glimpse of Julia and could see she and the crew were preparing for departure.

Needing a stall tactic, Madeline glanced at the book display to her right. Out of reflex, she grabbed a copy of *A Vintage to Die For*. She was heading for the register when she flipped the book over, receiving a mild shock as she put everything together.

P.A. Collins. Collins must be her maiden name, Madeline deduced as she quickly covered her surprise and got in line with the other eager shoppers.

"Ready?" Julia asked. It was more of a directive than a question.

"I'll be right out. I just want to buy this…for my dad."

Julia let out an impatient huff, but didn't challenge her. "Please make it quick. I've got to get back to the station so I can get this piece produced for the six o'clock news."

With Julia out of the way, Madeline was able to observe Vanessa and her mother again while Luke struggled to keep up with the flurry of sales. She figured this small operation was unaccustomed to such brisk business. Two people had gotten in line behind her, each holding a bottle of Rancho Vista Encantada's first vintage.

"Thank you so much for stopping in today," Vanessa said as she passed customers on her way to the front of the store. Madeline continued to eavesdrop as Vanessa mingled with the crowd, though she really was more curious about the first Mrs. Bartholomew whom she'd last seen working the other side of the room.

"I see you've got good taste in books as well as wine," Patricia said, surprising Madeline as she sidled up next to her.

"Oh…ah yes, thanks. It's for my dad, actually… He's sort of a mystery junkie," Madeline lied.

"Excellent! I do hope he enjoys it. If he does, tell him to spread the word!"

"Oh, will do!" As Patricia sought out another target, Madeline managed to regain her attention. "Would you mind signing it?"

"Not at all! I'd be delighted to!" While Patricia procured a pen and a place on the counter where she could autograph the book, Madeline's eyes roved over her as if committing everything about her to memory.

Nick plus Patricia plus Lindsay plus this land grant rancho. A recipe for disaster? Apparently so.

But only one of the players in that three-sided drama still had life and liberty. The question nagging Madeline was who had the means, motive, opportunity and the will to intentionally maim or kill Nick?

TWENTY

Madeline sat in the driver's seat of Mike's Mercedes, staring at the entrance of the derelict movie theater with unseeing eyes. She was aware of her hunger, thanks to her grumbling stomach, but she didn't want to take the time to find somewhere to eat. She had a lot on her mind, but found it hard to concentrate on any one thought long enough to make sense of it. She took a pad of paper and pen out of her tote in hopes of jotting down notes that would focus her mind and inspire a strategy or two.

"Think. Think. Think," she prodded herself. She reached over to the glove compartment for one of the energy bars Mike always kept on hand. After chomping it down in seconds, she realized hunger was largely responsible for her lack of brain power. Lack of valuable insights was the other culprit. She was half-tempted to call Mike to fill him in on the sighting at Natalie Sheckle's house and the trip up to the Bartholomew ranch, but she knew he was either with his property managers or already making merry with Jesse.

What made the most sense at this juncture was to go to the office and work the boards, add a few characters to the mix, see if that altered the picture in any way. Liking that idea, mostly because it was the only one she could come up with, she turned the key in the ignition and headed out onto the busy thoroughfare.

Rationalizing that the Sheckle home was more or less along the way, she decided to do another drive by. The goodbye she'd witnessed was not the type exchanged prior to a trip to the grocery store, so she didn't expect to see the guy with the muscle car. But it was still worth a chance. That kiss, with the lingering hands, was an *I don't want to leave you* kiss.

After gathering her hair back up and fastening it, she grabbed the wig from her tote, giving it a quick finger combing before she pulled it back on. She fluffed it around her face and called it good enough. She didn't bother with the useless glasses, since her sunglasses worked just as well.

The vicinity immediately surrounding the Sheckle home was still choked with parked vehicles on her return. She drove past Natalie's house and went to the end of the block, then made a rather ungainly Y-turn and headed back the way she'd come. No sign of the flashy muscle car. After passing her target a second time, she pulled into a neighboring driveway to turn around, then parked in a space that afforded a clear view of Natalie's front door from a safe distance. On the off chance the scene would repeat itself, she had her cell phone out and ready should she need to snap a photo.

Now the big wait, which gave her plenty of time to think. Mostly, what haunted her thoughts was that scene on Natalie's front porch. It replayed in a continuous loop, leaving her feeling disturbed and more convinced that what she had witnessed didn't quite jibe with the grieving widow M.O.

There's nothing wrong with Natalie Sheckle being involved with a man, she reminded herself. After what the woman had been through, she surely deserved a little comfort and affection to blunt the painful losses she had suffered. Losing a child to leukemia, finding your husband shot dead in your bedroom? Who could survive those kinds of hits and not have deep wounds in need of love and healing?

Intellectually, she got it. On an emotional level, she got it. But on a gut level, all she got was the message something about that scene earlier didn't fit.

She had just turned the key in the ignition when Natalie's garage door opened. Madeline shifted into drive, ready to follow once the Subaru pulled out of the driveway. Natalie cautiously backed into the street, then pointed the SUV in the opposite direction of where Madeline had parked. After waiting a few seconds, Madeline pulled away from the curb and followed the Subaru, keeping her pace slow and allowing Natalie to proceed at a comfortable distance.

Though the hope had been that Natalie would lead her to the man on the front walk, allowing her to get an address and maybe his license plate number, the route they were traveling led instead to the studio where Natalie gave her Pilates lessons. Feeling a little frustrated and out of sorts, Madeline pulled off the wig and tossed it onto the passenger's seat, where it lay clumped up like a hairy, feral animal.

"The office," she said out loud after weighing her options for the most productive move at this juncture. At least there she could scrutinize each piece of the Bartholomew puzzle and determine if what she'd learned today opened the gates to enlightenment.

TWENTY-ONE

The trudge up the stairs to her office was still a little challenging, but she could feel improvement over her first day back. The hallway was reassuringly quiet. Apparently, none of her neighbors felt inclined to work on a Saturday afternoon. The only sound she could hear was her own footfalls on the worn Saltillo tiles. No snatches of conversation seeped through the closed doors. She liked the feeling of solitude and looked forward to brainstorming without distractions.

As she unlocked the door to her office, she thought about Jack Waverly, the attorney in the office next to hers. She hadn't seen him since the day she got shot. Having him to bounce her misgivings off of had been invaluable when she discovered Hannah Cavanaugh's secret. She had been waiting to thank him in person, but she hadn't had a spare moment since she'd been officially back to work. Had she gone into that situation ignorant of certain facts, she probably wouldn't be standing there right now.

She was half-tempted to try his door, but thought better of it. She needed focus, not distractions, regardless of how pleasant they might be. She unlocked the door, closing and relocking it before going straight to disarm the alarm. She stopped short as she realized the alarm was off.

"Hello?" she said loudly, her voice firm, her ears straining to hear the slightest movement. Her heart did a quick flip as a lumbering hulk came out of Lauren's office, headed her way.

"Charlie!" she exclaimed, exhaling with relief. "What are you doing here?" she asked, her voice automatically switching to the dulcet, modulated tones reserved exclusively for encounters with four-legged friends.

"Maddie, is that you?" Lauren's voice preceded her as she came out of her office to rein in her oversize protector, who was now busy licking the lotion off Madeline's right hand. "Charlie, come here," she said, more of a polite suggestion than a strict command.

"What are you doing here on your day off?" Madeline asked as Lauren collared Charlie and tried to give her room to pass.

"Go lay down," Lauren instructed in her most authoritative voice, taking a few seconds to make sure Charlie was going to cooperate before turning her attention back to her boss. "Sorry about that. I think he really missed you while you were out."

"I missed him too," Madeline said as she headed in the direction of her office.

"I hope you don't mind me working on the weekend," Lauren said sheepishly as she tagged along, getting a laugh out of her boss.

"Of course not, though I was hoping the new assistants would lessen your load." Madeline dropped her tote onto the conference table and turned to face Lauren. She didn't need flashing red lights to alert her to a change in her trusted employee. The way she had trouble holding eye contact was a dead giveaway that something was bothering her. The longer Madeline held that thought, the more convinced she became that bad news was on the way. Hiding her suspicions, she went to the water cooler and filled a glass.

"Oh, I think they'll work out okay," Lauren said without much enthusiasm. "It's all still so new to them. Having to support two completely different businesses takes a while to get used to." She averted her eyes as her finger traced an unseen pattern on the conference table.

Madeline caught the absence of eye contact, a sure sign something was on her assistant's mind. "Did you make coffee?"

"No, but I can."

"Why don't you make enough for both of us, then come into my office so we can get caught up?" Madeline asked, keeping her tone light.

"Sure. I'll be right there."

Madeline walked into her office, pausing to look around at the space where she'd spent most of her waking hours the last four years. She still hadn't had a chance to go through the clutter that had sat more or less as she left it when she made the rash decision to confront Elise Cavanagh at her home. She had hoped to file or shred most of what lay spread out across her desk, file cabinets and credenza by now, but having two new cases to deal with on her return had stalled that project.

Promising herself she'd get to it the following day, she turned on her computer. She had managed to shift clutter from her desk to other less trafficked areas when Lauren appeared with coffees for both of them.

"I'm sorry I haven't had a chance to clear some of this stuff out of here," she said as she handed her boss a mug.

"Well, that's not really your job anymore, is it?" Madeline said with smiling eyes, hiding the fact she was studying Lauren's body language and facial expressions to figure out what was going on.

She's going to quit.

The thought hit Madeline like a fierce jab to the solar plexus. In truth, she couldn't blame Lauren. She had just been given the added responsibility of handling all the event business two days prior to her boss being shot, only to be completely on her own while Madeline languished in the hospital for three weeks. It was not how Madeline had envisioned the hand off. On top of all that, Lauren had to hire her own assistants, whom she then had to train. And that was in addition to not knowing if there'd be a company for her to run if her boss didn't come out of her coma.

Madeline let out a resigned sigh as she tried to prepare herself for the worst. The obvious casualty was MDPI. In reality, it couldn't exist without the revenue generated by Current Affairs. Samir would have to go, and probably one of the new hires. But the most painful part would be giving up what she loved doing for something that paid the bills but made her cringe to think about.

Lauren continued to fiddle with a loose thread on the cuff of her sleeve, avoiding eye contact with her boss. Madeline didn't like to see her loyal employee and friend struggle with something that was obviously causing her a great deal of stress and conflicting emotions.

She's going to start her own event planning business.

This bulletin hit twice as hard as the first. It meant she'd have to fight to hang on to the clients she'd foisted off onto her employee while she'd been sleuthing.

"I feel really bad about what I'm going to say, and I hope you won't be upset with me…"

Madeline felt the sting of perspiration under her arms while her throat muscles contracted.

"I appreciate all you've done for me, but I feel it's best if I…" Lauren drew a deep breath before forcing the words out, "give Charlie to someone who needs him more than I do. I couldn't have gotten my confidence back without him, and it feels wrong for me to hang on to him when I know there are others going through what I did who need his help now."

Madeline's startled expression was frozen as though it had been caught in a camera flash.

"You want to give Charlie to someone else," she stated flatly, as if she didn't comprehend the words coming out of her own mouth.

"You're disappointed, aren't you?" Lauren asked, averting her gaze to her lap.

"No. No, not at all," Madeline rushed to reassure her. "I…think that's very commendable of you to put other's needs above your own. I know it will probably be difficult to say goodbye…"

Lauren struggled to hide her emotions, flashing her eyes at Madeline as she nodded. "I know I'll miss him a lot, but I can't let that stop me from doing what's right. The truth is, I've got more responsibilities now, and it doesn't feel right to put Charlie's wellbeing last. He needs to get out for walks more often than I can manage at the moment. I've even had Jessica take him out a couple times a day, which makes me feel bad because that's not what she was hired to do," Lauren admitted sheepishly.

Madeline found it hard to argue with Lauren's concerns. They wouldn't be the only ones to feel the loss; Charlie seemed perfectly content to hang out at the office all day, greeting visitors and making the occasional rounds. But he had been specially trained to serve those who had suffered traumatic events—in Lauren's case, being kidnapped and shot by a psychopath. And her point about letting his talents go to waste when others were in need was also valid. If there was any reluctance here, it was on her own part. He had been her gift to Lauren to ease her own feelings of guilt, as well as giving Lauren the support she needed to reenter the world.

"I'll contact the trainers this coming week to let them know Charlie's available," Madeline said, earning a bittersweet smile from her most valued employee. "And by the way, it's time for another increase in your salary. You more than deserve it, handling everything so well in my absence."

Lauren's face colored as Madeline's gesture made her feel emotional again. "Thanks, Maddie. But you know I was happy to do it. I'm just so grateful you pulled through."

Madeline reached across her desk and gave Lauren's clasped hands a squeeze before getting down to business.

Once Lauren gave her a complete update on all the events on their calendar, Madeline gave her additional ideas to give more pizzazz. It eased her mind to realize minimal oversight was all that was needed from her at this stage of her career as an event planning maven. Lauren had always been good at doing as directed, and now she was exhibiting a real flair and understanding of what made events of different stripes shine. It occurred to her as she headed to the conference room that once Jessica and Sydney got a feel for the business, they could take on even more events. And maybe, just maybe, she could turn the whole operation over to Lauren some day and just take a cut of the profits.

That idea put a smile on her face until she confronted the storyboards of MDPI's latest puzzles. Two dead husbands. The big question concerning both cases was cause of death: accident, suicide or murder?

Though she felt lingering apprehension regarding the man on Natalie Sheckle's front porch, she put that case aside for a moment to focus on what had gone on the day Nick Bartholomew died.

The tour of Rancho Vista Encantada had been helpful. She had gotten a feel for what life was like for the remaining Bartholomew family members, and had seen both of Nick's children in their natural habitat. She now had a feeling for the privileges they had enjoyed since birth and had gotten a taste of a lifestyle that was quite different from what most human beings could ever imagine. As idyllic as their circumstances might be, their perception of what was normal for them had been altered dramatically upon the death of their father. But even with that huge loss, neither of them appeared to be suffering, at least not outwardly.

It was also safe to say their lifestyle had not been adversely affected in any way; in fact, it could be argued their lives had been enhanced now that they had received their inheritance and were able to run the ranch as they saw fit. Vanessa had moved into the main house and had installed her mother in the one her father had built for her. Madeline surmised that whatever money and other assets Nick had at the time of his death had passed to his children, outright or in trust. After winning the wrongful death suit against Lindsay, Vanessa and Sean had made sure she would never get a penny of his estate, effectively canceling her access to a first-rate criminal defense.

This fact brought up another key point: having control over Rancho Vista Encantada had allowed Vanessa Bartholomew to initiate other actions her father would've never approved, actions that gave her the ability to create a name for herself with her own retail winery on the Gaviota coast, the first of its kind and probably the only one that would ever exist on that undeveloped stretch of highway. This was not only a feather in her cap, it was also a distinction that could cement her future as a winemaker and potentially make her a wealthy woman in her own right.

Madeline gravitated to the board. She took the photo of Vanessa and pinned it to the top. As she rested her backside against the conference table, she reviewed what she'd seen and heard at the ranch earlier, focusing on her observations of the young winemaker.

To be in Vanessa's position at this stage in her life was impressive. It showed determination and drive not often found in a privileged twenty-something. She had been guaranteed a problem-free, cushy life, yet she had become seized by the desire to learn winemaking at UC Davis. Prior to the breakup of her parents, she had been focused on mastering Western Pleasure horsemanship, with a view to competing, an expensive hobby that generated little to no income. But that pursuit went out the window when Patricia was essentially sent packing.

Now that Madeline thought of it, she had to wonder how that all came about. Using a mid-life crisis as a justification, how was Nick able to discard Patricia so easily? Certainly, there was ample room on the ranch for her to stay without being in his way. She could've resided in one of the many houses on the property and been accessible to her teenage children, which would've been a lot less traumatic, especially for Vanessa.

Setting aside who was at fault, what mechanism allowed Nick to banish Patricia from the ranch? Even with a prenup, that seemed a little harsh in view of the fact that they still had a minor child living at home. Had there been a precipitating event, something that warranted breaking up the family, like infidelity on Patricia's part?

Hmmm, Madeline thought, warming to the idea that there had to be a reason events had unfolded the way they did. She regretted not being able to pump Lindsay for the details of the breakup. Unless Nick had some powerful leverage over his first wife, the facts didn't add up. Or they may have received the sterilized version of what caused Patricia to become the ex-Mrs. Nickolas Bartholomew.

Madeline could understand why Nick and Patricia would want to shelter their kids from the infidelity of either parent. And it could be that Nick had taken the high road, choosing to preserve Vanessa and Sean's view of their mother, even at his own expense. He had gone to great lengths to earn back his daughter's good favor—building her a home of her own, planting a vineyard to keep her happy.

But it could also be true that if Nick had been having an affair with Lindsay, Patricia may have wanted to completely distance herself from her cheating husband, even if it meant abandoning her kids and giving up what was rightfully hers. Rationality can go right out the window when trust and hearts are broken.

But on the other hand, if Nick had been the injured party, and Patricia had remained mute on the subject of their divorce, then there was nothing to dispel his daughter's contempt for him and Lindsay. If Patricia had been the cheating spouse, chances were she wasn't inclined to alienate her kids with the truth about the breakup. Nick stayed silent on the matter and Patricia agreed to leave the ranch.

However the events unfolded, the divorce had been a shocker that sent waves of heartache and loss through the family. Everyone involved had been adversely affected by the fallout. Yet, by the same token, there had also been a few winners, namely Lindsay and her daughter. To say Vanessa had reason to resent or even hate her former friend-slash-stepmom was a huge understatement. It was also fair to imagine she felt the same for her father, though maybe not quite as acutely. But then again, maybe even more so...

Madeline stood up to get a closer look at the photo of Vanessa that Samir had found on the Internet. By the expression on her face, Madeline guessed it had been taken during Lindsay's trial. There was a hard set to her mouth and steely disdain glinting from her eyes for whomever had the gall to accost her outside the courtroom. Though it was taken two years earlier, she looked older then, hardened and bitter.

Where's my perfect life? I want it back, Madeline imagined her saying.

By her own admission, Vanessa had been in the kitchen when Nick came in prior to the accident. She and Sean alibied each other. They also testified that no one else had been present while the three of them were there. From day one, they were unified in their statements to law enforcement that there had been no note warning the tractor was unsafe.

Madeline let the air seep out of her lungs as she returned to her perch and scanned the board again. Though there had been several others on the ranch during that window before Nick's death, none of them had more to gain than his kids. There was the unsubstantiated rumor that Lindsay had been seen kissing Seth Arnold, who was supposedly let go shortly before the accident.

Maybe he came to say goodbye to Lindsay…

"…if in fact they had been having an affair—wait, scratch that," Madeline said aloud, becoming animated as her thoughts fought for center stage. "There could be no truth to that rumor, and he still might want to say goodbye to Lindsay. She's a nice person, loves horses…" Madeline's voice trailed off along with her thoughts. *Wouldn't Lindsay have mentioned that fact when we were at the prison?*

Madeline let out a frustrated sigh and began to pace, running her hands through her hair as she struggled to order her thoughts. *She would've told us about him coming in to say goodbye. She's had almost two years to go over every single detail of that day. Especially now that we're looking into Nick's death on her account.*

Suddenly aware of her thirst, Madeline went over to the mini fridge and grabbed a cold bottle of water. *The ranch hand lets himself in—the doors are probably never locked. Rancho Vista Encantada's not the kind of place where just anyone can wander in off the highway. And there's no way of even know-ing homes exist up there.*

So, the doors to Nick's home being unlocked was entirely possible. This meant anyone who had access to the ranch could come or go if they were so inclined. But how bold would someone be who'd just gotten fired? Would they care? They'd have nothing to lose at that point.

Instead of playing guessing games all afternoon, Madeline took her phone out of her bag and searched for Yolanda's number.

"Hello?" Yolanda answered cautiously. After giving the housekeeper a reminder of who she was, Madeline got right to the point.

"Do you have the ranch foreman's phone number? There are certain facts I need to establish before I go any further on this case." There was a pause during which Madeline imagined Yolanda torn between her compassion for Lindsay and her daughter and her allegiance to the family who signed her checks and provided her housing. "What I'm really trying to do here is eliminate suspects. Right now, there are too many variables."

Though this disclaimer was vague to the point of being irrelevant, it did prod Yolanda into giving her the foreman's contact info. She could hear rattling as the housekeeper scrounged around for her address book.

"Please don't tell anyone who gave you this number," Yolanda said, waiting for Madeline's assurance that this act that felt inherently disloyal wouldn't come back to haunt her.

"You've got my word," Madeline promised before thanking the housekeeper and ending the call. She entered the number for Lester Prinz while she reviewed her strategy. She had to give him an explanation of who she was and why she was calling, which probably would be met with resentment and a good telling off. But she had to try. Right now, the unsubstantiated rumor of Lindsay kissing a ranch hand was the only thing that gave her a motive for killing her husband.

"Hello?"

"Is this Lester Prinz?"

"Who's calling?" the foreman barked irritably.

"My name's Madeline Dawkins. I'm a private investigator looking into the death of Nick Bartholomew."

"Why the hell would you be doing that?" he demanded.

At least he hasn't hung up yet, Madeline thought before deciding which card to play.

"The warden at the prison where Lindsay Bartholomew is serving her twenty-year sentence has intervened on her behalf. We've been retained to look into her case to see if we can find any reason for it to be reopened. As far as we can tell from the transcripts of Lindsay's trial, the rumor of her having a relationship with one of your ranch hands, backed up by Nick's kids, is what tipped the scales of justice against her. Since you were the one who supposedly let Seth Arnold go, I'd like to hear your version of events. Was Seth let go because he'd had an inappropriate relationship with your boss's wife?"

From the silence on the line, Madeline couldn't tell if the call had been ended until she pulled the phone away from her ear. It was still going.

"Mr. Prinz?"

A deep sigh of resignation came through loud and clear. "I hate like hell to have to dredge up that godawful time," Lester growled before his voice softened. "If I'm going to be truthful—and I'd appreciate you keeping this to yourself—I never could imagine Lindsay being capable of a spiteful act like that. I mean, hell, that's an awful thing to accuse someone of, deliberately letting someone get mangled by a tractor…? I didn't believe it for a second."

Madeline was taken aback by this revelation. "Did you speak on Lindsay's behalf at her trial?"

"No. I wasn't asked to," Lester added defensively.

This time, it was Madeline who was momentarily speechless. The Public Defender they'd spoken to admitted he hadn't had the resources to depose the ranch hand in Wyoming. Was it possible he was so overwhelmed he didn't interview all the relevant witnesses close at hand?

Yes, Madeline thought, *it's entirely possible.* He would've been playing catch up since he was assigned the case after the trial against Lindsay had already begun. He may have been relying on the defendant to do her own detective work. But surely, if an alleged affair with a ranch hand was supposedly the motive behind the depraved act of not telling her husband about the tractor being unsafe to use, then the public defender would want to counter that, wouldn't he? The ranch foreman was the most likely witness to be called, either by the prosecution or the defense, depending on the veracity of the claim. Why wasn't he called?

A sick, dizzy feeling came over Madeline. With a hand to her head to steady herself, she pushed on. She couldn't retry this case herself, but her hope lay in finding evidence that would lift the cloud about the note Lindsay supposedly wrote. The farther she got into the case, the murkier it became. It felt like a frameup, something she had firsthand experience with. The irony of having this case handed to them by the very man who had framed *her* made her feel like she was being gaslighted.

"Okay, so if you'd been called to testify at Lindsay Bartholomew's trial, what would you have said regarding the rumors of her kissing one of your employees?"

"I would've said I knew nothing about it."

Madeline let a couple beats pass as she absorbed this newsflash. "You hadn't heard the rumor, so you hadn't fired him because of it," she summarized for the foreman's clarification.

"That's correct."

"Okay then, why was he fired?"

"He wasn't fired. He left on his own accord. I would've preferred more notice, but he had just found out his brother-in-law had been killed in a bar-room fight, and his sister needed his help running their ranch in Wyoming."

Madeline felt as nauseated as if this injustice was happening to her instead of Lindsay. *How was this even possible?* she queried herself. She wasn't naïve enough to think justice was always served in a court of law, but she certainly never imagined such a high-profile case would be conducted in such a haphazard manner.

"Would you be willing to swear out an affidavit attesting to what you just told me?" she asked. Her question was met with throat-clearing and resistance. "Mr. Prinz, a woman is stuck in prison for a crime she vehemently denies committing, while her young daughter is being raised in foster care. The very least Lindsay Bartholomew deserves is a fair trial where all the facts are scrutinized. If you can't find that a compelling enough reason to get involved, think about Nick and what he would want you to do to set the record straight."

"I wouldn't even know who to tell my story to," Lester drawled.

"I know the District Attorney personally. If you give me your consent, I'll set up a time for you to tell him what you've just told me." Madeline's offer was met with more silence. She counted ten beats before Lester answered her, during which time she imagined him weighing the consequences of his colluding with the enemy camp.

"All right," he relented, "I'll do it."

After thanking the foreman and promising to get back to him, she ended the call and scrolled through her phone for the D.A.'s contact info. She tapped the phone option, then thought better of it. Even though she knew this would probably be enough to warrant a new investigation and possibly a new trial, it could take years to secure Lindsay's release, and first she'd have to get Conrad on board.

She backed out of Conrad's profile and clicked on Mike's. Again, she ended the call before it went through. This was the pivotal piece of information they had been hoping to uncover, but she didn't want to jump the gun. She wanted to have all the pieces of the puzzle first.

Now that they had possible testimony that refuted the D.A.'s case against Lindsay, she was more driven than before to find out who was responsible for Nick not seeing the note she'd left for him. If they could determine who took it, and find some sort of proof, then Lindsay would go free, and whoever sent Nick to an early grave could take her place.

That would be justice. Now the hard part: cracking the carefully erected barrier that protected the person really responsible for Nick's death.

TWENTY-TWO

Madeline combed through the facts of the Bartholomew case until almost six o'clock. Lauren and Charlie had taken off around four, giving her the unique opportunity to think without interruption for two solid hours. Her mind was so jammed with questions and theories, she found it hard to keep it all straight. Before giving into her body's demand for food and a little downtime so that all she'd discovered could percolate in her brain, she reviewed the new notations she'd pinned to the Bartholomew board one last time.

Just reexamining the new bits of insight she'd gleaned that day gave her a boost. But she still had the presence of mind to caution herself. Staying detached from the personalities in this drama was vital; for all she knew, this could just be an exercise to prove Steven still had the ability to manipulate her life.

Thinking about Steven brought up the anger she had fought hard to suppress regarding how this case—this *pro bono* case—had been thrust on her. She could feel her hackles rising along with her resentment of Mike going behind her back to meet secretly with Steven after the nightmare he had put her through. Anger continued to mount as she went into her office to retrieve her bags and turn out the lights.

How could he do this to me—sneak around my back to meet with that son of a bitch? Here Steven is, manipulating my life again. And to what end? What is that bastard really looking to achieve?

By the time she armed the alarm and locked the door, she was in a black mood, one that gave itself life by preying on her fears and pent up anger. The only way she had been able to forge a new future for herself after what Steven had done to her was to constantly reassure herself that he was locked away in prison and would remain there until he was in his seventies. Getting out, having the blessing of the governor, flying around in the Falcon 900…it was all too galling.

Feeling poisonous hatred as it pumped through her veins, Madeline forced herself to take deep breaths as she navigated the stairs out to State Street. Letting her mood be blackened by thoughts of her ex-husband was a self-inflicted blow. Yes, Steven had insinuated himself into her world again—through her partner. But she alone controlled how she reacted to his actions. If she continued to let him manipulate her from afar with her own thoughts, then she was essentially handing him the power to rule her life.

And that would never do.

By the time she made it to Mike's old Mercedes, the chilling breeze and her instinct for self-preservation had boxed Steven up and relegated his role in the Bartholomew case to the archives. So what if he had brought the case to them? His involvement was irrelevant at this point. *Poof! Gone and forgotten.*

Forcing her mind to focus on other matters, her thoughts turned to getting something in her stomach, which had been justifiably growling for the last two hours. She could rely on hopefully finding something edible in Mike's fridge, or she could stop and pick up something at the market on the way to his house. Since she had to pass by it anyway, she thought that was the smartest move.

But as she headed down Carrillo Street toward the Mesa, she decided to take a detour to her place. She would change out of her funky duds and grab enough clothing to last a few days. Then she would assess the situation after that. There had been a few discussions over the last year about her and Mike living together, maybe renting out one of their homes, but that had been more testing the waters than anything serious. At least not on her part. She loved staying at Mike's, enjoyed that sweeping view of the ocean and the coastline to the east, but she just wasn't comfortable with the idea of not having a place to call all her own.

Thinking of Mike stirred up emotions she'd rather not think about. She loved him and considered him her partner for life, both professionally and personally. But there was a part of her that would never feel completely comfortable giving up her heart and her independence, no matter how much Mike meant to her. The whole business with him meeting secretly with Steven had reignited her innate fear of trusting another human being unreservedly.

After pulling into her driveway, she walked around the front of the Mercedes, using the flashlight on her cell phone to guide her up the path to her front door. As an afterthought, she swung the light in the direction of her lawn, panning around in search of any colorful, malevolent tokens of her nasty neighbor's disdain.

Later, she would wonder if that simple act had saved her life, giving her that half-second to detect the presence behind her.

Her phone flew from her hand as her assailant grabbed her from behind, landing on the lawn with its flashlight beam shooting straight up into the dark, overcast night. It provided enough illumination to give her an idea of her opponent's intent as light flashed off the blade of his knife.

The assailant's left hand covered her mouth as he pressed the knife to her throat. No warning was issued to keep quiet; no move to take her tote or force her inside the house where he could rape her and steal her valuables.

Madeline instantly recognized the situation for what it was: a contract hit, with a knife instead of a gun. Quiet, quick and absolutely effective.

While her mind froze, her body went into survival mode. She grasped the fist wielding the knife with both hands and twisted it as she pulled it down and away from her, taking his whole arm with her as she stepped forward, using that torque to flip him over, dislodging the knife in the process. Had he not been savvy in martial arts and knew how to roll with such a move, she would've broken his wrist and possibly his elbow and shoulder in the process. Instead, he tumbled and landed sprawled across her lawn for a split second before bouncing to his feet.

Once the grip around her chest had been broken, she let loose a guttural yell, puncturing the night air with an unmistakable call to action. As he lunged for the knife, she unfurled a powerful kick to his side with her right leg that knocked him off balance long enough to deliver a series of strikes and kicks, which he countered with his own. She dodged them, though they brought him back within range of the knife. As he went for it again, she launched a kick to his head that knocked him sideways.

She was now closer to the knife than he was, but making a move for it would've been too risky. Despite his obvious pain, he flew at her again. She dodged him, then jabbed her elbow sharply into his neck. He staggered but remained upright and came at her, most likely calculating his chances of completing his mission and getting away now that she'd managed to alert her neighbors.

Madeline sidestepped him again, using that torque to deliver a powerful thrust to the side of his head with the heel of her hand. She reflexively reared back, her left knee coming up to protect her as he twisted and unfurled a mighty punch at her face. She tucked into herself, dodging the strike, then pivoted on her right foot while letting loose a brutal side kick to the gut with her left that knocked the air out of him.

As he fought to draw breath, she lunged for the balaclava, snagging enough of it to yank his head downward while she thrust her right knee into his face. Momentarily stunned, her attacker wobbled backwards in a crouch while Madeline put a safe distance between them. She panted, her body quivering as she braced herself for her assailant's next move. Her phone was only a few feet away, yet trying to retrieve it was out of the question.

She realized lights that hadn't been on earlier now blazed from her neighbor's house to the west, the good neighbor as opposed to the bad neighbor. Later she would remember wondering for a fraction of a second if this stunt was just the latest affront from her frustrated and likely deranged neighbor to the east. But that thought was quickly replaced by a more obvious scenario.

Sensing his window of opportunity had just closed, her assailant executed an ungainly exit, thrashing through the towering scheffleras and disappearing into the night.

"Hey!" she heard her neighbor yell before speaking rapidly to someone on his cell phone. "Hang on…hang on a second," he called into the phone as he hurried up Madeline's driveway. "Are you okay?" he asked anxiously, taking in her disheveled condition as she panted for air.

"I'm okay," she managed to say as she looked down at the balaclava in her left hand, right before her legs gave out and she slumped to her front steps.

"The police are on their way. Do you need an ambulance?" he asked, relaying the dispatcher's question. Madeline shook her head. "She says no. Are you sure?" Madeline nodded absently, her mind reeling from trying to process all that had happened in under two minutes.

"You might want to send one anyway," she heard her neighbor say, though his voice sounded like it was coming from far away. "I think she might be going into shock."

~~

Madeline refused the paramedics' advice about going to the hospital to be checked out more thoroughly. Her disclosure about the recent gunshot wound and protracted convalescence had them understandably concerned. She was operating in a partially numb state, but she knew herself well enough to know she wasn't physically hurt, just shaken by what she'd been through. She sat on the sofa in her living room in a state of confusion, as if she couldn't quite accept what had just happened to her. She tried to be as helpful as possible so the medical and law enforcement professionals could finish quickly and get on with their jobs.

The police had taken her statement and made a thorough search of her property and the neighboring homes on her cul-de-sac, their hunch being the assailant had fled the scene through one of the properties at the end of the street. That would've given him easy access to the brush-covered hillside, allowing him to disappear into the night. They were hoping someone would have security camera footage of the perpetrator, but even if they did, the way he'd been dressed would make identifying the guy virtually impossible.

The two officers had taken down her description of the assailant from the split-second she'd seen him unmasked: a male in his late-twenties, early-thirties, approximately six-feet, dark hair, medium complexion, stocky build, no distinguishing features that she could see. If he had tattoos, they were hidden by the dark clothing that covered his entire body. He hadn't uttered a word during their brief but intense skirmish, so she didn't even have a voice to draw clues from. Their only hope was to get DNA from the balaclava. Otherwise her assailant would never be found, unless he was crazy enough to take another run at her. She planned to be ready for him next time.

Before the officers left, they urged her to come into the station the following day to look at mugshots. If she could recall any physical details of her attacker, a sketch artist would be available. Though Madeline hadn't gotten a good look at him due to their darkened surroundings, the officers assured her they could learn a lot from very little with the current composite technology. She told them she'd think about it.

Mike arrived as the policemen were leaving, an indication that he'd been going well over the speed limit to get there, probably close to a hundred, considering Madeline had called him right before the cops showed up. When he didn't answer the first time, she called back rather than leaving a message. He answered immediately the second time, correctly sensing her urgency of needing to speak with him. Judging by her flat delivery and the icy vibe coming over the airwaves, he speculated she was putting the ambush down to Steven Ridley, which in turn implicated Mike due to his recent dealings with him.

"How are you doing?" he asked after he saw the officers out.

Instead of answering him, Madeline just stared at him, the muscles in her jaw quivering with pent-up anger and fear. Mike took a deep breath before sitting down beside her, careful to give her plenty of room.

"I'm so sorry this happened to you," he said, his voice low, his words heavy with regret. Madeline looked briefly in his direction before getting up. "What can I get you?" he asked, making the mistake of grabbing her hand.

"What are the chances of an attack like this being random?" she demanded, pulling her hand away. Mike let his breath out in one big gush, then got to his feet. Madeline glared at him before heading to the kitchen.

"Look, Maddie, I know you think Steven is behind what happened tonight—"

Madeline swung around at him so fast, he froze in his tracks. "What happened tonight is I almost got killed."

"I know that," Mike responded more forcefully than he had intended. "Jesus Christ, I know that," he reiterated more calmly, his right hand moving reflexively to cover his mouth so she couldn't see the depth of his pain. "I also know odds are Steven's behind what happened tonight. And yes, that makes me feel responsible as hell."

Mike's admission caught Madeline without a stinging reply to hurl back at him. She regarded him sternly, hands on her hips as if challenging him to dissolve her rancor and release her from the hold Steven had managed to get on her once again.

"Look, can I get you a drink, a glass of wine or maybe something stronger?"

he asked as calmly as he could, his own emotions a hair away from smashing everything in sight.

Sensing how hard the situation was on Mike—regardless of her need to blame him for conspiring with her nemesis—Madeline shook her head, her eyes downcast as she let the air seep from her lungs.

"Come here," Mike said softly as he bridged the gap and held her close to him. Their bodies came together in solidarity, forming to one another as they had thousands of times in their long history together. The comfort they found in each other's arms made it impossible to give any more fuel to bent feelings, whether they were justified or not. Their corporeal beings instinctively knew they were much better, much stronger united than they were divided. To have almost lost her to the savage ambush made Mike feel almost as sorrowful as if her attacker had succeeded.

"You're starving, aren't you?" Mike asked after he got a handle on his emotions. He kissed her tenderly on the top of her head before pulling back to look her in the eyes. "Let me see what I can find in the fridge."

"No," Madeline said as she let go of him. "You won't find anything. Plus, I don't want to stay here. I really just stopped by to pick up some clothes to take to your place. I haven't eaten a thing since this morning—except a bar—but I don't want to be here another minute."

"Okay, you grab your stuff, and I'll have some food delivered to my place. How does that sound?"

"It sounds like the first step on the path to redeeming yourself," Madeline said with dead seriousness before heading to her bedroom.

Mike got busy on his phone, searching for the appropriate cuisine to eat after a brush with death. If he could've found a place that served crow, he'd have gotten a double order for himself. The only way he could come out of this with any honor was through a full confession. He just hoped it wouldn't blow up in his face a second time.

~~~

Madeline and Mike kept their thoughts to themselves during the five-minute drive from her house to his. Mike wouldn't hear of her driving, not after what she'd been through, so they left the Mercedes on her driveway. The food arrived right after Mike brought in all of Madeline's assorted baggage, a variety of totes to disguise the amount of stuff she suddenly found indispensable. He guessed at the real reason for not putting it all in a couple of suitcases: that would look too much like she was moving in on a more permanent basis, something he knew she wasn't ready to do. Especially after his perceived treasonous act.

The silence continued as they ate their Thai feast, aside from occasional sighs of pleasure at having something warm and deliciously spicy to take their minds off the attack, at least momentarily.

"I'm guessing you hadn't eaten anything yet when I called you," Madeline said.

"You guess right. Up until that time, it had been all about the drinking. I'm actually relieved I won't have to witness the effects of all that alcohol."

"I bet," Madeline said, picking at what was left on her plate, her eyes downcast. "Thanks for getting here so fast." A bolt of insight hit her, causing her to gasp.

"What is it?" Mike asked, alarmed by the expression on her face. He couldn't tell if she was in pain or having some sort of epiphany. Her eyes traveled from the middle distance to meet his, the beginnings of a smile replacing the look of apprehension. She stood up suddenly, almost knocking the chair over in the process.

"The surveillance cameras!" she cried out triumphantly. When Mike's face failed to show the appropriate enthusiasm for her "aha!" moment, she gave his memory a nudge. "The ones you installed in the front of my house to keep an eye on me."

She nearly laughed at her good luck. Instead of seeing the same look of excitement reflected back at her, Mike's expression went from startled to grim.

"I know it was too dark to see much, but we might be able to learn *something* from the footage."

Mike wiped the corners of his mouth, stalling as he mentally prepared himself to deliver the bad news.

"I disabled the cameras the day you came back to work," he admitted glumly. Madeline's countenance fell, her mouth hanging slack at her rotten luck. "I never wanted to intrude on your privacy—I only wanted to keep tabs on your house while you were convalescing. I didn't want you to think I was spying on you like some kind of control freak."

Madeline sank back into her seat dejectedly. Since she was already down, Mike figured this might be as good a time as any to make another confession. He pushed back his chair and cleared his throat to get her undivided attention.

"I know you're beyond pissed I talked to that scumbag Ridley, and even more pissed that I hid our conversation from you."

Madeline stiffened and leaned against the chair, crossed arms creating a physical and emotional barrier. Mike sucked in a deep breath and forged on.

"When I saw his call come in, I didn't take it. I know how repulsed you must be after what he's done to you, because I got an inkling of that when his call showed up on my phone. It really pissed me off that he had my contact information and the gall to use it. But I was really ticked when I saw he had the nerve to leave me a message." Watching Madeline squirm against the chair prompted him to suggest they get more comfortable.

"This is kind of a long story," he said as he picked up their plates and took them to the kitchen.

"In that case, you better top up my wine on your way back," Madeline said as she pushed her glass toward him.

Once they were reseated in the living room, Mike continued his confession. "I still have the message, by the way, but I won't subject you to hearing it right now. If you're ever curious, we can play it."

Madeline let out a contemptuous snort, her eyes averted. She couldn't imagine what more there could be to this story that she didn't already know. She hoped Mike wasn't trying to tap dance his way out of what happened earlier; she was nowhere near absolving him of his involvement in her near-murder, unintentional or not.

"After I listened to his B.S. story, I nearly deleted the message. I couldn't give a damn about his bogus crusade, and I sure as hell wasn't about to do anything that might put him in a favorable light with the powers that gave him his freedom."

Madeline fought the impulse to tell her partner to speed things up. This was way too much throat clearing for her taste. If he didn't get to the point soon, she was going to get up and go sleep in his guestroom.

"Then I got to thinking… In his message he said he wanted to meet with me face to face to discuss this female prisoner's situation. My first thought was he was trying to set me up. My second thought was I could set *him* up…"

This admission broke through Madeline's flagging attention, fatigue and resentment. She sat up a little straighter, her eyes now glued to Mike's.

"What did you do?" Her rancor took a backseat now that the prospect of hanging Steven with his own rope had presented itself. "And please…cut to the chase…" she said with a meaningful look.

"Before I met Steven out on Highway 1, I had arranged for a P.I. out of Lompoc to follow him after our meeting." Madeline leaned forward, a look of cautious optimism radiating from her eyes. "As soon as I got back in my car, I texted the investigator a description of Steven's government issue car and the license number. I knew Steven had to go back the way he came, otherwise he'd be within your thirty-mile sanctuary zone, so there was no risk of losing him. Bottom line, except for when he's flying around the state in his 'official' capacity, I've got eyes on him."

Madeline absorbed this news with an expectant look on her face as she worked out what all they could learn about this shark masquerading as an angel.

"You've got someone covering him in Sacramento?"

"Yep. I chose a large firm with satellite offices, so whenever he's traveling by car, he's on our radar."

"So, you know where he's living…?"

"Sure do."

"But he still managed to hire someone to kill me," Madeline said as she got up and began pacing. "And don't say we can't know for sure he's behind what happened tonight. That was a hit, and you know it. Though we've made a few enemies in our line of work, I can't think of anyone who would go to such drastic lengths for the sake of retribution. The fact that Steven contacted you under any pretense tells me he's enjoying this little cat and mouse game. He probably knows you've got him under surveillance, and this is his way of thumbing his nose at you."

Mike had no comeback for her accusations. He'd been played, no doubt about it. Had he been thinking, he would've never left Madeline unguarded. But self-recriminations would have to wait until later. The question for the here and now was what to do about Steven, and more specifically, how could they neutralize the threat he posed?

"We can drop the Bartholomew case," he said. He knew she wouldn't go for that suggestion, but he felt obligated to make it anyway. Madeline came to a halt and braced her hands on the back of the chair she'd been sitting in.

"I wouldn't give him the satisfaction," she said. "Besides, I'm curious as to how and why he chose Lindsay's case to champion. Plus, nothing we do on one of our cases would have any impact on him. We're going to have to catch him in the act of something that will land him back in prison, for good. Though honestly, I think the only way I'll ever feel safe is when he's six feet under, or better yet, burnt to a crisp."

Mike totally understood Madeline's feelings. She was justified in hating Steven, and he agreed with her sentiments. But what she had said about the Bartholomew case seemed curious.

"You think there's something suspicious about him advocating on Lindsay's behalf?" he asked.

"Doesn't it strike you as beyond self-serving that he just happened to find a bona fide injustice he could take credit for righting?" She paused to think about what she'd just said. Everything she thought she found out earlier that day now came into question. She had run it all through a prism geared to the supposition that Lindsay was an innocent victim of cruel circumstances. Now she was forced to look at this case in a different light.

"What if picking Lindsay's case wasn't a random act?" she suggested.

"What do you mean? You're not thinking Steven and Lindsay knew each other before she ended up in Chowchilla...?"

"For all we know, Steven might be trying to get Lindsay out of prison because they've got something going on."

"What would make you think that?" Mike asked, clearly finding the suggestion dubious.

"They could've been seeing each other prior to Nick's death," she said, ignoring Mike's skepticism as she warmed to the idea.

"You mean when Steven was in prison...?" he asked doubtfully.

"No, before Steven went to prison."

"Like before he set you up as an adulteress and started romancing that wealthy divorcée? Let's not forget that up until a few months ago, he'd been stuck in prison for four years. That means they would've had to have met while you were still married to him and Lindsay was married to Nick, and we both know Steven had been pretty busy at that time trying to keep his felonious dealings from blowing up on him."

Madeline let her head loll back in defeat, realizing her imagination and paranoia had jumped the rails. She came around the chair and slumped into it, her fingers to her temples as she tried to ease the pressure in her head.

"Okay, never mind," she conceded.

"Don't get me wrong, I'm all for brainstorming on how this all fits together. It seems too farfetched to think he could've planned the whole Lindsay thing. Sure, he could've had an idea in the back of his mind, and when the warden offered her opinion of Lindsay's conviction, he saw the link to Santa Barbara as a carrot he might use to draw us out into the open."

Mike's speculation only made her feel worse. He might not have been on the right track in terms of means or method, but the motive—at least at this juncture—seemed to be revenge.

Bottom line, Steven didn't need to employ any subterfuge to get at her. He could have easily obtained her address and hired an assassin to carry out his revenge. The guy who attacked her was definitely skilled, someone who didn't need to rely on marksmanship to carry out a hit. Bringing the case to them was just a twisted way to get back in her head.

"You know what, I'm just too wiped out to speculate about his motives right now. I don't know how much sleep I'm going to get tonight, but I at least have to try to get some," she said as she stood up on unsteady legs and took her glass to the kitchen.

"What can I do to help?" Mike asked as he came up next to her and draped an arm around her.

"Let me sleep in tomorrow, if I actually do fall asleep."

"Want one of my world-famous foot massages?" Mike asked hopefully.

Madeline gave him a wan smile before declining his offer.

"Not tonight," she said, grabbing her handbag and trudging off in the direction of the bathroom.

Mike sank onto one of the barstools, head in hand as he berated himself for ever meeting with Ridley. He was following his thoughts in circles so intently, he actually jumped when Madeline reentered the living room.

"I think I'm too keyed up for sleep."

"You want me to run a hot bath for you? Make you some hot tea?"

"No. Not yet. I think a drive would calm me down."

"A drive…? Okay," he said as he slipped off the barstool. "We can do that. Drive along the coast…does that sound good?"

"Actually, I was thinking more in the direction of Goleta." When Mike stared at her blankly, she confessed her real motivation. "I saw something today, and I know I won't get any sleep until I at least drive by Natalie's house to see if her boyfriend's car is outside."

"*Boyfriend?*"

Madeline drew in a deep breath and explained how she went to speak to Natalie Sheckle prior to her assignation with Julia and Rancho Vista Encantada. "I know what I saw wasn't a familial show of affection. It was a real kiss, a loving, 'I hate to leave you' kind of kiss."

Mike gave her an open-mouth stare as he tried to get his head around this latest development and his partner's sudden obsession with the case.

"I don't want to go over there and confront anyone, I just want to see if the car's there and get the plate number."

Mike seemed like he was resigned to doing as she wished, but skeptical about the justification.

"Look, we already know that things are seldom the way our clients present them," Madeline continued to lobby. "If we can get a plate number, we can run it and at least get a snapshot of this guy she's apparently involved with. After that, we can decide if we want to confront her with the fact that we know she's involved with someone and see how that fits in with this whole 'Andrew would never take his own life' thing. Either way, I'm not going to feel comfortable about pursuing her case until we get a handle on what's really going on in Natalie's head."

When Mike let out a frustrated wheeze and threw his head back, Madeline closed the deal. "See why I won't be able to sleep, knowing I might be missing the opportunity?"

"Yeah, I get it," Mike said, glancing around for his keys. "You going to go like that?" He looked pointedly at her slippers and lounge pants.

"No, I'll just be a minute," she replied as she brushed past him, pulling off one of his old T-shirts en route.

By the time they reached Natalie's housing tract, it was almost eleven o'clock. Whatever event had attracted all those extra vehicles to her neighborhood had apparently disbanded. Madeline's hope of getting a second gander at the slick guy's license plate fizzled as Mike did a slow drive-by of the Sheckle house.

"Darn," she said, letting out a discouraged huff. It had been a longshot, but it would've niggled at her all night if she hadn't checked it out. Mike was in the middle of turning left into a driveway when his headlights panned across a vehicle on the opposite side of the street and about five houses up from Natalie's.

"Stop!" she cried out. "Go forward so I can see that vehicle." Mike put the Audi in reverse, then pulled up alongside the car that matched Madeline's description.

"Is this the car you saw this morning?" Mike asked, craning to see inside the tinted windows.

"It is," she answered excitedly, leaning over him for a better look. "See if you can get the lights on his license plate so I can take a photo."

Mike complied, gliding the SUV gracefully forward before making a quick U-turn to come up behind the tricked-out muscle car. He put the Audi in park while Madeline took the shot. "What did the driver look like?"

"Tall, lanky, dark hair. Moved with ease. Came across as being pretty confident, a little cocky, even."

"Well, the car definitely says he's not a family man. Two-door muscle cars tend to go out of the picture when kids come on the scene," Mike observed.

Madeline was inclined to agree. There was something about the way he had handled himself that said he was lone wolf, someone who put his wants and needs above everything and everyone else.

She replayed what she'd seen from the Mercedes' rearview mirror in her mind, coming to the same conclusion as before: the way he'd casually but intently scanned the street as he quickly glided toward the automotive version of himself, his furtive glances forward and back before he clicked open his doors and slid inside. She remembered hearing the muffled growl as the car came to life and the deep rumble as it quickly passed her by.

"Happy?" Mike asked.

"Yes," Madeline replied, turning to face him. "Thanks for indulging me. I knew it was going to hound me all night if I didn't get over here. I would've been too worried that I'd oversleep and miss this opportunity, not that I had any guarantees that he'd be back."

"You want to pound on the door and demand an explanation?" Mike baited her. That wouldn't be a particularly professional move, but then again, it might be the most expedient way of getting to the heart of what was really going on.

Madeline bit her bottom lip as she entertained the idea, knowing it had only been offered in jest. Still, it was daring enough to suit her frustrated state of mind. Having clarity on even one of the perplexities hounding them would be a great satisfaction.

"It's probably not the smartest move right now," she conceded. "With our luck, we'd end up losing our licenses."

"Maybe not if we solve a murder," Mike said before he could stop himself. Madeline weighed the pros and cons of going rogue. She let out a frustrated sigh of having no clear path on any of the three quandaries they were now embroiled in.

"Home, James," she said.

Her thoughts tumbled over each other as Mike guided the Audi through the maze of streets that would eventually lead to the freeway. She turned to watch the tract houses flick by, wondering idly what went on in these seemingly ordinary pods of everyday life.

"Are you going to stay up the rest of the night creating a file on this mystery guy?" Mike challenged her as they turned right onto Turnpike.

Madeline smiled sheepishly. "No, that would definitely wire my brain up too much. I have a feeling I'll be able to let go of this and the Bartholomew case until the morning. Maybe my subconscious will have sorted a few things out by then."

"All I care about is you feeling safe," Mike said as he merged the Audi onto the 101.

TWENTY-THREE

A terrifying shriek startled Mike out of his coma-like sleep. He knocked over the lamp as he lunged to turn it on, barely catching it before it crashed to the floor. Madeline let out another scream before he managed to get it turned on. Once he could see, his eyes panned the room as he searched for intruders. His heart hammered in his ears while he rushed to Madeline's side of the bed, where she fought for release from the down comforter.

"Maddie, Maddie! You're safe. I'm here. You're just having a bad dream," he said, trying to sound calm for her sake. Madeline flailed for a few seconds longer until her mind was able to assimilate what was really going on around her.

"Are you okay?" Mike asked as he steadied her. After a few confused seconds, she nodded her head and drew in a shaky breath as she tried to calm herself. Seeing that she was awake and aware of her surroundings now, Mike pulled her into his arms and held her tight, feeling the pounding of her heart as it collided with his own. "Was it about the attack?" he asked, loosening his hold so he could see her face.

"I don't know what it was. I don't actually remember anything... I just... It just... I don't know," she said weakly, shaking her head in dismay. She let out a long, quivering breath that allowed her body to relax somewhat.

"It's okay. It doesn't matter. You're safe, and I'm here, and hopefully you can get back to sleep." With slow, gentle moves, he helped Madeline settle back down on the bed, then pulled the duvet up over her shoulders before sitting back down next to her. It took her heart another painful minute to stop its flailing.

"Can I get you anything? Some water?"

Madeline shook her head and drew in another deep breath, this one a little steadier and calmer.

"I've wrecked your night's sleep, haven't I?" she asked in a voice left raspy from her guttural screams.

"Don't be worrying about me," Mike hushed her, smoothing back a few matted strands of hair, wet from tears and perspiration. Even after all she'd been through, she still had a radiant beauty that could take his breath away.

He sat vigil until her eyes had been closed for a few minutes and her breathing had slowed to a faint rising and falling of her chest. He moved off the bed as gently as he could and headed for the front of the house to make sure the alarm was still set and all doors and windows were still locked.

"Did you hear something?" she asked groggily. Mike watched as she struggled to keep her eyelids open long enough to hear his answer.

"No, I didn't hear anything," he replied, edging back to her side to reassure her. "I was just going to get a glass of water." Madeline's gaze softened, and her eyes fluttered until they closed again.

Breathing easier, Mike went out of the bedroom and systematically checked all the windows, doors and the security system to make sure nothing had been breached. Satisfied, he filled a glass with water and came around the kitchen island where he planted himself on one of the counter stools. He set the glass down on the counter and pressed the palms of his hands against his brow. He ran his hands down his face, then let out a gust of breath that held years of old apprehensions and doubts.

After downing the glass of water in one long guzzle, he turned his mind to practical matters. The most urgent item on the agenda was keeping Madeline safe. Taking Ridley out of circulation permanently was the only way he could see that happening. A slow, painful death would be his first choice, but that would come with its own baggage, namely a prison sentence of his own.

But a return to prison was the most obvious solution to the threat Steven Ridley posed. He'd managed to convince everyone all the way up to the Governor that his revolutionary plan to reintegrate convicts back into society efficiently and safely couldn't be done from his own prison cell, but there had to be certain conditions attached to that. Surely, any breach of the law would violate the terms of his release. So, the logical answer to the Ridley problem was to somehow catch him out.

And there lay the big snag. Whoever Steven hired to kill Madeline knew what he was doing. Thanks to his four years in prison, Steven had probably made many useful contacts among a wide variety of felons. It ate at Mike to think of the power Steven now wielded, due to his role as an advocate for his fellow inmates.

Mike grudgingly admired how Steven had created this new model which gave him the ability to fast-track an inmate's reintegration back into society. Those he helped leave prison early would naturally feel beholden to him. He probably had a stable of ex-cons he could call on for any type of favor, including making a problem disappear forever.

Mike opened his emails and reread through the latest correspondences from Turner Private Investigations. They had been following Steven's movements for ten days, since Mike's roadside meeting with him. Now all the seemingly mundane facts that had been collected needed to be analyzed for their potential to compromise Steven's cushy setup. No doubt he would take pains to maintain an upstanding profile. But there had to be some way to breach that slick veneer and expose whatever less than kosher shenanigans he was orchestrating from a safe remove.

According to the reports, Steven spent most of his time in Sacramento. The assumption was that he only used the Falcon 900LX owned by a rich benefactor when he visited one of the thirty-three state prisons in his official capacity. But there was really no way for anyone to confirm that he wasn't using the plane for his own private errands. The owner of the jet was a big political donor, a shipping magnate by the name of Harrold Green. Mike made a mental note to research him at a later date.

The latest report, which had come in earlier that day, held what he was really looking for. Knowing Steven's appreciation for the roles women play in any society, finding his latest entrée into the mainstream of Sacramento's movers and shakers would've been a high priority. According to TPI, Steven had been seen with Sarah Strong-Hartmann on three separate occasions, two of them at high-profile social functions.

Mike clicked on the link and was taken to TPI's secure site to view the photos of Steven and his new benefactress. Though not a beauty by anyone's gauge, Ms. Strong-Hartmann seemed fully self-possessed and capable of handling any situation she might be thrown into. Mike opened a new browser and did his own search. Without getting too in-depth, he surmised Sarah was a powerhouse fundraiser and a champion of several pet causes, including shelters for abused women, mentoring programs for at-risk youth, and...*ding ding ding*...prison reform with an eye toward reintegration back into society.

A match made in heaven, Mike thought with a cynical smile. He had to wonder if this association was purely serendipitous, or if Steven had done a little long-range planning. In either case, Sarah Strong-Hartmann would be key to the plan Mike had in mind.

After another hour of research, Mike's eyes started to close of their own accord. It was after two a.m. He wouldn't be good for anything if he didn't get a least a couple more hours sleep. He shut down his computer with a solid kernel of hope that he and Madeline could put "paid" to the Steven Ridley threat. He had to believe it; if not, there was nothing to ensure Madeline would be safe.

TWENTY-FOUR

Mike straggled in from the bedroom looking like he'd gone ten rounds with a kangaroo and lost. His chin-length, sun-bleached hair was sticking up in various directions where it wasn't matted flat. His eyes struggled to stay open, squinting at the sunlight that streamed in from the living room windows. Sitting cross-legged on the sofa that afforded a view of the coastline and the harbor, Madeline looked up from her laptop and laughed at the sight of him.

"I made coffee," she informed him, not even trying to disguise her amusement.

"Thanks," Mike croaked as he pulled her robe more tightly around him, making Madeline laugh harder. Seeing that he had a good sixty-five pounds on her, the cashmere knit was hard-pressed to adequately cover him. Whereas it hung almost to her ankles, it barely covered Mike's knees.

"You should wear lilac more often," she ribbed him as she got up and went to refill her own cup.

"Please go easy on me," he cautioned as he plodded into the kitchen. "My pitiful condition is a direct result of your heart-stopping nightmare. I'm surprised the neighbors didn't call the police."

Madeline came up behind him, snuggling into his large frame for a moment before reaching past him for the coffee pot.

"I'm just lucky I didn't end up in ICU with a massive coronary," he groused somewhat seriously.

Recalling her own near heart attack, Madeline leaned against the kitchen island and gave him a sheepish, apologetic pout.

"I'm truly sorry about the nightmare," she said, dropping her eyes to her coffee mug. Eye contact with each other only held for a couple of seconds as both of them struggled with the seriousness behind the joking. Mike set his cup back on the counter and crossed over to take hers away before folding his arms around her. They swayed in each other's embrace as all their silent apologies passed back and forth. Mike kissed the top of her head before letting go of her and reaching for the much-needed caffeine.

"I'm glad you were able to get some sleep," he said as he opened the refrigerator doors and hunted up breakfast fixings. He pulled out a carton of eggs and a loaf of bread, then went to search the cupboard for something to liven them up.

"And I'm glad you were able to get back to sleep after I scared you half to death," Madeline replied, coming up beside him to see what the verdict about breakfast would be.

"It took a while. I had to come in here for a bit to calm down."

"I'm sorry."

"Don't be," he said as he carried his finds to the far end of the island. "I was able to lay a little ground work on our latest case—"

"What's our latest case?" Madeline asked, confused by his comment.

"The 'How to get even with Steven' case," Mike said as he cracked an egg and tossed the shell into the trash in one fluid motion.

Madeline digested this concept with growing interest.

"Okay, I like the idea, but where do we even start?"

"Well, it's funny you should ask…"

"You sound like a man with a plan," Madeline said tentatively, still not quite over the shock of nearly having her throat slit.

"That's because I am," he said confidently as another egg was cracked and dropped into the bowl.

"Are you going to tell me what it is, or do I need to guess?"

"I will enlighten you over my world-famous green chili and jack omelet," he said as he pulled out a frying pan from under the counter and set it on the stove. "Why don't you go see if it's warm enough to sit out on the deck, while I throw this masterpiece together?"

"You'll need to flatten out that fur on your head or you'll frighten the neighbors," she advised him as she went to do as he asked. "Is the alarm on?"

"Oops!" Mike held up a finger to stall her progress as he went to shut off the security alarm. "That would really aggravate the neighbors," he said as he padded back to the kitchen on his bare feet.

Despite the residual anxiety from the previous night's brush with death, Madeline found it hard to hang on to her anger and fear in the bright light of day. With the birds singing and the sunlight streaming into Mike's front room, that terrifying skirmish almost didn't seem real.

And there was something heartwarming and comical about Mike making breakfast in her robe that made it hard to hold on to resentment. Every time she looked over at him, she could barely keep from laughing.

She stepped outside and inhaled deeply, a sense of wellbeing seeping into her soul as she filled her lungs with the fresh ocean air. Even though she had been furious with Mike for meeting with Steven, she couldn't lay the blame for what had happened on her front lawn on him. Steven didn't need to have any communication with either of them to send a hit man after her. He had coaxed Mike into meeting him for the sheer fun of letting Mike think he was somehow in control of the situation. It was a way to show off his newfound freedom and his new, government-sanctioned program.

She let her breath out in a discouraged huff, then silently admonished herself for succumbing to negative thoughts. It only proved that Steven had once again managed to invade her psyche, and that was not okay. With effort, she banished him to the nether regions and got down to practical matters. It would be lovely to sit out there in the sunshine, listening to the birds and the waves in the distance, but the table and chairs would need wiping down first.

As she went back inside to get some damp paper towels, she caught a glimpse out the front windows of a small band of well-intentioned, door-to-door religious advisors. The thought of being politely ambushed during their breakfast out in the open put the kibosh on dining al fresco.

"I think we better eat inside," she said to Mike, not bothering to explain why. She took placemats out of the drawer and put them on the counter just as Mike was divvying up the huge five-egg omelet. "That smells heavenly," she said as she took the two pieces of toast from the toaster and buttered them generously.

Seated at the kitchen counter, they kept their thoughts to themselves as they voraciously consumed the omelet, toast and coffee. Not for the first time, Madeline pondered the restorative properties of food.

"Just what I needed," she said as she stood and gathered her utensils, plate and mug. "Thank you for that." She kissed Mike's cheek on her way to the sink. She had a split-second glimpse out one of the kitchen windows of the God Squad before they headed up Mike's front walk. She ditched the dishes and called out a quick warning. Mike wiped his mouth and got out of range of the front windows in a hurry.

A tentative rap of the door knocker was repeated more forcefully. Hiding from harmless folks brought on a fit of giggles that Madeline was powerless to stop. There was something so innocent and goofy about the whole situation, a stark contrast to what had transpired the night before. She supposed it was her mind's way of neutralizing her near-murder, giving her something benign to worry about.

"This is silly," Mike said, smiling involuntarily at how ludicrous it felt to be hiding behind his own front door. "I should just tell them I'm Jewish. There's really nothing they can say about that, right?"

"Wait, they're leaving," Madeline said as she peeked around the side light flanking the front door. At least the comical episode had dispelled the lingering apprehension of the night before. With food and coffee in her system, and her equilibrium mostly restored, her brain was whirring with various questions that needed answering. At the top of the list was getting to the bottom of what was really going on with Natalie Sheckle.

"So...I guess the idea of taking the day off to recuperate was just a silly pipe dream of mine," Mike said after watching Madeline gravitate back to her computer.

"You're welcome to take the day off, but I couldn't possibly sit around doing nothing, not when there's so much that needs to be followed up on."

"Where do we start?" he asked resignedly.

Madeline eyed him from head to toe. "Why don't you take a shower, then we can go pay Widow Sheckle a house call."

"Is that what you were working on before I got up?"

"It sure was."

This admission piqued Mike's curiosity.

"What have you found out about that car we saw?"

"It's registered to Mathias Tischler of Newbury Park."

"That's a bit of a drive."

"It is. Over an hour each way." Madeline glanced up and gave her partner a look meant to spur him into action. "If we hurry, we might be able to catch both of them in residence."

Mike let out a *humph* and headed off to do as he was told. If he had to work on his day off, he could at least console himself that with everything they had going on, it would surely not be boring.

~~~

At ten o'clock on a cool Sunday morning in November, there was little action to be seen in Natalie Sheckle's neighborhood. They passed one earnest jogger and an elderly man walking an elderly Chihuahua, and that was it. In the light of day, they had no trouble seeing that neither of the two vehicles parked on Natalie's street were the anthracite gray muscle car. Madeline was grateful she'd followed her gut instinct and gotten that photo the previous day, when she had the opportunity. At least they had something to work with now; without that license number, they'd have nothing but conjecture to fill their thoughts.

"Maybe they went out to breakfast," Mike suggested as Madeline studied the front walk, her mind replaying the visual she'd gotten the day before. "What do you want to do now? Do you want to knock on the door, see if Natalie's home?"

"Sure," Madeline replied absently. Mike backed up, then pulled into Natalie's driveway, a move Madeline thought was an interesting strategy. There was something subtly assertive in the ploy, effectively eliminating a quick getaway should Natalie feel the need to flee them. It definitely sent the message that she was cornered, on a subliminal level.

Mike rang the bell twice, knocked on the door and called out Natalie's name for the sake of thoroughness. "Okay, now what?"

Madeline looked to the house directly across the street. Jill Smalls had been quite open and willing to talk to them when they knocked on her door a few days earlier. Madeline was half-tempted to pick her brain, this time with the hope of learning more about the guy she'd seen yesterday morning. But she didn't feel like she had any suitable questions at this point.

"I guess we can come back later," she said, giving Mike a conciliatory look.

She took out her phone and began tapping out a message. "I just sent Natalie a text letting her know we'd like to speak with her."

"Good. So, where to now? The office?"

"Sure. We're certainly not lacking things to keep us occupied."

"Think we should swing by the police station first?"

"What for?" Madeline replied sharply.

"They wanted you to sit down with a sketch artist, remember?" Mike asked as they made their way back to the car.

"I already told them what I saw last night, which was virtually nothing," she said crossly, not relishing the idea of prolonging that aggravation. "No, we've got more useful ways to spend our time. And besides, we know who's really behind that attack. Getting the goods on Steven is our only real option."

"Which reminds me, I haven't filled you in on what I was able to learn while I was burning the midnight oil after your night terror," Mike said as he opened the driver's door. He waited until they were both inside before he gave Madeline the condensed version of what Steven had been up to since his release from prison.

"Now, why am I not surprised?" Madeline said flatly, her mouth hanging slack with indignation as she studied her partner. Despite her rhetorical question, she actually was a little surprised. She had to remind herself that just because she had learned firsthand what a conniving, ruthless monster Steven could be, anyone who hadn't heard the details of what he'd done to her would never suspect him of being so calculating and cruel.

"Figures there's a woman in the mix," she added as all the pieces fell into place. Men held most of the state government offices, but women still wielded a lot of power, sometimes in a more under-the-radar fashion. "And no doubt she's loaded."

"To the teeth."

This bulletin hit Madeline in her most vulnerable spot. Steven had already demonstrated he could talk his way out of anything, even prison. He'd only been out a few months, and he had already reeled in a rich benefactress. He had a private jet at his disposal and flaunted his access to her by baiting Mike into meeting with him one on one. And all of that was just foreplay. He made sure he got into her head before he made his lethal presence felt.

There was a part of her that was screaming deep down inside, where no one else could hear it. Until they could find a way to neutralize the threat Steven posed, she had to keep her wits about her at all times. And more importantly, they had to come up with an effective counter offensive. Quickly.

Mike could feel the tension radiating off Madeline. It was stupid to think she had dodged a bullet when more were sure to follow. From now on, whoever came after Madeline would have to go through him first. Was he foolish to believe he could protect her? In reality, there was probably a target on his back too.

"I do have a plan," Mike said, intentionally breaking through Madeline's dismal musings. "For Steven, I mean."

"Good. Let's hear it."

"I'll let you read the reports from the P.I. firm I hired, but what I took away from what they've gathered is there's a situation we can possibly exploit, and that's the new benefactress, Sarah Strong-Hartmann."

"Okay, what's the plan?" Madeline prompted as she shifted in her seat to face him.

"I say we fly up to Sacramento tomorrow morning and drop in on her, give her a firsthand account of what Steven put you through four years ago and this latest attempt on your life."

"Do you really think she'll even want to hear what I have to say?"

"I don't think we should give her a choice."

"So, we track her down, and I spew all the gory details like an aggrieved ex-wife...? That should go over really well. I'll probably get mowed down on the way back to the airport."

Mike let out a sigh and turned his attention to merging onto the freeway.

"I'm sorry. I know you're trying to tackle this problem head on, and I don't have any brilliant ideas how to defuse the threat he poses to both of us. And really...taking any kind of action is going to feel better than standing still and waiting for the next assault," Madeline said, sighing at all the conundrums haunting them.

"Well...if that means you're on board, let's make a plan," Mike said, turning to gauge her true feelings.

"Okay, I'll leave the planning up to you. You find out the quickest way to get to Sacramento and figure out our best strategy for confronting Ms. Strong-Hartmann. In the meantime, I'm going to concentrate on our two cases. We've learned a fair amount about both of these widows and the circumstances surrounding their husbands' deaths. Now we just have to study what we know and see if we can figure out what really happened to Nick Bartholomew and Andrew Sheckle."

TWENTY-FIVE

Mike was impressed with the additional facts and observations Madeline had added to the Bartholomew board. Though nothing stuck out as evidence of Lindsay's innocence, there were several new facts that kept alternative scenarios in play. In reality, there were plenty other potential suspects who hadn't gotten the kind of scrutiny Lindsay had received right out of the gate, thanks to her irrational stepdaughter. At this juncture, no one was above suspicion. Not even Lindsay.

The fact that Steven had brought them this case now counted as a suspicious event. Even if Madeline hadn't come up with a plausible circumstance to link Steven to Lindsay, they couldn't discount some ulterior motive. Still, it would be just like him to orchestrate some involved ruse to distract them from the fact that his release from prison put Madeline in his crosshairs. But there could also be something else behind his actions that they hadn't yet uncovered.

"Oh, with all the drama last night, I forgot to tell you what I learned from the foreman on the Bartholomew ranch," Madeline said, her features lighting up as she recalled that pivotal moment.

"What?" Mike asked, an expectant look on his face as he settled himself on the corner of the conference table.

"Two things, actually. Contrary to what Vanessa said during the taped interview, Lester Prinz did not fire the ranch hand who Vanessa alleged was having a fling with Lindsay. Seth Arnold gave his notice and abruptly left the Bartholomew gig because his brother-in-law had been killed, and his sister needed his help to run their ranch."

"Okay. So, he wasn't fired, but he still could've been sneaking around with Lindsay," Mike replied.

"That's true," Madeline acknowledged before making her second point. "But here's the crucial point—Lester Prinz was never called to testify against or on behalf of Lindsay."

"Well, once Nick's kids won that wrongful death suit, Lindsay had to resort to using a public defender to represent her," Mike reminded her unnecessarily. "We both know how overwhelmed and under-budgeted that department is. And I agree she didn't have a strong defense, which probably isn't uncommon with people who believe their innocence alone will keep them out of prison."

"Yes, I know all that. But still, if Nick's kids hadn't moved so fast to strip Lindsay of the means to a proactive defense, any legal counsel worth their salt would've quashed the notion of Lindsay having a motive to kill her husband based on unverifiable hearsay. Lester Prinz would've been deposed, along with Seth Arnold. With adequate funds, they could've used that unsubstantiated rumor to their advantage by pointing out that someone was trying to frame their client. Without a motive, there was no argument for Lindsay killing her husband. The best they could've gotten would've been depraved indifference or involuntary manslaughter."

"Okay, I see your point. But all those things only tell us that Nick's kids— especially Vanessa—used everything in their power to discredit their stepmom."

"That's true. But if there's no logical reason for Lindsay to want to cause her husband great bodily harm, then we have to consider other potential suspects and other motives."

"I agree," Mike said diplomatically, though he felt like they were talking in circles. "Now, if we can get past the abstracts and find a solid motive for someone wanting Nick dead, maybe we could get somewhere."

Madeline couldn't dispute her partner's point. What they needed was an alternate scenario, something that would explain why the note Lindsay had supposedly written had not been found anywhere on the ranch.

"All right…for argument's sake, let's say that Lindsay's version of events is correct, and in reality, there hasn't been anyone who can prove Lindsay *didn't* leave a note—"

"That's because you can't prove a negative," Mike countered.

"Yes, but let's assume for the purpose of this exercise that Lindsay is inno- cent," Madeline said, undeterred by Mike's role as devil's advocate. "Who had the most to gain? Or maybe more to the point, who *has gained* the most since Nick's death?"

"From what we've learned so far, that would be Vanessa."

"Exactly. She had managed to guilt her father into planting ten acres of grapes, but her ambition was much greater than what could be fulfilled with a hobby vineyard. Not only has she expanded her vineyards to thirty acres and counting, she managed to do a land deal with the state that gave her the only commercial business on the Gaviota coast, giving up half of the Bartholomew ranch in the bargain. Forget everything else—that in itself is a huge game changer. And if Lindsay's claims about Nick's desire to preserve the integrity of the original land grant parcel are true, then that gives Vanessa another motive. Considering how things have turned out, I'd say it gives her a strong motive."

"Yeah, but could she really have been that ambitious or that pissed off at her father to kill him?" Mike asked skeptically. The look on Madeline's face told him he was being naïve to even pose that question.

"Let's just review what we know so far... Vanessa and Sean alibi each other. They were both in the kitchen at the same time—or so they say. They both observed the freshly baked pie, and they both maintain there was no note."

"I'm with you so far," Mike said as he shifted his weight, clearly uncomfortable with the scenario she was presenting. It meant they had to prove that both Nick's kids were lying, and with what they knew so far, they had no way to do that.

"But let's say the note was tucked under the pie, sticking out just enough for someone to see it. It would be so easy for either Vanessa or Sean to sneak a peek at the note, realize the significance of what it contained, then palm it. Nick comes in, sees the pie his loving wife made for him, they all dig into it. Then Nick wanders off contentedly to go till the soil..."

Mike let out a heavy sigh as he stood up and went to scrutinize the exhibits on the board. "Okay, all of that is possible and even plausible. But how do we prove it?" he asked as he turned his focus back to Madeline. She had no other retort than an exasperated laugh.

"That is the whole crux of the matter, isn't it? Nothing was ever actually proven one way or the other regarding Nick's death. In truth, Lindsay should be looking for someone who can appeal her case. With what we've learned so far, it seems like there are enough holes in the argument that she willfully caused her husband's death to warrant an appeal."

"So…you're ready to give up, hand this off to someone else?" Mike asked skeptically.

"No," Madeline snapped, her tone defensive. "I'm not saying that at all."

"Oh…okay…it just sounded like you're convinced we can't find out what really happened that day, so we might as well throw in the towel," Mike said, purposely baiting her.

"I never said any such thing. I'm far from giving up. I was just getting you up to speed on what I learned so far."

"Um hmm," Mike murmured, head down as he pretended to be engrossed in something he'd taken from the exhibits box. Recognizing the ploy, Madeline ignored him as she tried to figure out the logical next step.

"It would be the perfect crime, you know—framing someone else for the murder," she mused out loud. "How does someone live with themselves when they know they're responsible for ruining so many lives?"

Mike shrugged. "It happens every day. Not all human beings regard life as something sacred. They regard life as their one chance to get what they want, what they think they deserve. If they perceive that someone is standing in their way, they have no qualms about eliminating that person."

"You're right. You're absolutely right." Madeline stood with her hands on her hips, her gaze lost in the middle distance, her thoughts far away.

"Okay…for argument's sake, let's say Vanessa acted on a split-second urge to dole out some justice. She's the one closest to the pie while Sean scrounges around in the refrigerator for something to eat. She's got that note in her pocket the whole time her father, brother and she are eating Lindsay's blackberry pie. She watches her father wander off to do some tractor work, knowing full well it's unsafe to operate. Maybe she thinks he'll notice right away that it can't be ridden. No harm, no foul. He might get royally pissed off at Lindsay for not warning him, and that would suit Vanessa just fine. Or maybe he'll start it up and figure out there's a problem and bail.

"Think about the sense of power Vanessa is feeling at that moment. When her parents were going through the divorce, she had no say in what was happening to her life. She was a victim of circumstances, powerless to control her parents or her feelings of abandonment."

Madeline paused to take in Mike's reaction. Gone was the urge to argue for the sake of it as he stared at her with admiration. There was nothing she'd said that he could refute, for it was all completely possible, maybe even accurate.

"There was a rush to strip Lindsay of her assets so she couldn't mount a proper defense, thanks to the way Vanessa maligned her from the get-go," Madeline continued. "Lindsay was kept off-balance by the wrongful death suit Vanessa and Sean filed against her right after Nick's death. It took everyone's attention away from the fact that Vanessa not only had the means, motive and opportunity, she had a score to settle with Lindsay and her father. She couldn't afford to have anyone question her own means, motive or opportunity. But the big problem now is how do we prove it."

"Maybe the best way to prove it would be to try to *disprove* it," Mike offered.

"Disprove it? How?"

"Let's follow Vanessa's actions, starting with the statement she gave the sheriff's deputies. Was she or was she not out to frame Lindsay from outset?"

Still unsure what could be gained by this approach, Madeline crossed around to the other side of the conference table and turned on her laptop. Once it booted, she brought up the taped interviews with the sheriff's deputies. She clicked on the interview with Vanessa and turned the screen so Mike could see it.

"*Please walk us through your actions and observations on the afternoon of April 21*ˢᵗ *, starting from the time you last saw your father before the accident.*"

After watching to Vanessa's interview again, Madeline hit the pause button. In light of what they were now suspecting, it seemed even more obvious that Vanessa was trying to fit Lindsay up for her father's death from the outset.

"Okay…I think it's safe to say that Vanessa was gunning for Lindsay right out of the gate. But that still doesn't prove or disprove anything," she said.

"No, but we can't disprove that Vanessa didn't do it, either."

"What? You lost me."

"Yeah, I think I lost myself too," Mike said with a weak laugh. "I had something, but… it vanished."

"Okay…you were on the right track. We both feel that Vanessa wanted

Lindsay to go down for her father's accidental death. The only reason this was even investigated so vigorously was because the repairman told the deputies that he had made it perfectly clear to Lindsay the tractor was not safe to use. Lindsay could've played stupid and said she forgot to leave a note, but that would've really put the suspicion on her. She *could've* forgotten to leave it and lied about it…" Madeline said with a shrug.

"Yep, she could have. I'm not sure she could've gotten a twenty-year sentence for manslaughter, though," Mike pointed out.

"No, I think the D.A.'s office would've had to aim for involuntary manslaughter and bargain down. But maybe this is a point we can work with to disprove that Lindsay intentionally caused Nick's death…"

Mike's brows furrowed as he tried to unravel the point Madeline was trying to make. "Okay, that was a dumb idea I had," he admitted. "Just forget trying to prove a negative. Tell me what you're really thinking."

Madeline drew in a long breath as she put her thoughts in order. "If Lindsay wanted to get rid of Nick—for whatever reason—she'd have been better off just playing dumb. If she put on a charade of remorse for having forgotten to leave Nick a note, she would've had to go through a fair number of legal hoops, but she would've ended up with very little jail time, if any.

"In fact, I remember a case where a drunk driver killed a pedestrian, and she managed to get off with no prison time. She didn't come clean until two days later, and her excuse was she didn't realize she'd hit anyone. If Lindsay admitted she'd made a horrible mistake by forgetting to leave a note, then Vanessa's accusations would've been seen as nothing more than justifiable hysteria over her father's death. And I doubt Lindsay would've been charged with murder or stripped of her community property assets."

"Good point. Okay, but that could've been a tactical error on Lindsay's part," Mike argued.

"You mean, not thinking it out carefully enough?"

"Yeah."

"But I just don't think Lindsay was unhappy in her marriage. Yolanda would've picked up on that, I'm sure of it. She was there six days a week for the whole time Lindsay lived there. And Yolanda had every reason to disparage Lindsay, given that Nick married her after he divorced wife number one, a woman who was like family to Yolanda. And she'd been working for Nick for many years before Lindsay came along."

"You've got a point there," Mike said. "Yolanda didn't have anything negative to say about Lindsay." They stared at each other for a moment while their minds came to a consensus.

"I think we need to go speak to the housekeeper again," Madeline said. "It's Sunday, her day off." She looked at her watch; it was almost eleven o'clock.

"There's one other thing that's been niggling at me," she said as she went back to her computer. Instead of hunching over it, she took a seat as she hunted up the file she was looking for. Once she found the surveillance footage that was turned over to the sheriff's office, she watched it from the beginning. The date stamp on the first frame was taken two days prior to Nick's fatal accident.

"What are you looking for?" Mike asked over her shoulder.

"I don't know, really," Madeline confessed as she skipped to the next activity caught on camera, then the next. "I've just been having a hard time getting a sequence of events straight in my head." She said as jumped ahead again.

Each time a vehicle came into the ranch or exited, she stopped the tape to scrutinize the occupants. It would've helped a lot to have Lindsay there to give names to the faces of those free to come and go from Rancho Vista Encantada during that time.

Mike tired of bending over and took a bathroom break while Madeline continued her fishing expedition. He was just coming out of the loo when Madeline struck pay dirt.

"What'd you find?" he asked as he came up behind her. Madeline turned the computer so he could see it better. He pulled out the chair next to her while his eyes strained to identify the faces in the white Range Rover. "That's Vanessa." He pointed to the driver. "Who do you suppose that is?" His finger slid over to the passenger.

The film was not high resolution and the passenger was partially in shadow. Madeline had to get close to the screen to make sure of what she was seeing. She got chills up her arms as she confirmed she was looking at an older version of Vanessa Bartholomew.

"That's Patricia Bartholomew, Nick's ex-wife."

Mike got the same prickly sensation she'd gotten when he processed the implication of what they were seeing.

Madeline got all the way through the footage, having paused on every vehicle to look for the first Mrs. Bartholomew. As there wasn't all that much traffic going in and out, it didn't take very long to realize she never appeared again, at least not on the day of the accident or the day after.

"Smoking gun?" Mike asked as Madeline looked him directly in the eyes, a slow, triumphant smile breaking out across her face. Just as quickly, the smile was replaced with a stern look of doubt. She backed up the footage and repeated the process, stopping to reexamine the second occupant in the white Range Rover.

A memory from the day before had Madeline jumping up to grab her tote bag, belatedly recalling the reason why it felt heavier than usual. She pulled out the hardcover copy of "*A Vintage to Die For*" by P.A. Collins and flipped it over. Triumphant in her discovery, she flashed the photo of the pretty blonde at Mike before holding it up next to the grainy image on the screen.

"This is Vanessa's mom. Patricia Bartholomew. Nick's former wife. I met her yesterday at the tasting room during the interview. Well, I didn't actually meet her, but I did get her to sign my copy of the book," Madeline said, flipping to the dedication page to see what she'd written. The author's signature was a bold, slanted scroll—confident and a tad flamboyant, kind of like the woman herself.

"If what we're seeing here is Nick's first wife, this changes everything," Mike uttered cautiously, his expression more troubled than triumphant.

"It sure does," Madeline said as she looked back at the woman in the passenger's seat. "Well, it looks like we've got one more reason to pay Yolanda another visit."

"You think she knew Nick's ex was on the property the day of the accident?"

"I think it's entirely possible. I also have a hunch this wasn't a one-off visit. It was never mentioned by anyone we've seen so far that Patricia visited the ranch, on that day or any other. That right there is a huge omission. My gut's telling me this was a secret arrangement between Nick's first wife and his kids. Who knows? Maybe he even knew about it, but kept it a secret from Lindsay. I can guarantee you that if Lindsay knew Patricia was there the day of the accident, she would've made that abundantly clear. Unlike Lindsay, Patricia had a motive for removing that note."

"No argument there," Mike agreed. "This really is starting to feel like a cover up and frame job."

"It sure is. Let's take that drive," Madeline said as she stowed the novel back into her tote before hiking it onto her shoulder. She silently cautioned herself not to get too excited, but she couldn't help thinking about Lindsay and her daughter. If she and Mike were right about what they'd seen, their nightmare could be over soon.

TWENTY-SIX

Madeline and Mike had been sitting on Yolanda's front porch bench for twenty minutes by the time the housekeeper returned home. They stood as she pulled into her accustomed parking spot and remained on the porch while she took her time getting out of her weathered Honda. The stalling put all three more on edge. Her visitors wondered if she was about to do a runner, while Yolanda tried in vain to convince herself the two detectives weren't there to implode her world.

After a couple tense minutes, Yolanda freed herself from the confines of her car and trudged toward her front door, her handbag clutched to her bosom like a life preserver.

"Sorry for the surprise visit," Madeline said, keeping her tone neutral and professional.

"We promise not to take up too much of your day off," Mike offered with a wan smile that Yolanda was hesitant to return. She moved to her front door, key in hand, her eyes trained on the task of unlocking the door to the house she enjoyed as part of her compensation.

"Would you like some coffee?" she asked after she set her handbag on the hall table, keeping her eyes averted from them the whole while, as if she could pretend in some part of her brain this visit wasn't really happening.

"We're fine, Yolanda. Thanks, anyway," Mike said as he and Madeline followed her. They came to a halt at the kitchen table, where they had sat two days earlier. After watching the housekeeper go through the ritual of measuring coffee and water and setting the machine to brew, Madeline got to the point.

"How long had Patricia Bartholomew been staying on the ranch prior to Nick's death?"

Without any other props or tasks to occupy her hands, Yolanda stood there wringing them, her lips pursed as she struggled to find the best way out of this situation.

"We've seen the surveillance footage of her in the Range Rover with Vanessa two days before Nick's accident," Mike told her, indicating the tablet in Madeline's hand with a nod of his head. His tone was neither aggressive or accusatory, simply matter-of-fact.

"In the seventy-two hours covered on the tapes provided to law enforcement, we couldn't find any footage of Patricia leaving the property," Madeline told her as she showed the frame with Patricia in the passenger's seat. "Which has to mean she was on the ranch—and more specifically, that side of the ranch—when the note Lindsay left for Nick disappeared." The housekeeper remained rooted to the spot in the middle of her kitchen, her trepidation palpable.

"I'll pour you some coffee, Yolanda," Mike offered as he moved past her.

"Why don't you have a seat and tell us the truth of what happened that day?" Madeline asked as she pulled out a chair for her. She waited until Yolanda was seated before settling into the one next to it. Mike placed a cup of steaming coffee in front of Yolanda, which she quickly grasped, grateful to have something to steady her hands.

"Whenever you're ready," Madeline said, leaning back against the chair, her eyes never leaving Yolanda's face. She could sense they were on the brink of finding the missing piece to this case, the reason behind why an innocent woman had been unjustly imprisoned.

While Yolanda fought for composure, Madeline signaled to Mike to grab the box of tissues from the corner table in the living room. When he placed it in front of Yolanda, she reached for a tissue preemptively.

"I understand the position you were in, Yolanda," Madeline said in a soft, compassionate tone. "But were you really okay with letting the woman who killed your employer get away with murder while another woman took the blame?"

Yolanda looked up at Madeline, then Mike while she snuffed back tears. "It was a terrible time. Everyone was so upset. I couldn't even think. Everyone was saying that Lindsay didn't leave a note, that she was lying. Everyone said right away it was Lindsay's fault Nick had died."

"So, you believed Lindsay would intentionally put Nick's life at risk?" Madeline asked. Yolanda shook her head slowly.

"No. I didn't believe that."

"Do you believe she *forgot* to leave a note?" Mike asked as he lowered himself onto the chair to Yolanda's left. She sniffed, then let her eyes meet Mike's.

"I didn't know what to believe during that time. I couldn't believe any of it was really happening. Such a terrible time." Yolanda let her eyes drop to the table, her stare fixed on something only she could see.

"What did you tell the deputies when you were interviewed the following day?" Mike asked. Even though he'd watched the taped interview, he wanted to hear what Yolanda would say. She shifted in her seat, obviously troubled by the question.

"I told them I didn't know anything about the note. I left before the repairman came."

"Then what makes you believe Lindsay didn't forget to leave a note for Nick?" Madeline asked. She wouldn't have guessed Yolanda could get any more uncomfortable, but the look on the housekeeper's face was cause for concern. She looked as if she were a couple ticks away from a stroke.

"Yolanda, we're only looking for the truth, and we don't believe for a moment you had anything to do with taking the note or Nick's accident. But there are two other people whose lives have been ruined because of what happened that day and the events that followed, people who also loved Nick very much."

Yolanda's watery eyes glanced furtively back and forth between the two detectives before she looked down into her coffee cup. Her hands shook as she raised it to her lips.

"Take your time," Mike said softly, shooting a glance at his partner. Yolanda took a sip of the coffee, then another before setting it back down. She seemed more composed as she turned to Madeline.

"I saw the note," she said.

Having gotten the words out, she lowered her eyes back to the coffee cup while Madeline and Mike looked at each other in shock. On one hand, they had corroborating testimony that Lindsay had in fact written the note of warning, which meant she was innocent of intentionally harming Nick. But there was something sinister lurking underneath Yolanda's confession, and it wasn't just the fact that she hadn't told the sheriff's deputies about seeing the note when questioned.

"Where did you see the note, Yolanda?" Madeline pressed, leaning in to force Yolanda to look at her. The housekeeper swallowed hard as her head swiveled from one interrogator to the other.

"I found it in the wastebasket under a bathroom sink in Vanessa's house, in the guest bathroom Patricia used when she stayed with her."

This revelation had Madeline's heart thumping as her mind raced.

"When was this?" she asked more forcefully than she had intended.

"It was a few weeks after Nick died. It was after the memorial service, after Lindsay was charged with his murder. Nothing was normal anymore. That whole period is like one big, horrible nightmare." Yolanda paused as she took a deep breath. "I went over to clean Vanessa's house. It hadn't been cleaned since before…before the accident."

She drew in another deep breath and let it shudder out of her lungs before continuing.

"I had set the wastebasket by the bedroom door. It was completely full, and I was going to empty it into the kitchen trash once I finished the room, but the vacuum cleaner cord knocked it over. When I was picking up all the bits and pieces, I found the note. It was all wadded up. If I hadn't recognized the blue paper, I wouldn't have even noticed it. But I knew right away it was from the pad Lindsay kept on the kitchen counter by the telephone. It had horses running along the bottom of it. A funny feeling came over me. I remember how scared I was when I smoothed it out. I recognized Lindsay's writing, and I knew finding it in Patricia's wastebasket was bad."

"What did you do with the note, Yolanda?" Mike asked, hand on the back of her chair as he leaned toward her. The tension in that small nook was electrifying.

"I put it in my pocket."

"And then what did you do with it?" Madeline asked cautiously, as if she were afraid to find out the answer.

"I will go get it," Yolanda said, startling her visitors with the idea that tangible proof of Lindsay's innocence still existed. Yolanda appeared lighter as she rose from her chair and moved in the direction of the bedrooms. After exchanging nervous looks, Mike and Madeline followed her.

They reached her bedroom in time to witness Yolanda pulling open the lowest drawer of a heavy mahogany dresser and then removing a wooden keepsake box. She carried it to the bed and carefully laid her mementos aside until she uncovered what she'd been looking for. She picked it up and held it out to the detectives as if she were taking the most frightening and definitive step of her life.

Mike reached for the crinkled notepaper. He unfolded it and gingerly held it at the edges so both he and Madeline could read it. The sight of the flowing cursive letters in bright blue ink sent waves of emotions through them. Triumph, pain, empathy, sorrow came at them in turns. Their eyes had gone glassy when they looked over at Yolanda, who was now shedding the tears she'd kept pent up inside for far too long.

"I didn't know what to do with this when I found it. I knew right away it meant Lindsay didn't lie about leaving a note, but I couldn't face the truth about finding it in Patricia's trash. She'd been almost like a daughter to me. I came to work for her when Vanessa was only three years old."

Madeline fought for control of her tongue. There was no point in grilling the housekeeper about her decision to keep this evidence to herself; she had been living with the knowledge that she had become a party to Lindsay's wrongful conviction ever since she found the note. The only upside Madeline could see was that Yolanda hadn't destroyed the concrete proof that Lindsay had been telling the truth. Without this tangible proof, it would be more than an uphill battle to overturn Lindsay's conviction.

"What will happen now?" Yolanda asked as tears began to run down her cheeks. "Will I be arrested?"

Madeline and Mike sighed in unison. Whatever happened after this point was entirely out of their hands.

~~~

Yolanda's kitchen table became an ad hoc office while Madeline and Mike broke the news to the District Attorney. With Madeline's cell phone lying between them, they gave Conrad the details about the existence of the note that proved Lindsay Bartholomew's innocence, while Yolanda sat with her back to them on her living room sofa. They had taken a photo of the note and sent it to the D.A. so he could see it with his own eyes. He would surely have the original copy analyzed, but Yolanda's testimony would carry a lot of weight, despite the fact she had failed to turn it over sooner.

After they filled him in on the circumstances in which the housekeeper had come by the note, they set up a Skype session so Conrad could hear Yolanda's testimony firsthand. When she had finished her confession, Conrad had them end the interview so he could speak to the detectives without including the witness in their conversation. They took Madeline's phone out to Yolanda's back patio and spoke in hushed tones as Conrad outlined what would need to happen next.

Though they had been successful in their mission to find out what had really gone on the day of Nick Bartholomew's death, the aftermath of the discovery was going to be very messy. On top of having his Sunday ruined, Conrad was seriously rankled to have one of his closed cases jeopardized by previously unfound evidence. He was furious with the way the case had been carried out, though he knew that the buck always stopped at the top.

But this was more than egg on his face; this was a case where an innocent woman had been imprisoned while the guilty party was at liberty to enjoy what she had taken back after orchestrating her ex-husband's death. Just in terms of legal ramifications and procedural hoops—not to mention the negative media coverage—this was going to be a royal pain in his ass for weeks to come.

Though Madeline and Mike could sympathize with his situation, they were most concerned with those whose lives had already been upended by Patricia Bartholomew's deception. Lindsay and Joni and Yolanda were all collateral damage, more innocent victims of Patricia's treacherous actions. And so were Sean and Vanessa, assuming they weren't somehow complicit in concealing the note written for Nick.

By the time they ended the call with Conrad, Mike and Madeline were wrung out. The adrenaline rush brought on by discovering proof of Lindsay's innocence had worn off. Grappling with all the steps that would have to take place between that moment and Lindsay's release and her reunion with Joni had their minds boggling.

Fortunately for them, their involvement would be ending soon, except to give formal sworn statements. The case would have to be reinvestigated, unless Patricia was willing to do everyone a favor by confessing. Still, there were a lot of innocent people who'd been harmed by Patricia's actions, Yolanda being one of them. Not only was she guilty of concealing evidence, her housing situation and employment were now in jeopardy. And then there was Sean and Vanessa; on top of losing their father, they now had to face the cold reality that their own mother was responsible for his death.

Mike and Madeline had agreed to escort Yolanda to the sheriff's office so she could give a new statement. Mike offered to drive Yolanda in her car, seeing how shaken she was by the whole ordeal. Two sheriff's deputies would be dispatched to bring Patricia and Vanessa Bartholomew to the station separately for questioning. Thankfully, whatever happened after that was out of their hands.

As they came out of the ranch on the frontage road parallel to the 101, Madeline decided to cross the highway so she could witness the fallout of Yolanda's bombshell firsthand. She let Mike know she'd catch up with him at the sheriff's office. After investing so much in unraveling this case, she had to see how it all played out. Just imagining what the impact would be on Vanessa and her mother gave her chills. It wasn't going to be a pretty sight, but she wanted to be sure Patricia didn't wriggle out of it somehow.

As soon as she got out of the Audi, two sheriff's cruisers pulled into the parking area. They had been advised to check the tasting room/gift shop first; if Patricia Bartholomew, aka P.A. Collins, and Vanessa Bartholomew weren't there, they would procede up to the residences.

The two deputies casually surveyed the immediate area as they each hitched up their service belts and made their way inside the retail establishment. They had not issued any warning to her or the other visitors who were coming out as they were about to enter. They were playing it cool in hopes of making this visit come across as benign as possible.

Madeline gave the deputies a minute head start before following discreetly behind them. She crossed the threshold in time to see them turning away from Luke at his post behind the register as Vanessa and her mother responded to his signal. The remaining handful of curious browsers glanced over without thinking too much of the scene unfolding around them until Vanessa's voice rose in righteous indignation.

"Who the hell gave you the authority to come on to my private property to pull this *outrageous* stunt? You are disrupting my business, not to mention causing distress to me and my mother."

The deputies kept their voices calm, focusing instead on their assignment. They advised both women they had been sent to bring them in for questioning in connection to the death of Nickolas Bartholomew.

"Are you out of your minds?" Vanessa roared, clearly on the verge of hysteria. She was determined not to make this affront easier for the deputies. "Who sent you? I demand to know—what the hell is this all about?"

While Vanessa unloaded on the lawmen, Patricia was doing her best to hold herself together, despite her shock and disbelief. The mere fact that this was happening was enough to put her in panic mode. Madeline could feel the fear just below the surface as Patricia's face paled and her eyes grew wide with trepidation.

"Please, ma'am, we're just following orders," one of the deputies said while his partner spoke discreetly into his radio.

"Whose orders?" Vanessa demanded, clearly frightened now that the perfect life she'd built on the foundation of her father's death threatened to morph into a surreal nightmare.

"If you don't come voluntarily, ma'am, we'll have to cuff you and take you out of here by force," the same deputy advised as his partner began to clear the gift shop.

"I really have no idea what you're talking about," Patricia stammered, throwing her daughter a panicked, pleading glance as the deputy gently grasped her bicep and maneuvered her toward the exit.

Madeline reluctantly yielded to the directive and fell into step with the other visitors. Even from the front porch, she had no trouble hearing Vanessa's outraged protests.

"You can't do this!" she shrieked as she watched in horror the tarnishing of the enterprise she'd worked so hard to create. "Mom, don't worry—we'll sort this out. I'll get our attorneys on this so fast, whoever's behind this will regret it, big time!"

Despite her bravado, Madeline detected real concern in Vanessa's teary eyes.

Does she know? Madeline wondered as she stood inside the Audi's driver side door as the Bartholomew women were helped into the backseat of separate cruisers. She imagined things would get pretty dramatic once they got to the station. She slipped into the driver's seat and pulled out onto the highway, anxious to learn how this was all going to play out.

Mike wanted to wait for Yolanda to be questioned at the sheriff's office, so Madeline took advantage of the close proximity to Natalie's house to drive over to see if she'd returned yet. She had witnessed the arrival of the squad cars carrying Nick's daughter and former wife, but they were taken inside the station through a rear door. She was curious to learn whether either or both women would be held after the interview, but she supposed that depended on how fast the attorneys responded to Vanessa's distress call. Madeline would've loved to see those separate dramas unfold, but her main concern was securing Lindsay's release from prison.

She also had another drama that had yet to resolve itself, one that continued to niggle at her. It bothered her that Natalie hadn't replied to the text she'd sent several hours earlier, but a face-to-face confab was more to her liking, anyway. When she asked Natalie about the mystery man, she wanted to see her reaction. After Natalie's emotional breakdown during their interview, the idea of her being romantically involved with someone just didn't fit. Unless Madeline had missed the obvious, she would've bet Natalie was nowhere near ready for a new relationship, not with all the doubts and denial she harbored over Andrew's death.

At 4:15, the sun was already casting long shadows through Natalie's neighborhood as it descended. A chilly breeze ruffled Madeline's hair as she stepped out of the Audi and made her way up Natalie's driveway. She stood at the front door and listened intently for several seconds, trying to pick up anything besides the ambient sounds of the neighborhood on a day of leisure.

She rang the doorbell and strained to hear anything coming from inside the house. After about thirty seconds, she rang again, this time with three long presses on the button. Still nothing.

With all that Madeline had on her mind, she actually found it annoying that not hearing back from Natalie was bothering her so much. She had more than enough to angst over with the Bartholomew case and the recent attempt on her own life without creating problems where they didn't exist. But she knew herself well enough to know that when her brain fixated on something, there was usually a sound reason behind it. She rang the bell one last time, then gave up and headed back down the driveway.

She was in the process of tapping out another text to Natalie when voices coming from across the street caught her attention. She hit "send" on her phone and shoved it into her pants pocket as she headed to the other side of the street.

"Hello, again!" Jill Smalls called out as Madeline approached her property.

"Hi, Jill," Madeline replied, coming to a halt on the sidewalk where Jill had raked together a pile of fallen leaves. "It really feels like autumn, doesn't it?" she asked convivially as she cast her eyes around Jill's property. The placement of her windows gave her a direct view of Natalie's house and specifically the entry. With no tall vegetation blocking the line of sight, it would be possible to see anyone coming or going from the property.

"Yeah, it sure does. I really like the change. It seems like we've had nonstop summer for six or seven years," Jill observed with a laugh.

"I agree. We might even get some rain next week," Madeline added before getting to the reason for her visit. "Have you seen Natalie today?"

Jill stopped her raking to think. "No, I haven't seen her."

"How about yesterday?"

"Hmm…yesterday. Oh, yesterday was a zoo around here." Jill used her rake as a staff to support herself as she recalled the scene in her neighborhood. "There was a christening a few doors down. You would've thought it was the event of the season!" she said with a laugh. "At least it didn't go late into the night." After Madeline gave her an inquiring look, Jill remembered the question she was asked. "No, sorry—I didn't see her yesterday."

"How about this guy…?" Madeline said as she retrieved her phone and pulled up the photo of Mathias Tischler she'd copied from his driver's license. She handed the phone to Jill, who shook her head doubtfully as she studied it. A man in his fifties with the onset of male pattern baldness came up behind Jill, a bulging garbage bag filled with fallen leaves in each hand. After shooting a brief smile at Madeline, he peered over his wife's shoulder. Jill turned and held the screen so he could get a better look.

"Have you ever seen this guy around Natalie's house?" Jill asked. "This is George, by the way," Jill said to Madeline as she handed the phone to her husband. George set down his bags and took the phone, his expression changing as he recalled where he'd seen that face before.

"Is he about…yea tall…?" George asked, raising his hand to the six-foot level.

"Yes," Madeline said, checking her optimism.

"I haven't seen him over at Natalie's," he said, handing Madeline her phone.

"But you do recognize him…?" Madeline asked.

"Yeah, he was the jerk who broke my new computer screen when he literally dumped it in front of the garage, didn't even have the courtesy to bring it to the front door. Remember that?" George asked his wife.

"How could I forget? That's him? Are you sure?"

"Of course I'm sure. PDS made him come back to pick it up so it could be returned to the retailer in order to get a replacement. I was so aggravated," George said in an aside to Madeline. "It took another week to get the new one."

Madeline was way past the insult to the injury and fully attuned to how this realization impacted the Sheckle case.

"So, this guy delivers parcels to your house?" Madeline asked as she held Mathias Tischler's likeness where they both could see it.

"*Did*," George qualified. "For about a week. Jerk. He was just filling in while our regular driver was on vacation."

Madeline could hardly contain her thoughts; they were racing in half a dozen directions as a variety of scenarios flitted through her mind. Now that she had new fodder for a variety of speculations, she was anxious to get back to Mike to give him the news.

In reality, what she'd just learned wasn't much, not on the face of it, anyway. But like anything else, you had to pull a thread to see where it would lead. But a fill-in delivery guy who is suddenly romantically involved with the grieving Widow Sheckle was an aspect to the situation that definitely deserved deeper scrutiny.

"Sorry we couldn't be of more help," Jill said as Madeline stowed her phone back in her tote bag.

"Oh, you've been very helpful. Now we know who his employer is. If you happen to see him around here again, I'd really appreciate you letting me know," she said as she handed George her business card.

"Sure…we'll do that," George said after studying Madeline's card. Madeline thanked them both and headed back to her SUV. She smiled to herself as she overheard George's comment to his wife. "I would've *never* figured her for a *P.I.*!"

~~~

Back in her vehicle, Madeline was reluctant to return to the sheriff's office after what she'd just learned. She was antsy to speak with Natalie to find out about this guy she was seeing.

Natalie had given them the impression she was still very much in mourning. Trying to understand what really happened that day seemed at odds with having moved on with her life. She seemed pretty invested in believing that Andrew hadn't killed himself, which told Madeline that Natalie couldn't move on until she knew for certain, one way or the other.

Could it be a coincidence this guy came into her life at the same time she sought help to find out the truth behind Andrews's death? Or was Natalie orchestrating the outcome she needed in order to collect on Andrew's insurance policy? If that was the case, what role did the guy in the muscle car play?

"But how could we prove someone else pulled the trigger?" she asked herself out loud, her hand clutched to her forehead.

"Evie saw Andrew react to a text message he received. Fact," she said out loud. "He left the shop without saying where he was going or when he'd be back. Fact. Okay, that's something."

Madeline eyed the clock on the dashboard, knowing she needed to get back to the sheriff's office. She pushed that thought aside and gave voice to another likely truth about this case.

"The scene in the bedroom had been tampered with after Andrew's death. That would obviously be impossible for Andrew to do. Fact. So, that fits with someone else either killing him or messing up the scene, intentionally or otherwise. Fact. Question is, do I believe Natalie *inadvertently* altered the scene when she rushed to see if Andrew was still alive, or did she realize his suicide meant no life insurance payout?"

Madeline glanced over at Natalie's front door, willing her to emerge.

Since Andrew's insurance policy had been in effect for less than two years, which meant no payout on a suicide, to take his own life would be a cruel blow to Natalie, in addition to leaving her a widow. But maybe he was too grief-stricken over the loss of his son to consider what Natalie would go through upon his death. Maybe he blamed her for Jeremy's illness. Or maybe he knew she was having an affair.

All of those scenarios had plausibility. She tried to put herself in Andrew's shoes, tried to imagine the grief he was feeling due to the loss of his son. Whatever pulled him away from his shop may have set off remembrances that were too hard to bear. Or maybe the text tipped him off that Natalie was having an affair. Maybe she told him herself in a text, the text that had been deleted by someone. Either way, he could've come home and faced his desire to end his own pain, regardless of what it would do to Natalie.

Madeline looked at the clock again, but didn't make a move to start the SUV. She stared out the windshield, coaxing the missing pieces to fall into place. Natalie had admitted to possibly disturbing the scene when she rushed to Andrew's inert body. Was it calculated? How much time elapsed between finding Andrew's body and calling law enforcement? There was no way to know, since no one in the neighborhood was aware of the shot.

Madeline rocked her head back against the headrest. She wondered if her brain was too frazzled to make sense of this case. It didn't help that the questions kept coming at her while the answers remained stubbornly elusive.

Without even wanting to entertain them, more unknowns floated to the top of her head, taunting her, like how did this Mathias guy and Natalie end up together? His license had a Newbury Park address, yet he had been a fill-in delivery driver in the Sheckle neighborhood. Maybe he was just a floating substitute. Maybe he was used as a fill-in wherever needed.

A thought occurred to Madeline out of nowhere, making her heart thump. Andrew's high school yearbooks were from a school in Newbury Park. It was a good possibility that these two men were acquainted, and that would explain the connection to Natalie. Maybe he was a friend from school who came to the memorial service. Or maybe he and Andrew had remained friends all these years, which would also explain the connection to Natalie. Old friends can fall in love, especially after a tragedy. These were certainly possibilities, and benign ones at that. But she wouldn't know anything for sure until Natalie answered her messages.

Madeline's phone chimed, signaling a new text message. She grabbed her phone, anxious to see if it was Natalie. Her short-lived hope was immediately dashed when she saw Mike's message:

Yolanda is on her way back to the ranch. I'm ready when you are.

Madeline started the Audi, giving Natalie's front door one last look before pulling away from the curb.

TWENTY-SEVEN

Mike filled Madeline in on the conversation he'd had with Conrad Adams while Yolanda was being interviewed by the sheriff's detectives. Once the note Yolanda found in the wastebasket in Vanessa Bartholomew's house was thoroughly vetted for authenticity, and assuming the story Yolanda told was validated, Conrad would initiate steps to get Lindsay Bartholomew released from custody and begin the prosecution of Patricia Bartholomew, unless she had a change of heart and gave a full confession. According to the D.A., she had already lawyered up and was keeping her mouth shut.

"Wow, this is quite the turn of events, isn't it?" Madeline remarked as she reclined her seat and propped her bare feet up on the dashboard. The events of the last twenty-four hours had left her head spinning. How quickly things had proceeded from nearly being killed on her front lawn to finding proof that Lindsay had been telling the truth about the note she left for Nick.

As if reading her thoughts, Mike provided a sharp pin to burst her bubble.

"One sticking point of Lindsay's note is when it was actually written. Patricia's lawyers will try to make mincemeat of it in court. Conrad is anticipating all kinds of theatrics on that subject. They will insist it was written after the fact, in collusion with Yolanda."

"Oh boy. I'm glad we're not on that end of the justice spectrum," Madeline said, a good deal of her sense of accomplishment evaporating in a tired sigh.

"I imagine we'll get dragged into the circus, along with everyone else. The only people who are going to come out on top are the attorneys."

"You know, there is one aspect of this drama we haven't really considered, and that's how Vanessa is going to take all this," Madeline said. "In time, she might have serious doubts about how that note ended up in a wastebasket in her own house. Even if she believes her mom's claim that the note was planted there to incriminate her, Vanessa's still going to have her doubts about Yolanda's involvement."

"It's funny you should say that. I was out in the lobby when mother and daughter were brought in through separate entrances. They didn't exchange words, but Vanessa looked at her mom like she'd been betrayed in the most devastating way."

"Oh, I can imagine! Yikes. Talk about life-altering moments," Madeline said, letting her head fall back against the headrest. "Lindsay writes the note like she was told to, and if Patricia hadn't been on the premises, Nick would've found it and avoided a fatal accident." She turned her head toward Mike, a sad smile on her face.

"I don't know what went through Patricia's mind when she took that note, but it probably *felt* like such a benign act, and she may have been just as shocked by the outcome as everyone else. I mean, how likely is death by tractor, anyway? The whole thing is so surreal."

"I agree, but tractor accidents are more common than you think. Most of them aren't fatal, though. What I find really bizarre is how we got involved in this case," Mike said, regretting the words as soon as they left his tongue. Madeline's head swiveled around to look at him, but she surprised him by not taking offense.

"Speaking of bizarre cases…" She proceeded to fill Mike in on what she's learned from Natalie Sheckle's neighbors.

"Hmm…that is an interesting coincidence," Mike agreed, though he really didn't put a lot of stock in what she'd learned. Without malice, he dissected everything she had said, point by point.

He agreed it was interesting that the man Madeline had seen kissing Natalie on her front walk was the same guy who had damaged the Smalls' package. But it was probably just a coincidence that the delivery guy happened to live in Newbury Park, where Andrew went to high school. Those leads would be worth investigating, especially since they didn't have anything else to go on.

After having her speculations discounted, Madeline knew Mike was right; at that juncture, all they had were ifs and maybes.

She took out her phone and debated whether or not to call Natalie again.

She hit call and listened to Natalie's recorded greeting while deciding if she should leave a message or just hang up. Either way, Natalie would know she called, so she left a quick message asking Natalie to call her, no matter how late.

"You're going to obsess over this, aren't you?" Mike asked, his tone more probative than critical.

"I already am." Madeline studied her partner's profile while she struggled with her doubts.

"Do you want to drive by her place, *one last time* to put an end to all this sleuthing stuff for the day, after we grab a bite to eat?" he asked, making his point perfectly clear.

"Yes, I would definitely feel better if we just had a look around," she replied, expanding on his offer of a drive-by.

Mike raised his brows, but held his tongue.

"Okay, pick a place that has good burgers. I can't remember feeling this hungry. Must be all the excitement of the last twenty-four hours," he said.

"Feels like the longest day of my life," Madeline agreed as she got busy on her phone, looking for a good hamburger joint close by.

***

"Doesn't look like any lights are on," Mike said as he pivoted around on Natalie's front step to look at the neighboring houses. It was only quarter after six, but it looked like everyone was in for the night. A few lights glowed through windows unguarded by blinds or draperies, a stark contrast to what it felt like standing on a cold front walkway in total darkness.

"I don't like the way this feels," Madeline said under her breath.

"The way what feels?" Mike replied warily. His tone grated against Madeline's already frazzled nerves.

"The whole thing. This case. This Mathias dude. Natalie not returning my calls or texts."

Mike said, "C'mon, let's call it a night. We've been through a lot the last couple days and we're both exhausted. Let's go home."

"I'm not ready to leave," Madeline said crossly as she headed down the walkway and disappeared around the garage.

"Where are you going?" Mike asked, clearly losing his patience.

Madeline ignored him as she used her flashlight app to guide her to the gate on the other side of the garage. She reached over and undid the latch, then pushed the gate open. Mike caught it as it swung back at him.

"What are we doing?" he asked in a fierce whisper.

"There's something wrong here," Madeline whispered back. "Think about it," she said as she came to a halt long enough to enlighten him. "I've called and texted Natalie throughout the day, with no response."

"She could be out with friends, or doing any number of things," Mike said with thinning patience.

"All day long, without ever looking at her phone? Sooner or later she's going to get annoyed with me and get in touch just to stop all the notifications."

"What if she's got her phone turned off?"

"Why would she do that? She just hired us to find out about Andrew's death. She seemed desperate to know the truth. It doesn't fit," Madeline said with finality.

"You can't know that for sure. Besides, just because she hired us doesn't mean she's given us permission to snoop around her own house," Mike hissed, setting out after her again as she made her way to the back of the house. Instead of answering him, she came to a stop after they rounded the corner to the backyard. She shined the flashlight on the windows and doors in the master bedroom, but all she could see were the closed blinds.

Undeterred, she moved on to the door leading to the master bathroom. The blinds weren't closed, but the room was dark. The blinds in the dining room/kitchen/family room were twisted closed, but no light showed through them. The bedroom next to it—Jeremy's bedroom—didn't have the blinds drawn, but there wasn't any sign of light coming from there or anywhere else in the house.

The second bathroom window was too high to see into. Madeline passed it in favor of the front bedroom, where Natalie had apparently been sleeping since Andrew's death. The blinds were twisted upwards so no one outside could see in, but they weren't closed.

"Satisfied?" Mike hissed in her ear.

"No. I want to see inside."

"*What*?" Mike yipped angrily as Madeline headed back the way they'd come. "Maddie. Maddie!" he called out, his voice barely above a whisper as he struggled to keep pace with her. He finally caught up with her at the gate.

"You're taking this thing a little too far, don't you think?" he said under his breath. "You're a little strung-out right now. You need to take a break, get a little perspective. Things will seem much different in the morning... Maddie...Maddie, *wait.*"

Madeline had no intention of waiting for him. He understood the depth of her conviction as she stooped down and grabbed the bottom of the garage door with both hands to force it upwards.

"I've got it," he whispered calmly as he bent down to assist her, staring directly into her eyes to let her know he was willing to get arrested for breaking and entering if it really meant that much to her. She backed away while Mike raised the heavy overhead door high enough for her to slip under. Now the moment of truth: would the door to the house be unlocked? If not, they'd have to go out the way they went in, and maybe then she'd listen to reason. Mike hoisted the door high enough for him to slip under it.

"Maddie," he tried again as he caught up with her at the door leading into the house, "you know that our *client* is probably going to freak out—and justifiably so—especially if we walk in and catch her in the middle of something she doesn't want us to see..."

Madeline remained deaf to his warnings. She had purposefully tuned them out because she had recognized the frame of mind she was in, that autopilot aspect of her brain that kicked in whenever extreme danger lurked, like it had the night before in front of her own house. It had taken her a few years to understand the survival instinct ingrained deep inside her, but now she got it. If the limbic part of her brain was screaming "danger," she knew better than to ignore the warning.

Madeline turned the handle and the door gave way. She pushed through, calling out to Natalie, Mike right behind her.

They only had to go as far as the family room to discover what had Madeline's radar squawking.

"Oh, God!" she cried out before flying to Natalie's inert form sprawled out in the hallway between the family room and the bedrooms. Mike had his phone out and was already in contact with 9-1-1. He succinctly gave the dispatcher the reason for his call and Natalie's address when prompted, then queried Madeline for the victim's status.

"She's breathing. There's a pulse, but it's very weak. I can't see any visible signs of violence. Judging by her non-responsive state, I think she may have overdosed."

Mike relayed her assessment to the dispatcher. "County Fire Department is on their way," Mike called out to Madeline as she tried to get Natalie into an upright position. Mike gave her a hand after he ended the call. "Fortunately, the station's not far from here. They should be here any minute."

Two minutes later, they could hear the faint wail of sirens in the distance. Mike lumbered quickly to the front door. He ran out to the driveway, spotting the flashing lights as the Fire Department vehicle blared toward him. He flagged them down and got out of the way as two firemen alighted from the truck and strode briskly up the walkway.

Shaking with the adrenaline rush and the fear produced by such a close call, Mike slumped against the exterior wall of the garage, his hands pressed to his head as if to keep it from exploding. He couldn't let himself think of what the outcome would've been if Madeline hadn't trusted her gut instincts. Having had way too much excitement for one twenty-four-hour period, Mike bent over and retched into the low bushes lining the front walk.

TWENTY-EIGHT

"She's gone into a coma," Conrad Adams informed Mike and Madeline as he joined them in the emergency waiting area. This news took all the remaining fortitude right out of both detectives. They looked so dejected and wrung out, Conrad couldn't even fault them for giving him the worst weekend of his career.

"There would've been no chance of saving her if you hadn't gotten there when you did," he added in hopes of giving them something positive they could take away from their ordeal. "All we can do at this point is hope and pray. And let's not forget, sometimes that kind of downtime can be exactly what the mind and body need."

They both knew Conrad was alluding to what happened to Madeline just four months earlier. As much as they wanted the same positive outcome for Natalie, they were afraid to get their hopes invested. If she didn't ever wake up, they may never find out why she had such a heavy dose of barbiturates in her system. They hadn't come across the source of the pills, but solving that mystery would have to wait…wait until Natalie either recovered or passed away.

This last thought caused Madeline's stomach to churn. She hated being in this kind of limbo. There were too many questions and too few answers for anyone's liking.

"Why don't you go home and get some rest? Maybe the universe will stop conspiring against us long enough for us to catch our breath," he said, hoping that wishful thinking would sustain them until they could process all that had happened the last two days. They were all in need of a release of some sort—a few drinks, a good night's sleep, maybe a crying jag—whatever it took to get past the events of the last forty-eight hours.

"You'll let us know if…if anything changes…" Mike said, his arm around Madeline's shoulder as he spoke for both of them.

"Yes, of course."

Mike was ushering Madeline toward the exit when she pulled away and went back to where Conrad stood consulting his phone.

"There's a person of interest the police need to speak to," she said, the intensity in her eyes telegraphing her concern. "I saw him and his car at Natalie's house twice in the last two days. We ran his plate number, so we've got his name and address," she said, using her tone to underscore the significance of their discovery.

"I found out earlier today this same guy was subbing as a delivery driver in the Sheckle's neighborhood around the time of Andrew's death. Think about it," she added when Conrad's blank stare didn't reflect the sense of urgency the situation warranted. "We can put him on the Sheckle's street prior to Andrew being found dead, and he was there again not long before Natalie went into a coma. I can't believe this is just a coincidence."

Madeline finally got the reaction she'd been looking for when Conrad's eyes registered the impact of her words.

"Send me what you've got. I'll make sure he's questioned, if we get to that stage," he assured Madeline as he squeezed her shoulder. "It's too early to jump to any conclusions." If he thought this would comfort her, he was wrong. Feeling dejected and frustrated, she reluctantly let Mike lead her out to the parking lot.

Conrad waited until they passed through the glass exit doors before succumbing to his own exhaustion. He conferred with the policeman on duty before exiting the way he'd come in, through the ambulance portal. His night wasn't over yet, not by a long shot.

Mike walked around the Audi and opened the passenger's door for Madeline. He hated seeing her in such a rattled state; he would've preferred chasing after her on some dubious hunch to seeing her so beleaguered by feelings of failure.

"Where to, partner?" he asked once he was belted in and had the engine running. It took her a few beats, but she finally let him break through her thoughts.

"Home."

"Your home, or my home?"

"Our beach home," she said with a smile so weak Mike almost didn't catch it before it faded.

"Shoreline Drive it is. I hate to say it, but I'm hungry again," he said, not letting on the reason his stomach was empty. Madeline let out a weak laugh, surprising him.

"I could eat," she replied. "When have you ever known me to not be hungry after a near-death experience?"

"I could stop at the deli on the way home, if that works for you…?"

"Fine. Just make sure you come out with a bottle of something good, I don't care what it is," Madeline warned him before turning to look out her window, watching with detachment as the darkened houses of the surrounding neighborhood passed in front of her.

~~~

"We killed that," Mike said as he leaned back against the sofa, stuffed and wrung out, but strangely at peace.

"That was perfect," Madeline agreed as she scraped the last bit of egg salad from the to-go container. In an uncharacteristic show of bad manners, she licked the fork clean and looked as though she were contemplating licking the inside of the carton, too.

"More wine?"

"I'm good," she answered as she slowly leaned back into his raised arm. He caught her neck in the crook of his elbow and pulled her close, kissing the top of her head tenderly.

"Well…I wonder how we're going to top today…" he joked, getting a weak laugh from his partner.

"Hopefully, this will be the day that tops 'em all," she said as she unwound his arm and got to her feet.

"Where are you going? I'll take care of all this," Mike protested as he tried to get up as nimbly as she had. It didn't come off nearly as graceful.

"Stay where you are—I'm just getting some water."

Mike wanted to be chivalrous, but his body was betraying him. He sagged back down on the sofa and let his head loll against the cushion. He would've fallen asleep like that if Madeline hadn't shocked him to alertness with an ice-cold glass against his arm.

"Arrrggg!" he growled before catching himself. He couldn't decide if Madeline's ornery smile was a good thing or a bad thing.

"Here—you need to hydrate," she said, offloading the glass to him as she sat back down beside him. "So, ready for the recap?"

"What are you talking about?"

"If we don't process everything that's happened today, we'll both wake up in the middle of the night stewing over it."

"Can't do it. I'm too pooped. You go ahead," he said, folding his hands demurely over his midsection. Though he was trying very hard to look and sound alert, Madeline could tell his eyes were struggling to stay open. She let out a sigh, then decided to carry on without her partner's input.

Lindsay's case: that was a monumental turn of events, though it was hard to know at this juncture how the pieces were going to lie when it was all sorted out. In any event, it was safe to say they had performed their task; what the legal system made of their discovery was out of their hands.

She put a check in the win column and moved on to the Sheckle case.

That one was more complicated. If Natalie remained in a coma, who knew what would happen? They would just have to play it by ear. She had given Conrad the license number of Tischler's car. She would summarize her conversation with the Smalls and pass that along tomorrow.

Because there were more questions now than when they started the case, Madeline couldn't check off that box yet.

"Hey, I thought you were going to do a recap," Mike said, breaking into her thoughts.

"I just did."

"I didn't hear anything."

"You didn't want to participate, remember?"

"I didn't say that. I just didn't want to have to contribute, that's all."

"Okay, here's the short version: we did our jobs, but the fate of our clients is still uncertain."

"Hmm…that's disappointing, isn't it? I mean all that sleuthing and we get is bupkis."

Madeline let out a breathy snort. *Bupkis, indeed.* She pulled away from him and stood up.

"Where're you going?" Mike asked as he sat up straighter.

"I'm going to get ready for bed. I'm done for the day," she called out as she disappeared from view. A minute later, he heard the shower water running.

A shower sounded like a good idea. Joining her would save him the trouble of having to run it himself. It would also be a lovely way to end a grueling day. With all the effort he could summon, he pushed himself off the sofa and lumbered in the direction of the bathroom, the sound of the water hitting the shower door calling him with its soothing patter.

For the second day in a row, Madeline was the first one to tackle the morning. She'd managed to get fully dressed and ready for the day without rousing Mike from a dead sleep. She was already at work on her computer when he wandered into the kitchen area, idly running his hands through his hair as he blinked at the too-bright morning glare.

"Did you sleep?" he asked as he took his coffee over to where she was seated on the sofa.

"I did," she replied, not taking her eyes or her mind away from her task.

He sat down next to her and sipped his coffee, a mistake that left him with burnt taste buds. He didn't feel nearly as refreshed as his partner looked. Even though they were the same age, Madeline's remarkable ability to spring back to her glowing, energetic self after all she'd been through the last two days hurt his pride and made him wonder if she were really human, and not some alien or supernatural spirit. A lady vampire, perhaps.

"What are you smiling about?" she asked with a raised eyebrow, her fingers continuing to tap out words as she gave him a sideways glance.

How did she know I was smiling? Mike wondered, concluding she must be a witch.

"Nothing. Just wondering how you manage to look so good after all that happened over the weekend," Mike fibbed with a straight face. This answer earned him Madeline's full attention. Her serious expression softened into an amused smile. She reviewed what she'd written and hit "send."

"I'd like to get to the office as soon as you're ready," she said as she stood up and took her computer over to the dining table. "Seeing as your car's still at my place, we'll have to go in together."

Mike drew in a long, strained breath, consciously holding his tongue until the appropriate response occurred to him. He knew any attempt he made at looking out for her wellbeing would be viewed negatively, like he was trying to exercise control over her. Suggesting she might want to lay low for a bit was out of the question. Stalling was his only palatable choice.

"Okay, I'll make some breakfast and take a shower. I kind of wanted to see if there was any surf," he said as he got up and went over to the big picture window that faced south toward the Pacific.

"Well, in that case," Madeline said after consulting her watch, "I can either take you to get your car at my place, or you can get a lift over there later. But don't forget—we need to be at the airport around ten, at the latest." The expression on Mike's face when he swung around to look at her gave away the fact that he'd forgotten all about their plan of going to Sacramento.

"You don't have to come with me," Madeline said, her tone and knee-jerk reaction betraying her agitation as she put her computer to sleep and stowed it in its bag.

"Don't be ridiculous. Of course I'm going with you," Mike answered in a huff. "If you really think it's the right thing to be doing now."

"What's that supposed to mean?" Madeline asked defensively, hands on her hips as she challenged him to say the wrong thing. Though she had elected to put last night out of her mind in favor of taking care of the things she could, her emotions were definitely frayed and lurking just below the surface. She didn't need the person she depended on the most questioning her judgment.

Mike hung his head and let out a frustrated sigh. "I'm not trying to tell you what to do, and I'm not saying that you aren't capable of dealing with ten times more than anyone else. I was just suggesting maybe we should give ourselves a chance to process our two cases, both of which had plenty of action yesterday." Mike's words and plaintive tone instantly deflated Madeline's righteous indignation.

"I'm sorry. I guess I'm still in combat mode."

"It's okay. Nothing to apologize for." Mike went over and gave her the first hug of the day. "And if you're really keen on going to see Ridley's new benefactor, then of course I want to go with you."

"It was your brilliant idea, remember?"

"Yeah, I do. It seemed a lot more brilliant yesterday, for some reason," he said with a smile before he pulled her to him and kissed her forehead. She met his lips with hers briefly before snapping back to practical matters.

"How long will it take you to get ready?"

"I'll be ready in a jiff," Mike said before downing the rest of his coffee as he walked to the kitchen. He grabbed a banana, which he peeled and ate as he wandered back to the bedroom.

Madeline watched his retreating figure with a sense of profound love, a love that had gone through many phases over the twenty-five years they'd known each other. It had become the kind of love she'd given up finding, yet it had been there for her all along. They both just needed to grow into it, was all.

Mike walked back into the main room as he buttoned his shirt, nudging Madeline out of her pleasant daydream. She grabbed her computer bag and tote, then walked through the door Mike gallantly held open for her.

Another challenging day, she thought as she drew in a deep breath. This was the kind of moment she would want to hang on to forever: posed on the brink of discovery, heading into uncharted territory with the man she loved and trusted most in this world.

TWENTY-NINE

Mike and Madeline had the office to themselves for half an hour before the staff got there, just long enough to get their heads around what they had accomplished on their two cases and what they needed to focus on next. Madeline was taking the contents out of the box Natalie Sheckle had given them, her heart heavy as she wondered if their client would ever regain consciousness.

Samir broke through her solemn thoughts with a cheerful "Good morning."

"Hi, Samir," Madeline replied, glad to see his smiling face. "Go ahead and put your stuff in my office, then we'll give you an update."

"It was a busy weekend," Mike added with a meaningful look. Samir caught the inference and hurried to drop his backpack on a chair across from Madeline's desk.

"Good morning," Lauren said as she popped her head around the doorjamb. Madeline returned her greeting and motioned for her to come in. Jessica and Sydney called out their greetings, smiles mixed with curious glances as they went to their desks to begin another busy week.

"Close the door, please," Madeline said, earning a concerned look from Lauren. Madeline conveyed to Mike with a quick flash of her eyes that they would need to be careful about what they disclosed in front of her. After her own brush with death and Madeline's close call four months earlier, the less Lauren knew about Madeline's attack Saturday night, the better.

"Have a seat while we fill you both in on our two current cases," Mike said as he rested against the edge of the conference table, his back to the two case boards.

"Obviously, this doesn't pertain to you, Lauren, but we still want you to have a sense of what's going on with this side of the business," Madeline said.

"Thanks. I appreciate that."

"So…we had a huge breakthrough on the Bartholomew case." Mike got up and pointed to the photo of the note Yolanda Cisneros had surrendered to them. "It appears that Bartholomew's ex-wife had been on the ranch when the accident occurred. Apparently, she was there often, without Lindsay's knowledge. She took the note that warned Nick the tractor was unsafe to use. Madeline discovered a frame in the surveillance footage that showed the first Mrs. Bartholomew sitting in the passenger's seat of her daughter's vehicle two days before Nick had his last tractor ride. There was no footage of her leaving before Nick's accident, which meant she was still on that side of the ranch when the accident occurred. When we confronted the housekeeper, she confessed to knowing that the ex was a frequent visitor to the ranch."

"She's also the one who produced the note Lindsay had left for Nick," Madeline added.

"How did she get it?" Samir asked, his eyes wide with amazement.

"She came across it in the daughter's house while she was emptying a wastebasket," Mike supplied.

"Wow, that's a game changer," Lauren said.

"Yes, it is," Madeline agreed. "Without that note, it would be next to impossible to prove Lindsay's innocence."

"So, will Lindsay get released from prison now?" Samir asked.

"We hope so, but that part is out of our hands. It'll probably take longer than it should, but hopefully she'll get out and be reunited with her daughter soon," Mike said.

"Awesome!" Lauren said, always pleased when justice was achieved.

"Unfortunately, we don't have good news regarding the Sheckle case," Madeline warned, wiping the smile off Lauren's face.

"I don't really know anything about that case," she said.

"The client doesn't believe her husband committed suicide. She thinks he was murdered," Samir informed her.

"And it's gotten more complicated than that," Mike interjected. "The wife is now in a coma after apparently ingesting a large dose of barbiturates." Both assistants groaned in unison at the tragic news.

"So, there you have it," Madeline said as she pushed away from the wall, calling her troops to action.

"All right," Lauren said as she and Samir stood up slowly, processing what they'd just learned. "Thanks for including me in the huddle. I appreciate knowing what you guys are up to."

"Well, you're an important part of the team, even if you don't work this side of the business anymore," Mike said.

"We're flying up to Sacramento soon, but we'll be back mid-afternoon. We can go over the event pipeline when we get back," Madeline said as she walked with Lauren to the door.

"Sounds good. I'd like to get your opinion on something before I place the order."

"You got it." Madeline closed the door and leaned against it for a moment before parking herself on the table corner nearest to Samir. "I don't want Lauren to know about this," she said, her eyes locked on his. "And I'm only telling you about this because you saved my life during the Cavanaugh investigation."

Samir's normally sunny expression clouded over with concern. He nodded his understanding, his lips pursed. Madeline stood and motioned for him to take a seat before she got right to the point.

"Someone pulled a knife on me on my front lawn Saturday evening." The horrified look on Samir's face prompted her to put his mind at rest quickly. "I was lucky. I managed to fend him off. I wasn't hurt, but it made me realize that my ex-husband still has it out for me."

"He was the one who attacked you?" Samir asked incredulously.

"No, it was someone else, but I feel pretty sure he was behind it."

Samir fell back against the chair, his mouth hanging open in shock, his gaze averted while he assimilated the implications of this close call.

"You think he'll try it again, is that why you're telling me?" he asked as he leaned forward expectantly. "Do you need me to be your bodyguard?" Samir's suggestion made her smile, in spite of the circumstances.

"I'll never let her out of my sight," Mike assured him. "We just want you to be vigilant—extra vigilant."

"We'd like you to keep an eye on the girls, walk them out when they leave at night. Maybe arrive a little early in the morning and wait for them in the parking lot."

"Just be extra cautious and aware right now," Mike added.

"Sure. I will," Samir said as his mind geared up for this new duty.

"The reason we're going up to Sacramento has to do with Steven and his current liberties." It was a vague description of their mission, but Madeline didn't feel the need to elaborate.

"Let me know if there's anything you need me to do while you're gone," Samir offered.

"You can help us process everything we learned this weekend," Madeline said as she went over to the box containing Andrew Sheckle's memorabilia.

"Oh, that reminds me—there's a person of interest we'd like to learn more about," she added as she turned to Mike, nudging his memory of the events that had taken place prior to finding Natalie unconscious.

Mike gave Samir a quick rundown on what they had discovered prior to finding Natalie comatose, starting with what Madeline had glimpsed on the front walk Saturday morning.

Madeline listened as she continued digging through Andrew's memorabilia, setting aside everything until she came to Andrew's high school yearbooks at the bottom of the box. Samir got up and grabbed a notepad from the center of the table, readying himself to take notes.

"Despite earlier reservations," Madeline said, "I believe it's no coincidence that Andrew Sheckle went to high school in the same town where the guy in the muscle car lives," she said as she held up a yearbook for Mike to see. Newbury Park was a fairly small community, by Southern California standards.

"Probably not," Mike conceded, coming to peer over Madeline's shoulder as she scanned the first page she'd flipped to. "He could be an old friend of Andrew's. That would explain why he's spending time with Natalie now that Andrew's gone. Even if she hadn't known him prior to Andrew's death, they may have met at the memorial service."

"I don't remember seeing his name in Andrew's contacts," she mused as she flipped through the pages looking for last names beginning with S. No Sheckle. She flipped ahead to the Juniors' section, her finger gliding through the photographs. Taking the cue, Mike reached for Andrew's cell phone to double-check. He scrolled through the all the contacts without coming across either first or last name.

"Mathias Tischler, right here," she proclaimed triumphantly as she handed the yearbook to Mike. Samir got up and came to take a look while Madeline's mind whirred. Andrew and Mathias Tischler had been juniors together in 1997 at Lincoln High School in Newbury Park. Now maybe they were getting somewhere.

"No question, this is the same guy," Mike agreed. "Okay, so that proves they both went to the same school at the same time. We still don't know for sure if they knew each other. Let's see if this Tischler guy wrote anything personal in Andrew's book." Samir took the yearbook from 1996 and went to sit back down at his provisional desk.

Mike flipped to the front and began scanning the messages left by Andrew's fellow students while Madeline grabbed another yearbook, the one with 1998 on the cover. She flipped through the pages until she found Andrew's name near the bottom. She had to turn to the next page to find Mathias Tischler's. Eerily, and without ambiguity, Tischler's photo had been completely blacked out with an ink pen, to the point that the page had become indented. If that didn't say hate, nothing did.

"Check this out," she said, handing the book to Mike.

"Wow. That's pretty telling."

"I'll say. Samir, see what you can do with the inscriptions in these yearbooks. Hopefully, you can find last names to put with these first names. Then you can start trolling social media for Lincoln High alumni. See if you can find anyone who has stayed in touch with either Andrew Sheckle or Mathias Tischler."

"Will do," Samir said as he got up to gather all the yearbooks.

"Here's Andrew's phone too," Mike said as he handed it over. "If you can find any of his high school friends in his contacts, that would be your best bet."

"I'm on it," Samir assured him, his smile so full of team spirit, Madeline could barely suppress a laugh. He was fast becoming one of her favorite people.

But even Samir's good nature couldn't keep her mood up for long. There was a possible killer in the wind, one who may have pulled off a second murder dressed as a suicide if she hadn't chanced upon seeing him at the Sheckle's front door. Before she got too invested in this theory, she needed to run the scenario backwards to see if it had any stumbling blocks.

Even if Andrew and Tischler hadn't been in contact since high school, Tischler could've discovered where Andrew lived when delivering a package to him or a neighbor. They could contact the delivery company to find out the exact dates Tischler had been subbing.

She went to her laptop to pull up the screenshot she'd taken of Tischler's driver's license and printed it. She retrieved it from the printer in her office and brought it back to the conference room to tack on the Sheckle board.

"Are you keeping an eye on the time?" Mike asked.

"Yes, it looks like we need to leave pretty soon," Madeline replied as her eyes traveled from Tischler's image to Andrew's and back again.

"If you do locate anyone from Andrew Sheckle's or Mathias Tischler's past, see if you can find out if they knew each other," Madeline added.

"Right. You want to know why he's hanging around Andrew's widow."

"Exactly. Plus anything else you can learn about him. I really don't like the fact that the last time I saw Natalie upright, she was with this guy." Turning to Mike, "I guess we need to get going," she said, resignation in her voice.

Mike could understand why she'd have reservations about the dubious mission they were about to embark on, but he was not going to be the one to suggest they call it off. He watched her gather up her things, then let her lead the way, exchanging a look of solidarity with Samir, who seemed to be picking up on the fact that Mike was more concerned about Madeline's safety than he was letting on.

"Send us anything you find out about Tischler," he said before exiting the conference room.

"You got it," Samir called out agreeably before succumbing to worry. That Ridley guy was about as cold and calculating as Ted Bundy. It didn't ease his mind any to realize Madeline probably wouldn't have real peace of mind until the scumbag was dead.

THIRTY

Boarding for their flight had just been announced when Madeline's phone buzzed. She looked at the caller ID as she and Mike ambled toward the line of fellow travelers bound for Sacramento.

"It's Slovitch," she said to Mike as she dropped behind to take the call. "John, hi." She signaled to Mike to hold on a moment as she moved to a spot that was a little quieter. When Mike joined her, she put the call on speaker so they could both hear what the detective had to say.

"Looks like trouble's been following you around again," he said.

"I'm going to guess you heard about the close call Saturday night."

"Yep, I did. The case landed on my desk, naturally."

Mike raised his brows to telegraph their need to speed things up or the plane would leave without them. Madeline's unspoken reply said he needed to be patient.

"Do you need anything from me? Mike and I are just about to board a flight."

"Just wanted to give you some good news. Two hairs were found inside the balaclava, presumably belonging to your assailant." This bulletin left Madeline and Mike momentarily speechless. "Are you still there?"

"Yes," Madeline hurried to reassure him. "We're here, just a little surprised that we got lucky."

"Lucky twice, by what I see from the report."

Mike motioned to Madeline with a wag of his head before heading back to the gate and the awaiting attendant.

"Yes, it seems so," Madeline agreed as she took the call off speaker and set out after her partner at a slower pace. "When do you expect to get the hair analysis back?"

"I can't say for sure. I put a rush on it."

"Thanks, John. I can't tell you how much better that makes me feel."

"Well, good. I'm glad. Now, catch your flight. I'll be in touch."

The cramped commuter plane ferrying them from Santa Barbara to Sacramento was definitely a step down from their last air travel experience. Conversation was not worth the effort of competing with the engines to be heard. Mike occupied the forty-five minutes of flight time by checking his messages and getting caught up with world events, which didn't serve to improve his mood any.

He was trying to be open-minded and Zenlike in his expectations of what this trip would yield, if anything. His gut feeling was this could be a complete waste of time and money, even if they were lucky enough to find Ms. Strong-Hartmann at her office.

Uncharacteristically for Madeline, instead of wringing the most productivity out of every second, she sat with her arms crossed, staring out the window or at the back of the headrest in front of her for the duration of the flight. Mike left her to her thoughts, knowing that when she was pensive like that, it was better to just let her think. He knew more than anyone how many unknowns she had vying for her attention.

Once they were in a taxi headed for the prestigious Plaza Tower on 9th Street in downtown Sacramento, Madeline became hyper-alert, her eyes roving from side to side as she took the measure of California's capitol city. She had only passed through there once on the way to Tahoe, and that had been many years earlier.

The first thing that struck her as they came in for the landing was how small the state's capitol seemed. Considering how much went on there, it didn't come across as a major hub of government activity, and certainly not as hectic and overbuilt as Los Angeles or San Francisco. The buildings grew taller and grander as their taxi turned onto 9th and headed into the heart of the business district.

The folly of what she had embarked on hit her as she stepped onto the sidewalk in front of Plaza Tower. Looking upward to take in its twenty-six floors gave her momentary vertigo, which mixed badly with her anxiety and almost made her get back in the cab.

"You okay?" Mike asked as he came up next to her. Madeline drew in a deep breath and let it out in a gush.

"Yes. I'm fine," she bluffed, giving him a breezy smile that didn't fool him for a second.

"Well…shall we?" he asked, his outstretched hand pointing the way.

Once inside, they found the bank of elevators in a gleaming marble-tiled corridor. Madeline kept her eyes on the contrasting shapes and colors of the geometric flooring as she silently rehearsed her spiel. She reminded herself that the sole purpose behind this extravagant errand was to give Steven's benefactor a word of warning. She knew from her own experience with the man how wonderful he could be when everything was going his way. What she wanted—needed—to impart was how quickly that could change when things didn't.

Maybe she'll never see that side of him, Madeline argued. With the kind of wealth Ms. Strong-Hartmann enjoyed, Steven might never have the need to betray this woman's trust the way he had with her.

A sharp ding signaled the arrival of an elevator car behind them. The ride to the twenty-fifth floor went quickly, cutting her inner debate short. They stepped out into the corridor, directly in front of Sarah Strong-Hartmann's office. Mike gave Madeline a reassuring smile as he held open the thick glass door for her to enter. She approached the young woman at the reception desk, her eyes making a quick assessment of the minimally furnished yet refined space. From where they were standing, they had a glimpse at the impressive view through the doorway of the office on the other side of an intersecting hallway.

"Hello," Madeline began with a congenial smile for the receptionist's benefit. "We're hoping to have word with Ms. Strong-Hartmann." The smile she and Mike had been greeted with dissolved into a wary, tight-lipped barrier.

"Do you have an appointment?" the receptionist asked with a raised brow to underscore her doubtful tone.

"No, we don't. We were just hoping she could give us a few minutes of her time. We understand how busy she must be, but it's very important we speak with her regarding a personal matter."

This last remark was met with a puzzled and alarmed frown.

"We feel what we have to tell her is important enough for us to fly up here from Santa Barbara to meet with her face to face," Mike offered in hopes of gaining the gatekeeper's assistance. "Could you please just check with Ms. Strong-Hartmann to find out if she'll see us? We promise we're not here to sell her anything or get a donation out of her."

The receptionist found it more difficult to take such a hard line against Mike's persuasive appeal, especially when he sweetened it with one of his slightly flirtatious smiles. Madeline fought to keep a straight face as the young woman blushed from her neck up to her hairline.

"I will ask, but I can't promise she'll see you. Her schedule is just packed today."

"Thank you. We appreciate that," Mike said as Madeline's eyes took in the completely empty waiting area.

"Your names?"

Mike deferred the question to Madeline.

"Please tell her that the second Missus Steven Ridley and her partner would like to speak with her about an urgent matter," Madeline said, noting the look of recognition on the receptionist's face. She rose up out of her seat as though being levitated by an unseen force, her eyes roving skeptically from one visitor's face to the other.

"I'll let her know you're here."

Mike and Madeline strained to hear what was taking place just out of their line of sight. They didn't have to wait long to see the effects of their opening gambit. As the receptionist moved to the right and turned their direction, Steven's new champion came into their line of sight as she rose out of her seat and leaned to the side to take a look at them. After speaking to her employee in hushed tones, she moved from behind the desk and headed their way.

The look on Sarah's face was neither hostile nor congenial as she came out into the reception area. Her intense appraisal of the visitors made it clear to them this was not a welcome interruption of her busy day.

"I can spare five minutes," she said after Madeline introduced herself and her partner.

"We appreciate that," Madeline said as Sarah turned on her heels and led them to a conference room to the right of her office, out of sight and earshot of the front desk.

The short walk gave Madeline a few moments to process her initial reaction to Steven's latest champion. She was a little more care-worn than the photos she'd seen of her online. Most likely, her various civic-minded and charity works were of greater importance to her than her looks. Her clothes looked expensive though dull. Taking into account the heeled shoes, Madeline put her height about a couple inches short of her own five-foot-seven. Sarah's expertly highlighted brown hair fell past her shoulders in a fashionable cut, though Madeline guessed she was in need of essential nutrients. When she turned to face them, her expression was hard and flat, her gray-blue eyes narrowed warily.

"What is it you traveled all that distance to tell me?" she prompted as she folded her arms in front of her. "I already know about what landed Steven in prison, so if you've come to enlighten me about that, I'm afraid you've wasted your time coming here."

Madeline glanced at the chairs they had not been invited to sit in before responding to Ms. Strong-Hartmann's opening salvo. She hadn't expected this to be an easy sell. Instead of being deterred or put off by Sarah's open hostility, she remained calm and focused.

"To be honest, I never felt compelled to share insights about my former husband until I was attacked by a knife-wielding assailant Saturday night." Madeline saw a flicker of uneasiness flash across Sarah's features before they hardened again.

"You have evidence Steven had something to do with your attack...?" she countered cynically.

"The link to Steven hasn't been proven...yet."

"You have my sympathies for your misfortune. Is that all you wanted to tell me?" Sarah challenged her with raised brows.

"I understand why you'd be leery about taking the word of the ex-spouse of the new man in your life. And really, I came here for my own benefit. I wouldn't have been able to forgive myself for not at least warning you of Steven's...darker side."

"You are quite presumptuous, coming here like this, making assumptions about my relationship with your former husband."

"I can certainly understand why you would resent my interference. Ordinarily, I would never do something like this. But Steven Ridley is a shape-shifting parasite. He has an uncanny talent for projecting exactly what someone wants to see in him. Believe me, I was happily fooled for twelve years—until he needed a wealthy woman by his side."

The air between the threesome was charged with animosity as Steven's new advocate digested this intrusion into her personal life.

"I consider myself warned," Sarah replied in a hollow tone of voice, not giving Madeline a speck of encouragement. "Now, I really must ask you to leave," she said as she reached for the door handle.

"I didn't come here because I still have an axe to grind with my ex-husband, though I don't believe he should've been let out of prison early, no matter what good deeds he did while he was there. And I didn't come here because I was under the impression you can't take care of yourself. I made this journey because I know my ex-husband better than anyone. You will be fine as long as you don't work at cross purposes, or he doesn't set his sights on winning a bigger prize, or if you don't deny him what he wants out of you."

"Are you finished?"

"Not quite. You're obviously an intelligent woman of means. I trust that you protect what you have from self-serving snakes like my ex-husband. I will also consider that I've done my due diligence. I only wanted to give you a different version of whatever Steven told you about the reason he was incarcerated. For the record, when Steven ran into financial problems, he had me drugged and raped so he could blackmail me into a quick divorce, so he could then marry a rich heiress. When that didn't work, he released the video of my rape on the Internet, after which I was kidnapped at knife-point, then bound and left to die in our wine cellar."

Madeline walked right passed Sarah and through the now open door, stopping over the threshold for one more parting shot. "I'm guessing Steven failed to mention how he managed to swindle his *first* wife out of most of her late-husband's estate. If he has, ask him about it. Better yet, hire someone to look into it for you. I think you'll find her story quite eye-opening and compelling."

After a tense stare-down between Madeline and Steven's latest conquest lasting all of ten seconds, the detectives headed to the exit. As they stood waiting for the elevator, Sarah Strong-Hartmann appeared in her hallway, arms crossed, her mouth a hard line of disapproval as she glared at Madeline.

The *ding* announcing the arrival of their escape hatch seemed to break the flow of negative energy emanating in their direction. When Madeline turned around to face the closing elevator doors, she saw Sarah's glare had shifted to a concerned inward gaze.

Maybe this mercy mission hasn't been a complete failure after all, Madeline mused. If even one grain of doubt had worked its way past Sarah's pride and Steven's impressive charms, then she felt justified in having invested time and money into this counter-offensive. Other than undermining his reputation in the eyes of those he had impressed enough to facilitate his release from prison, she didn't see any other way to protect herself, short of hiring a full-time bodyguard.

Besides, she thought as she gave Mike a weak smile, *I've already got one of those.*

The question still niggling at her was how far would Steven go to get his revenge? She envisioned a scene in which Sarah told Steven about her visit from his second wife. *Will that fuel his lust for vengeance, or will he play it safe and leave me alone now?* After all the years she'd known him, she still couldn't predict his behavior. He was a predator, capable and cunning, adept at shape-shifting to fit his agenda. As someone had once put it, Steven could be whoever you wanted him to be.

As long as he's getting what he wants, Madeline amended as Mike held the elevator door open for her.

THIRTY-ONE

Madeline found a table in one of the airport's cafés while Mike placed their order at the counter. As she took her tablet and cell phone out of her tote and set up a makeshift office, doubt raised its ugly head, making her wonder why she had been so insistent on making this trip, especially in light of everything else going on. Had she really believed Steven's new champion would take her warning seriously? Would she have, if the tables had been turned?

She pulled her hair back and fashioned it into a loose knot as she tried to tamp down the feeling that she'd been foolish and impulsive, dropping everything to convince a total stranger that Steven was not to be trusted, based entirely on her conviction that he'd been behind Saturday night's attack on her. She hadn't for a moment changed her mind about that, but coming up here to make her case to Steven's ally was not only a miscalculation, it probably put her right back in the bullseye.

While berating herself for acting rashly, her phone vibrated. It was Samir.

"Hi, Samir. What's up?"

"Can you talk right now?"

"Yes, we're at the airport, waiting for our flight back to Santa Barbara. What's going on?"

"I found out some pretty interesting stuff about Mathias Tischler through social media."

"Oh, good. What have you learned?" Madeline asked, looking up at Mike as he took a seat across from her. "It's Samir," she informed him as she put the call on speaker and laid the phone on the table between them. "Tell us what you learned about Tischler."

"In his senior year in high school, a fellow student was allegedly raped at knife point. She named Tischler as her assailant."

"That's quite a bombshell," Madeline remarked, her mind already racing as it tried to calculate how this figured into the current situation with their comatose client. Andrew had been the common denominator between Mathias Tischler and Natalie Sheckle. But what did that mean, exactly? Had Andrew introduced them? Had he and Mathias stayed in touch? That didn't seem likely, considering Tischler's photo had been blacked out in Andrew's yearbook.

"Who told you this?"

"I got the same story from two different sources, both fellow students in the same graduating class as Andrew and Tischler. Stephanie Caso and Becky Williams. They both knew Andrew, Mathis and the victim, Clarise Hammons. Neither one of them had a good thing to say about Tischler."

"That doesn't surprise me. So, what happened with the sexual assault allegation? Was Tischler formally charged?"

"According to Stephanie and Becky, he was brought in for questioning. But he had a solid alibi, so it came down to the word of one against two. Unfortunately, since he was a minor at the time, those records are sealed."

"Then we don't know for sure if the accusation against him had merit or not," Mike interjected.

"That's true. Anyway, according to Becky and Stephanie, Clarise had been really roughed up—split lip, scratches and bruises all over her body, especially her thighs. A few superficial cuts on her arms and legs backed up the knife accusation. There was proof that she'd been sexually molested, rather violently," Samir said, sidestepping the graphic details.

"The girls' soccer coach found her out behind the gymnasium. Clarise never went back to that school. The family was so bitter, they left town. Stephanie said they moved to Indiana, but I haven't confirmed that yet. I'll keep digging to see if I can find any other connections to her."

"Did Stephanie or Becky know who Tischler's alibi was?" Mike asked.

"Yeah, this is the best part. According to both women, Andrew Sheckle was Tischler's alibi for that afternoon."

Chills raised the hair on Madeline's arms as she and Mike silently stared into each other's eyes, processing the implications of this new piece of information.

"I'll keep looking for other alumni who can corroborate their claims and have any details to add."

"What do we know about Clarise Hammons?" Madeline asked.

"Becky said she was a straight-A student. Nice girl, kind of shy. She didn't hang out with the wrong crowd, was dedicated to getting good grades. Supposedly loved animals and wanted to be a vet."

"Have either of them reconnected with Clarise online?"

"No. Neither of them heard from her after she left town."

Madeline distinctly remembered getting a bad vibe when she saw Tischler with Natalie on her front porch. And there'd been something telling about the way he handled himself as he got into his car. Too slick by half. He gave off an air of being quite taken with himself. God's gift to women.

"Great work, Samir," Mike congratulated him.

"Yes, excellent job, Samir. You've filled in a lot of holes and given us a quite a bit to work with."

"We should be back to the office by two-thirty or three," Mike added.

"Okay, I'll keep digging," Samir replied, trying to keep his enthusiasm and pride in check.

Madeline ended the call and sat there with her phone in hand as she and Mike just stared at each other for several seconds.

"Good job," Mike said at length.

"That was all Samir," Madeline demurred.

"We wouldn't have any of that if you hadn't been so obsessed about the guy on Natalie's front porch," he reminded her.

Madeline shrugged modestly.

"But that was some pretty good detective work on Samir's part."

"It sure was," Mike agreed, a slow smile spreading across his features.

Madeline sat back against the banquette, her gaze drifting as she reviewed the Sheckle puzzle pieces. "Since Natalie is in a coma and there's no proof that someone else is responsible for the overdose, I don't imagine this case will be getting much scrutiny until Natalie either comes out of the coma or…passes away."

Mike's head seesawed back and forth, conceding that given the circumstances, she was probably right.

"Still, I don't think there's anything to stop us from continuing our investigation…"

Mike responded to this with raised brows and a slow nod of agreement. "How do you want to proceed?"

Madeline thought about this for a moment. "According to Mr. Smalls, Tischler had been subbing in the Sheckle's neighborhood the week Andrew was found dead. We can check with the delivery company to confirm this."

When Madeline became lost in thought, Mike asked, "What are you thinking?"

"I'm just wondering if the delivery route includes the commercial complex on Turnpike."

"You mean where Andrew's shop is?" Madeline nodded. "Oh…so you're wondering if that's how Tischler reconnected with Andrew…? That's definitely a possibility."

"I think we should drop by the shop on our way back to the office," Madeline said as their lunch arrived.

"Good plan. Maybe Tischler's photo will jog Evie's memory."

"Yes…that's what I'm hoping." Madeline had a faraway look in her eyes as she poked around her salad with little interest. "Here's a scenario," she said, her features brightening as she sat back. "Let's say that Andrew and Tischler hadn't had any contact since their high school days. But when Mathias fills in for a vacationing driver, he runs into Andrew while delivering a package to the shop."

Mike nodded as he chewed a bite of his sandwich.

Madeline fell silent for a moment until she found a sequence of events that fit the known facts of Andrew's death. Mike kept devouring his Reuben as he imagined the gears in his partner's head turning, chewing thoughtfully before he offered another possibility.

"If his employee was standing there, Andrew might've been put in an awkward position."

"That's what I'm thinking," Madeline replied, her eyes alert now as the pieces began to fall into a plausible hypothesis. "To get rid of Mathias, Andrew may have given him his cell phone number, thinking it would be much better to deal with this unwelcome reminder of the past somewhere private, away from his business."

"I could see that happening," Mike agreed before taking another sizable bite.

"Andrew was Tischler's alibi, but I'd bet any amount of money that he wouldn't have blacked out Tischler's photo in his yearbook if they had remained chums after that incident."

"Tischler coerced an alibi from Andrew for a crime he really did commit," Mike supplied as he followed the natural progression of that theory. Madeline nodded pensively.

"And whatever qualms Andrew had about giving a false alibi, he managed to move on with his life, putting that lie in the past..."

"Until Tischler shows up at his shop."

"Exactly." Madeline leaned across the table as she continued to theorize. "It's not farfetched to think that Andrew had done a lot of soul searching during his son's illness. That kind of experience will make you question everything about your life, what kind of person you've been, what kind of bad karma you've racked up."

"Yeah, I can vouch for that," Mike agreed. "Been there many times."

"What if Andrew told Tischler that he planned to come clean, admit to the police that he had lied about being with him the day Clarise Hammons was raped?" Madeline fell silent while she envisioned that exchange.

"Tischler texts Andrew while he's at the shop, convinces Andrew to meet him somewhere private—maybe tells him he's going to confess, but wants Andrew to be there with him. Andrew meets Tischler at his house, but Tischler has no plans of coming clean to the police. He conceals a gun in his work uniform, argues and pleads with Andrew from one room to the next, then shoots him in the bedroom, thinking that's far enough away from the street so the shot won't be heard. He wipes the prints off the gun, deletes the text on Andrew's phone, arranges the scene with Andrew's body and the chair and hopes it will pass as a suicide."

"There was no forced entry, no sign that anyone else had been there..." Mike said, picking up the logical thread. "So, then Tischler hops back in his delivery truck and he's out of there, with the perfect cover."

"Exactly. When the neighbors are questioned, they all say they didn't notice anyone around the Sheckle's house at the time of Andrew's death because we tend to overlook people like delivery men and trash collectors, meter readers...

door-to-door evangelists," she said with emphasis. "We're accustomed to seeing these folks in our neighborhoods, so we don't attach any significance to
them. But Mr. Smalls recognized Tischler's photo immediately because of the
confrontation over the damaged package."

She put down the fork she'd been absently holding in favor of her phone.
"So, who do we call? Both Slovitch and Conrad are not especially thrilled with
us right now..."

"No, but Conrad initially brought us the case."

"True." She inhaled a deep breath and placed the call, but hung up before
it could go through. "I think a text is the best method of communication for
now. That way, he can get back to us when it's convenient for him."

"And you won't have your head bitten off if he answered your call while
in the midst of one of his nightmare cases," Mike offered.

"That's right. But I think I'll hold off on that too, for the moment. Let the
dust settle, see what else we can learn first," Madeline said with a smile before
skewering a large bite of salad, her appetite suddenly revived.

"We may be on the brink of closing the second case in two days,"
Mike observed.

Madeline raised her glass of mineral water for a toast.

"Hold that thought," she said as they clinked to that hopeful outcome.

THIRTY-TWO

The first stop after they arrived back in Santa Barbara was The Frame Job. It occurred to Madeline as they approached the storefront how apt the name was in light of Andrew's murder. He'd been framed for his own death, while a suspected rapist and murderer drove off into the sunset, his violent past securely buried. Or so he thought…

Evie was ringing up a sale when Mike and Madeline walked in. They watched as the sole customer exited, then asked if they could speak to her privately.

"We can talk here. Len had a doctor's appointment, so he had to leave early."

Unfortunately for them, because of their need to know if Evie recognized the man in the photo they were about to show her, they also had to be the bearers of bad news. "It still might be better if we go in the back," Mike suggested.

"Whoa, now you're scaring me," Evie said as goosebumps ran up her arms. She motioned with her head to follow her as she led them into the back room. "Okay…what's going on?" She wrapped her arms protectively around herself, bracing for bad news.

"Natalie's in the hospital, in a coma," Madeline told her, reaching for Evie's arm when it looked like her legs were about to give out.

"Oh my God…what happened?" Evie asked, her voice weak from shock. "I need to sit down." She blindly groped around for a stool to sit on. Mike found one under the long work table and set it next to her. Madeline braced her by the left arm as she settled on it. After several seconds of stunned silence, Evie asked for particulars.

"We found her unconscious on the floor in her family room last night," Madeline told her. "She had a high amount of barbiturates in her system."

"*Barbiturates?*" Evie exclaimed weakly. "Natalie would so not take drugs of any kind. She thinks they're poison. She was not happy about all the chemicals the doctors pumped into poor Jeremy. No way would she ever even touch a pharmaceutical. And downers? No way. Where would she even get something like that?"

Mike and Madeline had no answer to offer her. They had their suspicions, but nothing concrete yet.

"So, you don't think Natalie could ever get depressed enough to take an overdose of narcotics…?" Madeline hadn't even finished her question when Evie began adamantly shaking her head.

"Show her the photo," Mike prompted. Madeline took her tablet out of her tote and brought up the photo of Mathias Tischler.

"Can you recall ever seeing this guy in the store? He's about six-feet, slender build."

"He's been identified as being a fill-in driver for PDS." Mike's words acted like magic. Evie's expression immediately turned livid with recognition.

"*That* guy! Yeah. Prick. Yeah, I remember him really well. What a jerk. I had to get Andrew involved because a glass order was delivered in pieces. I heard it rattling as the guy brought it into the store. I called him out on it, but he just shrugged, told me to make a claim for it online and started to walk out of the door."

Evie stopped, her expression frozen as she recalled other pertinent details of that episode.

"That was so weird," she said as she shook her finger at the recollection forming in her mind. "I remember the look on Andrew's face when he came out of the back room. He turned ash white. I didn't know what to make of his reaction until this guy," Evie said, indicating Madeline's tablet, "this *jerk* called out his name, all happy-like."

"But Andrew recognized him," Mike asked for clarification.

"Oh, yeah. It was…*awkward*," Evie said with emphasis.

"Do you recall what Andrew said to him?" Madeline asked.

"No, sorry, I don't."

"The day Andrew died, do you recall him saying anything before he left the shop? Did he mention going to meet someone at his house?"

Evie was already shaking her head before Madeline finished asking her question.

"Sorry, I still don't." Looking from Madeline to Mike, she asked, "Do you think this guy had something to do with Andrew's death?"

"We're just trying to put the pieces together right now," Mike hedged. "But if you happen to see this guy, call us right away." He handed Evie another one of their cards to make sure she had their numbers handy.

"And if you remember anything at all about that day or anything else you feel we should know, please contact us immediately," Madeline added.

"And will you call me if you hear anything about Natalie?"

"Sure," Mike said. "Just write down your cell number for us," he said as he leaned over the work table for a pad of paper and a pen.

"I wonder if they'd let me see her. I wish I knew who to call. I don't really know any of her friends," Evie thought out loud as she scrawled her number and tore off the sheet to give to Mike.

Madeline smiled weakly and gave her shoulder a squeeze.

Evie let out a long sigh as she slipped off the stool. She grabbed her backpack from a cupboard and walked with them into the front of the shop. She turned the OPEN sign around to CLOSED and locked the door on the way out.

"We've got another piece of the puzzle," Mike said as he clicked open the doors of the Audi. Madeline, lost in thought, didn't say anything until they were both buckled in their seats.

"I'd like to go visit Jill Smalls, the Sheckles' neighbor across the street."

"Okay," Mike said as he started the car and backed out, wondering when she was going to clue him in on her plan. They were halfway to Natalie's neighborhood when she put her thoughts into words.

"Mr. Smalls filed a complaint for the damaged package he received. There would've been some kind of a communication trail—an email, I'm hoping."

Mike thought this through, picking up on her line of thinking.

"So, you're wondering if the text Andrew received the day he died was sent by Tischler."

"Right. If he had made a delivery on that street the same day—say before or after he shot Andrew and made it look like a suicide—we might be able to tie those events together, giving us an exact time and date—"

"Placing Tischler at the scene when Andrew met his end," Mike finished.

"Exactly. Let's just hope we find Jill at home."

"That still won't prove anything."

"No, not conclusively," Madeline admitted. "But it will help tie everything together, once we get all the facts assembled. Besides, we know Tischler was sub-bing in this area. So, there's a good chance these two events coincided. If they did, we'll have our opportunity and motive. The means becomes almost irrelevant at this point. If someone has a strong enough motive, they will find the means."

Though there were no cars in front of the Smalls' home, Jill answered the door when they rang the bell.

"Hey," Jill greeted them, surprised by their visit, but happy to be of help if she could. "Come on in." She stepped back to let them through. "I thought I saw you last night, when the fire crew was over at Natalie's place." Madeline nodded sadly. "Is she going to be okay? One of our neighbors said it was a drug overdose, but I didn't believe it," Jill said as they came to a halt in the family room, just off the entry.

"She did have narcotics in her system, but it's unclear at this point whether she took them voluntarily," Madeline said, earning a raised eyebrow from her partner, which she ignored.

A hand flew to Jill's gaping mouth, her eyes wide with shock. "Is she going to be okay?" she asked again as she sagged against the back of a nearby sofa.

"She's in a coma right now," Mike said.

On unsteady legs, Jill moved around to the front of the sofa, where she slowly lowered herself. After a few beats, she motioned for her visitors to join her. Perching on the sofa perpendicular to the one Jill sat on, Madeline got to the point of their visit.

"We're hoping you can help us with our investigation."

"Me? Sure. What can I do?" Jill asked, sitting up straighter as she roused her energy and focus.

"The incident with the damaged monitor that was delivered here…we're hoping to find out exactly what day that happened."

"Okay, sure. Umm…let me think. George might still have something. He took care of it on the phone, but knowing him, he probably made sure he got some sort of written confirmation, like an email he could refer to until the issue was resolved. It's possible he may have not gotten around to deleting it yet." Jill got to her feet and went to the kitchen to grab her cell phone. "I'm going to give him a quick call," she said as she waited for her husband to pick up. When he did, she turned and went back into the kitchen while she explained the situation.

Mike and Madeline waited as patiently as they could, straining to learn the fate of their hunch. After a few more exchanges, Jill returned to the living room.

"He's going to forward the email between him and PDS to me, then I can forward it to you," Jill said.

"That would be great. Thank you," Madeline said with relief as she and Mike got to their feet. "Did he tell you what date that happened?"

"No, but I've got the email right here…" Jill opened the email on her phone and confirmed that the incident date was the same as the date of the original email correspondence. "August tenth."

Heat radiated through Madeline's body as her mind verified their hunch.

"Same date?" Mike asked, his own spine tingling in anticipation of her answer.

"Same date," Madeline confirmed.

"Give me your email address and I'll forward this to you," Jill said, excitement and emotion making her voice quiver. It wasn't every day she got to participate in solving a crime. Madeline spelled it out for her. They waited expectantly until Madeline confirmed receipt of the forwarded email.

"Got it," she announced, giving Jill a big smile of thanks.

"You've been a huge help, Jill. Thank you," Mike said as they made their way toward the front door.

"Will you let me know what you find out, especially about Natalie's condition?"

"We will," Madeline assured her. "Thank you so much for giving us this piece of concrete proof."

Jill stood on the threshold, her arms wrapped tightly around herself. This was not the kind of situation she ever expected to encounter in her seemingly ordinary, peaceful neighborhood.

"We'll be in touch," Mike promised before following Madeline down the front walk.

THIRTY-THREE

They sat parked in front of the Smalls' residence while Madeline reread the forwarded attachment Jill Smalls had provided. She then typed out a detailed email to Conrad. Before sending it, she turned to face Mike.

"Did you send Mr. Smalls' email to Conrad?" Mike asked.

"No, I'm going to hold off for the time being. I need to think something through first."

"Can I help?"

Madeline was too engrossed in her thoughts to answer right away.

"I need another minute," she said, doing a quick search on her phone. "I thought so." She turned back to her partner. "The main distribution center for PDS is just a mile and a half from here. Maybe we can get someone to give us the current whereabouts of our prime suspect." She seemed cheered by the prospect. "And we can verify the time the damaged monitor was delivered to the Smalls' address."

Though Madeline was clearly buoyant due to this lucky break, Mike was feeling a little wrung out. He groaned as he sagged against the seatback. *Where does she get all her energy?* he wondered, hoping there was a drive-thru coffee shop close by.

"Shouldn't this case be in the hands of law enforcement now? Other than scouting for background info, like we just did with Evie and Jill Smalls, we don't really have a role in this drama anymore."

"We most certainly do," she countered. "Natalie hired us to find out the truth about Andrew's death, and she hasn't relieved us of that commitment. Until we line up all the facts in an arrow pointing back to Tischler, our work isn't finished. Besides, so far, there's nothing to suggest foul play as far as Natalie's overdose is concerned."

"*Yet*," Mike reminded her unnecessarily.

"Exactly. So that means we're still on the case. Only now our scope has been expanded to include Natalie's overdose."

Though it was kind of cute to see Madeline get all high and mighty on him, she was cherry picking which facts she wanted to adhere to.

"Do you honestly feel like we're done here?" she asked skeptically. "We haven't really sorted out anything until we can solidly prove Mathias Tischler killed Andrew to keep him from exposing the truth about the rape in high school. If you recall, that's what Natalie hired us to do—find out the truth about Andrew's death."

"All right, okay—we'll play it your way. Just tell me where we're headed," he said as he turned the key in the ignition.

Mike sipped his coffee discreetly in the background as Madeline negotiated with the employee manning the counter at the PDS sorting facility. He could tell the twenty-something was reluctant to disturb her boss, but Madeline managed to get her point across. The employee vanished for a few seconds before returning with an equally harried guy in his early forties. By the look of him, he wasn't sufficiently compensated for the toll his job was taking on him.

"How can I help you?" he asked perfunctorily.

Madeline displayed her P.I. license and asked if there was somewhere they could speak in private, her gaze going to the line of customers who had appeared since her arrival. She glanced at Mike before disappearing into a back room. She returned five minutes later as Mike was depositing his empty coffee cup in the trash bin.

"Were you able to confirm Tischler was the one who delivered the damaged package to the Smalls?"

"Yep," Madeline said as they fell into step.

"How about the time?"

"The Smalls' package was scanned by Tischler at 2:36 on August tenth, which ties in quite nicely with the coroner's report."

"Excellent!" Mike gave her a big smile for her keen instincts. "Did he tell you which route Tischler's working today?" he asked as he held the door open for her.

"Nope."

This didn't really surprise him. Just because they were licensed investigators didn't mean anyone was obligated to share information with them. They weren't law enforcement, after all.

Madeline let Mike ruminate for a moment before dropping the bomb on him. "Tischler isn't with the company anymore."

"Did he quit, or was he fired?"

"He was fired. Failing to show up for his shift was the last straw, on top of all the complaints they'd received about his rude behavior and damaged packages. I suppose the only reason the manager gave me the time of day is because he had his own questions about Tischler's actions. His sudden disappearing act left this facility shorthanded."

"I thought Tischler was a floater," Mike said, unlocking the doors remotely as they approached the Audi.

"He was, in that he rotated from branch to branch. He would fill in during employee vacations and leaves of absence at any particular processing facility in his radius for a particular length of time—usually for a few months—then he'd be sent to the next facility in the rotation."

"I see," Mike said as he closed his door and stuck the key in the ignition. A cloud passed over his features as a thought registered.

"How about his last day on the job?"

"August tenth."

The look on Mike's face was priceless.

"Wow, that's more than a coincidence," he admitted. "Things are really starting to add up against Tischler. Where to now?" Mike asked as he started the engine.

"Nowhere."

"What do you mean?"

Madeline turned in her seat to face him, knowing what she was about to propose would be a hard sell. She wasn't even sure she should trust her instincts or intuition or whatever it was that was making her think such crazy things. If she hadn't eaten at the airport in Sacramento, she might try to blame her irrational thoughts on low blood sugar.

"What's going on?" Mike prompted again.

"I've got this feeling."

"About what?"

Madeline looked around, stalling. "Just hear me out, okay?"

"Okay," Mike relented, already getting tense. "Just answer me one question—are you all right?"

"Of course I'm all right. Why do you ask that?"

"Because you've been going gangbusters since you came back to work—less than a week ago, may I remind you. Don't you think you're pushing yourself too hard?"

"No, not at all. I feel perfectly fine. I had four months of taking it easy. I'm very well-rested and in top form. Don't worry about me," she said, trying not to sound testy.

"And you were also attacked two days ago," Mike said, earning an indignant huff from his partner.

"You don't have to remind me. Anyway, as I was saying…" Madeline's voice trailed off, her original train of thought lost for a moment. When she found it, even she had a hard time justifying what her instincts were telling her.

She drew a deep breath before forging on. "If you were Mathias Tischler, and you had killed Andrew Sheckle to make sure he didn't tell anyone about giving you a phony alibi, why would you romance his widow?"

"Because I'm a sick puppy to start with…?"

"Maybe it started out as something like friendship—on Natalie's part. Maybe without knowing the real history between Andrew and Mathias, she found his company comforting. But she can't really get over Andrew's death. She struggles with the whole idea of him committing suicide and hires us to find out the truth…"

So far, everything Madeline had said seemed logical and plausible. But Mike had the distinct feeling he wasn't going to like what was to follow.

"I think we already established the fact that Tischler wanted to shut Natalie up before we or anyone else discovered what really happened that day. That's why he slipped her a Mickey."

"Yeah…" Mike cautiously agreed with her.

"I want to go back to Natalie's house."

"What for?" The look in Madeline's eyes was making him nervous.

"I want to look for her phone."

"What for?"

"Quit saying that. I obviously have my reasons." Her features hardening with impatience. "I want to see what we can learn from it," she said, her arms crossed in front of her.

"Breaking and entering while it's still light out is much riskier than under the cover of darkness," Mike pointed out.

"We don't have to go through the garage this time. I left one of the doors in the family room unlocked." Mike leveled a quasi-stern look at her. "Just in case we needed to get back in. I see nothing wrong with that. Natalie retained our services, and we're working on her behalf. End of story."

After shaking his head in dismay, Mike turned away and started the engine.

THIRTY-FOUR

With all the windows closed, the air inside Natalie's house was warm and stale. The house was also eerily silent, a stark contrast to the dramatic scene that played out less than twenty-four hours earlier. Madeline motioned for Mike to leave the door open to let some fresh air in as she pulled on a pair of latex gloves, then tossed a pair to him. Like thieves, they moved around silently until they were sure they were all alone.

Despite the warmth, Madeline felt a chill as she surveyed the site where last night's drama unfolded. Furniture had been shoved out of the way to make room for the gurney. Various bits of trash left over from the firemen's efforts to assess Natalie's condition lay scattered on the floor.

Madeline cast her eyes around the open space comprising the kitchen/dining room /family room as she headed for the wing with the smaller bedrooms, while Mike went to check out the living room and the master wing. She made note of the dishes sitting in the kitchen sink. The wine glasses, plates and silverware, along with other items in the house, might hold Tischler's fingerprints, which could tie him to the scene should this become a murder investigation. Though she was curious to see if he had planted a cache of barbiturates to frame Natalie for her own overdose, she wanted to leave any evidence for the crime scene investigators should Natalie die as a result of the overdose.

Once they had ascertained no one else was in the house, Madeline pulled her phone out of her pocket and dialed Natalie's number.

At first, they didn't hear anything except for the ringtone coming from Madeline's own phone. As she walked toward the front bedroom—the room Natalie had moved to after Andrew's death—she heard a faint, intermittent chime. She followed that sound until the call went to voicemail, then redialed the number. This time, she was able to pick up the chime emanating from a handbag hanging from the ladderback chair by the front window.

After ending the call, Madeline dug around for Natalie's phone. When she tapped the button below the screen, a list of recent activity showed up. There were the two calls she'd just made in addition to others. When the screen went dark, she swiped it to bring back on, inadvertently bringing up all of Natalie's apps. Madeline let out a huge sigh of relief. This was going to be easier than she had expected.

"I found Natalie's phone, and it's not password protected," she called out as she made her way back to where Mike was consulting his own phone in the kitchen.

"That's a nicely placed bit of luck." He came up next to where she had pulled out a stool from under the kitchen counter but had yet to take a seat. "What are you checking first?" he inquired, looking over her shoulder.

"I want to see who else called her besides me."

There were a few calls earlier that day from some of her contacts—all female names—most likely due to Natalie not showing up to teach her Pilates classes. She would listen to those messages later, just in case there was anything relevant to Natalie's current condition. At some point, she would need to contact these women to let them know about Natalie's status and see if they could shed any light on her relationship with Mathias Tischler.

She then checked all the other recent activity. It appeared that Natalie was more active with text messages than phone calls. As she suspected, there were several from puzzled clients wondering if something was wrong. Scrolling down farther, she found what she was really looking for.

"Matt," she exclaimed as she flicked through the thread of text messages going back several days, maybe several weeks. "Got to be short for Mathias." She switched tactics by pressing on his name and choosing the "info" option.

"Matt Tischler," she informed Mike triumphantly. "Listen to this." She shivered with distaste. "'Been thinking about you all day. Sorry about what I said to you on the phone this morning. I totally get why you need to find a reason for Andrew's death. I guess I just don't like seeing you so sad. From now on I'll just keep my big mouth shut. You need to grieve in your own way and I want to be there to support you while you go through it. Anyway I understand if you don't want to see me tonight. But I'm here if you need me.' That message was sent by Tischler on Friday at 3:05 pm. I saw Tischler leaving the next morning."

"What did Natalie write back?" Mike asked, sufficiently intrigued as he tried to read over her shoulder.

"'I know it must seem like I can't let go but like you say it's just something I have to work through in my own way. Thanks for understanding. And I do want to see you tonight,'" she read aloud.

"Heart," Mike added as Madeline looked up at him.

"Yuck…this makes my skin crawl. I wonder if this is incriminating enough for Conrad to issue a subpoena," she thought out loud as she went back to his contact info. All Natalie had for him was his name and cell phone number.

"I don't know," Mike said doubtfully. "We've found absolutely nothing to suggest Tischler is responsible for Natalie's overdose."

Madeline sighed heavily, knowing he was right.

"Well, we need to do something. Since we've discovered this in the course of our investigation, I think we might have some latitude, considering our client was drugged and left for dead."

"We have no proof of that," Mike reminded her. "We're in a pretty gray area right now." Madeline scoffed at his sudden adherence to walking the fine legal line. She was usually the stickler for protocol.

"So, what do we do with this?" she asked, wagging Natalie's phone, her stare intense and hard, leaving no doubt what she'd like to do with their discovery.

"What do we do about our client who's hanging on to life by a thread?" she rephrased after Mike shrugged. "Natalie hired us because she believes Andrew was murdered. Now suddenly she's in a coma from a drug overdose, and we're pretty sure who's responsible. We can waste time trying to get a legal opinion about our duty to our client and our responsibility to the law, or we can try to solve this case and turn it over to law enforcement."

"What do you suggest?" he asked gamely. If she was willing to stick their necks out, he had to be one hundred percent on board or not at all.

"I say we send him a text now…"

A couple beats passed before Mike figured out what she was getting at. "You mean as Natalie from her own phone…"

"Yes," Madeline said as she worked out the particulars. "We found Natalie in a coma, but 'Matt' doesn't know that."

"Not unless he was hiding in the bushes when the Fire Department showed up."

"You really think he camped out there all that time?" Madeline asked skeptically. "He'd want to make himself scarce. He had no real reason to suspect anyone would go nosing around her place in the dark of night. Besides, we didn't see his car anywhere on the street."

Mike could've presented another argument, but he had to agree it wasn't likely for a killer to lurk in neighbors' bushes for hours, maybe overnight, just to see how the plan he set in motion played out. It could've been days before anyone discovered Natalie's body.

Mike held her stare, almost afraid to admit he knew where she was going with this scenario.

"You want him to think Natalie is alive and well and what...none the wiser that this 'Matt' dude tried to kill her?"

"We could say something like...'What happened last night? Did I get drunk and pass out? Woke up feeling like death warmed over'...or something to that effect."

Mike pulled out the stool next to her and sat down, pensive but not dismissing her idea outright. "For all we know, Tischler could be in the wind," he said at length.

"Very true. But this may bring him back."

Mike pondered this notion for a moment before voicing his reservations. "If Tischler is the one responsible for Natalie's overdose, why didn't he take her phone, or at least delete his messages?"

"Maybe he thought it would be too suspicious if her phone wasn't with her," Madeline countered. "You don't drug someone to steal their phone. Plus, that would really make her death look like foul play, don't you think? On the face of it, this was a suicide, tragic but understandable after all she's been through."

"Okay, I'll go along with that. But why would he come back now? Wouldn't he just stay gone?"

"I think he'd want to make sure the truth about his past didn't get out. There's no statute of limitations on rape in California if a weapon is used, as was the case with Clarise Hammons. If Natalie died, the investigation into Andrew's death would stop. And as we just learned from the texts, she *had* told Tischler about hiring us. He needed to put a stop to that. He couldn't risk her private investigators digging into Andrew's past, thus exposing the likelihood that Andrew's death wasn't suicide. And if it wasn't suicide, who'd have a motive for staging it?

"Besides," Madeline continued as she got up and paced, "what other reason would Tischler have for killing Natalie, someone he obviously didn't know while Andrew was alive? I think her desire to continue with the investigation is the reason Tischler staged her suicide too."

"How do you think they got involved in the first place?" Mike asked.

"I think he sought her out, being the twisted creep that he is. It's very likely he introduced himself at the memorial service. Maybe he wanted to be certain no one suspected foul play. Maybe he's just a sick bastard who thrives on manipulating people's lives. Who knows?" she replied with an indifferent shrug.

Mike shook his head, not sure what to think or which was the right move at this juncture. Sensing time was getting away from them, Madeline lobbied harder.

"What would be the worst-case scenario in sending Tischler a text pretending Natalie's right as rain? Even if he's already gone to ground, as you suspect, it's no real loss. It also might draw him back. Either way, we're not really forfeiting anything."

Mike inhaled deeply, throwing his head back to let his breath out in a gust of resignation before reluctantly giving his consent.

"Let's write a script, see where it could lead us," he suggested as he got up and went to search Natalie's kitchen drawers for a pen and paper.

"Good idea," Madeline agreed. "Any objections to the opening dialog I came up with?"

"No, that was fine," Mike said as he came back to the other side of the counter and retook his seat. "Let's start there."

Madeline wrote it out and slid the paper towards Mike so they both could see it.

"'Did I get drunk and pass out on you? Woke up with a major hangover.

Hope I didn't make a fool of myself,'" Mike said out loud before adding, "'I can't remember a thing.'"

"Good," Madeline said as she tacked that to the message. "Now, what would Mathias likely say…something to the effect of, 'yeah, kinda' or 'you're funny when you're drunk.' Let's look at their past texts…"

Following the dialog all the way back to when it started, they not only got a feel for their texting style, but they were also able to establish the date they began to communicate, which was only a month after Andrew's death.

"This whole thing is really vile," Mike said, disgusted. "I mean, scamming on the wife of the guy he probably killed to keep his crime under wraps."

"I know, it's beyond coldblooded. It's sociopathic," Madeline agreed. "Okay…where do we want this conversation to go? I think whatever he replies—if he replies—we need to coax him back up here. Like tonight."

"Okay," Mike agreed. "We don't really have anything to lose, I guess."

"No. He'll either lay low or want to finish what he started."

"But what happens if Natalie *does* come out of the coma? Aren't we setting her up for another attack?" Mike worried.

"No, because hopefully we'll be turning over everything we've found out to Conrad, and he can go after him. Ideally, we'll be handing him enough evidence to prove Tischler was involved in Andrew's death and that he drugged Natalie. And sadly, the truth is we don't know if she's going to pull through or not. It could go either way. We've potentially got two murders here, and Conrad's the one who got us involved in this mess in the first place."

"Yeah, you're right," Mike was forced to concede. "At least this gives us a chance to confront him or alert the authorities to his involvement and-or his whereabouts. Okay, let's do it."

"Before we start, I'd like to set up the scene here first. We need to tidy up so he can't see what really went on here last night. Then I'd like to pick up some stuff from my house."

"What kind of stuff?"

"I have that long, dark wig that's very similar to Natalie's hair. If I pull it back in a ponytail and wear my black yoga pants and top, I could pass as her from a distance. Even closer if I had my back turned."

"Now, wait a minute," Mike protested, "we never talked about you masquerading as the intended victim."

"I know, but think about it. If we get Tischler's attention, he will probably be a little leery. I can turn a couple lights on low in the kitchen and living room, with the blinds down but opened a little, just to give him the visual that Natalie is in fact alive and well. Once I let him in—"

"Yes...? What do we do then, fearless leader?"

"We'll subdue him and make him talk."

Mike let out a dismissive sound that was part snort, part throat-clearing, and one-hundred-percent disparaging. Madeline chose to ignore it and plowed on.

"We can hold him until we have a chance to fill Conrad in on what Samir learned about the rape of that girl in high school, about Andrew providing an alibi for Tischler, how Tischler and Andrew met again after all these years at the shop, and we can put him right here, on this street, on the date and time Andrew was shot. That's enough to get him brought in for questioning. After that, it's up to law enforcement," Madeline finished, clearly sold on her own vision of how this sting operation would go down.

"Oh, lordy..." Mike groaned. "You know it's just our speculation that the alibi Andrew gave Tischler was false," he said in a last attempt at being devil's advocate.

"It does fit, and without an overuse of imagination," Madeline countered.

After a moment of pained reflection, he nodded his consent. "I guess we're not really forfeiting anything. Go ahead. Send the first text."

"No, not until you pick up those things from my house."

"Why am *I* going to get them? I won't even know where to look."

"Because I don't really want to go there by myself, not after what happened the other night—"

"Oh...right," Mike groaned, running a hand down his face.

"...and I think one of us needs to stay here. Call me when you get there and I'll tell you where to look. Just be on the lookout."

"What if Tischler shows up here of his own accord, just to check on his handiwork?" Mike hypothesized, his brow creased and his arms crossed in a challengingly manner.

"I'll be on high alert. If I see or hear anything, I'll let you know immediately.

And I won't text him until you're leaving my place. It'll only take you twenty minutes to get there and back, and I'll keep out of sight in the meantime. But you need to hurry. It's going to be dark soon and we don't want to waste this opportunity to catch a rat," she said as she took him by the arm and led him in the direction of the door they'd come in.

"Keep a low profile and be quick," she cautioned as she closed the door behind him.

~~~

"Okay, here goes..." Madeline hit "send" on Natalie's phone. "Let's see what happens," she said into her own phone for Mike's benefit.

"I should be there in a few minutes. Let me know as soon as Tischler responds, which hopefully he will."

"I will. But even if he doesn't respond, that doesn't mean he won't show up anyway, unannounced, and make another attempt on 'Natalie's' life," Madeline pointed out.

"I know, don't remind me. But it could also be a very long night if Tischler doesn't show," Mike said as he fought down feelings of fatigue, wishing he'd picked up another coffee along the way.

In order to establish some peace of mind, he decided to give Samir a role in this operation. As he expected, Samir was more than willing. After Mike parked his Mercedes several houses down from Natalie's, he paid a visit to Jill Smalls. Once he got permission for Samir to use their front yard for surveillance purposes, he gave Samir specific instructions on where to position himself and how to react if given the signal.

He was just crossing the street from the Smalls' house to Natalie's when he received a text forwarded from Natalie's phone:

I really wish I could see you tonight but just got called in to sub in Burbank. 6 people are out with the flu. I don't know how long I'll be on that route but that's too far for me to commute from your place. I'd have to get up at 4am and you know I'm not really a morning person :) we'll talk soon. <3

Mike let out a grunt as he placed a call to his partner. "I'm coming up the walk right now."

"I'll let you in the front door," Madeline replied before ending the call.

"So…there goes that brilliant idea," Mike said as he passed over the threshold.

"Not necessarily."

"And what makes you say that?" Mike halted in the entry, almost daring her to come up with some implausible longshot.

"Well, think about it. His text says he has to sub in Burbank starting tomorrow. I'm not saying it's impossible for him to have gotten the same kind of position with another delivery company, but getting fired from his last job wouldn't look so good when someone verified his previous employment."

"So, you don't believe his excuse for not coming up here…and you don't believe he told Natalie that he lost his job…?"

"No on both counts. It wouldn't surprise me at all if he'd seen this attractive young widow with her nice house and two incomes as someone he could sponge off of indefinitely. But then Natalie hired us to look into Andrew's death, so now I think he'll definitely come up to finish what he set out to do last night."

Mike took a few beats to absorb what his partner had suggested. He didn't like her line of thinking, but other than arguing for the sake of it, he tried to weigh the likelihood of the scenario she'd just outlined.

Sensing his faltering resolve, Madeline nudged him closer to her view of what Tischler was probably up to. "If he was worried enough to slip her a lethal overdose—"

"We don't know that for sure."

"—and her latest text would prove it didn't take, then as far as he's concerned, she's still a real threat to him. I don't see that there's anything that would stop him from making sure he got it right the second time. And if he wasn't smart enough to erase his text conversations with Natalie last time, he now has that option."

After listening to and weighing Madeline's argument, Mike pursed his lips and shook his head almost imperceptibly before conceding she had a point.

"Okay, I guess we're in for a long night," he said as he ambled resignedly toward the kitchen. "Wish I'd had the foresight to pick up something to eat. I'm already starving."

Madeline followed behind him, arms crossed, mind in overdrive. "I don't think it's a good idea to mess up the kitchen," she said as she watched her partner hunt through their client's cupboards for something to eat.

"You're right," he agreed, surprising Madeline with his nonchalance. He wasn't one for letting his stomach go unattended. "I'll get Samir to pick up something for all of us," he said as he whipped out his phone and began to tap out a text. "I'm sure we've got plenty of time. Tischler will probably wait until she's gone to bed before he makes his move."

"Samir?" Madeline asked, perplexed.

"Yeah. He's over in the Smalls' bushes. I cleared it with Jill," he added when he looked up at his partner's startled face. "What do you want? What's close by?"

~~~

The take-out Mexican food had long been consumed by the time their stakeout began to take its toll on their nerves and stamina. By 12:30, even Madeline was beginning to think she had miscalculated Tischler's desire for peace of mind. She sent a text to Mike, who was keeping a low profile in the master bedroom.

Looks like our guy is a no-show, she conceded. Mike responded with a loud yawn that could be heard all the way to where Madeline was playing decoy in the front bedroom. He stood up and gave his tired body a powerful stretch before ambling out of his strategic post. One look at Madeline as she came into the family room told him she was also struggling to keep her eyes open. Still, he knew how much she hated to admit defeat.

"Let's give it until one o'clock," he bargained, surprising her enough to shake away the tiredness.

"Okay, but maybe we should send Samir home. He's been out there in the cold damp for hours. He's probably stiff as a board by now."

"Yeah, I'll relieve him of his duty. I'll tell him he doesn't have to come in until eleven tomorrow." He tapped out a text and sent it.

"That's a good idea," Madeline agreed as she stood up and began some gentle stretching to get her body unkinked. All the shutters, drapes and blinds had been closed, and all the lights had been turned off since 9:45, to give anyone watching the impression that Natalie had gone to bed. She turned a table lamp by the sofa on low just so they could move about and gather their stuff without having to fumble around in the dark.

In hindsight, baiting Tischler had been a longshot, but it had felt worthy of pursuing since they really didn't have a lot of other plays outside of trying to track him down. Now it would come down to making the drive to Newbury Park and possibly hiring a firm down there to find Tischler's whereabouts, if he hadn't already done a runner.

We could always ping his phone, Madeline thought as she made a note on her phone to do that first thing in the morning, which they could do now that they had his cell number.

After stalling for as long as they could stand it, Mike consulted his watch and declared there was really no point in hanging out any longer.

"Okay, let's pack it in," Madeline agreed as she turned on her phone's flashlight and switched off the table lamp. Mike was heading for the French doors to the back patio when he froze in his tracks. With a finger to his lips and a nod to Madeline's phone, he alerted her that he'd heard something.

Madeline doused her flashlight app, the only illumination now coming from the oven clock and the various electronic devices in the entertainment cabinet. She slunk up to the left side of the doors, bookending the entrance with Mike on the right. She carefully set her tote on the ground, her heart thumping in anticipation.

With the sound of blood coursing through their ears as their pulses raced, they had to strain to hear what was happening outside. The slight scrape of metal on metal telegraphed that Tischler had his own key.

Of course he did, Madeline realized as she thought back to the previous night when all the doors had been locked.

There was a tentative tug on the levered door handle. The door moved a fraction of an inch, not enough to free it but enough to jostle the shades just slightly. Mike was a second away from blasting his foot into the door frame when his phone chimed with an incoming text.

What followed next happened quickly. The chime froze the movement of the handle. Mike's leg unfurled a kick so powerful the lock gave and the wood surrounding it splintered. In the two seconds it took to push through the now jammed doors, the thump of racing footfalls quickly receded. Mike gave chase, with Madeline right behind him.

Under the cover of a moonless, cloudy night, he wasn't sure if he saw or only imagined he saw a figure sail over the top of the gate. By the time he unlatched it and swung it open, Tischler had already disappeared either around the front of Natalie's house or in the opposite direction. Mike ran as far as the end of the garage and quickly scanned the street scene. Panting from the burst of exertion and the adrenaline rush, he shook his head as Madeline came up beside him.

"Shit!" he cursed under his breath, turning from one direction to the other, his agitation palpable.

Madeline was just about to comment that at least they now knew they'd been on the right track when a faint commotion stopped her short. She and Mike moved as one toward the sound not immediately identified. It was faint and too far away for them to be sure, but it sounded like a muffled thud and a gasp.

Mike used his phone to light the way as they sprinted in the direction of the scuffle. They didn't have far to travel before they saw a dark-colored, low-slung car.

"Got him!" a wheezy voice called out gleefully from somewhere out on the road. Lights from the houses on both sides of the street came on, shedding enough illumination for them to see an exuberant but winded Samir astride a man he had pinned to the ground with his hands and knees, the man they knew by the vehicle had to be Mathias Tischler.

"Samir!" Madeline gasped joyfully.

"What's going on out there?" a man's voice called out, sounding more aggressive than he probably felt. "I'm going to call the police if you don't answer me *now*!" A female voice could be heard in the background before Mike spoke up and told the concerned neighbor to go ahead and make the call.

It was almost 1:30 by the time the SBPD squad car carted Mathias Tischler off to the county jail. It had taken a good bit of sorting out from the parties involved before the arresting officers were sufficiently convinced the PI's were telling the closest version of the truth they were likely to hear. Mike and Madeline separately vowed that District Attorney Adams was not only aware of their operation, but he had personally asked them to take this case on behalf of a recently widowed woman, now languishing comatose in the hospital, most likely the work of the man sitting in their cruiser.

Tischler didn't help himself any by the way he carried on in the backseat, spitting expletives and threatening to sue for false arrest. In the end, the arresting officers cited him with trespassing, giving them enough reason to hold him until D.A. Adams brought more charges against him.

As the MDPI team watched the police cruiser drive away, Mike clasped Samir affectionately on the shoulder.

"You saved the day, Samir."

"You really did," Madeline agreed as she hugged Samir from the side, making him self-conscious but also extremely proud. "Had you not trusted your instincts and gone home when we told you to, he probably would've gotten away."

"I want you to take the day off tomorrow—today, I mean," Mike corrected himself as he checked his watch, realizing why he suddenly felt so drained. He and Madeline had been up for almost twenty hours. "In fact, I think we all should. The girls can cover the office while we lay low for a bit."

"I imagine we'll be hearing from Conrad bright and early," Madeline predicted, causing Mike to sag under the weight of his fatigue.

"Let's get out of here so the neighbors can get back to sleep," he said under his breath before giving Samir another clap on the back.

THIRTY-FIVE

This time, Mike was the first one up. He couldn't boast of having excess energy, but once he was able to shrug off the drug-like effects of his hard slumber, his thoughts began to bounce off each other. He lay awake for another hour before he felt rested enough to haul himself out of bed without waking his partner.

He brewed a large pot of coffee but put off making breakfast until Madeline showed herself. It was almost nine o'clock when he took his mug out to the terrace overlooking the harbor and the graceful sweep of Shoreline Drive. There was a crispness in the air and a faint whiff of orange blossoms that filled his senses and did wonders for his morale. From this serene perch, it was hard to assimilate all that had taken place in the middle of the night. The whole thing felt more dreamlike than real, especially from his current vantage point, sitting in the morning sunshine, beholding the Santa Barbara Harbor, the ocean and Santa Cruz Island on the horizon.

Like he had so many times in the past, he felt keenly grateful for the way fate had brought him and Madeline back together after all those years apart, the years when she'd been married to Steven Ridley, sleazebag extraordinaire. He would still be living in L.A., which he used to think he enjoyed. But in retrospect, it had felt more like surviving than thriving. The quality of life he'd found farther up the coast was unlike anything he'd known since he was in grade school. Santa Barbara was smaller, simpler, more laid-back and definitely friendlier. From where he was sitting, it really felt like he'd landed in paradise.

The word *paradise* stuck in his mind. Though it felt like a fitting word to describe his current view, he knew the concept of a place where everything was perfect was just wishful thinking. No matter how perfect and placid a place might seem, as long as there were human beings in the mix, the pretext of paradise was only an illusion. One just had to scratch the surface to find the lies and vicious acts that lurked just beneath a deceptive veneer.

That's the trouble with living in paradise, Mike mused as he took a long sip of his coffee. *It's easy to be blind to danger when everything seems so peaceful. It makes it easy to forget what human beings are capable of.*

He had just set down his mug when a slender pair of arms encircled him from behind. Had he not caught the whiff of rose and jasmine a split-second earlier, he might have grabbed those arms and hurled his assailant to the ground. Though his heart thumped as he fought off his natural response to defend himself, he was filled with an acute surge of love. That's what a mere touch from Madeline could do to him, even after all these years.

"How long have you been up?" she asked as she slid into the chair on his left and hijacked his coffee.

"A little while. Just enjoying a little peace and quiet."

"Oh…well, I better get out of your hair, then," Madeline joked as she started to stand up.

"Stay right where you are, little lady," Mike drawled in a laughable impersonation of John Wayne. Madeline tittered happily as she sat back and glanced around at the beautiful day.

"It's kind of fun having a day off in the middle of the week," she said, stealing another sip.

"Let me get you a cup," Mike said as he started to get up.

"No, stay where you are. I'll get some in a minute. Let's just enjoy this peaceful moment for a while."

"It is pretty nice," he admitted after listening to the sweet chorus of rose finches in the jacaranda tree behind him.

"Besides, there's something I want to discuss with you…" The mysterious way in which she said this, her offhanded manner and the tilt of her head, took him by surprise. As well as he thought he knew her, he couldn't imagine what she was about to say.

"What's on your mind?" he asked as he grabbed the mug and drank most of what was left.

"Just something I've been thinking about for a while…"

"Oh, you mean how incredibly fortunate you are to have me as a partner…?" came his glib reply.

Madeline held his stare, her expression unreadable.

"Something like that." She scooted her chair closer to his and took his left hand in both of hers. After a moment of silent reflection, she looked up into his eyes again and smiled ever so slightly. Mike couldn't remember the last time he'd felt so nervous. His chest contracted and his skin prickled with fear.

"Mike Delaney, partner and love of my life, will you marry me?"

Nothing was said while Mike's ears became deaf to all ambient sounds around him. He had consciously given up hope of ever making what they had legal, as in the "until death do us part" pledge backed up with a marriage license. He had actually gone through the mental gymnastics of planning, plotting and rehearsing lines similar to the ones he'd just heard, but everything he knew about Madeline's mindset told him he'd be setting himself up for rejection. It had always seemed the wiser, safer approach to just enjoy what they had together and forget convention.

"You don't have to give me an answer right away," Madeline said, the shadow of a smile playing at the corners of her beautiful lips. Before he could stop himself, he dragged her chair next to his and enveloped her in his arms, pulling her onto his lap, giving her his answer with a long, passionate kiss.

When their lips came apart and they could breathe again, Madeline asked coyly, "Is that a yes?"

Mike threw back his head and laughed, a deep, joy-filled sound that made her heart swell. "Yes. Yes. Yes," he said as he pulled her to him again, holding on to her tightly, trying to mesh his soul with hers. They laughed, their eyes welling up with tears as they became a little self-conscious. They caught each other's eyes and laughed, giddy at the thought of actually doing something they had sidestepped for years. With hands entwined, they smiled at each other almost shyly, but with a familiarity that assured them words weren't necessary.

Mike was the one to break the silence. "Since you're the wedding expert, I guess I'll leave all the preparations up to you," he said, getting a smile out of his partner.

"Thank you. As a matter of fact, I already have something in mind..."

"You were rather sure of yourself," he quipped playfully. Madeline shrugged a shoulder and smiled benignly. "Okay, just tell me when and where I need to show up."

"Really?"

"Sure," he replied with a big, goofy grin.

"Okay. Then I'll go ahead and make the reservations while you shower," she said as she got up.

Grabbing her by the arm as she headed into the house, he asked, "What's the rush?"

"Well…it's getting late."

"I thought we didn't care about the time. We declared this our day off."

"I know. And we're going to take advantage of it by flying to Las Vegas so we can get hitched. No fuss, no muss. Just you, me and the wedding chapel of our choice."

"Are you serious?"

"Of course I'm serious."

Mike blinked back his surprise. For a moment he was dumbstruck. He looked at the hand he still held in his, then followed her arm up to her face. Her expression was partly amused, partly impatient.

"All right, future Missus Michael Alan Delaney, Vegas it is." Madeline bent down and kissed him on the lips before she started into the house again. "Hang on a second," Mike called out as he grabbed her by the wrist again and guided her back to him.

"Where did this sudden urge to tie the knot come from? You made it very clear you never wanted to get married, you just want to enjoy what we have without the 'complication' of marriage. Now, out of nowhere, you want me to run off to Vegas with you for a quickie wedding. What gives?" he asked, his tone soft but serious, catching her off guard.

Madeline shrugged and tried to make light of his question, but he wasn't buying it. When he cocked an eyebrow and leveled one of his plaintive stares at her, she exhaled slowly and seemed to lose a good measure of her buoyancy. As he kept his eyes riveted to hers, she sank back into the chair next to his and regarded him somberly.

"I know that I've kept you at arm's length because of what I went through with Steven. In hindsight, I clung to the fear of being betrayed as a means of convincing myself I would never be that vulnerable again." She gathered her thoughts and the resolve to expose feelings she had never planned to share with anyone. She inhaled deeply before continuing, averting her eyes as she took a leap into perilous territory.

"This last week—my first official week back at work—I was exposed to two women who had lost their husbands. At first, that factor didn't mean anything to me. These were just cases that happened to involve the deaths of two men, both of whom left behind grieving widows. But as we dug deeper, I started to feel their losses, even though I reserved judgment about their guilt or innocence."

Madeline turned away, her eyes seeking the vast blue of the ocean as she confronted her emotions. "It hit me that I have a love as deep as theirs, a love that has spanned twenty-five years, yet I had been so guarded with my emotions, so afraid to love again because of how grotesquely Steven had betrayed my love for him."

With eyes that had become glassy, she met Mike's and offered an apologetic smile. "You are my rock, my one true love, my partner, my best friend. You've loved me since I was nineteen without hesitation, even when I cut you loose. But most of all, you're the one person in this world I can always count on to make me smile and give me hope that everything will be okay. If I was afraid of voicing my love for you or spilling my guts only to find out you're still commitment-phobic, those days are behind me. I love you and I want to be your wife, forever and always."

Moved by her testament of love, Mike wiped at the tears welling up in the corners of his eyes. He fought the strong urge to weep. He was surprised by the array of emotions bombarding him. Joy was foremost, though there was the residual of past pain and the fear of losing her, in the past and in the future.

There was also something less definable behind the constriction of his throat, the vague sense that he was missing something, that nothing this perfect could actually be happening to him, or if it were, it must be short-lived.

Sensing his underlying reservations, Madeline jostled his hand, drawing his gaze to hers, seeking affirmation that he did in fact want to spend the rest of his life with her. Mike wiped roughly at his teary eyes again and laughed, breaking the tension that had settled on them like a cloud obscuring the sun.

"If I'm going to be married today, I guess I'm going to need to shave," he said as he rubbed his stubbled jawline. Madeline gave him a purr of a laugh through her smile as she rose up and planted a kiss on his lips.

"I better get the reservations taken care and get my act together, too," she said over her shoulder as she went back inside.

❧

Twenty minutes later, Mike emerged from the bathroom, showered and shaved, the faint scent of cologne announcing his presence as he crept up behind his wife-to-be, whose fingers tapped vigorously on the keyboard as she tried to get her instructions to their staff typed up in an email. He leaned down and kissed her first on the top of her head, then on each side of her neck. She scrunched her shoulders as the ends of his damp hair tickled her skin.

"If we're leaving soon, you'd better get your booty ready."

"I know." She sent the email. "I'm going to shower right now. We're going to need to stop at my place so I can pick something special to wear. Got to look my best on my wedding day," she said with a laugh as she rose up and turned into Mike's awaiting arms.

"If you're ready, take a look at the email from Conrad," she called out as she headed into the bedroom. "You can read my reply in my sent emails."

After watching her retreating figure, Mike settled himself at her computer and scanned the inbox for the message from the D.A. Had he not been so high on life at that moment, any missive from Conrad after all they had dumped at his feet the last few days would've made his stomach clench. Though what they had managed to accomplish felt like clear victories to him, there were many facets to the law and law enforcement, and being free agents on the periphery meant they occasionally worked at cross-purposes.

Because Conrad had brought them into the Sheckle case as a personal favor to him, he couldn't really complain too much about all the mayhem that had ensued during the course of their investigation. And fortunately, he didn't.

While the D.A.'s office didn't currently have enough to hold Tischler in Santa Barbara County Jail for his possible involvement in Andrew's death and Natalie's overdose, Conrad had already been in contact with the Ventura County District Attorney regarding the brutal rape of Clarise Hammons. Though the crime took place twenty-five years earlier, Tischler could still be held accountable if the D.A. wished to pursue it.

If Natalie pulled through and could testify to not intentionally taking a near-fatal dose of barbiturates, then Conrad could bring attempted murder charges against him. And he could also go after him for Andrew's murder, which Tischler had been trying to cover up with Natalie's overdose.

With all those possible charges staring Tischler in the face, Conrad believed that something was going to shift in their favor. With Tischler in custody, there was hope whichever judge presided over the bail hearing would keep him locked up, citing him as a flight risk, at the very least.

After that nice, roundabout pat on the back, Conrad was less pleased to be in the position of having one of his convictions overturned, with a new suspect to prosecute. *Still, justice must be served*, Conrad stoically admitted before signing off without congratulating them on another case solved.

Success is its own reward, Mike thought blithely as he opened Madeline's reply.

So glad things have worked out for Lindsay Bartholomew. We hope she can be reunited with her daughter ASAP. We sincerely hope Natalie will pull through. Things will fall into place in the case against Tischler if she does. It won't bring Andrew back, but it will be some consolation for Natalie to know he didn't intentionally leave her all alone.

Mike and I will be unreachable for the next 24 hours. If you need anything from us during that time, please contact the office.

Best, Madeline

Mike liked her reply: short and to the point. They had done what was asked of them, and they had every right to be proud of their investigative work. Though they weren't the law, per se, they took their responsibility to their clients and the law seriously. They were a good team, on the job and off. And now they'd be husband and wife, a personal dream he hadn't been bold enough to hope for.

He closed the laptop and went to pack what would have to pass as his wedding suit and a few other items of clothing into a garment bag. The realization of what they were about to embark on made him laugh out loud. Madeline had been so right to spring this on him and to plot a wedding in Las Vegas. As corny, cliché and campy as running off to Vegas used to seem to him, this was without a doubt the happiest moment of his life.

THIRTY-SIX

With all that had happened in the previous twenty-four hours, the "situation" with her badly-behaved neighbor to the east had been completely pushed from Madeline's mind. She was so focused on what to wear and what to bring to Vegas, the familiar blue bags on her lawn came as a fresh affront. The jolt caused by their appearance was made more acute due to the fact that she couldn't hide the cowardly slight from Mike this time.

"What the hell?" he blurted as he stopped in his tracks and assessed the tableau in front of them. Madeline shot him an apprehensive look as her mind scrambled to find a way to keep this stunt from tainting their special day.

"I think my neighbor has a rare case of Tourette's Syndrome that manifests itself in rather peculiar ways," she said as she gingerly picked up one of the blue bags with the intent of depositing it in her garbage can.

"Don't touch that," Mike said, his tone laced with anger as he took the nasty parcel out of Madeline's hand and put it back on the lawn. Without a word, he pulled his phone out of his shirt pocket and snapped photos of the four bags. Madeline pursed her lips and pinched them closed with her teeth to prevent herself from saying something she would later regret. She was fed up with this kind of passive-aggressive behavior, but she didn't want a nasty scene to ruin her wedding day.

As she stewed, her foot tapping at the strain she was forced to endure for the sake of keeping the peace, the answer to the conundrum flashed on her in an instant.

She set her assorted tote bags on the lawn and hunted around until she found the wig she'd used to impersonate Natalie Sheckle. She haphazardly tugged it onto her head and quickly stuffed her own hair up inside it, using one of the Audi's windows as a mirror while she ignored Mike's demands that she clue him in on what she was up to.

Once satisfied she had the wig on properly, she donned the black-rim glasses she'd worn to Rancho Vista Encantada, then collected the offensive blue bags in one hand and set off to have a chat with Good Neighbor Doug.

"Am I just supposed to watch you go off to confront your neighbor?" Mike asked under his breath, doing his level best to corral his resentment. He'd waited way too long for this day to have it spoiled by some petty act of cowardice.

"No," Madeline said as she paused to look back at him. With a wag of her head, she beckoned for him to follow her. When his long strides brought him within a couple feet of her, she whispered for him to hang back until she signaled for him.

As she passed her schefflera hedge and came to the low bed of agapanthus lining Doug's driveway, she motioned for Mike to stay out of sight. She approached the front door and rang the bell before averting her face so that she'd only be seen in profile if he looked through the peephole.

The anger and resentment she felt at being put in this position kept her from becoming anxious. She wasn't quite sure about what she was going to say, but she knew how she was going to say it.

Muffled barking grew louder before she heard the door handle turn and the ineffectual commands for the dog to stop its high-pitched yapping that were as annoying as the yapping itself.

"Can I help you?" Doug asked irritably as he restrained his apoplectic mutt with one foot. "Be quiet!" After shooing his snarling lap dog away, he turned his attention back to the source of the interruption. Madeline stood on the doorstep, a bouquet of blue bags dangling from her outstretched hand. She let them drop with a soft thud on Doug's hardwood flooring, making him wince involuntarily.

"I believe you misplaced these on my property," Madeline said as she removed the glasses. Doug's first cowardly response was to close the door on her, which she effectively blocked by wedging her foot between the door and the threshold.

"Get off my property, or I'll call the cops," Doug spat, his pasty-white face coloring with red splotches as his misplaced indignation swelled.

"Oh, please do. I think it's time to put your harassment of me to an end."

Madeline turned to give Mike the signal, only to find he was just a few feet behind her, which explained why Doug had suddenly grown silent and paler.

"Look, I don't want any trouble," he said nervously.

"Good. Neither do we," Madeline said as Mike came and stood beside her. "In addition to letting you know that all your not so subtle, meanspirited taunts will not be tolerated from this moment forward, we wanted you to be the first to congratulate us." She turned to Mike and smiled before fixing her eyes on Doug again.

"From now on, any time you feel the need to vent your spleen by banging your trash can lids, launching poop bags over the hedge, or spying on me from your upstairs windows, you will be seriously offending this strapping hunk whom I will be so proud to call my husband.

"So, this is it, *Doug*—from now on, you will cease all aggressive acts against me. You will do your level best to be invisible and unheard. When you walk your dog, you will make sure to give *our* property a wide berth. You will be considerate when depositing trash in your cans. You will refrain from violating our airspace with projectiles of any sort. You will not spread nasty rumors about me or my husband. Have I made myself clear?"

Madeline almost felt sorry for the shamefaced coward who could no longer maintain eye contact with them. She was fairly sure he had understood the terms she'd laid out for him, but she knew they wouldn't have had any impact had Mike not been there to back her up.

Still, a victory was a victory, and she felt lighter as she and Mike walked back to her house hand in hand. She was also relieved that she had found the right way to defuse the situation.

"Sorry to get you involved, but I had to put an end to that," she said as they walked up her driveway. Mike put his arm around her and pulled her close, placing a kiss on her cheek.

"Don't be. I'm glad I was there for backup. I think you handled that perfectly. I seriously doubt he will be bothering us in the future." Madeline looked over at him and smiled. "I just wish you had told me about it. How long has he been harassing you?"

Madeline shrugged and gave him a weak smile. "It's been on and off for years. Since I moved in, really."

"I didn't see anything like that when I was coming over here all the time after you were shot."

"That's because he keeps tabs on what's going on here from that window up there," Madeline said as she gestured to her neighbor's upstairs bedroom. "I've caught him watching me from that back window when I've been out in my backyard."

Mike stopped and stared at Madeline with his bottom jaw hanging slack. "That son of a bitch," he growled under his breath. "Why didn't you tell me about any of this?"

"So you could beat the crap out of him and end up in jail?" Madeline shook her head ruefully. "I just had to handle it myself, in a way that would stick. And fortunately, I think you provided one. Now, enough about that idiot," she said as she started humming the "Wedding March." Mike grabbed her around the waist and pulled her to him, humming along as smiles broke across both their faces.

THIRTY-SEVEN

Because the only daily flight from Santa Barbara to Las Vegas wasn't going to work for them, Mike and Madeline decided to take the airbus down to LAX. They could've driven, but getting on the bus made them feel like their adventure was starting earlier. Nobody knew where they were, where they were going, or what they were about to do. It made them feel giddy, like young lovers realizing a whole new life lay ahead of them.

They were lost in their own world, their hands entwining of their own free will, only mildly cognizant of the people around them as they luxuriated in the knowledge that somehow their lives had finally meshed and become one. They had been partners for four-plus years—in and outside of business; now they would be partners for life, pledging to love and protect each other for the rest of their days. This official union would take any ambiguity out of their relationship. They would now be able to refer to each other as husband or wife, a huge step to take for both of them.

Though they had turned off their phones and left their laptops at home, in light of the loose ends they were leaving behind, they decided to check their phones one last time before boarding started for the flight to Las Vegas.

As Madeline stared at the three voicemail messages that had come in from Conrad while they were on the airbus, she hesitated before listening to the first one, promising herself whatever he had to say would not change how this day unfolded.

"*Your assistant told me you and Mike are taking the day off, but I just wanted to pass along the latest news. Detective Slovitch wanted me to let you know the lab results on the hairs found in the balaclava. They're a match for Octavio Guzman, twenty-nine, recently released from Lompoc after completing the career training program implemented by your ex. Small world. But that's not really much of a surprise. A warrant has been issued, and since we've got Guzman's employer info as well as his home address, we'll probably be able to bring him into custody shortly…"*

Mike had already checked his messages and was waiting silently as he tried to glean insights from Madeline's facial expressions. After debating whether to share this news or not, she backed up the call and put it on speaker so he could hear Conrad's message for himself.

"…I'll be sure to keep you posted on that. This could be big if we can make a direct link back to Steven. That would put the kibosh on his new career as champion of prison reform. They can keep the program and throw his rotten hide back inside. As for Natalie, she's still comatose, though her vitals are steady. We just have to wait, hope and pray she'll come out of it.

"As for Mathias Tischler, our office is working with the Newbury Park D.A.'s Office to review that rape charge against him. D.A. Williamson knows we've got two possible felony charges against Tischler, but in the meantime, he can be held on the rape case until we've got hard proof that he shot Andrew and drugged Natalie.

"So, good work, you two. Enjoy your time off. You deserve it. It'd be nice if you could lay low long enough for this crime wave to settle down. I'll be in touch."

Mike and Madeline let out a collective sigh as they digested Conrad's news. "Wow, that's a lot to take in," Mike said.

"No kidding. No wonder we're feeling so stretched. We've been up to our ears in complex cases. Which reminds me…Conrad didn't say anything about the Bartholomew case," Madeline said as she tapped on the second voicemail.

"Me again. Forgot to give you status on Bartholomew. Patricia has lawyered up, naturally, but I got a very strange call from her daughter late last night. I'll forward the voicemail so you can hear it for yourselves. Sounds like there might be some dissention in that camp. Talk to you later."

"We should run off and get married more often," Mike joked, enjoying how everything they had worked so hard on had come together.

"Here's the forwarded message from Vanessa Bartholomew," Madeline said as she tapped the arrow.

"Hello, Mister Adams. I think you might remember me from a case your office prosecuted a while back. Lindsay Bartholomew, my stepmom, was convicted of killing my father, Nick." There was a brief period of silence that made Madeline

check her phone to see if the message had ended. *"Excuse me...there's new evidence...um...with the note my stepmom wrote...you may already know this. I don't know what to think. I just want to know the truth behind my father's death."* A sound like throat-clearing—or choking back tears—could be heard before Vanessa spoke again.

"When I testified at both of Lindsay's trials, I was convinced she had delib-erately set my father up. I never imagined for a second...well, I just wonder now if we got to the truth or not. Anyway...I'd like to make an appointment to see you, if that's possible. I'll call your office in the morning. Thank you. Bye."

"Hmm. That was strange. What do you make of it?" Mike asked. Madeline took a moment to make sure she trusted her initial response.

"I think Vanessa pushed so hard for Lindsay's conviction because she had so much resentment toward her stepmom for displacing her mother. I think the loss of Nick was so brutal for her because her relationship with her father had been so badly damaged by the divorce.

"From what we've been able to piece together, Vanessa was never really able to forgive Nick for falling in love with Lindsay. When he died, she lost the chance to forgive him and to love him the way she had before. How could she even bring herself to consider that Lindsay wasn't responsible? I'm sure it never occurred to her that her own mother could've done something like that."

Mike didn't take long to consider what his wife-to-be was saying. "I think that sums it up pretty well. I get the impression Conrad—who's seen hundreds of cases—is reading the same subtext here. The fact that Vanessa made con-tact with him so soon after her mother was arrested is pretty telling." He gave Madeline a sad smile and pulled her to him.

"Whatever happens, I think our job is done," he said after giving her a tender kiss. When she pulled away to look at him, he added, "Lindsay will appeal the conviction now that her note has surfaced. One way or the other, she will get out of prison and be reunited with Joni. That's what we were after, so we can chalk that up as a win."

They stood with an arm around each other as they silently relegated the Bartholomew case to the archives and let their thoughts drift to the adventure ahead of them.

"What's the drill? Do you know?" Mike asked.

Madeline looked up at him, trying to catch what he was referring to.

"The wedding thing? I don't really know much about quickie Las Vegas weddings, so I'm counting on you to lead the way."

Madeline smiled.

"Don't worry. We're going to be in good hands."

Madeline had a full-fledged giggle attack on the drive to The Golden Promise Wedding Chapel, located away from the glitz and the extravagant hotels Las Vegas had become famous for. Mike suspected the stress of the past few days had taken its toll. But it was wonderful to see her so happy, regardless of the reason.

Once inside the small white chapel with a spire higher than the church was wide, a calm settled over her. She had made the reservation over the phone prior to leaving Santa Barbara, and the woman she spoke to greeted them warmly before having them fill out the paperwork for the marriage license. After the formalities had been seen to, she showed them where the service would take place and introduced them to the pastor.

Madeline had chosen a standard but brief service designed to get the job done as quickly and efficiently as possible. Everything they needed to say to one another about their love and their promise to stand by each other in good times and bad had already been demonstrated by their long association and a love that took little time to rekindle once Madeline was freed from Steven Ridley. All she wanted out of a wedding service was the paper that legally declared them husband and wife.

On the ride back to the Bellagio, Madeline sat close to Mike in the backseat as she admired her plain gold wedding band. She gazed up at her husband and smiled, her face radiant with contentment. She giggled as she felt Mike's silenced phone vibrate through his jacket pocket as a text came through, until she felt the same thing from the clutch sitting on her lap. When it happened again a few seconds later, they eyed each other cautiously as they silently deliberated whether they should see who was trying to get in touch with them.

Since checking Mike's would require shifting away from her, Madeline took hers out of her handbag just as the alerts buzzed again.

Sensing this could be urgent, Mike also went for his. They read Conrad's latest message simultaneously, gasping in unison as they learned what had sparked this wave of communiqués. Madeline read the first of the texts aloud.

"*'Just got an alert from the Board of Parole that Ridley's million-dollar bond has been withdrawn.'* What do you suppose that means?"

"I don't know," Mike answered. "Oh, he goes on to say in the next text, *'Bond was put up by a woman named Sarah Strong-Hartmann. Without that bond, Ridley goes back to prison.'*"

Mike and Madeline stared at each other, mouths agape as they received the most wonderful wedding gift they could've ever hoped for.

"Yes!" Madeline cried out, making the driver look up at her in his rear-view mirror. She gave her husband's leg a squeeze, then kissed his cheek, her face radiant.

"There's more," Mike said, his voice somber, the muscles in his jaw twitching.

"What is it?" Madeline eased away from him as chills prickled her skin. "What?" she prompted again as Mike's worried gaze alerted her to real danger.

Mike looked into Madeline's eyes that were now glassy with nascent tears. He looked down at his phone and read, "*'Ridley's ankle monitor is pinging from the middle of Sacramento River. Somehow suicide seems unlikely.'*"

Madeline's eyes locked on to Mike's, willing them to reassure her.

"He can't hurt us," Mike said as he pulled her closer to him. "He was going back to prison anyway because of the attack on you. He's running scared, but he has totally cooked his goose this time. He'd be *insane* to come anyway near Santa Barbara."

Madeline continued to stare at him, but his words did nothing to reassure her.

"Even if he makes it that far south, you've got me as your around-the-clock bodyguard."

Madeline tried to smile for Mike's benefit, but it just wouldn't hold. She knew that Steven would value freedom over revenge, but it was still hard not to fear the threat he posed. She closed her eyes and silently prayed for protection.

When she opened her eyes, she gazed at her new husband with love and trust and put fear out of her mind and heart. From this point forward, she would just have to grab life with both hands and live every day to its fullest. And the devil could take Steven Ridley, may he rot in hell.

Dear reader,

Thank you so much for reading Madeline and Mike's latest adventures in sleuthing. As usual, they proved quite adept at clearing the obstacle course I put them through. And as in the three previous books, they often called their own shots. As a writer, that's a very gratifying experience.

I wish to thank my husband Guy, my sister Melanie, and my brother Brad for their steadfast support and encouragement. Many thanks to Amy Marie Orozco, Caressa Basham-Schramer, and Krista Venero at Mountains Wanted Publishing for combing over the text so thoroughly; Rob Dafoe of Brick Barn Wine Estate for the tour of his facility and for sharing his vast knowledge of winemaking; Captain Evan Grosswirth for getting me up close and personal with the gorgeous Falcon 900XL and for sharing his wide scope of aviation knowledge; Master Coffee—AKA Teri Coffee McDuffie—and Ziggy Peake, for helping me fine-tune the scene on Madeline's front lawn, which resulted in Ziggy being throw to the ground numerous times by Master Coffee; and Deb Tremper of Six Penny Graphics for another beautiful cover design and flawless formatting. Their help was invaluable!

Feel free to contact me at cynthiahamiltonbooks.com, follow me @AuthorCynthiaH on Twitter, friend or follow me on Goodreads, BookBub and Facebook. Comments and questions welcome! Reviews are the writer's best friend; it's through them that we are able to grow our reading audience.

I hope you will join me again for MDPI's next adventure!

Warmest regards,
Cynthia

http://cynthiahamiltonbooks.com
https://twitter.com/AuthorCynthiaH
https://www.goodreads.com/author/show/434917.Cynthia_Hamilton

www.ingramcontent.com/pod-product-compliance
Lightning Source LLC
Chambersburg PA
CBHW031058270626
47155CB00026B/648